FULL CIRCLE

a novel

GITA GORDON

Author's Note:

This book is a work of fiction. Although it contains references to historical events, real people, and actual locales, these references are used only to lend the story an appropriate historical context. All other names, characters, and incidents portrayed in this book are fictitious, and any resemblance to persons or events is entirely coincidental.

ISBN: 978-1-60763-336-5

Editor: Miriam Jakubowicz
Proofreader: Elisheva Ruffer
Cover design: Rivkah Lewis
Internal design and layout: Nachum Shapiro

THE JUDAICA PRESS, INC.
123 Ditmas Avenue / Brooklyn, NY 11218
718-972-6200 / 800-972-6201
info@judaicapress.com
www.judaicapress.com

Manufactured in the United States

To my wonderful grandchildren
who give me so much pleasure

Shira Rivka, Rachel Yonah, Baruch Yosef, Binyamin Yedidya,
Tiferet Emunah, and Shabbtai David

and

Avrohom and Leah, Miriam, Shabsi Dovid, Rivki,
Yehuda Ze'ev, Esti, Yisroel Meir, and Hadassah

and

Ayala Tova, Shabtai Zev, Yehuda Chaim,
and Rivka Liba Hadassah

Acknowledgements

I would like to express my appreciation and thanks to Judaica Press and to Nachum Shapiro, the managing editor, for making this book a reality.

To my children for their support during this pandemic year, which made it possible for me to continue writing.

To my daughter-in-law Shoshana for all her help and encouragement, without which I don't think I could have continued.

To my editor, Miriam Jakubowicz, who did a marvelous job and was such a pleasure to work with.

Thank you to Rivkah Lewis for creating the beautiful cover.

Special thanks to Gwynne Schrire, historian and author, without whose help I would not have been able to write this book.

And to all the people who reviewed the manuscript and gave such good advice: Tehilla Brocha Notelovitz, Rachel Yonah Wisemon, Shira Rivka Wisemon (who also helped me in many other ways this year), Naomi Isaacson, Zimra Korp, Zamira Brooks, who made suggestions and encouraged me, and Moria Buznach for all her help.

Prologue

"The entire physical universe is interrelated, interconnected, intertwined. What I do here physically affects something somewhere else physically ... What I do here spiritually affects someone somewhere else spiritually."

— Rabbi Emanuel Feldman

Such a minor event it was.

The horse stumbled and was injured. The driver knew he could not continue for a few days, until his animal was healed. His passenger, Aharon Yankelovitch, was on his way to the next village to meet the daughter of the *rav*.

Just when he was so close to his destination, the young *bachur* was forced to sleep overnight in a strange place, on a hard bench in the shul. Suddenly he remembered that Dovid Miller, his friend from yeshiva, lived in this village. Dovid had been called home not long ago. Could he ask to sleep in his house overnight?

What if Dovid's family had no room for him but was embarrassed to refuse? In the end, the decision was made for him when the men were rushing to shul for Minchah. There before him stood Dovid.

"Aharon! Why are you here? Let's go *daven*, and then we'll talk."

In a small place, news travels fast.

"Your wagon won't be going anywhere soon," Dovid said. "There's a wagon going to the next village early in the morning. It leaves very early, so we must arrange now for you to be a passenger."

When they finally returned to the house, it was dark.

"Come quietly," Dovid said. "There's a new baby in the house. Come, we must go to bed now. You'll have to wake up early tomorrow to be ready to leave."

What the host forgot to tell his guest was that someone else who was staying in the house would also be traveling on the wagon. A young girl, who had been helping her sister-in-law with her new baby, was going home because her older sister was about to become engaged. Their father, a *rav*, had arranged for an elite *bachur* to travel to their village and meet his daughter. Soon thereafter, he was sure, an engagement and wedding would follow.

Why had Dovid not mentioned this? Perhaps he was longing for his days in yeshiva, even though he was needed at home. Aharon's sudden appearance, and the opportunity to learn with him and help him, had somehow put everything else out of his mind.

Early the following morning, Aharon went alone to *daven neitz*. When he returned, he came quietly through the kitchen door. Just then, a young girl came in from a different door. She gasped when she saw the stranger.

"I'm a friend of Dovid," he said quickly. "I slept here last night and will be leaving soon."

The girl steadied herself. How foolish to be so afraid.

"I came here early to light the fire," she said. "Soon I will also be leaving."

"Let me light the fire, then."

"Are you sure? That's so kind of you."

The girl went to the cupboard and placed bread and butter on a plate. "Once the fire is lit, you must eat." The wail of a baby could be heard in the kitchen. "I must go," she said, and ran off.

Aharon was struck by the girl's kindness. The girl was amazed that this stranger had offered so quickly to light the fire for her. From such small events do great things occur.

When the wagon departed for the next village, Aharon sat up front next to the driver and another man. The girl joined the women with their bundles in the back of the wagon.

The men were mostly silent. The women talked. Aharon listened as Dina, the young girl, spoke. He knew then that he had met his *bashert*. Now he was faced with a problem. Here he was on his way to meet the *rav's* daughter. Yet he knew that the one meant for him was traveling on that same wagon. What was he to do? The problem became even more complicated when he realized, as Dina talked, that she was the *rav's* younger daughter. Despair overtook him.

How could he know Dina's thoughts? When she wasn't talking, she was sitting quietly and dreaming. *I hope the man chosen for my sister is a good man, a clever man, a learned man. She deserves no less. After her, it will be my turn. I hope I meet a man like the one who suddenly appeared in the kitchen. How thoughtful he was to notice my fear and put me at ease. How kind of him to light the fire.*

Now they sat in the same wagon, the young man on his way to meet the *rav's* oldest daughter, and the selfsame *rav's* younger daughter.

What if the horse had not stumbled? What if the younger sister had not been only one year younger, and herself about to enter the stage of *shidduchim*?

What is the use of asking such questions?

Faigy heard the noise of the arriving wagon. Her sister had been away for so long, and at last she was coming home. Faigy ran out the door and met her sister a little way down the road.

"Welcome home, Dina!" Faigy said. "It's so good to have you back! Oh, I have so much to tell you."

"Yes, it's good to be home again."

Faigy thought her sister sounded subdued, not that happy to be back. But why?

How could she know that her sister was thinking of a fine young man she would never see again?

The midday service was over, and Rav Shimon Simanovitch had just given the afternoon *shiur*.

As he was about to leave, he saw a young man come toward him: Aharon Yankelovitch, the *bachur* he had met some weeks before and selected to meet his dear daughter Faigy.

Aharon's words were not to his liking.

"I...I know I'm meant to meet your older daughter but...I would like to meet the younger one instead."

The *bachur* wanted to meet Dina, his younger daughter! What was he saying? He was meant to meet Faigy!

"I have family in the village," Aharon said. "I can stay with them. I will not say a word to anyone. I'll wait until the time is right."

The *rav* was at a loss for words. Faigy, his modest, clever Faigy, had been so excited to meet this young man. What would he tell her?

Dina, her younger sister, was outgoing and able to charm everyone, from old women right down to the smallest of children. But she couldn't compare to Faigy. Such a fine mind, Faigy had. When he spoke to his sons in learning each day, he was aware that she was listening at the door, but he ignored her presence, allowing her to gain the benefit of what was being taught.

True, she was not as outgoing as her sister, she was less popular, but she was a fine girl nonetheless. How would he tell her now that there would be no meeting, no *vort*, that the man he had sent for desired only her sister?

At last Rav Simanovitch recovered and was able to get some words out. "How can that be?"

Aharon gestured helplessly, not sure what to say himself. Slowly, haltingly, he spoke of the fateful wagon ride and the decision he had come to.

Now the *rav* knew that he had no choice but to make different plans for Faigy, his dear daughter. A painful conversation lay ahead of him.

Rav Simanovitch walked home and called his wife from the kitchen. They sat in the front room, at the table where they ate their meals and where he sat and learned. How many people had come to this same room, pouring out their problems? How many people had he been able to help and comfort?

Right now, it seemed there was no way to help or comfort him.

Malka saw her husband's solemn expression. "What troubles you?"

What could he do but tell her?

"We must talk to our Faigy," she said when he was finished talking. "What else can we do?" She went to call her daughter.

The girl came. She was smiling. She had been overjoyed at the arrival of her sister, and she was aware that the same wagon had brought a *bachur* from the yeshiva, a young man who was supposed to meet her.

Before she sat down, she glanced at the door leading to her brothers' room. Soon this room would belong to her and her husband. He would live here in this house, so that he could learn each day with her father.

Of the decision that had already been made, she knew nothing.

"Sometimes our plans don't go smoothly," began her father, "but our role in life is to accept what is sent to us."

What could he mean? Had the young man not arrived?

She listened as her father told her, as gently as possible, what had transpired.

The *rav* watched as Faigy suddenly slumped back in her chair. "He wants my sister, not me! My younger sister!"

Her father wanted to ameliorate the hurt. "Dina knows nothing of this. Maybe he is mistaken that his wishes are reciprocated. But you will marry first. He will say nothing. He will remain here with his family. Meanwhile, I met another young man when I went to the yeshiva. I could hardly make up my mind between the two. I will send for him. Clearly, he is your *bashert*. Only once you are wed, will your sister's wedding take place."

Just then, there was a loud knock at the door.

"Tell whoever it is to come back later," the *rav* told his wife.

The door burst open before she even had a chance to rise. Yittel Beilinsky, the local matchmaker, hobbled in and sat down on an empty chair.

"Forgive me for coming uninvited," Yittel said. "I must say something I know you won't agree with. But what can I do? I don't have a choice. I promised I would ask you, and I will keep my word."

The *rav* tried to interrupt, to suggest that she come back a little later, but she continued.

"Well, it's like this. Pinchas, the carpenter's son — his father had to bring him back from yeshiva to help him after his accident — well, I have just come from his house. Fine offers I had for him. But what does he say? 'No, the only person who finds favor in my eyes is the *rav*'s daughter. Go to the *rav*. If they refuse, maybe I will consider another girl, maybe not.' That's what he said to me."

In the sudden silence that followed her speech, the *rav* said, "Tell him he is a fine young man. I wish him well, but he is not for my daughter. No, my daughter will marry a man in learning."

"Of course," Yittel said. "I knew that would be the answer. Now I can tell Pinchas about a fine offer I have for him, a fine girl." She struggled to stand up, then added, "I know who you have in mind for Faigy — that young man who arrived here today. He went into the shul earlier . . . a fine young man."

She felt relaxed now, since she had delivered the unusual message. Now she could return to the carpenter's son and talk some sense into him. No, he could not meet the *rav*'s daughter. She had asked and had received a refusal. Now he must listen to her suggestions. Such a fine young man! It was high time Pinchas was married, and she had just the right girl for him.

As she wondered how to convince him, she heard the *rav* say, "No, not that young man. You are mistaken — I am sending for another."

Rav Simanovitch was discomfited now. He wished the woman would leave. Faigy heard his carefully chosen words. Every word was true, yet it was not the whole truth. There was no mention of the way he had rejected her.

"What, they met and don't agree? But he has only just arrived!" The matchmaker's voice was shrill with surprise.

Faigy felt her whole body go rigid. One thing after another! Why this sudden offer? Had the carpenter's son already been told of the rejection? Did he think that since she would now be so downcast, she would just accept anyone?

"You are mistaken," the *rav* said. "That young man is not for my Faigy. The young man I have in mind for her has yet to be sent for."

Yittel smiled. "For weeks now I have been going to the carpenter's house, trying to talk sense into the young man. For three whole weeks I have made one suggestion after another. Now I can tell him that the answer is no."

Faigy sat up. The other man desired her sister. Pinchas, the carpenter's son, desired only her!

Three weeks, the matchmaker had said. Precisely three weeks before the carpenter's son had come to their home to repair a chair. Unaware that anyone was in the room, she had walked in and seen the young man, red-faced and hot, hard at work. She had quickly brought him a pitcher of cold water and a glass.

The carpenter had looked up in surprise. Then he thanked her warmly and gave her a smile that lit up his face. Although the entire exchange had taken only a few minutes, Faigy had been left hoping that the man who would soon be traveling to meet her would be as pleasant as the carpenter.

Faigy came out of her reverie. Why should she humiliate the carpenter's son with an outright refusal? Had she not just been rejected? The days stretched empty ahead of her. Why should she and Pinchas not meet?

The matchmaker was gathering up her long skirt, preparing to leave, when Faigy drew a deep breath and said, "Tell the carpenter's son I will meet him."

There was a moment of silence, and then the *rav* spoke. "My daughter, what are you saying?"

"The carpenter's son desires that we should meet. I wish to meet him."

The *rav* thought he understood his daughter's hurt feelings. She felt rejected and was willing to accept the very next offer. Yittel was stunned.

Faigy repeated again, "Yes, it would please me to meet with him."

Three pairs of eyes looked at her in astonishment.

"He says he will meet only with me," Faigy said. "Very well, then! Perhaps after meeting me he will change his mind, or perhaps I will not agree to another meeting. But for now I wish to meet him."

How could they know that she was remembering that first short meeting, that warm smile?

Momentarily, Faigy forgot about her sister and the young man. This meeting with the carpenter's son would likely come to nothing, but it would give her time to think, to reflect upon her situation.

The *rebbetzin* led Yittel to the door. Before she could leave, Faigy began to weep. She tried to stop, but the events of the day finally overcame her — waiting for her father to return from shul with good news, the disappointment, and now this strange offer.

The *rav* gave in. "I will meet him and learn with him. Your mother too will meet him. Then we'll talk again."

"No . . . surely . . ." Faigy heard her mother object.

"Yes, we will meet with him, my wife and I, and then we'll decide."

Yittel looked at the crying girl. Strange! The younger sister was known for her fits of weeping if she couldn't get her way. Faigy, the *rav's* older daughter, was not known for such behavior. She was known for her clever ways. Like her mother, she could follow all the prayers in shul, sometimes even helping others who lacked this skill.

This behavior, demanding what her father refused, these sudden tears — it was all very strange.

Yittel stood motionless at the door. Was the *rav* not known for his unbending ways once he had made a decision? Yet here he was, giving in to his daughter.

"Tell the young man I will meet with him and then make my decision," the *rav* said.

"Yes, yes, I will go to him now," Yittel said. As quickly as she had entered the house she now left.

The meeting was arranged for the following day. To his surprise, the *rav* was favorably impressed with the young man. He had a fine mind and was clearly longing for the days when he could learn all day. However, duty to his family, to his father, compelled him to limit his learning.

Rav Simanovitch was also well aware of the fact that Pinchas learned during any spare moments he had throughout the day, and always at the end of the day, after Maariv. Shabbos, he devoted totally to learning. The community was not so large that the *rav* was unaware of what went on in his shul.

The *rav* spoke to his wife. "He is a fine young man. If our daughter insists on meeting him, I will allow it."

"What, the carpenter's son?"

"Why not? Did not you, the *rav*'s daughter, marry the tailor's son? What is the great difference between a tailor and a carpenter?"

"But you were learning in a yeshiva. You were the top student. My father made careful inquiries."

"True, I remained in learning. Why? Only because I wasn't called home to help! This young man was. He obeyed his father. Can we hold that against him?"

———

Pinchas was surprised when he was told that the *rav* would allow his daughter to meet him. He hadn't expected his request to be taken seriously. True, he had been very impressed by the girl's kindness. Few people noticed him when he was in their home, busy working.

And she had brought him a fine glass, not a simple mug. She had treated him with respect and served with such dignity. His thoughts had been filled with her kindness long after the chair had been repaired. He could hardly believe that he was really going to meet her.

The meeting took place two nights later. The table in the front room was covered with the white Shabbos tablecloth. Faigy was wearing her Shabbos dress, and her hair had been brushed until it shone in a long braid.

Dressed in his Shabbos clothes, Pinchas looked like a regular yeshiva *bachur*. How different he had looked in his work clothes. At first, she had regretted saying she wanted to meet him, but now she was not so sure. Her first impression of him had been accurate. He was truly a fine young man.

Her parents were sitting at the kitchen table, and the door to the front room was slightly ajar.

Faigy was quiet, giving him the chance to speak first, but then the words burst from her. "Why did you want to meet me?"

Pinchas was not happy with the question. What was he to say? The door to the kitchen creaked suddenly, and he was aware that every word they spoke could be heard.

"Well, Rivkah gave water to Eliezer, but she also gave water to his camels." He gulped and reddened. Why had he said such words?

The answer amused Faigy and she laughed. "Oh, but where, then, are your camels?"

The laughter dissipated the tension between them, and now they spoke freely. Faigy listened as he talked of yeshiva and how he missed learning all day. She told him how she listened at the door while her father taught her brothers, how she liked working in the kitchen, but not sitting and sewing.

Pinchas spoke of his family, but Faigy did not. The pain her sister was causing her was too fresh. She was still feeling the brunt of her mother's words to her, when she had said she would meet the carpenter's son. She had been called stubborn and contrary. Did her mother not comprehend the hurt she had just sustained?

Instead, she encouraged Pinchas to talk about his sisters and brothers, and the mischief they caused.

After Pinchas left, Rav Simanovitch came into the room. He had only to look at his daughter to know how the meeting had gone.

"Perhaps it should be arranged that we meet again," Faigy said.

The *rav* looked at his daughter. "Are you quite sure?"

Faigy felt she must give some explanation. She couldn't say how much she had enjoyed the conversation. She couldn't say that for the first time ever, she felt that she was not just the *rav*'s daughter, or her beautiful sister's older, less beautiful sister.

What she felt like saying was, "For the first time ever I felt that I was someone in my own right, interesting to talk to, pleasant to be with." Instead she said, "He spoke about his love of learning, of the yeshiva. He is a learned man."

The *rav* knew where this would lead, but gave his consent. He knew that Pinchas would not be able to sit and learn all day. Faigy would not live in his home while he learned with her husband. That place would be taken by Dina, once the time was right.

He glanced toward the door of the room that had been meant for Faigy and her husband. He saw that Faigy was aware of what that meant.

"Are you sure?" he said.

"Yes. Some things I will lose, but there is more that I will gain."

A clever answer, from a clever daughter, he thought. Aloud, he said, "Very well. It will be arranged."

Rav Simanovitch knew that his wife was dismayed at his decision to allow a second meeting.

"This can only lead to marriage," she said. "One meeting, I agreed to, but I was sure it would come to naught. Now, a second meeting?"

"We can make all the plans in the world," he said to his wife, "but if they are not meant to be, they will come to naught."

A short time later, the *rav*'s older daughter married the carpenter's son, and soon after, the younger daughter married the yeshiva *bachur*.

Despite the prohibition against forbidden speech, tongues still wagged. People wondered about the arrival of the stranger, who was so quickly wedded to the *rav*'s younger daughter.

It began in the shop as Leah attended to customers and her husband sat in the back learning.

Tzirel, who had hoped that the matchmaker would suggest the carpenter's son for her daughter, said to her friend Breindel, as they waited their turn to be served, "Strange, is it not, that the younger daughter married so soon after the older one?"

Breindel was about to reply, but it was her turn to be served.

When they left, Leah said to her husband, "When did the *bachur* arrive here?"

"*Bachur*? Oh yes, you mean the one who married the *rav*'s younger daughter?"

"Of course! Which other young man came here these past months?"

Not knowing why his wife was asking, he said, "I remember . . . it was a few weeks before the *rav*'s older daughter was married."

The couple didn't notice a customer walk in. When she went home her neighbor came to visit.

"You know, the *bachur* who married the *rav*'s younger daughter came here a whole month ago, right before they made a *vort* for the older girl. Remember the wedding was soon after? Then hardly any time passed and the younger girl got married. Why was he here for such a long time before meeting his bride?"

Like a multi-armed octopus words spread in all directions, each version of the story slightly different than the one that came before it.

The newly married couple became aware of the whispers and soon went to live in Aharon's shtetl, where he became a *rebbi* in the *cheder*.

The *rav*, heartbroken at their leaving, gave a *drashah* about *lashon hara*. Still, there were those who didn't heed his words.

Pinchas overheard two men talking in shul.

"So you see, that's why the girl married him, the young carpenter. The older daughter—the one they say is so clever—she was rejected, so she took the young carpenter! I thought it strange when the *bachur* came and then stayed all those weeks, even though it wasn't *bein hazmanim*."

Pinchas left the shul very quietly. His heart plummeted. Was that the reason he had attained his dream? When Faigy had agreed to meet him he had felt a surge of joy. Now he felt doubt and insecurity.

Suddenly he felt second best, that he had been accepted only because of unusual circumstances. He felt no desire now to learn. He couldn't walk into the shul and feel the pitying glances of the other men. Maybe others also knew about this. He turned and saw his *chavrusa* walking toward him.

"Sorry, I can't learn this evening," he mumbled, and slowly made his way home.

That same day, Faigy had heard the same story as she waited on line at the butcher. It was crowded, and the two gossips were unaware that she was just behind them. Anger overtook her. Clearly, her younger sister had been talking, boasting even.

She was subdued that evening as she prepared the meal. Now she sat at the table and thought of her sister. Was it not sufficient that her sister had taken the man, her intended? Was it not sufficient that she had lived with him in her parents' home, that she heard the sweet sound of learning as her husband and father discussed a difficult *Tosafos*?

No, that wasn't sufficient! She also had to boast about her achievement. To cap it off, just a few days before, her sister and her husband had left. He was now a *cheder rebbi* in his family's village. What would people say now?

When Pinchas walked in a few moments later, his shoulders bent and eyes dull, she realized that he too had overheard the gossip.

Without even sitting down, he said to her, "Why did you decide to meet me?"

"Well, I never did get to see your camels that first day, when you came to repair the chair, but I knew we would meet again."

Pinchas understood her message. She too had heard the gossipmongers. The hurt was written on her features. Without repeating the hateful words, she chose this way to convey her caring for him. How wise he had been to insist on meeting her. Had there ever been such an understanding woman? Let everyone say what they wanted. He would not let them ruin what was good and precious in their lives.

Faigy was relieved when she saw his smile. Amity was restored between them, but anger toward her sister grew strong within her.

Slowly the gossip turned to other matters, yet the effect of gossip never quite disappears. It lingers, causing harm and spreading poison. After that day, shards of anger and bitterness remained deep within the young couple. Faigy, especially, could not forgive her sister. In spite of the reassurance his wife gave him, worry over why his wife had truly agreed to marry him would not leave Pinchas.

Faigy and Pinchas remained in the village, and though Rav Simanovitch and his wife had feared that only stubbornness and hurt pride had caused their precious daughter to make her decision, they saw that the marriage was a good one. Pinchas not only provided well for his family, but he was also a kind man, good to his wife and patient with his children.

His daily learning after work was a source of pride to Faigy. It was clear to her that her husband was respected in the village.

Yet, in spite of her happiness, her anger at her sister did not abate. Years passed and life in the shtetl settled down to its routine of work and rest. Although each year her sister sent her a letter, asking for forgiveness, Faigy remembered the pain she had felt and remained obdurate.

BOOK ONE

Faigy's Story

Chapter 1

"Please tell me how you came to live here," the young girl said to me. "Please tell me about your life in the shtetl."

She sat there with paper and pencil, looking at me, and suddenly I felt displeased with her. Why did I think of her as a young girl? She was twenty-two years old. At her age I was married with children, a young woman. But she sat there, no responsibilities, still in her parents' home—yes, a girl, not a woman.

"Maybe I will tell you, maybe not. Let me think about it."

She looked bewildered. "Oh, but I thought——"

"No, don't think," I interrupted her. "You need to go now. I wasn't expecting you and I have no time now."

As she left, I felt a great anger welling up in me. Did I not deserve some peace? Now, at last, those terrible dreams had left me. Talking of the past would surely bring them back to me. Thoughtless girl!

Then a great sadness overwhelmed me. I wanted to cry. But no, I was not one for crying. What did tears achieve? Nothing! So why then did I begin to sob?

So I forced the tears away, and though I tried to think pleasant thoughts, everyday thoughts, instead my mind went drifting back.

After I married Pinchas, life was good. As time passed, everything that had happened before was forgotten and life was pleasant.

The children started to arrive and my good husband provided sufficiently for us. We lived in a small but sweet little house, with a small patch of garden both at the front and back of the house. In the front, the garden with its apple tree provided a place for the children to play, while in the back, a vegetable plot provided extra food.

Pinchas learned every morning before work. He was always the first one in shul, and people remarked on it. Sometimes, men asked his advice on small matters that were too insignificant to trouble my father, the *rav.* Apparently, his advice was good. I heard all this and felt a great pride in my husband. His trade brought security, and his learning and standing brought pride. Could any yeshiva *bachur* have done the same? I thought not.

If my parents were disappointed by the choice I had made, they never showed it. We ate *shalosh seudos* with them each week, and they treated my husband with great respect.

If they were upset that my younger sister and her husband had moved away, they never referred to it. This surprised me, since my mother had always seemed to me much closer to her than to me.

So I was content. How could I know that all this would end? I still remember the day that my pleasant, secure life changed.

It was 1884, the fifteenth of April. That was the date on the letter, and I cannot forget it. I don't recall the Hebrew date.

In our little village in Lithuania, we went by the Hebrew dates. The outside world, with its different way of counting time, hardly influenced us. Our life was dominated by the little wooden shul, where the men davened and learned before and after work, and where we celebrated Shabbos and the festivals.

But on that day, my husband received a letter from Avraham Cohen, a friend of his who had left the shtetl to find a better life in England. He wrote how life there was so much more pleasant for him. *How foolish,* I thought at the time. What can be better than the life we lead here?

My husband read the letter and then handed it to me. On the top was written "15 April 1884." *What a strange way to write the date,* I thought. But then I read the whole letter.

Though he had been in England for only a year, he wrote in glowing terms of life there. He was earning a nice living. There was no unpleasantness toward Yidden.

"So he says he leads a good life over there," I said. "Good for him! What was wrong with his life here that he had to leave?"

My Pinchas reacted quite differently. "Listen, he says that over there, even around this time of year, when we celebrate Pesach and they celebrate their festival, there are no bad feelings, no threats against Jews. He says there are plenty of jobs there. You know he's a good learner, but somehow he could never make a success of a job here. So no parents wanted him for their daughter. But there he is making a good living."

"So the move wasn't the disaster I thought it would be," I said, and then turned to more important matters. I didn't say why the man hadn't married, because in such a small place everyone knew everything about each person. From the time he was a small boy Avraham had a terrible temper. It had not diminished as he grew older. What young girl would agree to marry him? No, for him it was necessary to travel far away. For us things were different. There was no reason for us to leave.

The little boys — Yaakov, Dovid, and Yosef — had gone to my parents to deliver some cookies I had made for Shabbos. Fraidy, my oldest daughter, was out in the garden, holding baby Bracha and singing to her. For the moment the house was empty and I could talk freely. I dismissed the letter and my husband's reaction to it and spoke of what was on my mind.

"The *rebbi* says that Yaakov is learning very well at *cheder*. He says you should learn extra with him on Shabbos, just him alone. He needs a bit more, to keep him interested, and there are too many boys in the class for the *rebbi* to give him what he needs. He says that one day he will go to yeshiva and make us all proud."

But my Pinchas hardly seemed to hear a word I said. "Yes, yes, our Yaakov is a good boy — but this letter. Maybe we should leave. This week, there's so little work to do. I fixed a chair. I made a small bookcase. The money I earned is barely enough for wine for Shabbos, maybe half a chicken. If not for the garden and the vegetables, and the cholent your mother sends over on Shabbos, I don't know what we would do."

The only word I caught was "leave." He couldn't be serious. Surely not! What a thought. Leave my family! Why? So we could have a whole chicken instead of half a chicken for Shabbos, maybe? Such foolishness! Really, he just missed his friend. He used to learn every night with him. Since Avraham left, he had never really found another suitable *chavrusa*. The letter, it reminded him of all that. But surely the idea would go away.

"So this week wasn't good," I said. "Last week was fine. Next week will be better. Now about Yaakov ..."

"Yes, yes. I will learn with him right after the Shabbos *seudah*. Someone will have to entertain Dovid and Yosef. That's usually when I tell the boys Shabbos stories."

So Shabbos passed peacefully. I made extra *kneidlach* for the chicken soup and a big potato kugel, so that when it came to the chicken course no one noticed that the portions were smaller.

The next day, after the Shabbos meal I took the boys and Fraidy out to the garden while the baby slept inside. I told them a story that my father had once told me, about a man who wanted an extra-special fish for Shabbos.

After that we walked over to my parents' house. They fussed over the children, happy that David and Yosef had come along. The boys enjoyed the attention and didn't complain that only Yaakov was with their father.

I was happy that father and son were learning together. One day Yaakov would go to yeshiva. He would stay and learn, and not be called home as his father was. My son would be known for his learning.

So Shabbos passed pleasantly, and when it was over I said "*Gut fun Avraham*" with great concentration. I was happy that Pinchas hadn't mentioned again the foolishness about leaving.

But after Havdalah, when the children were in bed, Pinchas returned to the subject, and that was when the trouble began. He was quite serious about this crazy idea.

"If we sell the house, we'll have money for tickets," he said.

"No, never. This house . . . my parents gave it to us when we married. I will never agree to selling the house."

"When we're living far from here, what good will this house be to you?" Pinchas said, as if leaving was a sure thing.

"This house will be ours when we return, when we see that life is better here," I said. "Besides, I'm not going anywhere. If you think that that place is so wonderful, you go ahead. If it's a paradise like they say, with lots of work and lots of money and no one who hates the Jews, then write to me and I'll follow."

"Do you remember that day, when we were both upset, and you talked of camels? Later that day you said you wanted to leave here. Do you remember?"

"Yes, of course I remember. Can I ever forget that time? I felt so betrayed. But that was long ago. My sister left. We stayed. Why leave now?"

"I said then that we would leave when the time was right. I didn't want you to leave then, when you were so bitter. But now . . . have you forgiven?"

Of course I still harbored that bitterness in my heart, but I spoke not of it. Instead I said, "How can you bring all that up? We're settled here now. People here have forgotten all about that time. We lead a good life here. We won't leave. Why do you want to leave? I cannot understand this.

"We have a good solid home, with separate rooms for us and for the children. The shul is always full of men learning. You can always find someone to learn with. So last week you didn't make much money. Did we starve? Were you hungry over Shabbos?

"So sometimes an ignorant person says a bad word to you, because this is their special festival when their priest talks against us. Do they harm you, those people? So they repeat what they hear the priest say. It's always been like that. Is that really a reason for us to go into the unknown?"

"I want a better life for all of us," he said.

"My husband, why do you say such things? Do I ever complain? You give me such a good life. Are we not content with each other?

"I'm not forced to go to the marketplace to sell goods, so that there is food in the house. I do not have to sit all day like the seamstress next door, while her husband is away, trying and failing to sell the books he carries around. You provide for us. You care for us. When did I ever say I was not happy and satisfied?"

It was as if he didn't even hear my words.

Was this my husband standing before me? Always he had been so patient, listening to my problems, even small ones, like the time the fire was too fierce and the *challah* burned, and the day when I had just cleaned the floor and the boys came running in, tracking mud everywhere. Always he listened carefully and then said just the right words that made me laugh and realize that nothing irreparable had occurred. Yet now, it seemed as if my words were floating in the air, unheard by him.

"If you won't come with me then I will go ahead, and when I have everything settled I will send for you and the children."

"What, you'll go alone? How can you say such a thing? When I agreed to marry you, you seemed so satisfied, so happy. Now you want to leave me?"

Did he really mean those words? How could he? Yet he sounded as if he truly would do such a thing. My heart turned to stone.

"No, I don't want to leave you," Pinchas said. "I want to leave this place. I want you to come with me. Maybe the people here have forgotten about your sister, about the *bachur* who was meant for you, but about me — the carpenter's son marrying the *rav's* daughter — that they will never forget."

"What's wrong? Are you not a fine learner, as fine as any yeshiva *bachur*? Did you not return from yeshiva only because your father needed you? You're a good husband to me. I have no regrets that I married you. Are you telling me now, after all these years, that you have regrets?"

"My Faigy, how can you say such a thing? When the matchmaker came to me that day, and I wanted to meet only you, I truly meant it. I was overjoyed when you agreed."

"So, I did agree, and we have a good life here. Because you work, I have no need to find a way to make a living. I can care for my children and my home. Do you think my life would have been so much better with ... with ..."

I found I could not even say his name. The anger was still within me, like the shame was still within my dear husband. I wanted to reassure him, to make him forget the hurtful words he had overheard long ago, but he continued speaking.

"Life here is not bad, but there, in London, it will be better. Look what it says in this letter. There in the carpenter shops they do fine carving on the furniture and are highly paid for it. When do I have a chance here to do fine carving?"

I thought of the beautiful box where I stored the cutlery, the delicately carved Havdalah container, and wondered again at my dear husband's talents.

Before I had a chance to respond, I heard him say, "And in that country there are no pogroms. Do you hear? Never any pogroms."

"When have we had a pogrom here? The government protects us."

"Ai, the government. And what of the next government? The Bloch family went to Nizhny Novgorod, just over the border. It was peaceful, like here, when suddenly came the pogrom. Now they're all dead — and not only them, but many others too. What happened there can happen here."

Really, for a man who studied Gemara, his thinking was skewed. What logic was there in his words?

"No, if they had remained here, they would have been safe," I said. "Our government does not allow such things."

"Faigy, I hear them talk. I hear them in the marketplace. I hear them when I go to buy wood. They don't love us. In London I will make money from my carving. In London we will never fear pogroms. In London I will give you a fine life. If you're afraid, then I will go ahead, and when I can send you good news, you and the children will follow."

So with that I had to be satisfied. But of course, I was not. I knew I would have to talk him out of this crazy idea.

Chapter 2

"The province of Lithuania as a whole was free from pogroms. Totleben, the governor of his province, strictly maintained law and order in his area. But even he was a party to the so-called 'legislative pogroms' that came into force in 1882 as a result of recommendations of the various gubernatorial commissions appointed by the central government to report on matters affecting the position of the Jews."
—Saron and Hotz, *The Jews in South Africa*, p. 66

The next morning, as soon as the boys were off to *cheder* and Pinchas to his workroom, I walked with my girls to my parents' house. My mother was surprised to see me so early in the day. Normally I would visit only once the housework was done and lunch was prepared and bubbling on the stove.

Still, she welcomed us warmly, gave the girls sweet cookies, and was surprised when I sent them out to the garden to play. Before she could get a word in, I said, "Pinchas received a letter from England . . . you know, from his friend who left about a year ago. Pinchas wants to follow him to London. He wants us to leave. He believes what it says in the letter about how good it is there."

"You don't believe it?" my mother asked.

"That one . . . Ach, he's a good learner maybe, but . . . Of course he left. Here, his friends were marrying, one after another, and who would take him for their daughter? All of a sudden, far away in a strange land, he's successful! I can't believe it. Anyway, even if he *is* happy there, good for him. My husband is a fine craftsman. He has no need to run away from here."

"You said all this to your husband?"

"Of course, but he didn't want to listen. He sat down and learned, and then when I started to talk again, he walked out and went to the *beis midrash*—to learn, he said, but more likely so he didn't have to listen to me."

My mother sighed. "Let this be a good week for him, and then, with Hashem's help, he will be satisfied here."

Feeling more cheerful, I walked home with the girls. Pinchas and the boys came home for the midday meal, and all seemed well. He mentioned no more about the move and returned to work. Later, when the children were in bed, he sat down across from me to talk.

"The shtetl nearest to us is building a new shul," he said. "The old one is about to fall down. They didn't know what to do. Then all of a sudden, they received money from a man who left years ago. Now, it seems, he has made it big in that faraway place called Africa—the Tropowitzes went there a few months ago, remember? So anyway, the man sent them money for a shul. He remembers it was nearly falling down when he used to *daven* there.

"They asked me to come in every day and help their carpenter. The pay will be good. I'll have to leave early every morning and return late, maybe even sleep there some nights—just on the days when there's work that must be completed on that same day."

Well, that was a relief. No more talk of leaving, a good job lasting for weeks, good pay. What could be better?

Such foolishness! How wrong could I be?

⟨⟩

The weeks went by peacefully. Pinchas came home most nights, exhausted from the work and the journey home. So tired was he that he didn't even set aside time for learning in the evening. On Friday he would hand over money for Shabbos. I had thought it would be a big sum, after all that hard work, but it was always the same—sufficient to buy wine and half a chicken.

Rather than cause problems, rather than ruin our *shalom bayis*, I did the best I could. I made lots of *kneidlach* for the soup. I made a variety of kugels—carrot, potato, and even cabbage. But no one liked the cabbage kugel.

Every Shabbos, after the *seudah*, Pinchas learned with Yaakov. Every week I took the other children out to the garden and told them stories, about Shabbos and about my family. Oh, I told all sorts of stories on those Shabbos afternoons. I had such a feeling of contentment as I sat there, in the garden, no longer living under the threat of a forced departure.

Then there was the great day when we all went to visit the completed shul. Pinchas hired a wagon and the boys missed *cheder* that day. We drove, together with his family and mine, through the countryside. The towns-people were assembled outside the new shul, dressed in their Shabbos best, though it was a weekday. The *rav* held the Torah, and behind him, the men waited. Between them the little boys jumped up and down with excitement.

First the men went in. Then the women followed, crowding in behind the *mechitzah*, peering through the delicate carving that I recognized as Pinchas's handiwork. I could just see the carving on the *aron kodesh*, but even when standing on my tippy-toes the carving on the *bimah* was hidden from me.

What a wonderful shul it was, with rows of beautiful wooden benches and a fine large *bimah*, and the roof, painted blue, with little white stars. Around the wall, below the stars, were pictures of the desert, the *Luchos*, and Noach's *teivah* and the animals.

The man who had done the paintings stood next to my Pinchas, in a place of honor, in the first row of the shul.

Then the *rav* began Minchah, and the women listened quietly. At home, when I went to shul, the women would always gather around me as I read the words for them from my *siddur*. But here, no one knew me, and I remained silent, drinking in the words of prayer, so grateful that this work had kept us home and made my husband forget the words of that letter calling him away.

After that we went home. I was so proud of my husband and the great work he had done in creating that shul. I was happy that I had married Pinchas, a fine man who could create such a marvelous shul. I knew that the carpenter in the next village was an old man who worked only a few hours each morning, and that it was my Pinchas who had drawn up the plans and supervised all the work. It was my Pinchas who had done the fine carvings on the *aron kodesh* and the *bimah*.

My sister's husband, who taught young children, could not compare with my Pinchas, who with his two hands could create a shul of such beauty. Now there would be no more talk of us leaving. He had made his talent known. Other work of a similar nature would follow. My Pinchas would make a good living, and my boys, starting with Yaakov, would one day sit and learn in yeshiva.

I was quite unprepared for the words that Pinchas uttered once we had bedded down the children.

"The money from that work—I was careful with it," he said. "That's why we had so little each Shabbos. Now I have sufficient funds to buy tickets for all of us. There's no need to sell the house. You can remain here, until I send you word to come, or you can travel with me. The choice is yours."

That was when the fight began, soft at first, but then louder so the children woke up and came peering at us. So we stopped. The next morning, Pinchas was at shul even before I woke up. He began leaving early and coming home late, and still we fought whenever he was home.

"Huh, him you believe?" I said. "Remember his fine stories as he tried each new endeavor! We will not go."

"Oh, my Faigy, why would he write these things if they are not true? If you don't trust him, if you're afraid to go, then I will go ahead and send for you."

"Why? Everyone knows now what fine work you do. There will be more work like this."

But Pinchas shook his head. "No. It will not happen again. Is it every day that a Jew living far away becomes so wealthy that he can send money to build a whole shul anew? Besides, now my brother wishes to remain here, to work with my father. He learned much over these last few months, working in my place here in the shtetl. There is barely sufficient work for two. In London, there is work, fine work, furniture for wealthy people that needs fine carving. So Avraham says."

"I'm afraid to believe those words."

"If you're afraid to go, then I will go ahead and make sure that all is well before I send for you."

It was too much for me. "I will not go," I said.

Out into the dark I ran. My mother was clearing away the dishes from the evening meal. My father sat with a big *sefer* in front of him, learning by candlelight. Words tumbled out of me while my father sat absorbed in his learning, but my mother listened.

"What, you want to remain here with the children?" she said. "You want to become an *agunah* like your friend Perel?"

"Her husband went off to Palestine. If it was the Holy Land we were going to, do you think I would remain behind?"

"Still, his friend says that in England they don't hate the Jews, that he will make a fine living."

"Foolishness! Who would believe such a thing? Pinchas can go. If by some miracle it's true, then I will follow with the children."

The words that followed hurt me. They pierced my soul.

"You married the man, you must obey him," my mother said. "You cannot remain here alone."

My mother wanted to be rid of me! I was dumbfounded. I stared at her and she sat very still, looking at me. Then she went out of the room and came back with her well-worn book of *Tehillim*.

"Take this. It will protect you and comfort you."

All this time my father hadn't looked up.

"Tatte, will you speak with my husband? Will you talk him out of his foolishness?"

"What can I do?" he said. "It is the duty of the wife to follow her husband's wishes."

Once again, my parents had let me down. They had allowed my sister to humiliate me, by taking the man who had come for me. The old bitterness welled up within me.

So my parents wouldn't help me. They wouldn't talk sense into my husband. My mother's only concern was that I shouldn't be left behind forever and become an *agunah*, a drain upon the family.

My father, who had been so against the matchmaker's suggestion years before, who had wanted me to wait until he could find another yeshiva *bachur* who would remain in learning, now supported Pinchas, the carpenter.

The duty of the wife is to follow her husband's wishes. The words echoed through my mind.

But what if the husband's wishes were bad and the wife knew better? Did the wife's wishes have no bearing? I had only myself to depend on. I would sit with my husband and explain to him carefully, patiently, why he couldn't believe his friend's words. I would persuade him that now that he had built such a fine shul, his reputation would go forth to other places and more work, similar work, would follow.

With these thoughts I returned home. I had never regretted my decision to meet with Pinchas and then to wed him. True, I had only had the courage to say that I desired the meeting because of the humiliation I had suffered that day. But after that very first meeting, as I realized that Pinchas was my true *bashert*, the yeshiva *bachur* who had desired my sister disappeared from my thoughts.

From that first moment, Pinchas became the central pillar of my life. He found favor in my eyes, and he too was pleased with me and with our marriage.

Now, as I walked home, I practiced the words I would say. I was sure that he would listen carefully and see that I was correct. We would remain.

Ach, how wrong can a person be?

Chapter 3

"By 1800, there were 20,000 Jews in the East End of London, and a great surge of immigration followed the assassination of Tsar Alexander II in 1881."

— Gerry Black, *The History of Jews' Free School, London*, p. 2

Faced with the decision of leaving all that I knew or being left behind, there was really no choice at all.

We left with the boys — Yaakov, Dovid, and Yosef — and the two girls, Fraidy and baby Bracha.

Yaakov was already six years old and understood what was happening. He was full of questions: "Where are we going?" and "When will we return?" These were questions I could not answer. Dovid, at four, had just recently begun *cheder*. He was unhappy there and so he asked no questions, happy to be told that for the next little while there would be no classes as we traveled far away.

Yosef had just turned three. He asked no questions, and the little girls simply watched all the activity with big wondering eyes.

I thought my heart would break, but what could I do except dry my tears and make sure everything was carefully bundled together, and that we would have sufficient food for the long journey?

First, though, we had to travel over the border and then endure a terrible journey, five days in the bottom of a ship, people packed in together, rows of bunks stacked one next to another. And the food — basins of herring lowered down to us, dry, stale black bread, sometimes potatoes. Not that I was able to eat anything, with the rocking of the boat, the dirt, and the crowds of people. For this we had paid good money! I was glad I hadn't sold my house. I had rented it out to a cousin, for a pittance. Now she could move out of her parents' house, with her husband and baby. So we were both satisfied. She had somewhere to stay and I knew I had a place to come back to.

Arriving in a strange country, where they speak a language you don't understand, is no simple matter. We were told to disembark and so we did, climbing up from the dirty hold and walking off the ship. Down the gangplank we went, carrying our bundles.

The land seemed to sway beneath us as if we were still at sea. It was just before dawn, cold and grey, and a thin drizzle misted upon us.

"America?" a passenger asked my husband.

"No, *Engeland*, London," my husband replied.

"Oh no, this is a place called Liverpool," someone else said.

"Soon my brother is coming to take us to our new home here," another man said.

He looked around hopefully, and sure enough, a man came hurrying toward us.

It was lucky that man came then. He explained that often people were sold tickets to what they thought was America, but instead were given tickets only to this place, Liverpool in England.

"Better you should stay here," he said. "There are many Jews here. There is work here."

Then he looked at the envelope that Pinchas held out to him. "Oh, London. You must go to the train station and buy tickets there to London. You have English money?"

My Pinchas looked lost and afraid. My Pinchas, the source of my strength, now afraid? What had he brought us to? How would we get English money?

Fortunately, the man took pity on us. He exchanged some of the money that Pinchas had for English money. He wrote on a piece of paper what kind of tickets we needed and told Pinchas to hand it in at the train station office. He told a man with a horse and cart to deliver us to the train station.

What can I tell you? We traveled many miles on that great long train, through green fields and many towns, arriving at last in the place called London. Then we had to find a horse and cart, and show the envelope with Avraham's address again and again, until at last we arrived, just as evening was drawing in.

By now, after so many shocks and disappointments, this one was to be expected. This room, so sparsely furnished, hardly clean — this was where Avraham was so happily and successfully settled?

At first we didn't recognize him, with his trimmed beard and strange clothing. "Welcome," he said, and then looked shamefaced. "I never thought you would really come."

Looking around the place I understood why. The letter had boasted of a fine life, but the room in which we now stood looked more like a storeroom for vegetables than a place where people ate and slept.

"Come in, rest, eat," he said. "Tomorrow I will find you a place to stay and a place to work."

Thoroughly tired, I slept on the floor with the children, with the big blanket filled with goose feathers covering us, feathers I had plucked myself.

In the morning we were taken to a large building and then up some stairs to two small rooms.

"See, there's one room for cooking," Avraham said. "The other room is for sleeping. I told them you would pay at the end of the week, when Pinchas brings money from work."

I was left there, with our bundles, with the children, and off they went, Pinchas and his friend, who apparently knew how to find him work. What was I to do for food? I had some dry bread left from the voyage. There was water dripping from a strange-looking pipe over a sink. I played around with it until the drips increased and water flowed.

But this water was strange, a murky liquid, quite unlike the clear water we drew from the well, and I was afraid. I did what my mother had done every Pesach. I took out a large pot from the bundle and found some muslin. After straining the water, it looked fairly clear, and then I managed to get the few bits of wood in the stove lit and boiled the water.

All this time, the children had been crying. They were thirsty and hungry, but I waited until the water had cooled. Then I wet the bread and fed it to the children. At that moment I knew that this move had been a mistake. They didn't even have pure, clean water in this place.

Later, much later, Pinchas returned. He handed me a small bowl with pickled herring and a loaf of bread. Yaakov looked at him and said, "But Tatte, where are we to eat? There are no tables or chairs here."

I had always been so strict about the children sitting when eating. I had always insisted that they never rush into the house, grab some food, and then run back out to play. Now I looked at the bare room, at Pinchas struggling to reply, and I said, "Just for today, we will sit on the floor in a circle. I'll put a cloth on the floor and we'll eat after everyone has washed their hands."

Somehow I had to find tables, chairs, and beds. But how?

It was clear to me that Pinchas, too, was having doubts about this move. The sadness was etched on his face. My anger dissolved and pity flooded through me. There would be time for talk the next day. We would leave this place and return home, but now was not the time to talk of such matters.

So we ate and bentched, and then, without much talk, we went to sleep.

That night I dreamed of the small cottage, the patch of ground with the apple tree, the little shul. The pink apple blossoms fell on me and the children laughed, and faraway I heard the sound of men davening.

Then suddenly, everything changed. I was standing beside the room where I had hoped to one day live with my husband.

"Go away!" my sister said. "This is mine now. Go away!"

She grew bigger and bigger, until she towered above me and I screamed in fear.

Just then I awoke. There was a cacophony of noise coming through one of the tiny, dirty windows.

Pinchas was already up and dressed. "I must go. Here they begin work early. I will return late. Here, this is the last of the money I have. See what you're able to do with it. Oh, my Faigy, I should have heeded your words."

"We can return," I said. "There is no need to remain here."

Pinchas gave a deep sigh. "What will we use for money? All our money went for the journey here."

"We cannot remain here. Look at Avraham. With all his talk, look at how he lives. Look at these rooms. Was not our home a much better place?"

"Faigy, we cannot go home. I cannot earn a living back home. Avraham, well, you know him—he has no training for anything, so he tries this and that. Remember the fine shul I built. I can work. Remember that man in Liverpool who helped us? He too came from far away. Did you see his fine clothing? He came here and now he's doing well. I will work hard. We'll soon move to another, better place. You won't be sorry we came."

My husband turned and left. At home he would stride out to work, a smile on his face. Now he almost stumbled out, his shoulders slumped, and though I wanted to say more, I took pity and was silent.

———

Since I had no choice, I began to make arrangements to settle in this strange place. Fortunately, my neighbor, Rivka, spoke Yiddish. She helped me settle in.

She lent me rags and a bucket and while the older children took care of the little ones, I scrubbed the place clean.

With that done, we left those miserable rooms, me and the children and Rivka. She showed me where I could buy kosher meat. She took me to a long street where everything was sold, and there she bargained for a table and some chairs, and some rickety beds.

My father had pressed some money into my hands when we parted. I used it now to pay the man. Though it was a foreign coin, he took it from me and sent his young son to transport the furniture to our house on a small wagon.

It was difficult, walking in that crowded street, with Yaakov holding his younger brothers by his hands and the girls clinging to my skirt, but with the little money I had left over we managed to acquire, with Rivka's help, not only furniture, but also a few vegetables.

When Pinchas returned home later that day, our bundles were unpacked, the rooms were clean and furnished, and a vegetable soup was bubbling on the stove.

Later, when I thought about it, I regretted the work I had done that day. Maybe if I had simply sat and cried, and not done anything, Pinchas would have relented. Maybe he would have somehow found a way for us to return. But now he smiled broadly, remarked on what an *eishes chayil* he had married, and we sat and ate. He spoke of his work that day, and how he would do fine carving, and how we would soon move to a larger, better place.

When the children were asleep, I said, "Please, no talk of another place. Large, small—it means nothing to me. We must return home."

"Very well. In one year, we'll talk about it again. Maybe by then you will want to stay. Maybe by then I will want to leave. Who knows? But please, let us not talk of this again until that time."

On the third day of our stay in London, I asked Rivka about a *cheder* for Yaakov. Had his *rebbi* not said he had a promising future? Had his *rebbi* not said that one day he would be a top learner at a yeshiva?

"Oh no, here we have no such thing," Rivka said. "What *cheder*? What yeshiva? No, here our children are educated in the English way. We have a fine school here, for boys and even for girls. It's called the Jews' Free School. I think it's the best school in all of London.

"Tomorrow, have your Yaakov be ready early in the morning. I'll send my Michael to take him to the school."

Yaakov went with Michael, as arranged, and returned home for lunch the following day full of exciting news.

"In that place they don't talk Yiddish," he said. "All day I sat next to a boy who speaks the new language, and he told me what was happening. Soon, I too will know this English. We learn in a large building with many rooms. We go to many different rooms during the day and learn from many different teachers. Here they say teacher, not *rebbi*. You know something? With these teachers we don't wear a yarmulke!

"With one teacher, we learn Chumash, and then we wear a yarmulke. But it's so easy, that lesson. It's *Bereishis*, and I learned that long ago at *cheder*."

Yaakov paused to take a breath, then continued. "Oh, I must tell you, Dovid can also go to this school. Tomorrow I will take him. And I forgot to tell you that they call me Jack, not Yaakov. The teacher said Yaakov is a name from the shtetl and here we are in a new land, with a new language and new customs. He also said there is no need for my *peyos* to be so very long, and I should tell you to cut them."

So that is how I forgot my dreams of Yaakov becoming a *rav* like my father. This was a strange place. Rivka had said there were no *cheder*s here. Her children went to this school, this Jewish school where they told Jewish boys to cut their *peyos*, where they went bareheaded for most of the day, where they learned Chumash for only a small part of the day.

Pinchas had spoken of maybe returning in one year — no, not returning, just discussing the possibility. What would be with my Yaakov, returning with hardly any *peyos*, and not having learned Chumash properly for a whole year?

"But if I cut my *peyos*, what will they say when we return?" Yaakov said.

The words cut into my thoughts.

"Yes, that's a problem. Tonight I will talk to your *tatte*. He will know what to do."

What can I tell you? I needn't have worried about such things, since we never returned to the shtetl. Where were we to get the money to return? Pinchas' wages were just sufficient for rent and food. I made sure that the rooms were clean and everyone was fed. I did what had to be done, but my heart was filled with sadness, with longing, for everything I had left behind.

Those first few weeks we faced one problem after another. First there was the decision about the *peyos*. Pinchas took Yaakov aside—no, not Yaakov; he insisted we call him Jack—and discussed the laws regarding how long the *peyos* had to be.

"But if I don't cut them, I'll look different from all the other boys," Jack said.

Pinchas was silent for a while, and then said, "When we *daven* with a different *minyan*, we're told to follow their custom. So if this is the custom here, I'll cut your *peyos*, but only to the permitted length and no shorter."

That is how we proceeded: one problem following another. Always, with some degree of compromise, a solution was found.

I was so tired those first few weeks, and then I realized why. Another child was on its way. Now I was gripped with terror. A child would be born here, in these strange surroundings, without the village midwife, without my mother by my side!

In the end, the delivery was an easy one. The midwife turned out to be competent. But oh, how I missed my family, my mother caring for the children, my neighbors bringing me hot meals. Here, after a day or so, I had to be on my feet and see to everything once again.

We held the bris in the small *shtiebel* that Pinchas now went to. We managed to provide wine, *kichel*, and herring. It was a hurried affair, as the men could not be late for work.

Afterwards I wrote my parents.

It was difficult to have a bris so far from you. But baruch Hashem, all went well. We have called the boy Shmuel, after Fetter Shmuel, who was a great scholar. May he follow in his great-uncle's footsteps.

What I did not say was that here we called him Samuel. Nor did I say that there was little chance of him being a great scholar. There were *chadarim* here, in small poky rooms, after school. But Jack had gone a few times when we first arrived, and then refused to return.

"I learn nothing there," he had burst out. "What I learned when I first began *cheder*, that's what they do each day. Besides, do we not have Chumash lessons in school, every day for one hour?"

All our children, one after another, went to the Jews' Free School as they reached the age of four. The girls were in one building and the boys in another. There was no chance that this new little boy would become a great scholar. By now I had realized we would never return home.

At first I thought I could work, perhaps take in piecework like some other women and save that money for the fare back home, but it seemed to me that there was always another baby. Either I was waiting for one or I was caring for one. I could not work and earn money. I realized that going back was an impossible dream.

Day to day, I managed. I learned the new language. I kept the house clean, no easy task because of the black soot that seemed to seep through every window and crack.

My anger at Pinchas for making us leave gradually left. What use was it?

I was taken up each day with caring for my family. I kept the children healthy, no easy task, as money for food was short and the water remained murky. Every drop had to be first strained and then boiled and cooled. Finding sufficient food each day was a nightmare. Here there was no small vegetable patch. There was no cellar where cabbages and potatoes could be stored when they were taken from the earth. No milkman came to the door with fresh milk, topped with sweet cream. Every bit of sustenance had to be bought, haggled for, and carried home.

Once again, Rivka helped me. Together we went to the market for vegetables as late in the day as possible. Then the best, freshest merchandise was gone, but what was left could be bargained down, since the seller knew it could not last until the following day.

The butcher sold us "bones for the dog," though of course he knew that no such creature belonged to us. Soup was made from that broth.

Though I managed to keep the family fed, keeping their clothing clean was even more difficult. Laundry day in the shtetl had been arduous, but there the garden provided a place to hang the washing. In the two small miserable rooms in London I had to drape wet clothing over a large wooden frame and then hoist it above the stove.

During the week, Pinchas returned home too tired to do anything but eat his meal, *daven* at the *shtiebel*, and then return home to sleep. By the time the children were bedded down, I was so exhausted I could hardly move.

Shabbos was different.

On Shabbos I managed to make a fine meal. Not as good as that at home, but adequate. The room was bathed in the glow of the candles. The entire family had been to the bathhouse. We sat in our Shabbos clothing and sang *zemiros*. Pinchas told Shabbos stories to the little ones and said *divrei Torah* for the older children.

Those twenty-four hours passed in a cocoon of rest and peace. By the time the week began again, with all its problems, I found I could face them. Once the children returned to school and Pinchas to work, I began the week with a letter home.

Since the Shabbos mood was still upon me, I could write with some degree of cheerfulness. I realized then why we had received the false letter from Avraham. It was because of shame — shame over admitting we had made a mistake, that the life we had left was far better than the new life — and hope, the desperate hope that somehow everything would improve, that we would move to a better area, or that we would somehow, by some miracle, earn enough money to return.

So I refused to complain, but I also wouldn't write false glowing accounts. I did not want to be responsible for influencing anyone else to come here.

Shabbos was so good, I wrote. *Pinchas gave a fine d'var Torah. My kneidlach turned out well, as light as air. The children looked so sweet in their Shabbos clothing.*

All this was true, of course, but it wasn't the real truth. There was nothing about the terrible greyness all around, the continual soft wet rain, the noise from the street, and the terrible, long weekdays.

In this way seven years went by.

By then the family had grown. Jack was nearly bar mitzvah. The children had new names. They were now called David, Joseph, Frieda and Bertha. The children born in England were known as Samuel, Ethel, Rose and Isaac. Even I was called Fay by the neighbors. Pinchas remained Pinchas. If called by any other name, he simply refused to respond.

All the children attended the Jews' Free School. They were strict about the way the children dressed, which was good even though it meant more work for me, since I had to iron everything carefully. But they gave each child a new set of clothes each Pesach, and I didn't complain.

What wasn't so good was that they told the children to speak only English, even at home, and to teach their parents English. It isn't good when children know more than their parents. They lose some respect and it makes it more difficult to get them to listen.

Then there were other things, small details, but they made things difficult at home. The boys only kept their heads covered during Hebrew studies, one hour a day. The rest of the time they had to behave like Englishmen, and apparently these people do not cover their heads inside. It was difficult to make the boys keep their caps on their heads at home.

The girls had some Hebrew lessons too, but they were also taught subjects such as cooking and laundry and needlework. They wore white pinafores over their dresses. It was so hard to keep them clean. They needed to be constantly washed and then dried in that rainy climate, and then that was followed by careful ironing. So much work it was.

I was just past thirty by the time all the children were in school, but I felt like an old woman, tired and unhappy. Somehow I found the strength to make food each day, to see that the children wore clean clothes, to clean the flat for Shabbos—but that was all.

My days seemed to be filled with work, from the moment I woke up until I went to sleep. It was no easy matter to live in such a place. The air itself was dirty, coating everything in black dust. This could not be good for us, so each morning, as soon as the children left, I cleaned and scrubbed.

I strained the murky water from the tap and boiled it, and then covered it and placed a dipper there so we could have clean drinking water.

Once that was done, I began to prepare for the midday meal. The children came home, but not Pinchas. He ate at his workbench. I would save any leftover meat from Shabbos to put between pieces of bread for Pinchas.

I learned to make what the English call "bread pudding." With stale bread bought from the baker, and any other sweet foods I could find, such as a few raisins or an apple, I added an egg and milk, and baked it all, so the children would have a hot and filling meal.

The children all came home together. The older ones collected the younger ones at the school gate, and they walked together, in a group. They would come bounding in, talking all the while. I made them wash their hands, although some of them tried to avoid this. But I didn't relent. Such illness there was in this land. There were so many dangers for growing children. No, the house had to be clean and their hands had to be clean before eating.

On other matters I gave in. I didn't stop Jack when he behaved as if he knew everything and the younger children nothing, and took charge of them. I didn't interfere when quiet David allowed Jack to push him to one side so that he always had the rickety stool, rather than the one solid chair. I didn't stop Joseph from reading at the table, though what he could find of interest in an old newspaper was beyond me.

The girls too behaved in a manner that would have been foreign to them back home. Frieda seemed to never stop talking. She sat beside Jack and they talked and talked, ignoring the other children, ignoring me. But I didn't have the energy to correct her. Bertha and Ethel sat silently, eating with serious concentration and ignoring little Rose, who sat beside them. Every now and then she tried to talk to them and get them to listen to what had happened in her class that morning.

"Yes, very interesting," came the usual reply. "Now eat up your food or we'll be late."

I should have spoken to little Rose. I should have corrected the girls, told them not to ignore their sister, but instead I just sat and watched.

Samuel and Isaac sat beside one another. Seven-year-old Samuel, three years older than his brother, was saying, "If you don't want anymore, then pass it to me. I'll finish it." Isaac determinedly held onto his plate and gobbled up the last remnants.

Really, it was too bad of Samuel. I tried so hard to give them enough food. How could he try and take food from his little brother?

Yet I said nothing and wondered what I would make for the evening meal, since the last bit of food from Shabbos had been used up that day, and there would be no money from Pinchas until Friday afternoon.

Jack seemed to read my thoughts.

"Oh, Mother," he said. "I still have some money left over from shopping at the butcher before Shabbos. I meant to tell you, but it was such a rush getting ready. Should I buy some bones on the way home from school this afternoon? Should I give some of the money to Frieda so she can go to the market on the way home for vegetables?"

Careless boy, not giving me the change! Still, his suggestion was a good one. There would be a meal that evening. As I nodded, he shouted, "Right then. Time to go." The children bentched rapidly and then ran out the door.

I was left there, staring out the window at a grey sky, and thinking about my family and the village we had left behind, with its clean air and sunshine.

How had I allowed myself to be brought to such a terrible place?

One would think that because Pinchas had caused us to come here, there were bad feelings between us. But it was not so. Here, far away from all our family, we had only one another, and never a cross word was spoken between us.

How was I to know, then, that though we were managing now, it would not always be so?

Chapter 4

"In Hanbury Street there were eighteen workers crowded in a small room measuring eight yards by four yards and a half and not quite eight feet high. The first floor was let out to lodgers who were also Jews. Their rooms were damp as water was coming through the rotting wall ... The kitchen range was falling to pieces ... It was in such a district, and amidst such surrounding squalor, that in the early days, the Jews' Free School set about the formidable task of educating the mostly immigrant Jewish children; it was in such accommodation that the Jewish mother contrived to keep a clean home and feed and clothe her family ..."

— Gerry Black, *The History of Jews' Free School*, London, p. 2

When I thought things couldn't get any worse, they did. The date is engraved on my mind. It was Pesach, the 22nd of April 1891. It was a Wednesday night, and such a disastrous night it was.

Good health is a blessing we take for granted. My Pinchas had never been ill when we lived in the shtetl. When others became ill, he would chop wood for them. He would see that money was collected for them and quietly give it to them so they would not be shamed.

That was how things were done there. Here, in this big city, filled with many people, things were quite different. Here each person cared only for himself.

How did it happen that my Pinchas, never ill for a day in his life in the shtetl, began to suffer from breathing problems in London? True, the air was heavy with the blackness that comes from burning coal, and on many days a dull drizzle made the air damp. Yet the little ones never suffered in this way — only my dear husband.

On the last day of Pesach, our family was sitting around the table. On one side were the boys, dressed in the new clothes they had received from school. They looked like little English gentlemen in white shirts with large white collars, and brand-new boots.

The girls sat demurely in their new dresses, without the white pinafores they usually wore on weekdays. They had also been to Petticoat Lane and returned with colored ribbons that now sat firmly at the end of each tight braid.

The house smelled of soap and scouring powder, and the white cloth over the table was bathed in candlelight.

At that moment, the sound that I dreaded began. My husband was gasping for breath. The children were silent. They too knew what this meant. I fought to keep calm, fought to help my husband breathe normally even as fear coursed through me.

I spoke soothingly to him. I called for Frieda to bring a cup of steaming water to place before him. Slowly, he began to take short breaths and his ragged breathing became normal.

"This has gone on for long enough," I said. "We're going to the doctor."

As usual, Pinchas responded, "How will we pay him?"

Two days later, when Pesach was over and the children were at school, Pinchas was still lying on his bed, making horrible rasping sounds as he fought to breathe. I went to the pawn shop with my Shabbos dress, the last remaining memory of the home we had left behind.

I glanced at the few pitiful coins the man gave me. Soon they would be gone. Then I went home and together with a still protesting Pinchas, we made our way to the last terrace house, where the doctor had his rooms. The rain had turned into a soft drizzle. We removed our wet outer garments and sat on the old wooden chairs. To our surprise, the room was empty. Did that mean the doctor was away? Then there was a clatter of footsteps and a young boy ran out.

"Next," called the doctor.

The walk through the rain had not been good for Pinchas, and he began to gasp for breath.

As we sat down, the doctor said, "Ah, so that's the trouble, is it?" Without waiting for an answer he continued, "And if I am not mistaken, this has been going on for some time now. Correct?"

Pinchas was unable to do anything but struggle to breathe.

"Why didn't you come to me earlier?"

How could I explain the hopelessness of our situation? Since arriving in this forsaken place, Pinchas the proud carpenter no longer worked for himself, but for others. He spent his hours in a room packed with people, wood, glue and dust, and at the end of the week received a pittance. A day away from work meant less money and the risk of no job at all. What then?

We still lived in the same two small rooms. There never seemed to be sufficient money for food, but somehow I managed each day to keep the children fed and healthy.

Clothing was another problem. Of course, the clothes were passed down, from the older children to the younger, but that meant the older children needed new garments. Well, not new, but purchased from the secondhand clothing stalls on Petticoat Lane.

These thoughts went through me, and I struggled for a response.

"There is nothing I can do, so I don't suppose it makes any difference," the doctor continued. "What he needs is a warm climate, not this rain and fog and cold. It's the colonies he needs, somewhere like Cape Town. Got a letter just last week from a young man! Couldn't do anything for him either! Now a year later he writes that in the Cape he is quite free from problems."

The doctor riffled through some papers on his desk. He picked one up. "He writes, 'This is a wonderful place where the sun shines all through the year. Even the winters here are not cold, no snow, just a little rain on a few days. As soon as I arrived, I began to feel better. Now, all these months later, I breathe easily, without even thinking about it.'

"Yes, that's what you should do. Leave here. Go to the Cape Colony. Cape Town will cure you, just like it cured this man. Making a good living too, it seems."

"But is there nothing you can do for my husband now?" I asked.

"Steam, a bit of hot water—that's the best I can suggest. Take my advice. Go to the colonies. Sixpence, please."

So I handed over the money, and we left. The waiting room was empty. I wanted to sit down and remain sitting. What use was the doctor's advice? The Shabbos dress was gone, for useless advice? I should travel with a sick husband and nine children on a ship to a strange place? Where would the money suddenly appear from? How could we endure another sea voyage, traveling steerage? The journey to England had been horrific, but the family had been young and healthy, and full of hope. Then the journey had only been for five days. The Cape Colony was so far away. How long would such a journey take? No, it was out of the question.

Pinchas had never been ill back home. We would return to the shtetl. There he would get well and once again work for himself. Yes, it was time to go home. I had been writing falsely cheerful letters to my mother ever since we had arrived. Now was the time to tell the truth, to forget false pride and ask for money.

First we had to get back to our apartment. It was no easy task, since Pinchas was weak and unsteady on his feet. I had to make food for the children, from what? The money was gone. We walked home slowly and opened the door. I heard Jack and David talking.

"Don't tell Mother we didn't go to school this afternoon." Jack's voice came from the corner of the room.

"How then will we explain where we got these vegetables?" David asked.

"Listen, just say we met old man Kahn, and he gave them as a present. No need for anyone to know we helped with the horses and the deliveries."

"Can we go again?"

Just then the boys became aware that they were no longer alone.

I glared at the boys but said not one word. I supported Pinchas as he walked slowly, painfully, each step an effort. I helped him into bed and then watched as he sank down and closed his eyes.

The sense of hopelessness that had engulfed me was now overtaken by a slowly rising rage. My children, my boys, had been doing things behind my back. That was the kind of mother I had become in this depressing land, one who could be easily fooled and ignored. This would never have happened in the old days, in the shtetl. If I hadn't noticed anything unusual, one of my neighbors would have told me. Here, in this vast place, where every day was a struggle, children could do as they pleased.

Already filled with despair over the doctor's words, this was too much to bear.

"Never lie to me," I said to them. "Is that clear? Never lie to me again."

What kind of children was I bringing up here? We had to leave and the sooner the better. For the sake of Pinchas, for the sake of my children!

We had to return home. Then the doctor's words came back to me: We needed a place where the winters were warm. In the shtetl the winters were bitter. Snow came down heavily, sometimes almost blocking the doorway completely. Only the thought of spring and summer kept us going. In this other place, Cape Colony, there was never snow.

No, there could be no return home. A way had to be found for us to go to these colonies, to this place called Cape Town. Determination slowly began to displace my despair.

In the shtetl, I had been known as a strong and capable person. Here I had taken the path of least resistance, lacking energy to do more than just keep going. I could no longer simply accept each day as it came. If I was to save Pinchas, we had to go to the Cape Colony without delay.

In order to guide my children along the proper path, I knew I had to take firm control and not let their superior knowledge of a strange language and a strange place overwhelm me.

In that split second, with Pinchas barely able to stand without my support, and with the two boys looking up at me, I knew I had to find that stubborn streak I'd once had, that my parents had tried so hard to eradicate. Only that would save us now. How, I didn't know, but somehow I would succeed. First I helped Pinchas to lie down.

"David, sit beside your father. Call me if he needs anything."

The bundle of vegetables lay by the side of the small stove. Well, that was one problem solved. At least there was food for lunch.

"Now, Jack, tell me how you helped the man while I use these vegetables to make soup. Tell me everything. How long has this been going on? How often did you miss school?"

Jack stretched out his hand and gave me six shiny pennies. "We help Mr. Kahn with his deliveries every Thursday and Friday afternoon. We write a note to the teacher that says we have to stay home, and we sign your name on it. Today we helped as well, because after Pesach, when Mr. Kahn didn't work, he wanted to make an extra delivery. We go far, to where the big houses are. We run in and out with the orders. Mr. Kahn goes to the door and then he comes out and tells us what to take in."

I took the money. Six pennies! What good could six pennies do? We needed a vast amount to escape from this *gehinnom* that Pinchas had brought us to.

"The girls will be home from school soon," I said. "Tell me now, before they get home, every single thing that I don't know about."

"It began when school started last year. We always passed the stables just as Mr. Kahn was taking the horses out. So, well, you know how I like horses, and one horse was making trouble. I patted it, and stroked it, and then Mr. Kahn harnessed it while I was talking. Then, on my way home from school that day, he said he could do with some help, especially on Friday afternoons when he goes to the smart areas on the west side. That's when I started helping him.

"When we got back he gave me vegetables, and I met the girls as they came home from school and gave it to them. They said they had bought it at the market, like you had told them."

I remembered then how I had noticed one day how much more the girls had brought home than I expected, but I had felt grateful and didn't question them. How could I have been so lax?

"The teacher noticed that every week on Friday I was away," Jack said. "He asked me about it. I told him I must miss school then, because we needed the money I made. He just shrugged his shoulders, and said, 'If you keep up with your good marks, I will say nothing.'

"One day Mr. Kahn told me that it made everything go much more quickly when I rode with him, and he was making more money. He said he would pay me if I could bring another boy along. Well, that's when David started to come."

"Why did you bring home vegetables today? Why never before?"

"We always got vegetables, the leftovers, the ones he couldn't sell, but usually we met the girls on the way home from the market and they just added it to their bundles. Today we got home earlier than usual, I think, or maybe the girls are late."

I felt as if I would faint. The whole family was leading a life of deceit and I was blind to it.

"What about the money? You said he agreed to pay you."

"Yes, sixpence a time, if we both came."

"And what did you do with the money?"

There was a long pause.

"Tell me," I said. "I'm asking you. Food he gave you, and you brought it home. What did you do with the money?"

"Stamps," was the answer.

"What do you mean, stamps? Who do you write to?"

"No, they're stamps that have already been used. My teacher told us one day that people collect stamps. He showed us his stamp collection. So I found the shop where you can buy them. I bought a few stamps, but then I thought of a better idea. I used the money for tram fare and traveled to places where men work in big rooms. First I went from room to room asking if they threw away their letters with stamps. They did, so I asked if they would keep the stamps for me. Some said they would. Now, once a week I go and collect them."

"You work for these useless stamps?"

"Yes, and I put them in my book, a special book for stamps, in a special way so that the stamps aren't spoiled. Then they're worth money."

"That book is worth money?"

"Oh yes, definitely, lots and lots," Jack said confidently. "One day, soon, there'll be enough money so I can sell the book and the stamps and we can go home, to Bubbe and Zeide. I dream of them often. If no one wants to come with me, I will go alone. But I think everyone will want to come. Do you remember our garden?"

Could it be true? Did this child really have something valuable that could be turned into money? How much money could it be worth? Was it sufficient to pay for the fare to the Cape Colony? No, surely not. It was probably not sufficient to pay half, or even a quarter of the fare. No, even that couldn't be possible. But it was clearly worth something. How much? Where to get a fair price? How could I tell Jack that he would have to part with it, not to go to his beloved grandparents, but to go even farther away—so far away that return would forever be impossible?

What would third-class tickets cost? I had heard people say that third class was acceptable, not like steerage, where there was no separation between men and women and the food was doled out from large buckets. I had endured that for five days on the voyage to London. I could not endure it for weeks and weeks as the ship made its way far down south. Besides, Pinchas wouldn't survive such a voyage. The money would have to be found quickly, enough money so that we wouldn't travel in steerage.

"We will talk of this again but from now on, there are no secrets from me," I said. "Do you hear?"

That day, I went through the normal household routines, the cleaning and cooking, but the doctor's words constantly echoed through my mind. *It's the colonies he needs, somewhere like the Cape Colony, Cape Town. My patient wrote from Cape Town...*

As the day went on, Pinchas seemed a bit improved and spoke about going to work. The next day he slowly made his way down the stairs, breathing heavily.

Was it possible? Would we ever find a way to leave this miserable place?

Chapter 5

"The ships that ply the route from England to Cape Town were mainly
from the two British rival companies, the Union Fleet and Currie's
Castle Line . . . The ships were powered by both steam and sail power."
— Gwynne Schrire, *Memories of an Epic Journey*, p. 20

After Pinchas had gone, the children walked to the door. I pulled Jack back.

"Today you will come with me," I said. "Go get your book, the one with the stamps, the one you say is worth money."

Jack came back a few moments later with his precious stamp album. He looked none too happy. I felt a moment of pity for him. Then I thought of his deception, how for months he had been so untruthful. True, he had only wanted to help, but it was unthinkable to be so deceitful. The book could possibly be worth money. Money was needed. Every avenue must be pursued, no matter how unlikely.

"Come," I said. "We will first go to the shipping lines and find out how much the fare is to the Cape Colony. Then we will go to that stamp shop you spoke about and see what the book is worth."

I did my best to sound confident, but in truth I felt only fear and hopelessness. Putting my trust in a book filled with old, used stamps — what could be more foolish? Yet what choice did I have?

The shipping offices were not easy to find. I had to ask many people, until at last, someone directed us to the correct address. Once there my courage almost failed me when I saw the notice on the wall.

The Castle Line

Extra intermediate steamer for London. To Cape Town.

Leaving on Wednesday, the 4th May. Calling at Madeira.
Fare: 30 guineas first class, 23 guineas second class, and 10 guineas third class
Steerage: 2 guineas

It was leaving so soon! But then I thought, *The sooner the better.* The doctor's words had been quite clear. Only by leaving, by going to the colonies, would Pinchas be cured. Pinchas could not tolerate traveling by steerage in his poor state. But where would I find 110 guineas? Perhaps they would charge less for children? Feeling that the world was crashing down on me, but with nothing to lose, I walked up to the heavy wooden counter, where a bored clerk was standing.

"What is the fare, third class, for children?" I asked.

"How many children? What ages?"

I reeled off their ages. "Jack here is nearly thirteen, and his brother David is eleven. Then comes Joseph, ten, and my oldest girl, Frieda, is nine, then Bertha, eight . . ."

"Well, let's see."

"No, I'm not finished, Samuel is seven, Ethel is six, Rose is five, and Isaac is four years old."

"Oh my, what a list to remember! How many is that altogether? Sounds like a baker's dozen."

"Nine children, all under the age of thirteen," Jack said. "What would it cost?"

"You want the ship leaving on Wednesday?" the clerk asked.

How would I find the money? How could we be ready so soon?

Jack saw that I was having difficulty replying. "Can we book now?" he asked in a confident voice.

"Well, we have two cabins left, small ones, each with three bunks. If you could all fit in there, the children sleeping two to a bunk, I could do it for sixty guineas for the lot. But I'll need the money today. I can't keep it for you. First come, first served."

"I'll be back soon," I said, finding my voice at last. Fit all of us into two small cabins? But what other option was there? Sixty guineas was better than 110, but still an impossible sum.

"Come, now we will go to the stamp shop," I said to Jack.

The walk seemed endless. Eventually we came to a narrow lane.

"Here we are," Jack said, leading me up a flight of dirty, narrow steps.

The shop was small. The man behind the counter seemed to emerge slowly from the gloom. Jack placed his precious stamp album on the counter.

"How much will you pay me for this?" Jack asked.

I think Jack knew the true value of the book. He looked confidently at the man, waiting as he looked through the book. It appeared as if he was carelessly flipping through it.

"Ten quid," he said.

Jack grabbed the book back. "Mother, it is worth much more. Let us go elsewhere."

What could I say? Disappointment seeped through me. I had nurtured such unrealistic hopes. As we went out the door, I said to Jack in despair, "Where will we get sixty guineas?"

"Sixty guineas," the man said. "Someone already offered you sixty guineas? Young man, perhaps I should look again at the book."

I saw that my son was angry. He said quietly to me, "Mother, the man is trying to cheat me. It was bad enough to be forced to give up this collection, but to be swindled in such a fashion? No, I will not allow it. Besides, what can we do with so little money? We need at least sixty guineas. I'll ask my teacher if he wants to buy some of the stamps. Perhaps he will know of others who want to buy them. It will take time, but I will not be swindled in this manner."

What could I say? My hopes for saving my dear husband's life were rapidly fading.

Jack spoke now, in a loud, confident voice. "No. I know where to get the price I want. We will not do business, you and I."

"Sixty guineas," I heard the man say. "Someone will give you sixty guineas! Sixty-two guineas I'll give you. I may be a sentimental fool, but it seems to me that you're in need of the money, and the heavens will reward me for my good deed."

My Jack, it seems, had learned much since coming to this land. He turned around, placed the book on the counter, and held it down firmly. I realized at that moment that my young boy, who I had hoped would one day study in a yeshiva, was a child of the East End. I watched in amazement as he said, "Seventy-five guineas. Why should I take less than it's worth?"

I wanted to shout, "No, we need sixty guineas. Take the money. Give the man the book," but I glanced at Jack, at his firm mouth, his narrowed eyes, his confident demeanor, and I remained silent.

"Sixty-five," the man said.

"Seventy," Jack said. "Not a penny less." He looked at me and winked audaciously. He held the book more tightly in his hands and began to walk out. What could I do, but follow him?

"No, I like you, lad. I'm prepared to give you more than the book is worth. Seventy guineas it is."

"Right," said my son and turned back.

The money and the book changed hands, and we left.

"We have the money," Jack said, "but why do we want to buy tickets to Africa? The money could take us home, could it not? We can be with Zeide and Bubbe again."

This child, who I thought had so adapted to English ways, yearned too for what we had left behind. I longed to be able to say yes, we would go home, but I knew it could not be.

"The doctor said that only in the Cape Colony, in a place called Cape Town, will Tatte be cured," I said. "There the sun shines and the air is pure, and there is never any snow. We must go there."

Our thoughts were filled with the shtetl as we made our way back to the shipping office and paid the fare. For me, the day was beginning to take on an air of unreality. Jack handed over the money and waited as the man wrote out each name on the tickets. Jack accepted the tickets and handed them to me, and we made our way out of the office.

I looked back for a moment and saw that the man was smiling broadly as he took the money and placed it in his pocket, though a large till stood directly in front of him. I thought that was strange and wanted to ask Jack about it, but just then he began to talk.

"That was a really good price for the album. To think that I paid the fares for the whole family! Well, I'm sorry to lose it, you know — such a lot of work went into collecting those stamps. But to think we're going on a big ship, to another land. How exciting!"

But I felt no excitement. Now that it was all done, I was afraid.

I was afraid of the decision I had made on my own, without even involving Pinchas. This was a major decision, and I had not even consulted with my husband! How would he react? Would the sea voyage be too much for him? Would he be cured in that faraway land? Would there be a need for men of his trade? What would our fate be? How long would ten guineas, all that was left from the stamp money, last us in the new land?

How clever of Jack to get that extra ten guineas. At least we would not arrive totally penniless. Would it pay for a place to stay? Would it pay for food? What about work? Would Pinchas be able to work out there?

The doctor had said Pinchas would get better there. Did doctors always tell the truth? Did doctors know better than Hashem what the future holds? What could I do, but follow the doctor's orders and put my trust in Hashem? Had He not provided the money to travel in a most amazing way?

So with these thoughts in my mind, and Jack chattering beside me, I forgot about that man and the money he had put in his pocket — a decision I was to regret later.

That night I had a terrible dream, a dream I had had so often. Once again I heard my sister screaming at me, and then growing larger and larger as she leaned over me, until I could hardly breathe. The dream woke me. It was early morning, and the only sound was Pinchas breathing heavily in his sleep.

The dream left me uneasy. I thought of my mother's words to me before I left. *You must go with your husband, even though you will be far from us. Take my Tehillim. It has brought me comfort and strength over the years. It will do the same for you.*

If ever I needed comfort, if ever I needed strength, it was now. I took out the small book, battered from constant use, and read the words with great concentration. David was a great king, and yet he faced many difficulties in his life. Despite it all, his faith remained unabated. I was struggling to keep my faith, to remain confident, to trust that my actions that day would be for the good. Yet my fear remained. Our move from the shtetl had not been for the good. What would this decision, mine alone, bring to us?

The girl came back about a week later.

All week I had been thinking of the past, and now I knew that I could not tell her what she wanted to know.

The past was gone and could not be recovered. Why spend time dwelling on it?

I gave her tea and cake, and kept offering more, so she had little chance to talk.

Then, as I cleared the table, I said, "Visit any time. I enjoy your company. But don't ask me to talk about what has been. Today is important to me, and also tomorrow, but the past cannot be changed and is not worth discussing."

"You won't mind if I talk instead to the others?" she said.

"Can I control anyone? They must do as they please," was my answer. I was relieved that she had accepted what I said, that she did not try to persuade me.

When the door closed, I sat very still, and so many buried memories came back to me.

I remembered those long-ago days and played them once again in my mind: greeting my sister as she arrived home from her journey. Her wedding day, and how I had looked at her and the man beside her. I had been happy to be married to Pinchas, and yet at the same time angry with her. Confusion reigned within me.

I remembered, too, the day both Pinchas and I overheard the gossip about us. My father spoke often of the evils of lashon hara, describing how gossip could kill. Pinchas had looked so downcast. Was that the real reason we had left our home?

Such painful thoughts! They had been quite banished from my mind. Now they once again surfaced. This young girl and her questions! What happened to that good maxim that children should be seen and not heard?

BOOK TWO

Family Lore

Chapter 6

I am persistent. Well, some say I am stubborn, but I don't agree. I needed to know more, and she said she had no objection to me talking to the others. I would talk first to her oldest son, Jack. He was more forthcoming. In the weeks that followed, I spoke to many people, carefully taking notes on everything they told me. This is what I learned.

Fay and Jack returned home to find that the children had returned from school, and Pinchas had returned early from work. He was half sitting, half lying on the bed, and his breathing made a rasping sound. Fay tried to force a smile onto her face.

Looking at her husband, who had once been so strong and fit, she said in what she hoped was an optimistic voice, "Soon you will be well. We're going to the Cape Colony where the sun always shines, and you will recover there."

Pinchas, exhausted from his first day back at work, looked at her with a grey face.

"But money," he said weakly.

Fay was relieved that he hadn't said an outright "no."

"We have a clever son," she said. "Do you know that Jack has been collecting old used stamps? Worthless, wouldn't you think? But no, they're worth money, a lot of money. They have been sold, and now we're booked to leave soon on a fine ship. Not like we traveled here, all together at the bottom of the ship, but in two fine cabins. Now what do you think of that?"

"Good boy, Jack," her husband wheezed.

Fay wondered now if she had made the correct decision. What if the sea voyage was too much for him? Was the doctor really correct about the curative properties of this faraway place, this Cape Colony?

Jack had brought his atlas home in his schoolbag and showed the family where they were headed. The other children were less boisterous than usual. Jack had told them they were leaving soon, going over the seas to a new land. He seemed unhappy, and his mood affected them all.

Jack was having second thoughts about leaving London. When he had first arrived from the shtetl, he had been horrified by the noise and lack of space in their new home. He missed the garden surrounding his old home. He missed his grandparents, his friends. Everything here was crowded and noisy.

Now, all these years later, he felt dismay at leaving the school where he had spent so many pleasant hours. He always made up for the lessons he missed, copying the work from a friend and learning the new material. He did well in his lessons. In fact, the headmaster had called him into his office one day and told him that clever boys were sometimes given scholarships to the university. He knew many boys in prestigious professions who were earning nicely.

"Keep up the good work, my boy, and then, when the time is right, I will recommend you," Mr. Angel had said, to Jack's elation.

Jack had a good command of English, as did all his brothers and sisters. Even though he had hoped fiercely to return to the shtetl, he felt a part of this new land. He was in the bar mitzvah class and had already received a new set of *tefillin* from the school. He knew his bar mitzvah *parshah*, and was just about to ask his father if they could serve some wine and cake and maybe even herring at the small *shtiebel* they attended.

Now, quite suddenly, they were leaving all this behind. Not only would he never see his beloved grandparents again, they would be traveling even farther away from them. Now there was no longer a chance of a scholarship to a university.

Besides, he had learned about Africa in school. It was a wild place, with jungles and lions and other wild animals. This is where his mother wanted them to go? How strange. He had made this possible, with his stamp album. Stranger still!

But the younger children looked to him when they were confused, since he understood their surroundings better than their parents. When some ruffians had pursued the younger children from school, taunting them and throwing stones at them, they told Jack. The following day, he and David left school early. When the ruffians appeared again, Jack and David stepped forward and attacked, using the skills they had been taught in boxing lessons at school. The young ruffians had gone running, and never started up with the children again.

Jack knew how to bargain at the markets. He knew how to navigate Mr. Kahn's wagon through the streets of London. He knew where to get and sell stamps.

Altogether, he felt capable and at home here in this city, and was looking forward to the future. At the same time, like his mother, he had harbored secret dreams of returning to the shtetl. His family would walk into his grandparents' home, wearing fine clothes and bearing gifts.

Now, there would be no return to his beloved shtetl and no further study at a university. There was only a frightening, unknown future.

What would life be like in a strange land? Would he even be able to continue his schooling? Would his father be able to work? Would he, Jack, have to find work to support the family? What kind of work would he be able to do?

It was already the end of April. Soon, very soon, they would be leaving. He had to put aside all thoughts of himself and help his mother prepare for what lay ahead.

Chapter 7

"JFS teachers were better qualified than the average schoolteacher at that period…Jewish children in the East End of London were more likely to attend school and enjoyed better health than their non-Jewish counterparts."
— Gerry Black, *The History of Jews' Free School, London*, pp.100–101

On their last day of school, Fay asked Jack to write a letter for each child to give their teacher, thanking them and wishing them farewell.

Jack went to the headmaster's office and told him that they were leaving for Cape Town. He wanted a report card for each child. There would, hopefully, be schools in the new colony.

"Well, young man," Mr. Angel said. "What an adventure. Here, I'll write a note and you can go to each class and see if the teachers will oblige. I will go to the girls' school and see that your sisters each get a report from their teachers.

"We're sorry to lose you and your family. I have been keeping an eye on your progress. You're a clever lad. You should keep up with your studies. They don't yet have universities in the Cape Colony, but if you ever return here to study and need my help, contact me. Whatever you choose to do, I am sure you will do well."

Jack went to his class first and gave his teacher the note his mother had insisted he write, along with the headmaster's note. The class waited silently as the teacher read the notes.

"Right, come back after the lunch break," his teacher said. "I will have it ready for you."

From class to class Jack went, worried each time about a refusal, but the response was always positive.

When Jack went into David's class, he found David excitedly telling the teacher that they were traveling across the sea soon, to the Cape Colony.

"Very good," the teacher said, "but now concentrate on your arithmetic, so you don't disgrace me at your new school."

Then he noticed Jack by the door. He took the notes, read them and nodded.

"David can come to me before he goes home," he said. "I'll have the report ready for him."

When Jack walked into Joseph's class, his brother was standing in front of the class, reciting a poem they had been told to memorize.

"Casabianca," he said in a low voice, "a poem by Felicia Dorothea Hemans."

"The boy stood on the burning deck," Joseph said, his voice trembling.

He was nervous, since forgetting any words or getting them wrong meant a sharp rap on the knuckles with a wooden ruler, but then he lost himself in the beauty of the words. Joseph had a passion for words and books, but mostly for poetry. He was no longer a student reciting by rote words painfully learned. It was as if he became the small boy pumping furiously to save the ship.

Now his voice no longer quavered, but was fierce with passion.

Whence all but he had fled;
The flame that lit the battle's wreck
Shone round him o'er the dead.
Yet beautiful and bright he stood,
As born to rule the storm;
A creature of heroic blood,
A proud, though childlike form.
The flames rolled on —— he would not go
Without his father's word;
That father, faint in death below,

His voice no longer heard.
He called aloud— 'Say, Father, say,
If yet my task is done?'
He knew not that the chieftain lay
Unconscious of his son.
'Speak, Father!' once again he cried
'If I may yet be gone!'
And shouted but once more aloud,
'My father! Must I stay?'
While o'ever him fast, through sail and shroud,
The wreathing fires made way.
With mast, and helm, and pennon fair,
That well had borne their part—
But the noblest thing which perished there
Was that young, faithful heart.

Now Joseph came out of his reverie. He was no longer the young boy in the poem, faced with a terrible ordeal. Now, he suddenly realized, he was about to travel far away, on a long sea voyage, and he was suddenly very afraid.

He must not cry. He must not. The boys would tease him in the playground if he did. He returned abruptly to his seat.

"Very good. No mistakes. Very well, class, history now. Recite the dates of the English kings."

The teacher suddenly noticed Jack. "What is it, boy?"

Once again the letters were handed to the teacher, and once again Jack received a positive response. He was beginning to relax. He had expected curt refusals from the teachers.

Now Jack only had to go to Samuel and Isaac's rooms. Within an hour his task was done.

Jack wanted to run out of the school gates and take a long, leisurely stroll around the familiar streets. But the thought of those letters stopped him.

He went back to his classroom and tried to concentrate, but could think only of what he was leaving—and wonder what they would find in the new land.

Later, Jack collected the letters and told his mother how the teachers had reacted.

"They were happy to give the letters," he said. "I thought they would say it was just extra work, and why bother if we were leaving, but they were really good about it.

"You should have heard Joseph recite that silly old poem. He made it sound so real. The teacher makes the class learn it each year."

Later, much later, Jack wished he had paid more attention to Joseph and had asked him about the poem. Perhaps then he would have been able to prevent the unfortunate events that unfolded just when they were to leave the East End of London for a new life far across the sea.

Frieda and Bertha were not at school that day. They had been kept home to help their mother prepare for the voyage.

Frieda was scrubbing the floor resentfully. She had been looking forward to telling her classmates about the grand adventure she was about to embark on.

"Why are we cleaning this place?" she said. "We came here and found it so dirty. Now we're working so hard to make it perfect?"

"What!" her mother said. "Remember how we felt when we came? Remember how you yourself said to me, 'But how could they have lived like this? Such dirt! Such a bad smell!' Well, I will not have anyone say such things about us. Besides, I heard that a Jewish family is to move in after us. We should make this a welcoming place for them."

So Frieda went on scrubbing and Fay moved to the last bit of packing, calling Bertha to help her with the pots and pans they had brought from the shtetl and that were now, once again, being carefully wrapped up in the Shabbos tablecloth.

"How long will it take us to get to the new land?" Bertha asked. "Where will we live? Will Tatte be better there?"

One question followed another, and Fay could answer none of them.

"Less talk and more work," Fay snapped, but then she felt regret. Of course the child was worried. But what could she answer her?

Meanwhile, in the Infants section of the school building, Samuel was very aware that today he had a big responsibility. Today he was to collect little Isaac from the kindergarten class and wait at the gate for the older children.

Samuel puffed up with pride. Normally, one of the older boys did this. The voyage seemed of less importance to him now that this important task had been given to him.

In his own classroom, little Isaac looked around. Oh, it was good to be back in school. At home it was so dull. Everyone just ignored him. It wasn't good being the baby of the family. Here, in the classroom, everyone was the same. Everyone had to learn, and the teacher noticed everyone. Well, that was just fine by him.

Besides, this week he had been ignored even more than usual at home. Strange things were going on there, but that didn't matter. Here, in the classroom, everything was good and normal and predictable.

In the girls' school, Ethel sat proudly in class, holding a small book—her prize for coming out at top when adding up the long row of figures on the blackboard. The other children glared at her. She always won the prizes their teacher brought to school. It wasn't fair.

Rose sat in the corner of her classroom, wondering what was going on at home. They were leaving their home, but why? No one had bothered to explain it to her. Fortunately, the teacher was busy with the naughty girl in the front row and didn't notice that she wasn't looking at her and following her every instruction. Rose suddenly thought about the ruler that could come rapping on her knuckles at any moment and forced her attention back to the lesson.

When the school day ended and the children returned home, they saw that their mother and older sisters had packed everything. The wooden trunk they had brought with them from Lithuania stood in a corner, piled high with many tight bundles. The rooms were bare and clean.

Their mother was sitting at the table, writing. Jack peeped over her shoulder and read:

My dear family,

We leave here soon for a new land. We have been told it is a good place. The voyage will take many weeks, so don't worry if you don't receive letters from me or if Pinchas's family receives no letter from him. As soon as we arrive at the new place, we will write.

Fay ended with the usual words, but she hoped that what she was writing would turn out to be true — that the land would be a good land, that both she and Pinchas would write to their families and say how good the place was, that Pinchas would be feeling so much better.

Now, all she could do was *daven* that Hashem would help her. She addressed the letter and sent the older girls off to post it.

Fay had not explained to her children why they were moving. She expected the children to simply accept that they were leaving. She hadn't realized that all their plans could come to naught because of one frightened child.

Chapter 8

"The ships that plied the route from England to Cape Town were mainly from the two rival British companies — the Union fleet and Curie's Castle fleet, with the heavily subsidized German East Africa Company, the D.O.A.L., after 1892. The ships were powered by both sails and steam power. It was not until the twentieth century that steam power alone was trusted. There were two kinds of voyages to the Cape — by the smaller slower intermediate service or by mail service."

— Gwynne Schrire, *From Eastern Europe to South Africa: Memories of an Epic Journey*, p. 20

The time had come to leave. The younger children were jumping up and down with excitement.

Jack was outside, waiting for Mr. Kahn and his vegetable cart to come and take the family and their luggage to the port. Finally, Jack came running up the stairs.

"He's here! Let's take down the trunk first. Then everyone can come downstairs. If the little ones sit on the bundles, there'll be room for everyone."

It was Jack who noticed that Joseph was missing. A frantic search ensued.

Now what? Fay thought frantically. *I can't leave the child behind, but I can't miss the boat either.*

Suddenly, it seemed, all her plans had come to naught. No, she couldn't leave the child behind. But where would her family go? Where would they live? Other people were about to move into their flat.

And the money — all that money on tickets, gone, for nothing!

Meanwhile, Jack looked in every corner. No Joseph. He looked at his frantic mother.

"Please, Mother, you must go," he said. "This is the only time Mr. Kahn can take you. He has more deliveries to make today. I will find Joseph and bring him to you."

"Joseph!" Fay shouted. "Where are you?"

"Mother, please, just go. Get Tatte and go. I will find Joseph, I promise you. We'll meet you on the ship. I know how to get there."

Soon the subdued family and their goods were piled on the jolting wagon. It began to make its way to the River Thames, where their ship was docked.

The ship was scheduled to leave before dawn the next day, and the passengers had been told to board the previous evening. This was a new venture. Ships usually left from Southampton. The captain wanted the boarding to take place under cover of the night, and the navigating on the Thames to take place on the following day, before dawn, when there was little river traffic.

Now Jack felt panic. How would he fulfill his promise? Where should he begin his search? Just then, a small figure came out from the corner of the building.

"I thought they wouldn't go," Joseph said. "I thought we would all stay here if they couldn't find me. They have gone. They have left us. Now they'll all die on the burning deck."

Three years previously Jack had been in the same teacher's class. He too had to memorize the poem about the boy dying on the ship. Suddenly, he understood.

The wagon was still visible down the street. Not a moment could be lost. Placing his two fingers in his mouth, Jack gave a piercing whistle. Would the horses hear him? Would they stop?

If the horses didn't stop, then what? It was a far walk to the River Thames. Suddenly, the horses ambled to a stop. Jack grabbed Joseph's hand.

"Run now," he said. "We'll be safe. I'll explain it to you later. Just come."

The boys ran. They reached the wagon, Joseph red-faced and out of breath. Fay first gave a sigh of relief and then exploded in anger.

"You naughty boy! Where were you?"

"Mother, there's no harm done," Jack said. "We're all together now. I'll explain later."

Pinchas, agitated by the fuss, began to gasp for breath. Fay turned to him and forced herself to be calm.

Jack spoke softly to Joseph. "That boy on the burning deck . . . it happened during a war. Didn't your teacher explain it to you?" Joseph nodded. "Well, this is not a war. We're at peace now. No harm will come to us. Would I let harm come to you?"

Joseph remembered how a bully had once tried to hit him in the schoolyard, and Jack had, somehow, appeared at his side. Now he felt foolish. He tried to smile, but still the words of the poem echoed through his mind.

⌒

The ship was waiting on the Thames. The adventure that lay before them became a reality. Fay worried how they would crowd into the two small cabins they had been allotted.

Then, quite suddenly, an officer arrived and called out to the crewman who was helping with their luggage.

He looked with dismay at the large group, and then at the tickets. Eleven names appeared on the tickets. Two cabins, each with three bunks, had been allotted to them. The clerk had written down only six names on the lists he had supplied to the shipping office, but he had written far more names on the tickets for the passengers. The officer had been expecting trouble ever since he had been told that the new clerk had disappeared with the proceeds of the day.

The sum of sixty guineas was inscribed in the top left-hand corner of the ticket. "You paid sixty guineas for you and your husband and all the children?" he asked.

Fay was worried now, but she nodded. Jack stood by her side, listening intently. Pinchas, tired from the journey on the wagon, was sitting on coiled ropes nearby.

"You were given these tickets for six bunks altogether?"

"Yes. The man said the younger children could share bunks and the two older boys could sleep on some blankets on the floor of the cabin." Fay watched the man, panic beginning to overtake her.

"Do you know the size of the cabins and the bunks?" the officer asked.

Jack began to realize that something was very wrong.

Fay remembered how the clerk had placed their money in his pocket. She had wondered why he did that, but hadn't thought to say something at the time.

The officer gazed at the group before him. There were so many children. How could they all fit into the small space allotted to them by that dishonest clerk?

"Did you want only two cabins?" he asked, though he knew the answer already.

"We had enough money for those cabins, no more," Fay said. "So the clerk said that if the children would share bunks, it could be done."

"No, impossible, it cannot be done. I will see that the money you paid is returned to you. You will need to pay a bit more money and get better accommodation—four cabins at least. The next ship leaves in a week. You had better return home and make a new booking."

Fay was horrified. What home was there to return to? New tenants would be in those rooms. What money could she find in a week? Pinchas was ill, so ill that he had barely made it to the waiting cart. How could they now remain in London?

The captain of the ship looked at the group standing there, and the people behind them muttering impatiently. He walked over to the officer.

"That thieving scoundrel took money and allotted only two cabins for all this lot," said the officer.

Jack decided to speak up. He knew the English had strict laws, even if he didn't know what they were. With a confidence he didn't feel, he said, "You cannot make us leave. It's against the law. We paid for tickets for the whole family to sail now. If the man at the shipping office made a mistake, that's not our fault. We will not leave."

The captain was angered by the brash youngster. He was responsible for the safety of his passengers. So many people in two small cabins? Impossible! The nerve of this cheeky youngster, telling him about the law. Momentarily, he paused. Could there truly be such a law?

He knew everything about the laws at sea, yet little of the laws of the land. What if he was truly breaking the law by forcing these people back onto land? Who would be held responsible — the company, maybe, or worse still, the man who gave the order to remove them?

Jack stood glaring up at the captain, his feet firmly planted on the wooden deck, yet aware of the quivering of his knees. What on earth had made him say that? What did he know of the law? All he knew was that his history teacher always said, "In England, everyone, rich or poor, Jew or gentile, is protected by the law." Surely there was a law to protect his family from being refused passage. If they were prepared to be squashed together in a small cabin, if that had been written on their tickets, how could they be told to leave?

Who knew what the outcome would have been, if not for the sudden presence of a sailor who approached the captain and held out a note?

Fay was devastated. What would become of them? Their flat had already been given to others. The only hope for Pinchas was leaving this country. Now they needed more money for more cabins? Where would that come from?

The captain read the note once, and then again. He looked at the group before him, dressed in their best Shabbos clothing. The young boy seemed to know what he was talking about. Such a situation had never arisen in all his long years at sea. It seemed that the family would not simply quietly leave and wait for the next ship. How could they force these people off? What would the other passengers make of it? This was not a good way to begin a long voyage across the ocean. He looked again at the note he had just received.

"Well, it seems the problem is solved. A family has just sent notice that they are not sailing with us. The company has changed their booking to America. They have three large second-class cabins booked. I can give those to you."

He looked sternly at the children and added, "In second class, people do not want to be disturbed by rowdy children. The children must behave. Do I make myself clear?"

Fay heard him mention extra cabins and second class. Did that mean they would have to pay more? How should she pay? What would it cost? She was about to ask, when Jack spoke quietly in Yiddish.

"Let me answer the man, please, Mother." Without waiting for a response, he said, "Thank you. I will see that my brothers and sisters disturb no one. Please, could we go now to our cabins?"

Their bundles were picked up and a sailor was called to escort them to a different part of the ship. He picked up the wooden trunk as though it was made of feathers, hoisted it on his shoulders, and began to walk toward a flight of stairs. The older children picked up the bundles and pulled the younger ones along.

The captain watched them go. Had he made the correct decision? The children did seem well behaved, but where was the father? Then he saw Fay help Pinchas stand up. The man looked as if he was on his last legs. What had he done? To take this sick man on, sailing on seas that could prove rough . . . It was madness! Why hadn't he used the excuse of the wrong payment to make the family leave? Did the woman realize what would happen if her husband died at sea? Burial at sea was not a pleasant thing. How could he not have noticed this sick man?

What a voyage this was turning out to be. First there was that dishonest clerk who had absconded with money and made impossible bookings.

Then there was the last-minute cancellation with a family that had needed special Jewish food. After all the trouble he had gone to, here was this family taking their place—and with such a sick father. He hoped the new ship's doctor was a capable man.

Fay walked slowly with Pinchas, trying to keep in sight the sailor leading them.

Why had Jack spoken up and not let her voice her concerns? They were apparently getting better and more spacious accommodations. How were they to pay for it?

What would happen when she didn't have the money? The nightmare of imprisonment reared up before her. Yet what option had she but to let things play out as they had? It was imperative that she get Pinchas to this place, where the sun was always shining, where he could be cured.

The sailor disappeared, and for a few moments Fay stood, not knowing which way to go. Then he suddenly reappeared.

"Right, follow me," he said. "The children are in their cabins—the girls in one, boys in another."

Pinchas was breathing heavily. The sailor took him by his arm.

"Lean on me, right, that's it. Slowly now, we'll soon have you comfortably settled." Although the sailor spoke cheerfully, his thoughts were somber. What was the captain doing, letting such a sick man on board?

Fay looked around the cabin once Pinchas had been settled onto a bunk and was resting.

Compared to the way they had traveled to England, this was luxury indeed. The cabin was large. There was a small porthole with a view of the far bank of the Thames. The bunks were fastened to the wall and were made up with sparkling white sheets and bright blue blankets. In a corner of the room was a washbasin.

Once again, the question frightened her. How would she find the money to pay?

She was alone now with Pinchas. He lay down and was soon asleep. Just then Jack arrived.

"Mother, a man came and knocked on your door, but when you didn't answer, he came to our door."

Fay realized that their walk had taken much longer because of Pinchas. They had not been in the room yet when there was a knock. Was this the news she feared? Would they have to get off the ship? Would they have to find more money? But no, Jack was beaming. It couldn't be bad news.

"Mother, are you listening to me? Guess what? These people, the ones who didn't arrive on the ship, are Yidden. A sailor arrived from the kitchen and said that all the kosher food and new pots and pans were in the kitchen, just as we had ordered. Now what do you think of that?"

"But you told him it's not for us?"

"Of course, I told him the other family had canceled, that we were family Levine, but we would be more than pleased to use everything that had been ordered, since we too are Jews."

"What did he say then?"

"He was pleased that the food wouldn't be wasted."

"But Jack, the money for all this — the extra cabins, traveling second class instead of third — where will it come from?"

"That's what you wanted to ask the captain, right? That's why I spoke so quickly. They made a mistake — well, not them, but the man who sold the tickets — so they must make it right. I didn't want them to get a chance to find a way out, to take us off the boat. If you had begun to ask such questions, I don't know what would have happened.

"Our cabin has two double beds fastened to the wall. We fit in nicely. David and I will take the top beds, and Joseph a bottom bed. Samuel and Isaac will sleep on the other bottom one. It's so long that when they put their heads on opposite sides, their feet don't even touch. The other room for the girls is the same, and they fit in nicely. There's even a cupboard for clothes. Oh, I see you also have one.

"You just look after Tatte, and Frieda and I will care for the children. All will be well."

Jack hoped he had convinced his mother. However, he was less convinced himself that his words were true. What if more money was required? What then?

Now, with the family comfortably settled, Fay began to feel a bit more hopeful. Calmed by her son's words, she felt the tension begin to leave her. She looked at Pinchas sleeping peacefully. Tired from the events of the day, she lay down momentarily on the luxurious bunkbed. The ship rocked gently on the River Thames and soon she too was asleep.

For Jack, there was no such relief. He returned to his cabin and found the boys clustered around the porthole, gazing out.

"We're on a river, the big London river, not the sea," little Isaac said.

Jack welcomed the distraction from his brother. He expected at any moment to hear a rap on the door of his parents' cabin and a demand for extra money. He pushed those thoughts away and carefully explained how the river ran to the sea, and how the boat would sail down the river, until it reached the great ocean.

Some time later there was a strange musical sound outside in the corridor, followed by a sharp rap on the door. Jack felt fear course through him. The boat had not yet begun to move. They would have to give more money or leave the ship. He hesitated before answering, but Joseph had already gone and opened the door.

"Supper gong," a man said. "Before every meal the gong sounds. Everyone else looked out of their cabins, but not you. Your first voyage?"

Jack began to breathe again. "Where do we go?"

"Down the passage and up the stairs at the end, then turn left and there you are."

It took some time for Jack to gather the whole family together and make their way as instructed. Pinchas needed help up the stairs, but soon they found the large double doors that opened into the dining room.

The family gave a collective gasp. What looked like hundreds of tables and chairs were covered with sparkling white cloths, as if it was Shabbos. A sailor dressed in a smart white jacket came up to them.

"Follow me," he said. "I'll take you to the special table for your family. See, we have different plates so they won't be mixed with the others. We can't give you the special Jewish meat — it was too difficult to get hold of — but we have plenty of fish, vegetables and eggs."

Fay thanked him and told him how good the food was. She watched as Pinchas ate, but he was clearly making a big effort to remain seated. He was tired.

Before their plates were removed, she said to Jack, "Help us get back to our cabin."

When Jack returned to the dining room, the children were staring in awe at a huge pile of fresh fruit that had been placed on the table.

"The man said that the chef told him that he hadn't been able to make a special dessert for us," Frieda said. "The first night is so difficult. He hoped we would be satisfied with just fruit." She broke into a wide grin. "I think I like this, living on a ship."

Chapter 9

"There was a place for passengers in all three stories, as well as a very deep hold below deck. In these were found a treasury of food and heavy cargo. The place of the engine that they fire with coal day and night is very deep, and two people work there for two hours..."
— Schrire and Schrire, *The Reb and the Rebel*, p. 54

The children woke early the next day and began whispering to each other that surely the ship was moving. The rocking of the ship was different, no longer so gentle. They could hear the cawing of seagulls. From the portholes a stiff breeze blew into the cabins.

Pinchas too was just waking. Fay was relieved that he was breathing evenly. However, fear overtook her. She had acted so precipitately. Should they have first paid another visit to the doctor? Was Pinchas fit enough to travel? Should they have waited until he was stronger? What were the dangers of the sea, to all of them? Although she had never read an English newspaper, she knew that shipwrecks were not unknown. Had she placed her family in danger?

Just then there was a knock on the door. She opened it and Frieda came in.

"We're moving," she said. "I think we are at sea. I looked out the small round window and could see no land. The girls are dressed, but Jack and David are lying in their beds and won't get up. Joseph is trying to get Samuel and Isaac to stop running around. They're dressed, but they're getting wild without Jack and David to see to them."

Fay had to see to the children, but didn't want to leave Pinchas alone.

"Stay here," she said to Frieda. "I will go to them."

Now Fay was more worried than ever. There was not only Pinchas to care for, but two sick boys. She found the cabin door open, swinging. A sailor was standing next to Jack and talking to him.

"Your little brother called me as I was passing," the sailor said. "He said his brothers are dying. Believe me, it's nothing of the sort, just sea-sickness, that's all. In a day or so you'll get your sea legs and feel fine."

"But why only me?" Jack said.

"The other young lad is also ill," the sailor said. "Look there, at the top of the other bunk."

Jack saw David lying quite still, groaning softly. Jack felt panic overtake him. If they both felt so sick, what about the rest of his family?

"What about the girls, my mother?"

Fay came over to him. "Everyone is well. You heard what the man said. It's nothing. Soon you'll be feeling better."

She spoke confidently, cheerfully, wishing desperately that her words were true.

By the time Fay returned to her cabin, Pinchas was fully awake. Would he too feel sick from the ship's movement? To her relief, he seemed the same, no better and no worse. Frieda returned to her cabin to supervise the girls and younger boys. She helped Pinchas dress and then watched as he davened.

The melodious gong echoed in the corridors, and Fay knew it was time to go to the dining room. Soon the whole family, with the exception of Jack and David, was sitting around the table. They ate scrambled eggs, toast, and hot, thick porridge, followed by tea.

Were the eggs checked for blood spots? Fay worried. *Who turned on the oven? Were the dishes and pots washed separately?*

What was she to do? She had brought very little food with her. With all the arrangements, the packing and the cleaning, she had given the matter little thought. Surely, she told herself, the Jewish family that had been supposed to travel in their stead had instructed the kitchen staff how to prepare the food.

The children wanted to go onto the deck outside. What should she do? Would they be safe? But they couldn't spend the entire voyage sitting in their cabins.

She gave her assent but spoke sternly. "You must all stay together. We'll be traveling for many days, and there are many dangers. Do not, under any circumstances, lean against the railing, or try and look over. I don't want you falling into the sea. Understand? Frieda, you're responsible. See that they behave."

Fay helped Pinchas down the stairs and back to the cabin, worrying about the children outside alone, worrying about Jack and David.

Not much later there was a loud knock on the cabin door.

A sailor appeared. "All passengers must go on deck for a lifeboat drill. Take your life jacket with you."

"Life jacket?" Fay said.

The sailor pointed to a hook behind the door. Three strange objects hung there. They had pieces of cork tree sewn onto them, making them look like a woman's apron. There were strings on each side so it could be tied onto the body.

"Life jacket?" Fay said again. She'd never heard the term.

"Lady, I don't want to alarm you, but in case of a problem, in case you need to get into a lifeboat, this will keep you afloat in the water."

"But my boys, my two older boys, are ill in bed."

"It's only seasickness. The fresh air will do them good. Leave them to me."

Pinchas had begun the dreadful wheezing once again. He walked up the stairs with great difficulty. By the time they reached the deck, his face was grey and he could barely stand.

The children saw them and came running, clutching their life jackets. Jack and David soon appeared, looking nearly as bad as Pinchas.

The deck was filled with passengers, some looking bored, clearly having gone through this process before, while others looked worried.

They must have been first timers like them, Fay surmised.

"I will now use the life jacket," a sailor said. "Watch carefully." He slipped the jacket over his head and began to tie up the dangling strings so he was firmly ensconced in the jacket.

"Now, if you hear three sharp tones of the whistle"—a high, piercing sound rang through the air—"you will slip on the life jacket once you are on deck and make your way here, next to the lifeboat you see on the railing. Understood?"

Pinchas chose that moment to take a deep breath and then slowly crumple to the ground. Fay shrieked, and Jack ran to his father's side. There was a moment of horrified silence and then a young man rushed forward.

"Ship's doctor," he said. "Move away. Let me attend to the patient."

He put his ear to Pinchas's chest and then called to the sailor. "Come! Help me take this man to the hospital cabin."

"I knew we shouldn't have come here," Joseph sobbed. "I knew we should have stayed home."

The other children said nothing. They just looked on in horror, their faces white.

Fay felt that she too would faint, but she looked at her husband as he was lifted up and knew she must be strong.

"Jack," she said, "take the children back down when the man is finished talking. Look after them. I must go with your *tatte*, to see he gets well."

At last, after climbing numerous stairs, the doctor and sailor came to a large cabin with a porthole open to the sea. Pinchas was laid down on a high bed. He started mumbling, "Where am I? What happened?"

"Madam, how could you board ship with such a sick husband?" the doctor asked.

"The doctor said his only hope of cure was to travel to the Cape Colony."

"What, a man with congested lungs, embarking on a long sea voyage?"

Fay stared at him. What could she reply? She was doing exactly what the doctor in London had told her.

The doctor took down a bottle from a shelf. He poured some liquid onto a small piece of muslin, then placed pillows under Pinchas to move him to an upright position.

"See now, this will make you breath more easily," he said. "Just breathe in and out very slowly. That's good. Smell the sharp odor? Good. Keep at it. Soon you'll be feeling much better. This eucalyptus oil is good for clearing the lungs."

After inhaling a few times, Pinchas began to breathe more easily.

"Where are the children?" he said worriedly. "Last thing I remember we were all standing on the deck, wearing that strange garment, and hearing about shipwrecks."

"The children are with Jack," Fay said. "There's no need to worry."

"But shipwreck!"

"Now don't fret," the doctor said, his voice soothing. "There's no danger. Lifeboat drill is just a routine that must be done at the beginning of each voyage. Relax now. I will boil some water and make an infusion for you to drink. Madam, stand by him and hold this muslin close to him."

Fay did as she was told, regretting, once again, that she had ever left the shtetl. She should have been stronger. She should have prevented Pinchas from leaving. Had it been even more of a mistake to embark on this voyage? Pinchas had been ill before, but never had he collapsed in this fashion. Fear gnawed at her, but she strove to keep herself calm, to smile at Pinchas and to whisper soothing words of encouragement.

"See what a good man, what a fine doctor is here caring for you," she said. "Soon you will be fit again."

Later, when Pinchas had fallen into a deep sleep, the doctor spoke. "Madam, it was foolish to embark on this voyage. I will do my best, but I'm a doctor, not a miracle maker. He must remain in this cabin. I can care for him during the day, but at night you will have to stay here with him. If at any time he begins that noisy, labored breathing, you must call for me at once. Now go to your cabin and rest, but first, instruct one of your older children to sit by the bed when the lunch gong sounds. I must go to my table to eat with the captain. Come back here when the sun sets."

So began long days of intense worry. When Fay wasn't saying *Tehillim* or sitting beside Pinchas, she was imagining what her children were doing on the boat, with all its dangers.

On Friday morning she began to think about Shabbos. Pinchas was in one place and the children in another. How would she light candles? What about Kiddush? What about *challah*?

It was the doctor who solved the problem. "Your husband is much better. He can return to your cabin. But every morning after breakfast I will send a sailor to help him up the stairs, so he can breathe in the good sea air. He can lie back on the deck chairs. Make sure to cover him with a blanket. At lunchtime someone will take him to the dining room, and then he can return to his cabin. But remain with him. Any time he begins that heavy breathing, call for me."

So, to the delight of the children, normality was restored when the whole family was together once again. Fay brought candles to the table and lit them. The cook came hurrying over and snuffed them out.

"So dangerous! It's madness to allow you to light them, but what can I do? Captain's orders. At least he said I can leave them lit for only a moment or two and then put them out."

The children watched, horrified.

"It is nothing," Pinchas told them. "Your *mamme*, she had the mitzvah of lighting the candles. Nowhere does it say they must remain lit, only that a Jew cannot put them out. Now stand for Kiddush. How fortunate we are that your mother packed a bottle of wine."

There was no *challah*, but there were small, sweet rolls for *Hamotzi*. There was no chicken soup, but there was a thick, delicious potato soup, followed by poached fish and baked apples. The family bentched quietly so as not to disturb the other passengers. Pinchas, tired but satisfied, was helped by Jack back to his cabin.

Fay contemplated that Shabbos with a serenity she had thought she'd never feel again. The caring young doctor seemed to be helping Pinchas recover. The older boys had felt much better after going up on deck. The children were behaving well. They were listening to her and doing whatever she instructed.

Yes, Fay told herself. She had been correct to follow the doctor's instructions to travel to the Cape Colony.

Yet all this changed abruptly, just one week later.

The day had started off well, with Pinchas resting on the deck.

Then, after a short time, the sky became overcast. The sea suddenly went from calm to stormy. A sailor came and ordered everyone below deck. Jack and Fay helped Pinchas down the steps. By lunchtime, after spending some hours in the cabin, Pinchas was once again struggling for breath. The doctor was hurriedly summoned.

He didn't come immediately. The breathing became worse. Once again Jack was sent to get the doctor. He came hurrying back with Jack, out of breath.

"This storm, so many people feeling bad," he panted. "First-class passengers, you know. They need immediate attention. Now let's see. Oh my. My boy, there's no time to call for a seaman! Help me with your father. We'll take him up to the hospital cabin."

An anxious time followed. The ship was buffeted this way and that. Fay sat beside the high hospital bed, clinging to it. She held different muslins soaked with sharp-smelling liniments near Pinchas. Sometimes this helped and his breathing improved. The doctor came and went. Everywhere people were suffering from the storm and calling for him.

Fay was stiff with worry. What were her children doing? Who was there to care for them? Had little Joseph been correct in not wanting to board this vessel? In her hands she clutched the little book of *Tehillim*, but the rocking of the ship and the need to keep the aromatic oils near Pinchas made it practically impossible to read.

Three days later, the storm dissipated as suddenly as it had arrived. Pinchas began a slow recovery. Jack came up and reported that all the children were well. He didn't tell of the terrible seasickness they had all suffered, except for Joseph, who had gone alone each day to the dining room and brought back for the children fresh water. That was about all they were able to consume.

On the fourth day after the storm, the ship docked in Funchal, the capital of Madeira.

"Perhaps you should all disembark here," the doctor said. "You can continue on when your husband is in a better state of health."

Fay was torn. What should she do? What would they live on if they left the ship? Besides, the doctor in London had said that the colonies would cure Pinchas. This was not the Cape Colony. She decided to remain on board. The doctor wished he had the authority to insist that the family disembark, but he did not.

Fear filled Fay's every waking moment as the ship resumed its voyage. What if she had made a bad decision?

However, the weather was beautiful and the sea remained calm for the duration of the voyage. Each day Fay noticed a slight improvement in Pinchas's condition. At last, some three weeks later, the cry rang through the ship. "Tomorrow we dock in the Cape!"

Pinchas had survived the voyage. Not only that, some color had returned to his face. His breathing was almost normal. He had even gained some weight. Though he tired easily, he could now walk up to the deck without assistance.

They had reached their destination. Now, surely, all would be well. How could Fay know that there were evil people in this new land, and that trouble was just around the corner?

Chapter 10

"In 1891 there may have been 4,000 Jews in the country. By 1899
the numbers had grown to maybe 10,000."

— Saron and Hotz, *The Jews in South Africa*, p. 8

After weeks of living on the rocking waves of the sea, it was the stillness that woke Fay. The ship hardly seemed to be moving.

Fay saw that Pinchas was sleeping peacefully. She dressed quietly and left the cabin. As she passed the girls' cabin, Frieda poked her head out. She was already fully dressed.

"Oh, good!" Frieda said. "You're awake. Everyone here is fast asleep. Where are you going? Can I come too?"

Fay looked at her daughter. She was wearing her Shabbos clothes, which had been freshly washed and pressed the day before, and she had managed to braid her hair.

Fay had spent five pence each for her boys to get a haircut at the barber. Normally she would have done this herself, with a large pair of scissors, and she hoped she hadn't been foolish to spend the money. She made good use of the laundry. She carefully ironed the clothes that the children would wear as they left the ship, then laid them carefully one on top of the other in a corner she had cleared specially for this purpose. Her children would arrive in this new land looking presentable.

Fay thought back to their long-ago arrival in London. The conditions on the boat had been dreadful. Their clothes had been creased and dirty, and smelled of the herring that had been doled out to them. There had been no proper washing facilities. This time things would be different. They would arrive looking clean and respectable.

"Of course!" Fay said. "Come, let us see our new land."

"Oh, but isn't this exciting!" Frieda exclaimed as they made their way up to the deck.

For a moment, the child's excitement caught hold of Fay, but then the familiar worry overtook her. Where would they live? How would they earn money in this faraway place?

Only a few passengers were on the deck, gathered at the rails and peering out. But sailors were everywhere, moving swiftly and quietly from deck to rigging.

Fay and Frieda moved to the railing. They both gasped. All around the water was still. In the distance the sun had not yet risen, and a silvery gray film seemed to cover everything. In the distance they could see a large, flat-topped mountain. There were houses close together, and others that were further away and more distant from each other.

"Look, just look!" Frieda said. "See that big mountain—it's so high, and has such a flat top. Our geography book had pictures of mountains, but none with a flat top."

"Are you new here?" said a woman standing beside them. "I've been away for more than a year, but at last I have returned. We call that Table Mountain. Looks just like a table, don't you think? Sometimes a white cloud covers it—we call it the tablecloth. That means the South-Easter is blowing, clearing the air of dust. We call the wind the Cape Doctor. It keeps the place clean, and keeps us well."

"You've been here before?" Fay said, hoping the woman could give her information.

"Oh yes, almost all my life. I had to go to England for a short while, but it's so very good to be back."

Fay was satisfied with that answer. Now she was eager to leave the boat, to face whatever difficulties would come up, to find somewhere to live.

"When will they put up the gangplanks and allow us to leave?" was her next question.

"Oh my dear, not for some time. See, the sun has not yet risen. The customs people must first get here. They must check our luggage — you know, for forbidden items, things of great value."

Fay found this strange. Check for what? Did they have anything of value? No one would want their humble possessions. Later she was to remember these thoughts. How wrong she had been. Now, though, she remained where she was, her hand on Frieda's shoulder as they watched the sun slowly rise. The sky turned a soft rosy pink, and then as if a fire had suddenly been lit, the whole earth was bathed in golden sunshine.

The mountain now seemed a symphony of greenery and stark black rock. The houses with their white walls and red roofs, surrounded by patches of green, appeared bright on the slopes.

"Look," the woman said, "look there. See where I'm pointing, at the bottom of the mountain? See that big square of green trees? We call that the Gardens. When the Dutch sailors first came here, they planted vegetables there to feed the sailors who were on their long voyage to India. Now it's a beautiful park."

"Dutch sailors?" Frieda said.

"Oh yes, my dear. Didn't you learn at school that first the Dutch came here, but then we took over?"

Frieda looked embarrassed at her ignorance. Then she recovered and said, in defense of her school, "The British Empire is so large, each year we learn about another part. Last year we learned about India. I expect that next year my class will learn about Africa."

Fay began to worry about Pinchas waking up alone in the cabin. What if he needed something?

"Come, Frieda," she said. "We need to get ready. It was so good talking to you and hearing all about the Cape," she said to the woman.

Mother and child hurried back to the cabins.

"Oh, but this does sound like a good place," Frieda said.

Fay felt more light-hearted than she had in weeks. Here they could start a new, good life. With the Eibishter's help, Pinchas would be well in the colonies. The doctor had promised that the Cape Colony would provide a cure, and she had davened that his words would come true.

A little later, Fay, Pinchas, and the children stood spellbound and silent as they gazed at the mountain and the small houses on the hillside, and the great mass of land stretching as far as the eye could see.

On the quayside, a scurrying mass of humanity in a variety of clothing and skin hues moved around in seeming chaos. Yet the gangplank was fixed into place with great efficiency.

Many people were below now, calling out their family's names, suddenly spotting someone and waving frantically. Oh, how Fay wished there was someone to call to them in that way.

They set about getting their things together and leaving the ship. A sailor came to their cabin and offered his assistance. Soon they were on the quayside. They went to the customs shed.

"Ah, from London, I see," an officer said. He quickly scribbled on some forms and stamped them vigorously.

The man behind them was not dealt with so quickly. He was struggling with his English, lapsing into Yiddish, and the official was getting angry.

"Foreigners!" he muttered. "Why don't they stay home?"

Pinchas, who had been walking slowly behind Fay, stopped and walked over to the man.

"I will translate for him," Pinchas said. His English was clear, though heavily accented.

The official shrugged in agreement and a few minutes later, the man's papers were being stamped. As the Levine family made their way out to their new land, a tall man came up to them.

"New here?" he said. "Need a ride with your things? Need a place to go?" Without waiting for an answer, he swooped down and lifted up the wooden trunk. "Wait here! I'll be back for the rest of the things."

Pinchas was breathing hard, but he said under his breath, "Not a good man."

Fay overheard and felt a sense of panic at seeing the man disappear into the crowd. She remembered how earlier that day, she had thought they owned nothing of value. Yet the trunk contained everything that was precious to her — the silver Kiddush cup, her candlesticks, the family menorah, and so much more.

"Jack, David, go with him," she said. "Follow him. Wait with our things until we come."

The boys, bored with standing in line, scooted after him. They'd spent many years in the East End of London and were used to such crowds. They found the man loading their belongings onto a cart. He spotted them and shouted down, "Right, young fellows, run to your parents and tell them we'll be with them in a minute."

"David, why is he standing on the cart, the reins in his hands?" Jack whispered. "He looks as if he wants to leave straight away. Why isn't he sitting down, waiting for the family to come?"

David looked up, troubled by the same thought. "What do we do now?"

Jack was already moving toward the horse, making low soothing noises and patting him gently. His hands moved toward the harness.

"Quickly get Mother," Jack hissed to David. "Tell her to hurry here." His hands groped for the part that held the horse to the cart. Slowly, he began loosening the clasp almost completely so that only a bit of leather remained inside. In a moment, with only the slightest movement, it would come away, and horse and cart would no longer be joined together.

"Get away from the horse!" the man shouted. "He'll hurt you. Horses bite and kick, you know."

"Don't worry about me," Jack shouted back. "Horses I know about. What a fine horse. Soon my family will be here, and then we can leave."

He moved to the other side of the horse, stroking him all the while. The man was shouting, but Jack worked quickly, repeating the process so the other clasp was loosened. The man lost patience.

"Stand away or you will be hurt!" he shouted.

Jack smiled to himself but followed the instructions. The man picked up a whip and made a great cracking sound over the animal. The horse pulled away, and suddenly the man was being pulled off the cart, along the ground, shouting in pain and calling out, "Whoa, whoa!"

At that moment, Fay and David arrived. Jack gave a piecing whistle, and the horse came to a halt. It seemed that horses in this place responded to the same signals as the horses in London. The man got to his feet. His clothes were torn, and his face and knees were scraped.

"What the dickens were you doing to my horse?" he growled.

A crowd had gathered now, watching and listening.

"Me?" Jack said. "What could I possibly do to your horse? Looks to me as though you didn't do a very good job with the harness and reins."

Fay saw Jack wink at her.

"Where were you going?" she said to the man. "You said you were coming back for us. Where did you think we would all sit? It seems to me that the cart isn't large enough for all of us."

The man looked unhappy. The crowd was following every word. After a few moments the man said, "My mate ... I was going for my mate, to bring another cart to collect the rest of you."

"Well now," Fay said. "I will wait here. Go then, fetch your mate and his cart, and then we can all set off together, with my boys on your cart and the rest of us on the other one."

"Right! I'll just see to the harness and go off and get him."

Fay realized that the wooden trunk was only standing safe on the cart because Jack had managed to loosen the harness binding the horse to the cart. Once they were reconnected, the man would surely take off, never to be seen again. She was afraid. She forced herself to sound bold and confident, as if she was used to giving orders.

"No," she said. "My boy will do a better job of it than you. You can walk to your friend. We will wait here with the cart."

Suddenly, there was a cry. "My horse and cart is here! It disappeared from the gates. I have been looking everywhere for it. How did it get here?"

The man with the torn suit was there one moment and gone the next, like a puff of smoke.

Now the crowd began giving advice.

"Chase him!"

"He was trying to steal. Every time new immigrants arrive, they try to steal from them."

"What about stealing from me?" shouted the owner of the horse and cart. "What about stealing my horse and cart?"

A well-dressed man walked up to the crowd. His authoritative manner made everyone quiet down.

"What is going on here?" he asked.

Fay felt that at last someone had taken charge of an impossible situation. Quietly, she explained to him what had occurred.

"We won't catch him now," the man said. "Lucky he didn't get away with your things. I came here to collect my sister and her family, and all I found was the captain with a letter to explain they had changed their mind and used the money I sent them to go to America instead.

"Now, all that the ship has for me is stock I ordered from London, but no family. So here I am, with a wagon big enough for you and your luggage. Do you have more family members? Where are they?"

Fay pointed to Pinchas and the other children slowly walking toward them. The older children were carrying the remaining bundles.

"Right, young lad," he said to Jack. "Get your belongings off this cart, and we'll all go together to my wagon." To make these newly arrived Jews feel welcome, he said, "My name is Davidoff, and yours?"

"Levine," Fay said.

"Welcome to the Cape Colony, family Levine," the man said. The children responded with smiles. Pinchas stuck out his hand in greeting while Fay looked on.

Ephraim Davidoff was in a quandary. He had arrived early in the morning, full of anticipation at seeing his sister after many years apart. He had gone to enormous trouble, arranging a place for the family to stay in London before boarding, booking spacious cabins, and ensuring they would have kosher food on the voyage. Instead of meeting his sister, her husband and her children, he was holding a note.

> *Dear Ephraim,*
>
> *The journey to England went well. I thank you for making all the arrangements.*
>
> *While we were in London my husband became acquainted with another family, also traveling, and they have persuaded him that we should go to America. The shipping office agreed to change our tickets. I was so looking forward to being with you, but I must do as my husband wishes.*
>
> *Your sister,*
>
> *Bayla*

It was clear, reading this letter, that his sister was upset at the change. How could her husband have done this? He had written to them about the house he had bought for them. They had such a place waiting for them in America? Surely not.

It was a fine house, further down the mountain from his home in the Gardens area. Truth was, he had been worried about how his wife and sister would get on together. He couldn't ignore Bayla's call for help, for tickets to leave the shtetl, but his wife, Shirley, was English, correct and proper all the way through.

His wife and his sister as neighbors? No, it was unthinkable. They were so different, the two women. Bayla was not one to look for the good. She would criticize whatever she didn't like. Shirley kept a kosher home, but she allowed the maid to do the cooking and washing up, checking on her only very occasionally. Shirley didn't cover her hair. What would Bayla say? Shirley rarely criticized anyone, but what would she answer when she was told she was doing something wrong? The women must be kept far apart for them to live in peace.

The small houses, lower down, were smaller and less expensive. Still, they were nice compared to the houses of the shtetl. Bayla would surely be satisfied with a house that was not as large and impressive as his.

Although his wholesale business was doing well, he didn't have an enormous surplus of cash. So he had found this nice little house on Kloof Street, cheaper than his larger house. Still, it was in a good, respectable area, with a few other Jewish families nearby, and it was near the shul.

He had turned the front room into a shop. Had his sister not run a small shop while her husband sat and learned? Well, here there was no place to sit and learn. Bayla's husband would have to find work. But Bayla, he was sure, would be able to run a shop as capably as she had done back home in the shtetl.

The house was in a good position, facing Long Street, but not near any other shop selling groceries. The people who lived and worked nearby could all do with a neighborhood shop.

Yes, Bayla's husband could find work, though he had no intention of hiring him. He remembered the man as a boy. He hadn't liked him then, and he didn't think he would like him any better now.

They would be close enough to come for an occasional meal, but not near enough to visit without an invitation. He had planned it all so carefully. Now Bayla had chosen to go to America, where her husband's brothers lived. Had they sent them money for fare? No, of course not! Anger and disappointment clashed with relief that his wife would not be burdened with his family.

Now, this new family—what to do with them? Should he take them to Mrs. Clain's boarding house in District Six? Yes, that was an idea. There they would be among other Jews like themselves, new immigrants, and they would help each other.

But other new immigrants arrived differently. Usually the husband came alone and worked as a peddler, or at some other lowly occupation, until he learned the language and saved enough money to bring his family over. The landlady could possibly wait a week or two for one man's rent, but an entire family? Where would the money come from? The man was clearly ill. The woman had her hands full. So many children! What would become of them?

Maybe he should take them to the rabbi's house. Was there not a small sum of money, charity for needy newcomers?

But the house he had so carefully prepared—what about that? What would he do with it? Turn the front room back into a salon and pull out all the shelving? The large counter, too, would have to be removed. How could Bayla do this to him?

This woman, and her husband and children, looked respectable. The children were neatly dressed. They seemed to be well behaved, sitting quietly and gazing at everything, not jumping about and screaming. Could they live in the house? Could they pay a reasonable rent?

Where were they headed?

"Where should we take you?" Mr. Davidoff asked. "Do you have family here?"

Pinchas was too tired to answer.

"No, no," Fay said. "No family."

"What arrangement did you make for a place to stay?"

"In London, Jews are cared for in the Leman Street shelter. Is there any such place here?"

The driver had come to a junction. He needed to know where to go.

The woman wanted a place of shelter, a place that was free. But here, unlike London, there was no such place. What was he to do with this unfortunate group of strangers?

He made up his mind. The house was empty. There was food in the pantry. For a week or so, until the woman and her husband knew what they wanted to do, until he decided how to dispose of the house, they could stay at the place meant for his sister.

"The house on Kloof Street," he shouted to his driver. "I have a little house," he said to Fay. "It was meant for my sister's family. They should have arrived today, but it seems that they wanted to go to America instead."

Fay could hardly reply. This man, this Jewish man, was going to take them to a house that he owned. What would it cost? Was the little money they had sufficient to cover the rent?

But what other option was there?

"That is kind of you," was all she could muster.

Fay turned her attention to Pinchas. He was sitting beside her, his breathing now much heavier. The walk from the ship, the shock of seeing the man run off with the trunk, had taken its toll.

"Soon we will be in our new home," Fay said. "There you can rest." She spoke with false confidence, not knowing what awaited them.

The cart stopped beside a detached house, with white walls and a red roof. Stone steps led up to a front door.

"Come, we have arrived," Mr. Davidoff said. "Children, get down."

He took Pinchas by the elbow and helped him to stand.

"Go with the children," Mr. Davidoff said to Fay. "I will help your husband. He's tired from the voyage, it seems."

Still assisting Pinchas, Mr. Davidoff mounted the steps. He took out a large ring of keys and opened the door. Fay and the children entered, followed soon by the two men.

"See, this was the dining room and salon, but I fitted it out to become a shop," Mr. Davidoff said. "Now come into the rest of the house—the living quarters."

The family entered a long passage.

Near the door was a wooden chair with a carved seat and back and wide arms. Mr. Davidoff felt Pinchas clutching his arm tightly.

"Sit now and rest, while I show your family the rooms," Mr. Davidoff said.

He went through a door on the left of the passage, with everyone following him. The room faced the street. Beyond the net curtains the family could see the driver standing beside the cart. There were two beds, with shiny brass headboards. They were covered with maroon material that matched the maroon curtains on the window. On the opposite wall, near a chair, was a large chest of drawers. Sun shone through the net curtains, making patterns on the floor.

The family stood and gazed in awe.

"The is the main bedroom, for the parents," Mr. Davidoff said.

Back in the passage he pointed to another door further down. "That one, I think, is for the girls. The daughters of the people who lived here before slept there."

There were four beds, two on each wall, with low wooden headboards beautifully made up and white sheets securely tucked in. On the third wall was a window through which they could see a street and a row of small houses. Next to the window was a large wooden wardrobe. On one side there many drawers, and on the other, a long door was slightly ajar, with a rod and hangers. But what made the girls gasp out loud was the mirror in the middle, a large, shiny mirror that showed their reflections.

Mr. Davidoff pointed at a door across the passage. "That was for the boarders. They had young men as boarders, so they told me. I think it will be good for the boys. Come!"

They all went, with the exception of Frieda. She fingered the white sheets, then went to the window and gazed out. She gazed at her reflection in the mirror. Was all this real? Were they truly going to live here, in this marvelous place? How was it possible?

The family trooped into a large room, with a small window looking out toward the mountain. There was a small garden filled with greenery.

"Oh, a garden, like we had in the shtetl!" Jack said.

"Look, four beds!" David said.

The beds were lined along the walls. Next to each one was a small low chest of drawers. Above the beds were four large hooks.

"Just look at the floors," little Isaac said suddenly. "Have you ever seen such shiny floors?" All eyes looked down and saw that the floors were indeed smooth and gleaming.

"My wife came here with the maids," Mr. Davidoff said. "They gave everything a good cleaning, and I see they did a thorough job polishing the floors."

He led them out of the room to the end of the passage, where there was a large bathroom with a giant tub sporting gleaming brass taps.

The family was unprepared for such luxury. They stared at everything with big eyes.

Ephraim Davidoff noticed this. He led them back up the passage and helped Pinchas stand up. He noticed the man seemed to clutch him less tightly, and was relieved. He hoped the man was simply tired, not terribly ill.

On the other side of the passage a door led to the kitchen. Here a large wooden table dominated the room. It was covered with a red checkered cloth, beautifully set with cutlery and crockery.

There was a large coal stove, and they were told to "Sit, sit." They watched as the fire was lit and a kettle was filled with water from a tap. Their host went into a small adjoining room.

"My wife said she would leave cake, butter, and jam in the pantry, to keep it fresh," he said over his shoulder.

He emerged with a large tray, and Jack ran to take it from him. Soon the kettle was boiling and tea was made, and the children were happily eating. Pinchas sipped the tea as color slowly returned to his face and his breathing became more regular.

Mr. Davidoff rose to leave. "Well then, I must go, but early tomorrow I will call again." As he reached the passage, he stopped as Fay called out to him, "Mr. Davidoff, I must talk to you. I must know more about our stay here." She came into the passage.

Oh no, now I will never get rid of them, he thought. *How can I explain to her that this is only temporary, that I must sell this house? I should have made it clear before we even entered that this would be a temporary solution.*

Fay spoke quickly, quietly, so her family couldn't overhear her.

"I have to tell you, marvelous though this house is, I cannot afford it. My husband is a fine carpenter, and when he is well again, he will work. Until then, I have very little money, and no idea how I will earn money for food and rent."

It hurt Fay to say these words. She wanted to believe in this dream, of landing here in this spacious house. But how could one not speak the truth? Impossible! These words must be said.

This plain speaking shocked Ephraim. Only a moment before he had been worrying about how he would tell them they must leave. Now here she was telling him that they could not remain here!

Memories suddenly flooded him. He remembered arriving, more than a decade before, a penniless boy. He remembered traveling to the diamond fields and finding, after only a week of scrabbling in the dirt, three large diamond stones, lying one beside the other as if waiting for him.

He had wanted to call out, to shout in excitement. Then he remembered his father quoting from the *Tehillim* he had said often: "Put not your trust on princes, nor on a human being."

The men around him were far from princes. They were very much human beings and clearly less than trustworthy. Ephraim thought suddenly of a man, who on the previous day had given a shout of joy when he found precious stones, and now lay dying of a stab wound.

Ephraim hid the stones deep in his pockets and kept digging. At the end of the day he went to the tent he shared with a few other men and said, "This is no good. I'm tired of filling my shoes and pockets and mouth with nothing but sand. I'm going home. Nothing can be as bad as this."

He had made his way back to the Cape. There he had gone to a top jeweler, a Jewish man, and shown him the stones.

The man was honest. He found a buyer and gave the money to Ephraim. "Be careful, young man. Money comes easily and goes easily!"

Ephraim had placed the money in a bank and bought some clothing to look respectable. He found a small room to rent in District Six, on Harrington Street, near the kosher café. He found a job delivering goods. It was hard work and paid little, but it was sufficient to live on.

Months later, he found a better job, working in a grocery shop closer to Adderley Street. In that shop, his English improved.

A few years later, he found a job in a wholesale business. This work intrigued him, and he learned all he could. Now he had his own business. He could afford to buy a house in the Gardens, on the slopes of Table Mountain, like all the other rich people. He even had a clever, refined English wife. Well, he *had* been surprised when her family invited him to eat with them, and even more surprised when this young woman spoke to him in a friendly manner. But after all, he had made money by then, and the family obviously considered him presentable enough for their daughter. Her younger sisters were already married.

He was no longer a newly arrived frightened boy. He was now a man of substance.

As he stood there in front of Fay, he remembered his father's parting words: "Remember, only Hashem can protect you. Keep His laws always."

Life had treated him well. Was it not time to "*maaser*" some of his good fortune, as his own father had been so meticulous to do?

Why had he not thought before that it was necessary to donate a tenth of his earnings to charity?

The woman before him was honest, clearly a good woman. The

children were cleanly dressed, no small feat after a long voyage. They were well behaved. This woman could be trusted.

As the moments passed, the woman stood silently, not saying anything. He pulled his thoughts together and pulled back to the present.

"For this week, you are my guests," he said. "I was planning for my sister to run a shop in this front room. Maybe you can do that instead, or maybe your husband, but we can talk of this later. I'll come back and we will discuss how you can earn a living and what you'll pay for rent. Rest now! Were Jews not set upon the earth to be of help to one another?"

Fay was taken aback. She had been preparing herself to leave this place, to find somewhere else to live. She had been wondering how to tell the children and her husband that it had been a mistake, that this fine place was not for them.

"Come, let me explain to you how things work here," Mr. Davidoff said, not giving her a chance to argue with him. "See, here next to the front door is the gas meter. This is for the lights of the house, and also for the boiler that heats up the water for the bath. When the gas is low, you place a shilling coin in the meter, over here.

"A man comes once a week and collects the money. I have ten coins in this tin box. I placed them here for my sister."

Fay began to say something, but he interrupted.

"Use them now, and in time you can repay me. In the kitchen, there's a large tap beside the sink. This fills the spare tank on top of the ceiling with water. Keep it filled. We have a reservoir, just a little way up the road, and another larger one on Molteno Road, just where the mountain slopes begin, but every now and again we have a lack of water. The pantry is filled with everything you'll need for the next few days. I hope you'll be comfortable and happy here."

Then Mr. Davidoff bade farewell and went out to his cart, where the driver was waiting for him. Fay watched him go, stunned. This man, this stranger, was allowing them to remain in this marvelous place, even though he realized that there was no guarantee that rent would be paid. This man was offering her a means to make a living. It all seemed unreal.

"Tatte, are you tired?" she could hear her children say. "Tatte, why are you leaning on the table?"

Fay ran to the kitchen. "Jack, help your father up."

She went to the door that led to her bedroom and said, "Come, follow me."

Jack helped Pinchas into the room as she pulled back the sheets. As soon as Pinchas put his head on the soft pillow he was asleep.

Fay and Jack walked back to the kitchen. Fay longed to sit down, to drink and eat something, but the children had clearly eaten their fill and were clamoring to know more.

"Is this our new house?"

"How did that nice man know we were coming?"

"Look through the kitchen window — it looks just like a park, with a big wall around it. Does it belong to the house?"

Fay needed time to recover, to think of everything she had been told.

"Now, just look at those sticky hands," she said. "Wash carefully at the sink, then *bentch*, and then we'll look at everything again."

While the children did as they were told, Fay hurriedly poured some tea and drank it, though it was by now lukewarm.

"Quietly now, Tatte is sleeping," she said.

They went first to the girls' room.

"A room just for the girls, like on the ship!" Frieda said. "How marvelous!"

"Now girls, each of you choose a bed and lie down for a little rest," Fay said. "I don't know about you, but I feel as if I'm still on a ship. The ground seems to rock. I suppose after a rest that will go away."

The girls hardly seemed to hear her. They were gazing into the large mirror. Frieda had her arms around Bertha. They stood stock still, just looking.

Ethel and Rose were right in front of the mirror, laughing as they touched the shiny surface and moved their fingers up and down.

As she left the room, Fay heard Frieda say, "Come away. Don't touch. Look, you're leaving marks. Come, look out of the window. See the shadows the people make as they walk past. Look, across the road there are more houses, and they all have a little garden in the front!"

The boys went to the next room. Fay followed, looking around.

"Jack, David, and Joseph will each have their own bed," she said. "Samuel and Isaac can share, one at the top and one at the bottom."

The children looked at their mother. In London they had slept in one room, with a curtain dividing the girls from the boys. The beds had been low, rickety contraptions, made of bits of scrap wood, and they'd had to share them.

Once again, little Isaac spoke up. "Shiny floors, lots of big beds, even our own bath. I like it here. I liked it on the boat, but I like it here even better."

"I wish I also had my own bed, but I suppose we can both fit into that big bed," Samuel said.

Jack and David were already making their way to claim the beds they wanted.

Joseph was at the window, gazing out at the green bushes and trees. "Well, I was afraid to go on that boat, but now I'm glad that I did," he said.

Frieda knew she had to settle the children so she could see to Pinchas.

"Jack, David, come with me," she said. "Take the dark blue bundle to the girls' room. Then come back and take the other bundle to your room. Unpack, but quietly, as Tatte needs to rest."

Later, much later, after the children had carefully laid everything in the spacious, cupboards, Pinchas woke up from a long sleep. He found the children seated around the table in the kitchen.

"Tatte is here," Frieda said. "Tatte is awake. Now we can eat."

Fay had made a good evening meal from the food that was in the pantry. When the children's excitement at last give way to tiredness, and they fell asleep, Pinchas and Fay were alone at last. Fay told him of her conversation with Mr. Davidoff.

Pinchas sat without replying for a while.

"It seems that the time of miracles has not passed," he said finally. "Here we are in a fine home, with food and bedding provided, and we only have to begin paying rent next week. But where am I to find work? What will happen if there is no work for me? I am useless. I am no good to my family."

Fay had been thinking similar thoughts. It seemed to her that one miracle had followed another. First there had been Jack's stamps, which were worth a lot of money. Then they had been taken to wonderful cabins on the ship. Kosher food that had been ordered for others was given to them.

Toward the end of the voyage she had plucked up her courage and spoken to the captain. He had assured her that she would not be asked for additional money.

What if he had demanded money? What would she have done?

She had figured out that the accommodations on the ship, the food—it had all been meant for Mr. Davidoff's family.

With her *Tehillim* clasped in her hands, she had davened for a miracle to transport them safely to the new land. How long could such miracles endure? Surely such things could not last forever.

With as much confidence as she could force into her voice, she smiled at Pinchas and said, "How can you talk like that? It was you who told me that the man who took our trunk was bad. That was why I told the boys to follow him. If not for your warning, what would have been with us?"

"Really? Is that why they went after him?"

"Yes, I heard you. I trusted you. I trust you now to rest and get well. Are you not the finest of carpenters? As soon as you're well, you will find work. Tomorrow that fine gentleman will come and speak to us about making a living. I am fit, well rested, and able to contribute something for the first time in our life together.

"The sea voyage was a wonderful holiday for me. Until you're well, I will earn for us, just as you have done in the past. Then, when you're well again you will find work."

Pinchas smiled as tiredness swept over him. As he shuffled his way to the bedroom, Fay knew that in this new country she would have to be the breadwinner. She would have to run the shop, but how? She could speak English but had never learned to write it. She could add up in a trice — buying at the East End markets had made that necessary — but was that sufficient to run a shop?

Fay was tired, but before she could sleep, she needed courage to face the coming days. She took out her small book of *Tehillim*, her mother's farewell gift.

While the household slept, and the sounds of the street drifted into the house, she read verse after verse.

Today, the man who had wanted to steal their belongings and leave them stranded had actually helped them. The outcome of his treachery was that they had drawn the attention of a man who had acted spontaneously to help a Jewish family in distress. He had brought them to this fine home and even spoke of a way in which she could earn a living. Was that not a miracle? Had she not experienced so many miracles in these past weeks?

How wondrous were the ways of Hashem!

But still the thoughts plagued her. What if she proved to be an inept shopkeeper? What if Pinchas could not find work?

Today, all her fears, all her worries, had been proven wrong.

Tomorrow was a new day. Tomorrow she would have the strength to find solutions. She left the kitchen and soon fell into a deep sleep.

Chapter 11

"The growth of the community inevitably entailed an expansion of the Minister's work. The Jews living in outlying country districts made increasingly frequent calls on the Rev. Mr. Ornstien's services with the result that he was often away from town. The Minister's absence gave rise to frequent complaints by his congregation, who felt they had first claim on his ministrations. To overcome this difficulty, the Rev. F. Lyons was appointed assistant Minister in 1889 ... Thus during the absence of Ornstien in 1891, his capable assistant acted in the multiple capacity of Reader, Shochet, and Mohel..."

— Israel Abrahams, *The Birth of a Community*, p. 50

Early the following morning, as the sun came up, Jack woke up and looked around the room. He had lost his precious stamp album. His bar mitzvah day, which fell out while they were on the ship, had been forgotten, ignored by all. The *tefillin* that he had received from school were now in the cupboard next to his bed.

They had left England as summer was just beginning.

"It's so hot already," he had said to a sailor before leaving the ship. "Summers here must be very hot."

The sailor had laughed. "Young man, this isn't summer, this is winter. The months of June, July, and August are winter here. The seasons were reversed once we crossed the equator. Just wait until December—that's midsummer. Then you'll see what hot really means!"

The room was pleasantly warm, and quiet. The whole house was quiet.

Jack looked out the window. Behind the high walls he could see the mountain, now covered in a layer of cloud. Jack gently opened the cupboard. He took out his *tefillin* and the new *siddur* his school had given him for his bar mitzvah. He already knew how to don *tefillin*, and each morning on the ship, before the others woke up, he had davened. Perhaps here there was a shul and he could *daven* with a *minyan*.

Where was east? Where was Jerusalem? Outside the sky was growing lighter, but on which side was the sun rising? Jack made a guess and then alone, without his father by his side, he began to place the *tefillin* in the correct position. He opened his *siddur* and began to *daven*.

Oh, how different this lonely davening was from the picture that had filled his mind when he received these gifts.

Once he finished and carefully put everything away, he felt better, comforted, and no longer afraid of what the future held.

This new country must be a good place. So far it had come with other surprises, besides a warm winter with a shining sun. They were living in a spacious house, instead of two small rooms. From his bedroom window he could see a small patch of green, a cluster of leafy bushes, and the three steps from the kitchen that led down to the garden.

Was he the only one who remembered living in the shtetl, in a house surrounded by a small garden? Did only he remember a mother who was always cheerful, with family and friends in nearby houses, visiting, laughing, and joking?

He remembered his father in those days, a cheerful, smiling man who came home from work and rushed off to shul for prayers and for learning.

Then came that terrible journey, and worse still, London, where his mother became a stranger to him, a dour, tired old lady who learned to speak the new language with difficulty and never learned how to write it.

The garden was gone. The mother who laughed and told stories was gone. The strong father was gone.

Now, as he carefully placed his *tefillin* in the top drawer of the chest beside his bed, Jack thought back to those last few weeks in London.

How had he not noticed that his father was changing? How had he not noticed that his father rarely smiled? How had he not noticed that his father was so ill?

Now they were in a new land. Here his father would get well — so the doctor had said.

They had left the ship to be taken to a palatial house. There was a bedroom for the girls, one for the boys, and one for his parents. There was a large kitchen, with an enormous table, big enough for the whole family to sit around. The sun shone. The house was warm. It would be good.

Surely, the loss of his stamps and his long-awaited bar mitzvah celebration was nothing.

But even though this new house even had a room for a shop, Jack was once again troubled. His father was too ill to run a shop. His mother clearly couldn't do it. Did Mr. Davidoff realize that although his mother spoke English, she couldn't read or write it? Did he realize how ill his father was? When he did realize, would he tell them to leave?

Why had his mother agreed to remain in this large house? What had she said to Mr. Davidoff as she spoke to him in the passage? Jack was aware of just how little money his mother had. How would they pay the rent for this large house?

In London, families were evicted for not paying rent. He would walk hurriedly past them as they huddled disconsolately on the pavement, their furniture and worldly possessions piled around them. Could that happen to them here?

He heard his mother moving about, and he shook David awake.

"Hey, come on," Jack said. "You can't sleep all day. Did you see a big park as we came here yesterday, not so far away? Come on. Let's go explore a little."

The boys dressed and walked to the front door. Back in London, they had come and gone as they pleased. Their mother had always presumed that they would go to school and come home afterward. She had never asked them where they were going. Now, they were soon to find out, things would be different.

Fay was determined that she would never again sink into the lethargy that had allowed her children to act behind her back. True, it had brought good, not harm. After all, if not for Jack running about on that horse and wagon, he would not have been able to save their trunk by undoing the reins on the horse. He would not have had a stamp collection. They would still be in London, with her desperately ill husband.

Yet, she told herself, here she would keep a firm control over her children. Was that not her duty as a mother?

So as the boys made their way to the front door, she followed them and said very firmly, "Now where do you think you're going?"

David moved behind Jack. Jack had woken him up and suggested they go out. Let Jack do the talking.

"Mother, we're just going to . . . going to find where the nearest shul is." Jack gave a small sigh of relief. That would be acceptable to his mother, wouldn't it? "See, Tatte will want to *daven* with a *minyan* as soon as he's better, so I thought . . ."

Fay was tempted to just let the boys go. She had so much to do, so much to consider, but then she forced herself to answer. "No, look at your clothes — they're all creased, the same clothes you wore yesterday. Is that a way to go out? First you will have a good wash at the tap in that fine bathroom. Then find a set of clean clothes and make sure your shoes are shining. Just look at them.

"Then you can go, but don't go far. Be home in one hour and don't get lost. When you return, I will have food ready for you."

Fay saw the surprise in Jack's eyes. Even David, who was hiding behind his brother, peeped out to look quizzically at her.

In London, where the sun never seemed to shine, she had struggled with being far from her family and coping with the laundry and keeping the house clean. She had been busy cooking food on a limited budget and coping with each new baby. Her children had become independent, too independent, coming and going as they pleased.

In this new land, in this amazing house, things were going to be different. Fay was unsure where money for the next meal would come from. She was worried about her husband, whose health had improved slightly but who still tired easily. Nevertheless, she would not lose control again. She glared at the boys.

"You heard me," she said. "Get going."

The thought of food was good. The need to return in precisely an hour was not.

"But how will we know when an hour has passed?" Jack said.

"If you can't manage such a simple thing, then just stay indoors. You have a mouth. You can ask a gentleman the time. There should be a clock tower somewhere nearby. You can tell the time from that."

Jack pulled David along with him. How long would it take to wash and change? Then, after all that, they had only one hour? Well, one hour would have to do. It seemed as if they had left behind one mother in London, taken another one on the ship, and now had quite a different one altogether.

The boys arrived back at the kitchen, their faces shining and their shirts clean, if slightly creased.

"Wait, before you go, first sit and eat," Fay said. "It's no good running around without some food in you." Fay placed two small dishes on the table and gave each boy a piece of bread heavily coated with jam. She wondered what she would do when the loaf was finished. Was there a shop where she could buy kosher bread? How much would it cost? How long would the money left over from buying the tickets last?

She watched as they ate and listened as they bentched. Then, as they stood up to go, she inspected them. She looked down at their shoes, still covered in dust.

"What did I say about cleaning your shoes?" she said.

"How should we clean them?" Jack said. "What can we use?" He was almost afraid of this fierce new woman that his mother had become, but he was determined to regain his sense of self.

Fay found an old cloth below the sink and gave it to him. She watched as both boys rubbed their shoes clean. Then she looked at their hair, wet her hands slightly, and patted it flat.

"Off you go, then. Remember, one hour, no longer. We have a lot to do today."

Jack was thankful that they had been allowed out altogether. "Yes, Mother, we will be back in an hour."

He grabbed David's hand and tugged him out of the kitchen, out though the front room, down the steps and onto the pavement.

"Let's go," he hissed, and they took off at a run.

Fay watched the boys run. She hoped she was doing the right thing, letting them out alone in this strange new place. She looked out the window, beyond the garden, and saw that a thick white cloud now covered the flat-topped mountain. So this was the "tablecloth" the woman on the ship had spoken about. The light outside was not as clear as the day before; instead, a hazy sunshine filtered through the clouds.

Just then, Fay heard a sound she thought she would never hear again: harsh, rasping breathing. She ran to the room and propped Pinchas up on pillows, which sometimes helped. She spoke soothingly to him. What else could she do? Hot tea! That would help. She went quickly to the girls' room.

"Frieda, wake up now," she said urgently. "Come sit here with Tatte while I make tea for him."

Fay brought the tea and watched as Pinchas sipped it. Outside, it was slowly becoming brighter. Just as slowly, Pinchas began to breathe normally again.

Fay forgot about the boys, forgot about the new house, thought only of the fact that this new land was not providing the cure the doctor had promised. Once again Pinchas was ill. She was afraid.

As Pinchas breathed more easily and settled down to sleep, Fay took out a pencil and paper and began to write.

To my family,

We are now in the new land, the place where the doctor said Pinchas would get well. We traveled for many weeks on the sea. We are now so far from you that I fear we will never return.

Oh, how I wish we had never left. Did I write we were managing in London? Oh, how falsely I wrote. We had terrible accommodations. There was no garden. The streets were filled with dirt. The air was black with soot, and nearly every day it rained. Why did I ever listen to you and leave?

Worse still, Pinchas became ill. He has difficulty breathing. The doctor said if we came here, to the Cape Colony, he would get well.

We arrived yesterday, very early in the morning. A kind Jewish man met us and brought us to our new home here. It has a shop in the front room that I will run, to make parnassah, just until Pinchas is well enough to work.

Yaakov will write the new address in English at the bottom of this page.

Love to all the family, from your daughter Faigy

Fay could hear the other children waking up, talking to each other, moving around the rooms. As she gazed out the window, she saw the sun beginning to filter through the clouds. Slowly, the sun grew brighter. By the time the sun shone brightly onto the street outside, Pinchas was breathing normally again.

Fay felt she could leave her husband, now that he had fallen asleep and was breathing without difficulty. Some color had returned to his cheeks. She went to each room and told the children to hurry and dress, and come to the kitchen for breakfast.

Later, the children went outside to explore the garden. Sunshine poured down. The flat-topped mountain was now clear of any clouds. Fay went back to Pinchas. He slept peacefully. How foolish she had been to doubt the doctor. Her husband would get well. This was a good place.

Fay reread her letter. Was she correct to tell them how bad it had been in London? Would they believe her now if she wrote that everything was good in this new land? Should she tear up the letter and write only of good things, as she had in the past? No, let them know back home of the true conditions in London. Should she give a false picture, for the sake of false pride, like Avraham Cohen had done? No, that was harmful. Let others know the truth.

Now, as she sat alone at the kitchen table, she wondered when the two older boys would return. Had she been foolish to let them out on their own?

Chapter 12

"UK Chief Rabbi Hermann Adler assumed the title The Very Reverend — as Cecil Roth said he had an inevitable tendency to interpret his position almost in Anglican terms. He feared that the uncultured ways of their East End brethren might threaten the Jewish position in England and he was resistant to the idea of ministers assuming full rabbinical status. If a minister sought a rabbinical diploma, he had to go abroad to get it and even then there was no guarantee that the Chief Rabbi would allow him to be called 'rabbi.'"
— Rabbi Raymond Apple, *United Synagogue, Religious Founders and Leaders, A Century of Anglo-Jewish Life, 1870–1970*

Jack pointed in the direction of where he thought he'd seen a large park. David trotted beside him, confident that his big brother knew exactly where he was going.

A few minutes later they were gazing at the most beautiful landscape they had ever seen. The park seemed to stretch endlessly before them. They saw two men coming up a path, tall, well-dressed men wearing top hats and smart suits, and white shirts that seemed to sparkle in the sunshine. Such men were rarely seen in the East End. Jack had sometimes seen such people when he collected stamps near the large fancy shops.

Perhaps this place was private. Perhaps it belonged to these rich men. Jack placed a restraining hand on his brother's arm and waited, just outside the entrance, as the men came closer.

Then came the shock. The men were speaking Yiddish! Well, not really Yiddish — it was a strange, formal sort of Yiddish — but it was still understandable. The men were Jews. They were talking about getting to Shacharis in time if they hurried.

Jack remembered that he had told his mother they were on their way to find a shul. He was afraid of these richly dressed men, but he was more afraid of the stern woman his mother had suddenly become. His Yiddish wasn't as good as his English, since he hadn't used it much in London, but it was passable.

"Excuse me," he said, "where is the shul? We are new here. My father needs a shul and a *minyan*."

The man turned to his companion, speaking now in English, "Oh, another poor family. Yet another family that comes here speaking only Yiddish and needing our charity."

Jack was deeply offended.

"Listen, guv'nor," he said, "I speak English, fine English. We come from London. Who said we would ever take charity? Have we ever taken charity, David?"

David stood quaking in his boots. This was no way to speak to such gentlemen. Next thing a copper would come, and then they would be in for it.

The man laughed. "Well, my apologies. Straight from London, are you? Welcome."

"Funny Yiddish you were talking," Jack said.

"German, my boy, it was German, not Yiddish. Our parents came here many years ago from Germany."

Jack, still smarting from the insult and brought up among cockneys, with their quick wits, responded immediately. "Ah, immigrants like us, only we speak English. Were you able to speak English when you arrived?"

The men began to laugh.

"Yes, lad, you're correct. This is a land of immigrants."

David began to relax and Jack began to calm down.

"Right, lads, come with us. See through the trees there, that big white building. That's the shul, the very first shul ever built in Africa. Come along. We don't want to be late."

The two boys saw the building emerge from the tall green trees. As they came nearer, they saw six white columns rising high up, and above them a triangular construction with a Magen David in the center. This was the shul? Amazing! Even Bevis Marks, the Sephardi shul near the East End where the rich people went, didn't look as imposing as this grand building.

They entered through large wooden doors and saw carved wooden benches, a beautiful *aron kodesh* and *bimah*, and high on the ceiling an ornate copper candelabra.

The men walked the boys to the front and said, "Rev. Ornstien is away in England, so come and meet our assistant minister, Rev. Lyons."

A well-dressed man looked at his watch and said, "Later we'll talk to the boys. Now it's time to begin."

Jack had already davened, but David took out a *siddur*. Jack was reluctant to leave. He held the *siddur* before him and looked around at everything.

This shul was so different from the *shtiebel* they attended in London. The room was so large and the wooden chairs they sat on were solid and beautiful, as was everything in this amazing building. But the davening was so silent. The men hardly moved as they quietly mouthed the words of prayer.

When at last the service was over, Rev. Lyons called them over and wrote for them the times of daily davening. Jack was feeling the strain of being in this place, with all these well-dressed men. He took the paper, thanked the rabbi, and then went down the aisle and out the front door as quickly as he could without actually running. David followed closely behind him.

How much time had all that taken? How much longer before the hour was up? Jack couldn't figure it out. Shacharis was generally nearly an hour, so they probably had a little time left. He saw an avenue in the midst of the trees.

"Come, let's see where that leads," he said.

The boys ran up the avenue, toward the mountain. At the end they found a wide road, and beyond they could see some large grand houses.

"Now let's see what's on the other end," Jack said.

Down they ran to the other end, until puffing and panting they found themselves gazing at a wide, sandy, traffic-filled road, lined with shops and with carts of every description. A sign proclaimed, "Adderley Street."

The street was like nothing they had ever seen before. It was more like Bond Street, where Jack had sometimes struck out in search of stamps. The only difference was that Bond Street was covered in tarmac, and here the sand lay, flat and tawny, on the ground and in the air, churned up by the carts and the horses' hooves.

Beyond the street, in the distance, Jack could see the masts of tall ships. So that was the sea. They had landed there only the day before. Jack turned and looked behind him, and saw that the thick cloud that had covered the mountain earlier had disappeared. The mountain's long, flat top was clear against a bright blue sky.

To the left, peeping out of the trees, he could see the top of the shul. Their new home was to the right, though it wasn't visible from where he stood, and towering above was a high mountain, round at its base but pointed at the top. Someone on the ship had told him it was called "Signal Hill."

Jack felt momentarily at ease, happy in this new place. Here he would not get lost, though he was a stranger in a strange land. This place would not be like London, where at first he kept getting lost in alleyways and narrow streets. Here he just had to look around to find the flat mountain or the pointed one, and immediately he could know where he was.

The disappointment over the bar mitzvah day that had gone unnoticed, the disappointment over the lost stamps, the fear of not having enough money, of having to leave his home, left him. Here, in this new land, the family would lead a good life. He, Jack, would see to that.

The sun was already bright in the sky.

"I'm so thirsty," David said.

"It's probably time to go back anyway," Jack said.

They made their way back slowly, wanting to tell of everything they had seen, but wary of again confronting the strange, strict woman that their mother had suddenly become.

She had better not forget that it was my stamps that brought us here, that I was the one who saved our trunk from the thief, Jack thought.

All too soon, he would learn that paying for the fare and arriving with all their possessions intact was only the beginning of the tremendous challenges that would face them.

Chapter 13

"The wealthy Mr. Isaacs, president of the local congregation, is a most estimable man, upright and devoted to his people. He is ever generous in his help to the poor, and is the first to contribute with outstanding liberality, to all philanthropic and communal causes..."
— Israel Abrahams, *The Birth of a Community*, p. 87

The sound of laughing children woke Pinchas. To his surprise, he found that breathing didn't hurt his chest. The pain had been practically unbearable those last few days in London. It had eased somewhat on the journey, but not so much that he hadn't been aware of each breath.

Had he dreamt it, or had he woken up earlier, with that same pain?

Now, he breathed deeply in and then out again, and there was no pain, nothing. Pain had become such a part of his existence that he wondered to himself if he was still alive. Yes, it seemed he was, since through the doorway he heard the sound of his children's voices.

He willed himself to get up. With each day that passed in idleness, his old energy, the energy he'd had back in the shtetl when he was a young man, seemed to have left him forever.

He had let his Faigy take over their lives. She had found money to buy the boat tickets. She had spoken to a strange man at the docks, and they had been brought to this house. The doctor had said that if he remained in London he would die. As he heard those words, all he could think was, *What will be with my Faigy and the children?*

Yet here he was, apparently alive, breathing easily, but still so very tired. He was in yet another strange land, with a family to support. How would he do it? Weariness flowed over him. All he wanted was to go back to sleep, to forget his concerns, but that wouldn't do. Slowly, he forced himself up and got dressed. Putting a smile on his face and compelling his feet to move more rapidly than he wished, he walked toward the voices.

Jack and David were standing at a table, applying jam to slices of bread. The younger children were seated around the table, demolishing the slices as they received them. Faigy was nowhere to be seen.

Jack saw his father first.

"Good morning," he said. "We found a shul for you. It's too late now for Shacharis, but Minchah is at five this afternoon. If you want to go, we'll take you there. Maariv is about an hour later, and sometimes there's a *shiur* in between, but not always. Maybe, when you go, you can talk to them about my bar mitzvah."

Pinchas looked at his son. So the boy hadn't forgotten after all. Yet it was his son who had found the shul, his son who knew the times of davening. Should it not be the other way around?

"Where is your mother?"

"She went out. A gentleman came, the same man who brought us here yesterday. He came with another lady — his wife, I think. They all spoke, and then they all went out."

Faigy was with strangers, in this strange new place? When they had arrived in London, Faigy had spent the first week alone, at home, refusing to go out.

"Mother said we must keep the children quiet so they don't wake you," Jack said. "They were quiet, weren't they? We must give you breakfast — the bread and jam that the gentleman left for us yesterday. We saved four pieces for you."

Pinchas went back to his room and davened. Then he went to the kitchen and sat at the table, empty now, as the children had run into the small backyard and were playing some sort of rhyming game. Only Frieda was in the kitchen. She was standing on a stool by the sink, carefully washing dishes.

"Mother said that when she returns, she wants to find everything spic and span," Frieda said. "When she comes back, she will make tea for you. Can you just imagine, we have our own yard!

"Mother said she was going to find a school for us. The lady who came will show Mother where the school is. See, once we're at school Mother can begin to use the room as a shop and earn money for us to live on."

Pinchas ate his food. He drank the water from the mug set out for him. Frieda hummed a little tune as she worked. From outside the sounds of the children rose and fell. His Faigy was going to earn money for them to live on. How could she run a shop? Yes, the front room had a counter and shelves, but running a shop? His Faigy! No, it was impossible.

Could *he* run a shop? That was a possibility, but a shop depended on customers. There was no guarantee they would come. He must find work as a carpenter straight away. He would get regular wages every week. Surely there was always a need for a good carpenter. But as he finished his meal and found that he barely had sufficient energy to make his way back to his room, he realized that for now, he would not be able to work.

A feeling of hopelessness, of being superfluous and not at all necessary to his family, came over him. He stumbled back to his room, back to bed, where he fell into a long, deep sleep.

He didn't hear the sound of children rushing to the door, of Fay's voice, cheerful and encouraging.

"Sit down in the kitchen," she said. "Come now. Listen to what I have found out. This morning I went with Mr. Davidoff and his wife to his place of work. He showed me all the things they have in their storehouse and gave me two lists. See here—this is what I'll pay him for anything I buy from him. This here is what I ask the people to pay, when they buy things from me.

"Jack, you will write down on top of each word, in Yiddish, what it says. I will soon learn this alphabet too." She paused and looked around. "Tomorrow the driver will come and bring things to fill the shelves in the empty room. Never take anything from those shelves. Do I make myself clear?"

Heads nodded.

"Right, now there is more. Mrs. Davidoff took me home in her carriage — such a kind lady! She spent the whole morning with me, waiting while her husband told me how to run the shop. We passed a school — it's called Mr. Thorner's school and isn't too far from here. The Jewish children who live around here go to that school. Isn't that wonderful? Tomorrow you'll all be at school!"

The questions came fast.

"Where is the school?"

"Is it the beginning of a school term?"

But their questions were cut short.

"If you want lunch you had better leave me in peace," Fay said. "Go outside. Isn't this marvelous, our own garden? Go now!"

Fay needed some time to herself. She had been told what goods she would need, and she had been assured that they would arrive later that day, but who would buy them? And where would she find everything else she needed? This place had many shops. There was a kosher butcher, but what about bread? In London she had been able to buy fresh kosher bread. Then there was the school, with Jews and non-Jews mixed together, boys and girls mixed together. Who had ever heard of such a thing?

When she had expressed amazement, Mrs. Davidoff just laughed.

"My dear, it is the best school in all of Cape Town," she said. "The children of the very best families go there, Jewish children too. There is no Jewish school here."

Fay went to see Pinchas. His color seemed good. He was sleeping soundly, and though his breathing was audible, there was none of the terrible rattling sound that had so terrified her on the boat.

She went back to the kitchen. There was plenty of food in the pantry, and soon there was a vegetable soup bubbling away on the stovetop. She mixed the leftover bread from the previous day with eggs and milk to make the bread pudding she had made in London. What would she do when the supply in the pantry was finished? How long would the small sum of money that was left in her purse last? When would the shop begin to make money?

Pinchas was even more disconcerted later in the day. Jack and David had walked on each side of Pinchas with a proprietary air as they led him to the shul. In London, their father had davened in a small *shtiebel*, with working men. His sons were worried now about how he would react to the upper-class congregants, with their suits and hats. They had insisted that their father don his Shabbos suit, even though it was a weekday. He would be ashamed to appear there in his weekday clothing. To their amazement, their father had complied without argument.

It seemed to them that their mother and father had swapped natures. Just as their mother was now bossy, giving orders, their father was now compliant.

As they entered the shul with their father, Rev. Lyons recognized them and came over to welcome them. Then the service started. Their father's davening could be heard above those of the other men. Not only that, but he swayed back and forth in the customary manner. He stood out in strong contrast to the other members, who stood stock still, occasionally swaying slightly.

As soon as it was time to sit down, Jack whispered to Pinchas, "Tatte, we are new here, and here they do everything very quietly. Perhaps we should do as they do."

Normally Pinchas would have reacted angrily to a son telling him how to *daven*, but the last few weeks had been disorienting. First his quiet wife had taken all affairs into her own hands, and before he knew it, he was traveling on a large ship across the ocean, weak and in pain. Somehow, his oldest boys and their mother had contrived to have them taken to a spacious, well-furnished home when they reached this new land.

This was a far cry from the rooms they had lived in during those years in London. Now he heard only his own voice and not the comforting accompaniment of others as he said the ancient words, and that had filled him with confusion. Jack's words made sense to him.

When he stood again, he looked about surreptitiously and said the words of the *siddur* in the same quiet, subdued manner of the other congregants. Both his sons sighed with relief. The other members, who had been getting ready to confront him after the service, were thankful that the man had enough sense to adapt so quickly to their ways.

No one could know the sense of despair that overwhelmed Pinchas.

He watched as a tall, well-dressed man walked up to him. "*Shalom aleichem.* Welcome to Cape Town, Mr. Levine. My name is David Isaacs. I have the honor of being president of this congregation. Your boys were here this morning. The Levy brothers were at the dock yesterday. They told me how the boys saved you from disaster, when crooks tried to make off with your luggage. Fine boys you have. You can be proud of them.

"I hear that you're settled in a good house nearby. I suppose your wife will run the shop. What plans have you for work? Is there any way I can help?"

In spite of the fancy way the man spoke English, and in spite of his fine dress, his manner was friendly and without condescension. Pinchas relaxed as he replied, "I am a carpenter. That's my trade." He hoped he sounded confident, that the weakness he felt after the walk to shul and davening wasn't obvious to others.

Not a hint of concern could be seen on Mr. Isaacs' face, though his thoughts were troubled. He owned D. Isaacs and Co, a factory. Would an old-fashioned carpenter be employable? In January of the previous year the entire factory had been destroyed by fire. They had started again in nearby Barrack Street, in makeshift buildings. Would he be in a position to offer this man employment? True, he did employ many carpenters from the shtetls, but they were young men, fit and able to learn new ways. This man looked pale—ill, even.

Now was not the time for voicing such negative thoughts. Instead, he said, "Later, tomorrow perhaps, we can discuss work.

"Meanwhile, what are your needs? How prepared are you for your stay in Africa? You know the saying 'All beginnings are difficult,' but this is a fine land. You did well to choose to come here."

I made no choice, Pinchas thought. *I hardly understand how it is that we are here. But I hope Hashem is listening to your words.* Aloud, he said, "Thank you. Hashem will provide."

With that they parted. Pinchas and his boys walked through the side entrance of the Gardens to Kloof Street. His thoughts troubled, Mr. Isaacs joined a few other men as they walked up the avenue, toward the large solid houses that lay in the quiet Gardens area on the slopes of Table Mountain.

Pinchas and the boys arrived at their new home to find the rest of the family peering out from the front door, waiting for them.

"Come on, come on," they called. "We've been waiting for you. Our neighbors brought food to welcome us. There are two Jewish families on this street, and they brought us such fine food."

Fay met Pinchas and the two boys at the door. "Come, wash, and sit down. See what a fine meal we have. What good people live here, so generous and kind! We have fresh white bread and fried fish — not gefilte fish, but large pieces of fine fish fried in a batter. It's like Shabbos. Listen now as Tatte says the *brachah* for bread. Surely we will do well in this land."

Pinchas felt as if he was a puppet whose strings were being pulled by others. He had always felt himself to be in control of events. Since those last few days in England, when he had been too ill to move from his bed, it seemed to him as if others were manipulating the strings and he was moving in the direction he was being pulled.

He had felt this sensation in shul, when Jack had whispered to him. This feeling had been reinforced when a strange man had come up and offered help.

Now he felt the sensation flood over him as he sat at a table in a fine house that his wife had somehow arranged, eating food brought by neighbors, and recalling the conversation in shul.

"I suppose your wife will run the shop," the man had said. What a strange thing to say.

How did he know? This man had, in the kindest manner, offered his help. Yet Pinchas was troubled. Was there no facet of this new life that he would be in control of?

Pinchas realized that Faigy was talking to him. He had been so deep in thought that he hadn't even heard her. He pulled his attention back to the present. How could he think such thoughts? Was Faigy not a good and loyal wife? What option did she have, but to arrange for them all to leave London, to come to this sunny place, so he could get well again?

"Sorry, my thoughts were far away," he said. "What did you say?"

Faigy laughed. "I was only asking if you were enjoying the fish."

Instead of being pleased at her concern, Pinchas was further irritated. He was being treated like a child. There was no discussion about their future, no questions about how they should proceed, just this concern if he liked the food.

"Wonderful!" he forced himself to say. "Yes, ask the neighbor how she made it."

Fay was taken aback by this reply. There were few occasions when they could afford fish. Still, was her fried fish not as good as this woman's?

She bit back her hurt and turned to the children. "Before you go to bed, make sure to put your clothes out for tomorrow. Check that everything is clean and tidy. The school is not far from here, and you have missed too much learning. The sooner you are enrolled the better."

Pinchas sat there with great effort. The walk to shul had tired him, and the service had been an ordeal. By the time he had come home with the boys he was beginning to feel slightly breathless, though he hid it as best as he could. Now he could think of nothing but getting to the bedroom without collapsing.

It was with a sigh of relief that he fell onto the bed. If he could not even walk to shul and back, how could he search for work? How long would they be allowed to remain in this fine house if he couldn't earn any money? What was to become of them, his beloved wife and his dear children?

Why had he ever believed the words Avraham Cohen had written to him?

As capable as his Faigy was, she had never worked outside the home. What did she know of running a shop? Before he could dwell on his troubled thoughts some more, sleep overtook him.

—☞—

Fay had noticed how unsteadily Pinchas walked to the room. She began to clear the table, then stopped and walked to the bedroom. She saw Pinchas sleeping quietly, his breathing even. The walk had been too much for him. He would have to *daven* at home for a while, but soon, in this new land, he would be well again. Had the doctor not said so?

Her thoughts, though she couldn't know it, were quite different from Pinchas's gloomy thoughts as he had drifted off to sleep.

When the kitchen was tidy, Fay took out the letter she was in the middle of writing. *Tomorrow the children will go to school,* she wrote. *It is very different from the school they went to in London, which was so large. This one is much smaller, but I hope that here too they will do well.*

She didn't add that the school wasn't a Jewish one and that here, boys and girls sat in the same classroom. What was the point? She felt a twinge of remorse. Why hadn't she thought to look into this new land and what it would offer her family before she made the decision to leave London?

She sighed. Had she had a choice, with her husband so sick? But the children . . . what would be with them?

She must try and find a *cheder* for the boys to attend in the afternoon.

In London there were many *cheder*s for the many Jewish children who attended non-Jewish board schools. She desperately hoped there would be one here too. What would she do if there was none? No, impossible. There was a shul. Surely there must be a *cheder* for the boys. She would teach the girls to read *lashon kodesh*, just as her mother had taught her so many years ago.

Fay put the letter aside. In the morning Jack would find out their new address and write it down for her. She must find a place to buy a stamp and post this letter.

She wished she had never left the shtetl. She was still hurt that her mother had not helped her to remain. When Pinchas had been so determined to leave, could anything her mother or her father have said to him changed his mind? Why hadn't they tried? She sighed again. What was the use of stewing in anger? It could change nothing.

They were in a new land. Pinchas would recover. She would find a *cheder* for the boys to attend in the afternoon. The shop would be a success. Would Mr. Davidoff have set up a shop for his sister if he had not thought it would succeed? No, surely not.

How could she have known that the house had been bought hurriedly, and that Mr. Davidoff had wondered just how good a location it was for a shop? Since time was lacking, and his sister and her family were due to arrive, he had gone ahead with the sale. He knew he could always supplement her earnings, if need be. What choice did he have?

Perhaps it was better that Fay didn't know.

Chapter 14

"The proposal to institute a Jewish denominational school evoked at first considerable enthusiasm . . . Parents were quite keen on other people's children attending the Jewish school. But their enthusiasm languished when it came to their own. The majority were adamant in their reluctance to withdraw their sons from Mr. Thorner's popular school."

— Israel Abrahams, *The Birth of a Community*, p. 55

David was the first one to wake up.

He was excited to go to school. The other children had enjoyed the freedom of the voyage, running around and exploring, but for David the time had passed slowly. He enjoyed school. He liked learning new facts. Besides, learning came easily to him. He had only to read through a page twice to have everything firmly imprinted on his mind.

At the old school, in London, his teachers had encouraged him.

"My boy," they had said, "keep up the good work, and when the time comes you can apply for a scholarship at University College. It's a fine place and there's no problem there with admitting Jews."

Was there a university here? Did they accept Jews? In time he would make it his business to know, but meanwhile, he was pleased to be returning to school.

David glanced around the room, marveling at its spaciousness. The small cupboards beside each bed and the hooks above them comfortably housed their clothing. No more squashing everything into wooden boxes beneath their beds.

The ship's bedrooms had seemed spacious compared to their cramped London home, but it was nothing compared to this fine place that exceeded all his expectations of what they would find in the new land.

Of course, all this had come about because of Jack. His brother didn't care much for schoolwork, though he was good at it, but my, how he knew the world and its ways. Only because of his stamps and his knowledge of horses had all this come about.

On a chair beside his bed, David saw that the clothes he had placed there the night before looked different somehow, and then he realized why. Everything had been ironed. He looked around the room. Yes, the clothes they had been told to put out were all carefully ironed. How long had his mother worked last night, while they slept?

This new land seemed to him an upside-down place. Here they were, in the middle of the winter, now that it was June. When they left England, it had been right before spring. The worst of the bitter cold was now behind them, but each day had been enveloped in a fine misty rain and a dull grey sky.

How could it be winter here? The sun shone all day. By midday it was as hot as the hottest summer day in London.

Quietly, he got out of bed and dressed. He heard a noise in the kitchen, and saw that his mother was busily setting the kitchen table for breakfast.

"Oh, David, you're up," she said. "Let me look at you. Fine, just let me give your hair a parting. Right, now you look fine. Go and wake the others. Tell them to hurry. We don't want to be late for your first day of school."

As David walked into his room, he suddenly remembered the letters for the teachers that Jack had collected at their old school. He must remind Jack to take them. No, he would take them himself.

Where had Jack placed those letters? The confusion of the move, the packing, the voyage — it had all been so rushed. Then he remembered. He went to the correct bundle, still unpacked, that stood in the passage and found the package carefully folded in newspaper. Relieved, he took out the letters and placed them in his pocket. Just then Jack came into the hallway.

"I need the letters for school," he said.

"Don't worry," David said. "I have them."

Jack, happy for David to take some responsibility, merely nodded his head. David could handle the letters. He, Jack, had other things on his mind. He must find work. How would his mother run a shop? True, she could speak English, but she could neither read nor write it. He would have to go through the lists from Mr. Davidoff with her, before she could even think of seeing customers.

Where would they come from, these customers? Where had they been buying till now? Why should they start coming to this new shop?

He wouldn't go to this new school. Instead, he would look for work.

Of course, his mother would never agree. When he was alone with her in the kitchen, he said, "I will remain behind with Tatte. One day will not make that much difference."

Fay had been worrying about leaving the house with no one to care for Pinchas. What if he suddenly began to struggle to breathe? She acquiesced readily.

Pinchas was still sleeping when they left the house. Fay looked at each child, applied a hairbrush, inspected their hands and necks, and then said, "Right, come along now. We go to the top of the road, and then turn right and then right again. That's where the school is."

David was the first one to spot the school building. He saw a woman looking out through a window. The family went through the main entrance, and then a petite woman came hurrying toward them.

"This way," she said. "This way to Mr. Thorner, the headmaster."

She led the way.

"Here they are, sir," she said.

"So," said a large man sitting behind a dark desk, "how may I help you?"

He looked over the group. Where had these children come from? Was there a new orphanage? He hadn't heard of one opening around here.

"My children," said Fay, but she was interrupted.

"Your children...all of them...are your children?"

Fay nodded proudly. True, she had been careless. She hadn't kept a close enough watch on her children. They hadn't always been smartly turned out. But she had managed to keep them all alive—no mean feat in those horrible, dank London houses. Butcher bones boiled with cheap vegetables left over from the market had kept them fed and well—and her *Tehillim*, every day her *Tehillim*.

"Yes, they are my children," she said with pride. She started to rattle off their names, pointing to each one. "David, he's the second one, and..."

But the man interrupted her.

"Now, let's see, where did you last go to school?"

David spoke up before his mother could answer. "I have letters from our teachers, Sir. From our last school, Sir."

The boy spoke a fine English. There was the slightest cockney inflection, but still, he spoke a good, clear English.

He looked at the letters the boy gave him. Levine. Ah, Jews! But the boys had no strings dangling from beneath their shirts. They had no long forelocks. Then he saw the name of the school. Ah, well then, that explained it. They had been at the large Jews' Free School. The rich Jews of London had created this school for the poor Jewish foreigners to turn their children, thousands of children, into English boys and girls.

Even here, far away in this English colony, he had heard about it.

There were Jews who sent their children to his school, not the newly arrived immigrant children, but those whose parents had been in the country for some time, who had learned how to make a living. Some had even become wealthy.

The boy sounded polite, so the younger children would probably cause no discipline problems. These children came from the slums of London, but they appeared to be well mannered. They were neatly dressed, but such clothes—they were so old fashioned. The boys were wearing tight woolen suits and hard white collars, and the girls had long skirts covered with white pinafores.

He was quiet for a few moments. Could this woman truly afford his school? Should he send them further down the road to the College school, where the poorer immigrant children went?

But obviously, someone had told them to come here. So maybe he shouldn't judge too hastily. So many children! It would be foolish to turn them away without first finding out if they could pay.

"Right then, Miss Springer," he said, turning to the woman. "Take these children and these letters, and see that each child goes to the correct class."

It was only when the children had gone to their classrooms, and their mother had left, that he realized he had forgotten to talk about money and ask for the fees in advance, as he normally did. No matter. He would write a note and send it home with the oldest boy at the end of the school day.

David, blithely unaware that his schooldays could be suddenly brought to an end, happily followed the school secretary as she herded the children down a long corridor. He was worried that Jack wasn't with them. Now he would have to care for the others. Oh, how he wished Jack had come with them.

It was lucky that he had brought the letters, he thought. Now, as they scurried after Miss Springer, practically running to keep up with her, he whispered to the children, "Wait for me at the school gate at the end of the day. Even if you finish earlier, and you probably will, just wait for me. We must all go home together."

They turned down yet another corridor, and here each door had a label. They could hear children reciting the times tables. The woman stopped before the first door, and there was immediate silence. The entire class stood up at their desks. The teacher stopped talking and looked at the group standing at the door.

Miss Springer took one of the papers and looked at it.

"Isaac, come here," she said. "This is the reception class. In you go."

The teacher came to the door and led Isaac into the room. They continued to walk to the next room. Now Miss Springer motioned to Rose, and said to a man, "New girl here, Rose Levine. This is her report from the previous school. In you go, girl." She gave Rose a slight push into the classroom.

"Come in, child," said the man. So he must be the teacher, Rose realized. A man teacher for girls? Then she noticed two rows of girls on one side of the room and two rows of boys on the other.

"Sit next to Mary," the teacher said. "See, there's an empty seat next to her."

The door closed and then Miss Springer was hurrying to the next room. One by one, the children were taken to their new classrooms.

David was the last child to enter his classroom, which was at the far end of the corridor. He was sent to an empty desk at the back of the room. All the other desks were taken.

"Cap off, young man," the teacher said. Then the lesson continued, and David sank happily into the world of learning that he so enjoyed.

He became more relaxed as the day went on. The lessons were easy. In Arithmetic they did sums that he had already learned to do. Then there was something called "nature study," which was quite new to him but so interesting. It was all about the trees and plants in this new land. The spelling test was easy, even though the words had been given to the class to learn on the previous day. The history was the same as he had learned in his old school, all about the kings and queens of England.

His class's break times were different from the other classes, so he didn't see his siblings at all. He hoped they would remember his instructions to wait by the gate. What then? Could he remember the way home?

As he looked around the playground, he realized that the boys were much bigger than him. Well, maybe here, in the sunshine, people grew more. They didn't seem to be more clever, just bigger. They were taller and broader.

What he didn't realize, and what no one would realize for some time, was that in England school began at age four. Here it only began at age six. The secretary had seen "class one" on the letter and gone into the room for six-year-olds, even though little Isaac was only four years old. Each child was in a class with children who were two years older than them.

As the day progressed, David began to realize how very different this school was. His old school was a Jewish school, and clearly this one was not. Were there other Jewish boys in his class? Besides, in this school, boys and girls were in the same classroom. True, the girls sat on one side of the room and the boys on the other, but still, it was very strange!

Then there was the matter of size. This school was more like a very big house.

His old school had been enormous, with long corridors, large class-rooms, and many different floors.

David stood watching as boys and girls separated into little groups and began to play. He wished Jack was there. What if the boys attacked him, like the non-Jewish boys did when they were on their way home from school?

But no one attacked him. Someone pulled a ball out of his pocket. Another boy went to a small shed and took out a cricket bat. A game began. David watched for a few moments and then one of the boys shouted at him, "You're backstop, on our side. Stand on the edge and catch the ball if it comes your way when we're bowling."

Cricket hadn't been played at the London school, with its small, crowded yard. Here the yard was large. David felt lost, but by watching carefully he got the idea. By the time a ball came his way he understood what to do. He caught it and threw it toward the bowler, and with that, his place in the class was established.

Just before school ended, Miss Springer came to the classroom and gave David a letter. "Be sure to give this to your mother as soon as you get home," she said.

David took it happily, not realizing that it was an account mentioning a large sum of money. Little did he realize that this first day at this new school could well be the last. He took the letter, placed it in his satchel, and walked to the school gate to meet his brothers and sisters.

Chapter 15

Joseph was terrified.

Jack had always walked home with them. Jack had always kept them safe. What if there were bad boys who came to attack them, as sometimes happened in London? This school was not a Jewish school, so how would they be treated by the other children? How would they find their way home without Jack?

Little did he realize that David, too, was concerned. Jack had always been there to care for them, to ward off school bullies, to see that they got home safely. Still, David had told each child, in as firm a voice as he could muster, that they were to wait until he arrived, no matter how long it took.

So Joseph felt his worries leave him and he managed to enjoy the day. His fears about the other boys treating him badly because he was Jewish did not materialize.

Like David, he found the schoolwork easy. He also found that the other boys were happy to include him in their games, even though they were much bigger than he was. After school, he walked confidently to the school gate. There he found his sisters and brothers, except for David.

"About time," Frieda said when Joseph arrived. "We've been standing here forever."

Joseph thought he knew the way home, but then he remembered David's instructions.

"Reckon it won't be long now till David arrives," he said, just as David ran toward them. It seemed that his class had finished later than the others.

David hadn't taken much notice of the way as they walked to school. He'd been too busy dreaming about what it would be like and what he would learn. Fortunately, Frieda had looked at all the landmarks very carefully and was able to point out the route home.

As the children walked through the door, Fay's face lit up with relief. She hadn't asked what time school ended. She had been planning to go and wait for them at half past three, the time school ended in London, but here they were, only two o'clock, and they were all walking through the door safe and sound.

Only Jack wasn't home. As soon as she had walked in the door that morning he had said, "I'm going out now, to look for work. Just for a while, until the shop is busy, and then I'll go to school."

She had wanted to argue with him, but found no words. The boy was correct. He would need to find work. He should be at school, but if he found some sort of work, at least there would be money for food, even if it wasn't enough to pay rent.

When would he be home? It was so silly, she thought, to worry about a boy who had roamed the streets of London without her knowledge yet had always come home safe.

Now she bustled about. "Right, wash your hands and sit down at the table. Lunch first, then tell me what you learned today. Quietly, your father has eaten his lunch already and is having a rest."

David looked at his mother. She was standing very straight and talking in that strange, strict voice. This was truly a topsy-turvy land. Instead of his father speaking strictly, he was sleeping. Instead of his mother plodding wearily from her room, there she was, standing ramrod straight, like a teacher, and giving orders.

Just then, there was a knock at the front door. Joseph ran to answer it. Mr. Davidoff stood there.

"Good afternoon, young man. Are your parents home?"

"Come in," Joseph said. "I'll call my mother."

When Fay was at the door, she gave a start.

"Joseph, you and Frieda dish out the food and look after the children," she said, then hurried into the front room, the room that was to become a shop.

Joseph heard his father's shuffling footsteps heading to the front room. He must have woken up when Joseph called to his mother. He could hear voices, the soft, quavering voice of his father, the firm voice of his mother, the hearty tones of the man whose house they were in. What did it all mean?

Joseph and Frieda gave out the food, but once the children were eating the bread, hard-boiled eggs, and pickled cucumber, curiosity overcame Joseph. He went out to the hallway and heard the adults talking.

"For now, at any rate, my sister and her husband are on their way to America," Mr. Davidoff said. "I hope everything works out for them, that the streets are truly paved with gold. For my part, I have heard stories of terrible crowded houses, poorly paid work, no gold in sight. Still, who knows?

"Meanwhile, after the discussion we had, Mrs. Levine, are you sure you can take on the responsibility of running a little shop from here? I'm not sure that just a small shop can provide for the family."

Joseph heard his father now. "Oh, but I'm a carpenter. I will soon find work."

"Oh no," Fay said. "You must first regain your strength. Then you can think about work."

Joseph tiptoed back to the kitchen. His mother was telling his father what to do? How strange. For as long as he could remember, his father had always been ill, coughing and wheezing when he came home from work, and recovering gradually as the evening wore on, but somehow he had gone to work every day and his mother had stayed home. His father had always told his mother what to do. Now everything was reversed.

Joseph looked into the kitchen and saw that the younger children were eating without much conversation. He returned to the hallway.

He was in time to hear Mr. Davidoff say, "Well, I'll be going then. The goods will be delivered later by cart, but remember, if my sister changes her mind and arrives here, well, I don't have any option but..."

"No, I understand," Fay said. "For the moment your offer is very generous. I will be sure to repay you for the things you're sending for the shop, as soon as I can."

Joseph heard the door close and hurriedly ran to the kitchen, sat at the table, and began to eat. However, his parents didn't come into the kitchen right away. First his father went straight to the bedroom. A little later his mother came in, her voice bright and cheery. "Well, how was your new school? How are the teachers? What did you learn today?"

Joseph looked hard at his mother. Her voice was cheerful, but her eyes were sad.

"Oh, the work is so easy, too easy," Frieda said.

Bertha nodded her agreement.

"Yes, it is easy, but it doesn't matter," Samuel and Isaac said. "At break time, when we go out, the schoolyard is like a big park. The boys play football. It's great."

"The children are so big, much bigger than me," Ethel said.

Little Rose nodded. "Yes, and in my class, there are only three Jewish girls. When they have scripture lessons the Jewish girls have to stand outside the door and wait. What are scripture lessons?"

"I don't like to stand outside the classroom all alone like I did today,"

Joseph said. "I didn't do this before. Why must I do it now?"

As she watched the children eat, Fay was deep in thought. *How amazing that Mr. Davidoff is! We don't have to pay rent until the shop makes a profit. He's supplying the goods from his wholesale business ahead of time, and I needn't pay until I have made a good enough profit. Such mazal! But what if his sister doesn't like America? What then? No, I won't think about that. Hashem has helped us till now. Why should I doubt that He will help us in the future? All I must think about now is making a living.*

Just then, David remembered the letter. He ran to his room, looked through his satchel, and brought it to his mother.

Fay took the letter. She opened it and looked at the English writing.

"Come into the front room with me, where the shop will be, and read this to me," she said.

When Frieda had read it over carefully, not once, but twice, mother and daughter looked at one another unhappily. Such a large sum of money! Where were they to find it? In London, schooling had been free.

Fay spoke first. "The money, so much! What now? What do I tell the children? Is it a good place?"

Frieda nodded.

"Well, we'll see. Who knows? For the moment we'll say nothing to the other children. Right?"

Frieda nodded. Her mother left her alone in the room and went back to the kitchen to see to the younger children. Frieda stood in the empty shop.

"Say nothing," her mother had said. But what would happen? Would they suddenly have to leave the school because they didn't have money? Did all schools in the Colony charge so much money? This new land was good, warm and sunny and clean. But what if they couldn't go to school?

London had been different, but she was used to it, and she had so enjoyed school.

No matter what her mother had said, she would tell Jack about the letter. Jack always knew how to solve problems.

Back in London, together with Jack, she had solved family problems. When the money her mother gave her to buy food wasn't enough, Jack would come with her and persuade the shopkeeper to let them pay at the end of the week. Somehow, by then, he'd always been able to earn the money they needed. If that didn't work, Jack knew to wait until the market stalls began closing down and the just rotting vegetables were being discarded. He had filled her basket with them, carefully peeling away the worst leaves, so that the purchase looked presentable.

She thought of how humiliating it would be if they walked into the classroom and then were told a bit later to leave because the fees had not been paid. Why must they pay? In London, schooling had been free. Well, not quite free. Each week they had to take a penny to school and give it to the teacher. A penny each—that was possible. But the letter David had brought home asked for a lot more money than a few pennies.

Maybe, just maybe, there were other schools here for children like them, children whose parents didn't have so much money.

But Frieda liked this new school. She liked the big house and the garden around it.

She liked the way the desks were far apart, not all squashed together. She liked the way the big windows were open and the smell of freshly cut grass and the sound of birds singing came through the windows.

Frieda stood by the door, waiting for Jack to return. Just as the sun was beginning to set, he came running up the steps, a grin on his face.

"Why are you here, all alone?" he asked. "Where are the others?"

"They're in the backyard. The girls found a piece of rope and they're skipping. The boys are playing with a spinning top. Mother is in the room with Tatte. I've been waiting for you."

She wanted to ask Jack about his day. Her mother had not replied properly when she asked about him earlier.

"Soon he'll come back and tell us everything," Fay had said. "Now stop asking questions. Eat your food, and then help me with the dishes."

Now that Jack stood before her, all she could think about was the money for the school.

"We're supposed to bring money to pay for school tomorrow," Frieda said. She told him about the letter and the sum of money they needed.

Jack gave a low whistle. "That's a lot of money!"

Frieda nodded unhappily.

"Look, I'm not going to school," Jack said. "I found a job working in a grocery shop. I was working there until now."

"Yes, Mother told us you were looking for work. You really found work? Really?"

"Trouble is, I only get paid at the end of the week, and it's not as much as we need to pay the school," Jack said, looking closely at the letter.

"How did you get the job?"

"I walked all around, just looking, just to work out where we were," Jack said. "I saw a sign in the window of the grocer shop that said, 'Boy wanted, to help in the shop.' The man looked me up and down, like he didn't like what he saw."

Frieda could empathize with this. That was exactly how those fancy girls in her class had looked at her.

"Well," Jack said, "so he says to me, 'Well, young lad. You stand there behind the counter. See, I'm the customer. Listen to what I say, and give me what I ask for.'

"So I went behind the counter, and he said, 'I want a half-pound bag of flour, and a three-pound bag of sugar, five naartjies and two squash, not too big and not too small.'

"I looked behind me and saw that everything was packed in brown paper bags and marked *one pound weight*. Was he playing some sort of trick on me?

"I knew then that I wouldn't get the job, but I didn't want him to feel he had made a fool of me, so I took a bag of flour and three bags of sugar, and I said, 'Here, a pound of flour. Half a bag will only last a morning and then you'll have to come back again. Sugar is stored better in smaller quantities, so we pack it in one-pound bags.'

"He said, 'Right,' but he wasn't smiling so much. 'What about the fruit and vegetables, then?'

"I realized that naartjies and squash must be fruit and vegetables. Who even heard of such a thing where we came from? He must have known that.

"I was getting ready to leave, then I had an idea. I said, 'Look, let's go over to the fruit and vegetables in the corner there. You can choose the best ones, just the size you want.' Well, then I was ready to run off."

Jack laughed now as Frieda watched him. This was like old times.

"So I watched as he took five round orange things, different looking from the oranges they gave us in Madeira, and he took round green vegetables, and then he began to laugh.

"'See,' he said to me, 'the Malays call these naartjies, so we do too. These are called squash. People eat them here, even though they didn't back home. Well, my lad, I had my doubts about you, but you'll do.'

"So now, I work there. There's a lot to learn, but it's a good place to be. He'll pay me three shillings at the end of each week."

Jack didn't say that the pay was for working from Monday to Saturday. He definitely would not be able to work on Shabbos. When he told the man, that would be the end of his job. He would wait until Thursday and tell him then. Maybe, just maybe, the man wouldn't need him so much on Shabbos. Maybe he would let him work only Monday to Friday.

Even as he thought this, he knew it was improbable. The man would probably be so angry that he wouldn't even get paid for the days he had worked. But it was a chance he had to take.

Then he remembered the letter, the money that was needed for school. What now?

"Maybe you can tell them that we've just arrived, and we haven't unpacked properly yet," Jack said. "When we do, you'll bring the money."

"What if they say no?"

"Listen, Frieda, when has anyone ever said no to you?"

Frieda laughed. Over the years, out of necessity, she had become an expert at asking for favors. But those favors had been granted by Jewish shopkeepers and stall holders, who had given in to her pleading. Stern Miss Singer and no-nonsense Mr. Thorner didn't seem the type to be taken in by Frieda.

"Well, I don't know, but I can try," she said.

"Such stories I heard today," Jack said. "This is a place to make one's fortune. Soon our worries will be over. I'll find a way for us to pay that money." He said it more to cheer her up than because he believed it himself.

Frieda wasn't convinced, but they went together into the house. She sat quietly and listened as Jack spoke to their mother.

A little later Fay left the room and came back with some money.

"Look, maybe I should use some of our spare money, the bit left over from the stamps, after we paid for the tickets," she said. "It's not the full amount, but maybe tell them that the rest will come as soon as we have properly unpacked. I don't know. Just try."

Jack took the money. "I'll put it in an envelope and write a note explaining that the rest will come soon. It will be fine."

Mother, son and daughter stood together. They all had their doubts but kept silent, hoping desperately that the outcome would be satisfactory.

A little later a cart arrived, loaded with boxes. Two men brought everything inside, so that the floor of the front room was covered. The children were called in to help, and soon the goods were unpacked onto the shelves.

The children were overcome with excitement. Fay felt quite differently. What had it all cost? Would she be able to sell all this? Besides, the lists were written in English. She could read Hebrew and Yiddish, but not English.

"Now, who wants to help me work out the prices?" she asked. In fact, she needed her children to do it for her. How humiliating. In the shtetl, children had asked their parents for advice and help. Here, their positions were reversed.

Jack, David, and Joseph quickly volunteered.

Frieda was relieved when her mother said, "Frieda, take the children to the kitchen and give them something to eat. There's bread in the pantry and a jar filled with pickled herring. Later, I'll make something warm, maybe soup."

Frieda did as she was told, but as she sliced the bread and gave each child a piece of herring, she worried about the school fees.

When the sun set that evening and the family sat around the kitchen table, only the younger children were worry free.

Pinchas was feeling a bit better, but he wasn't yet fit enough to seek work or to even attempt the walk to shul again.

Fay was worrying about all the goods that sat in her shop, waiting for customers.

Jack was worrying about what to tell his employer about Shabbos.

Frieda was worrying that they would be humiliated and told to leave school the following day.

At school, back in London, the teacher always seemed to favor those girls who were well dressed, the girls who came to school with ribbons in their hair. She knew her mother saved their ribbons for Shabbos. Would her mother allow her to wear ribbons to school the next day?

Her eyes fell on Bertha. She was just one year younger than Frieda, and she had something that Frieda herself lacked—a sunny personality and a truly winning smile. Frieda was clever, that she knew. She always knew the answers to the teacher's questions and was always at the top of her class. But she was definitely not the most popular girl. On the playground she became tongue-tied.

Bertha had a talent for charming everyone she met. Whenever Frieda had felt very desperate about shopping in the market with too little money, she had taken her sister Bertha, with her winning smile. Maybe, if she took along Bertha, and they both wore ribbons in their hair, Miss Singer would take part of the money and wait for the rest. Well, it was worth a try. It was the best she could do.

When the kitchen was clear and only her mother was there, clearing up, she said, "Mother, tomorrow Bertha and I need to wear the Shabbos ribbons to school."

Fay looked up. Her mind was on earning a living and though she wondered at this strange request, she didn't have the energy to question it. If that was what the child wanted, why not?

"You know where they are. I put all the Shabbos clothes in the top drawer in your room."

"Oh, and Mother, none of the girls wear white pinafores."

"So leave them off. Less work for me!"

Fay was exhausted. She wanted only for the last bit of her work to end.

Frieda walked into her bedroom and opened the top drawer. The ribbons were there, a different color for each girl. She looked around the room. Her sisters were fast asleep. It had been a long and exciting day. But Frieda was too worried, too tense to sleep.

There was a small stool beside the window. Frieda sat on it, gazing out at the street. On one side there was still a little sunshine, while the other side was shady. Here the sun rose early and sank down late.

From the front room, they could see Long Street, a long wide street lined with shops. From her window she could see other houses, like theirs.

A horse and carriage came up the street, with a driver up front. The passenger, a big man, wore a fancy suit and shiny top hat.

Then she heard from high on the hill a strange sound. The muezzin in the nearby Malay quarter was giving his last call for prayers, but she would only learn of such things much later.

Then the street became quiet, not a soul to be seen. Where in London had there ever been a street so quiet?

She thought back to the flat that had been their home, the crowded dirty streets. There were always people walking along through light rain on good days and through smog on bad days. Only very occasionally did the sun come out and shine between the houses onto the narrow streets.

Here, it seemed, the sun shone every day. The streets were clean, the pavements wide, and the people were like the pictures in her geography books, from every part of the world, their clothing different from one another.

How long would the street remain so quiet and empty? And most important, how long would they be allowed to remain in school if they couldn't pay?

How she wished she could read Hebrew like her mother. In London, in the girls' section of the Jews' Free School, there had been very few Hebrew lessons. She could read only haltingly. Her mother had told her that it was the same in the shtetl. But her grandmother had taught her mother how to read. Oh, if only she could take her mother's *Tehillim* and *daven* for success. What if she failed? She just couldn't bear thinking about it.

Tired out by the events of the day, she lay down and was soon asleep.

Chapter 16

"As a highly qualified and experienced pedagogue, Mr. Ornstien realized the need to reorganize the existing system of religious education ... but ... the plan collapsed ... The idea of a Jewish public school, though temporarily dormant, was not forgotten."

— Israel Abrahams, *The Birth of a Community*, p. 56

Bertha woke with the sun shining on her face. It was a marvelous feeling. She just wanted to lie there, warm and happy forever. All her life, it seemed, she had felt cold. The walk to school, along grey wet streets on cold, dark winter mornings, had seemed to last forever. The classrooms had been just ever so slightly warmer, especially as the day wore on, and funny smelling. Then, just when she finally felt her body relax somewhat, the school bell would ring, and once again they had to trudge down the cold wet streets. There was usually a soft rain falling, seeping into her shawl and dress.

Their time on the sea had been marvelous. She had been mostly warm, and though the food was not at all like her mother's food, there was plenty. Now, for some reason she failed to fathom, they were living in this grand house, as big as the houses in the fairy tales her teacher had sometimes read at the end of the school day.

Their bedroom, with its flowered curtains and white sheets covered by soft, thick pink blankets, enfolded her in their warmth each night. The wardrobe fitted all of their clothes with ease. And in the middle was a large mirror, where you could stare at yourself as long as you wanted. Would wonders never cease?

But best of all was the sunshine. This was winter, Jack had told her.

Well, then, what would the summer be like? Bertha opened her eyes and watched as the sun slanted its way into the room, slowly taking up more and more space, until the whole room seemed to glow.

Just then her mother came bustling into the room.

"Right, up, all of you, up now!" she said. "I washed and ironed your school clothes last night. Frieda, I don't know why you insist on wearing a ribbon on your braids today. You know it's only for Shabbos. But if you want it so badly, you must have a reason. So I ironed all the ribbons for the girls. If you and Bertha wear your ribbons, why not Ethel and Rose too?"

Bertha looked at Frieda. She didn't look happy. Why not? She had asked to wear ribbons and here their mother was agreeing.

Bertha wanted to ask what was going on, but there was no time. They dressed and ate, and then took the bread and jam their mother had prepared for them for break time and hurried to school. David and Frieda were whispering together the whole way, so Bertha didn't have a chance to ask Frieda about the ribbons.

When she got to school, she began to understand. She wanted to run to her classroom. Today they were doing the eleven times table. She already knew the tables, but the rest of the class had only learned up to the ten times table. She wanted to show off, to show them that she already knew the next table, and even the one after that.

Instead, Frieda held her hand tightly and said, "Come with me. Smile nicely at the man. Don't say anything. Just smile."

Bertha was used to hearing these words when they went to the market, not when they went to school. Still, smiling was easy enough. If that was what her big sister wanted, then that was what she would do.

They walked together down a long corridor, and then into an office. Frieda knocked on the door. Mr. Thorner opened it. The stern-faced woman wasn't in the front room. The headmaster led them through the room and into his office. He sat down behind the large desk.

Frieda handed over the envelope. "Here is some of the money. By the end of the week, I'll pay you the rest."

Bertha wanted to ask questions. Where had Frieda gotten that money? Then she remembered her instructions. The man took the envelope and looked at the girls. Bertha smiled. She couldn't quite figure out why she was smiling, but still she smiled.

There was a long silence. Bertha wanted to say something, anything, but she always listened to Frieda.

Mr. Thorner saw the sweet smile. He wondered how much money was in the envelope. Normally he insisted on full payment of fees at the beginning of each term. Years of experience had taught him that in the end, this was the simplest, most efficient way to do things.

Frieda was worried. The headmaster wasn't smiling.

"You see, we only arrived on Monday," she said. "We haven't properly unpacked." The man still wasn't smiling. "Also, we don't even know if English money is the same as money here. When we understand better, we'll bring more money."

"What, you only arrived this last Monday!" Mr. Thorner said. "You haven't even been here a full week!"

He was amazed. Usually during the first few weeks people kept their children home, to help unpack and run errands. These children had been rushed off to school at the first available opportunity. He felt more confident now that the balance of money would be paid. These people clearly valued education. There would be no need for more letters or the painful task of eventually having to tell the children to leave.

Bertha continued to smile. Frieda grew alarmed at the long silence.

"Yes, that will be in order," Mr. Thornton said. "Usually we want the money before you begin, but all the teachers came back with favorable reports on your brothers and sisters. Make sure then, by the end of the week, that you pay all the money."

Frieda gave a sigh of relief and pulled Bertha out with her. She wasn't sure if they would be able to pay by the end of the week, but for the moment, she had achieved her purpose. They were still in school.

When Bertha arrived at her classroom, she saw with dismay that the children were already at the end of chanting the eleven times table. She was just in time to hear, "Twelve elevens are a hundred and thirty-two."

"Oh dear, Bertha, this is only your second day and you are late," Miss Brown said. "Now you have missed a new table. The class has already gone through it three times."

This was just the opportunity Bertha had been waiting for. Without waiting to be asked, she began very rapidly, "One eleven is eleven, two elevens are twenty-two . . ." Before the amazed audience she went right on until the end. Then, without pausing, she went on to the twelve times table, ending triumphantly with "Twelve twelves are a hundred and forty-four."

"Well, I never," Miss Brown said. "Very well, take your seat. Get out your reading books, children."

Bertha felt pleased with herself. She was wearing her Shabbos ribbons. She had shown those children, who yesterday had laughed at her clothing, that she knew more than them. Frieda was pleased with her because she had stood beside her in front of the headmaster and smiled. The sun was still shining, day after day of sunshine. Oh, but she liked this new land.

Later that day, she wasn't so sure.

The children arrived home and went, as they had been instructed, through the side gate that led into the overgrown garden and then into the kitchen.

Frieda made sure that everyone washed their hands and sat down at the table. Rose sat beside Ethel and saw that she was scowling. She didn't have long to wonder why.

"A girl in my class is having a birthday party this afternoon, and everyone was invited, except me!" Ethel said.

Before Rose had a chance to commiserate, the youngest boys, Isaac and Samuel, started arguing about who could play with the spinning top.

Joseph sat in the seat normally taken by David, and the result was scuffling and shouting. Fay came rushing into the kitchen and slapped each child at the table.

The older children reacted with amazed silence. Physical punishment at school was not unknown. In fact, in England it had been a fairly regular phenomenon, but at home, it was practically unknown. Misdeeds normally received a long lecture, almost always ending with, "That is not how Jewish children behave!"

Bertha was devastated. Such a perfect day and then this!

"Why did you hit me?" she shouted. "I didn't do anything!"

The reply was swift. "If I am disturbed in the shop, then you are all to blame. If someone starts any disturbance, all of you together should put a stop to it."

By this time, Pinchas had woken from his sleep and stumbled to the door. He heard Bertha and Faigy. He turned back before anyone noticed him.

Instead of returning to bed, he went to the window. He stared out, looking down Long Street, at the horse-driven carts churning up dust and the people walking along the pavement.

He had to get well. He had to join those people. He had to find a way to earn a living. His Faigy was running the shop, taking care of the family, taking care of him as if he were a child. It had to end.

Living in this fine house was good and well, but such anger, such shouting—this was unacceptable.

At work, away from the tension enveloping his family, Jack was worried about losing his job. He decided to tackle the issue right away, rather than wait and worry.

"Mr. Grocott, Sir, I really appreciate you giving me work," he said. "I think you should know that I cannot work on Saturday. That is our Sabbath, Sir. We are not allowed to work on that day. Maybe you can pay me less and get another boy to work just on Saturdays?"

Jack saw the expression on Mr. Grocott's face and knew that this approach would not meet with success.

"Boy, why didn't you tell me before? Of course I knew straight away that you're a Jew. But see, lots of Jews have businesses, and they work on Saturday."

What could Jack answer?

"I thought . . . I thought, well, I thought that maybe if you liked my work, then you would agree."

"You can work until Friday. Then you'll leave. I will pay you for the days you work, no more, no less. Understand?"

Jack watched as the notice for help was placed back in the window.

"Foolish boy!" Mr. Grocott said. "Do you think anyone will employ you if you won't work on a Saturday? Don't you know that is the busiest day for shopping?"

Jack didn't answer. What could he say? If that was correct, how would he find work?

During his lunch break he walked up the road, looking in windows, to see if help was needed. He found nothing.

At the end of the day, he noticed that the vegetables that were no longer saleable were taken out to be thrown away. Jack asked for them and was relieved when he received permission. He thought about taking them home, but there was sufficient food at home. Money was what they needed now. He thought about the docks, about the people milling around there. Maybe if he went to the docks, he could make some money selling the goods cheaply.

After leaving work that day, he went down to the docks. He sold everything, and in return he received a few coins. But this would in no way match the wages he had been hoping to receive each week. What work could he do that allowed him to be off on Shabbos?

He went home in despair, but with a false smile plastered on his face. This soon faded after his mother asked how his day had been.

"If Frieda doesn't give the school the balance soon, they will all have to leave," she said.

Jack was aghast. He was about to lose his job. The shop had no customers yet. All they had in the world was the money left from England.

"We still have that money . . . from the stamps," he said. He was reluctant to say, "Use it." What if he never earned any money again and what if the shop was a failure? His mother must make the decision.

Fay looked at her son. She looked at her tear-stained daughter. She had only a few coins left. It was risky to give it away. Yet how much of a risk was it compared to the long and difficult voyage across the seas with an ailing husband? What would she do with all the children at home? How could she properly run the shop?

"Go, fetch the money, Jack. Give it to your sister."

⌁

The next day was his last day at work. Jack walked to work with a heavy heart. He was painfully aware that the family now had absolutely no money. They were in a wonderful home. They had a shop full of goods and no customers. His father was too ill to work. Now, even the small amount he could provide from his work would be lost.

He was hoping that no one had seen the notice, that no one would take his place. But later in the day, when he was standing behind the counter, Jack saw a boy looking at the notice. He saw Mr. Grocott go out and talk to the boy, and then watched as they shook hands. Now there was no hope for him.

Jack said nothing to his family over Shabbos, nor on the following day. Early Monday morning he began to search for work, but the few times he found something, he realized that they too wanted him to work on Shabbos.

He walked to Mr. Grocott's shop and wondered if he dared to ask for a favor. Finally, he went in.

"I'm sorry I couldn't continue working here," he said. "I really enjoyed it. Er...the goods that you throw away at the end of the day...can I still take them?"

"What a strange young man you are," Mr. Grocott said. "You know that they're collected with all the other garbage and just thrown away. Why do you ask me? Why not just take them once we close for the day?"

"This seemed the best way," Jack said. "It feels more honest. Does that mean I can take them?"

Jack was relieved that the man held no grudge against him, that he was agreeable. This would bring in some money each day — not much, but something.

As Jack left, carrying the goods in a paper sack he had brought with him, he turned to wave at Mr. Grocott and saw something strange. There was no customer in the shop, yet the new boy had his hands in the till. When he saw Jack looking back, he hurriedly moved away. Now why would he do that?

One week later the reason became clear to him. Mr. Grocott was waiting for him as he approached the bins.

"Boy, do you want to come back?" he asked. "Bit of trouble I had, so I decided to get my son in on Saturday. He's about your age. Goes to SACS, clever lad, but on a Saturday he can help me here. Wish you could work on a Saturday, but at least with you I don't have to worry about money disappearing from the till."

Jack went home, his mood buoyant. As he went in through the front door, he saw a man filling a large crate with goods and then hand his mother a number of gold coins.

"Going up country, at short notice," he said. "Thought I had to go into town for supplies, then we saw this place. New here, are you?"

Jack quickly offered to take the crate to the wagon waiting outside. Then he went back into the shop.

"Well, that was a good customer. Was he the first?"

"No, there have been some customers today, not many, but some."

Fay sighed. There had been a trickle of customers, but they had clearly come into the shop only because they had forgotten some small item after purchasing most of their goods elsewhere.

So much money she needed, to pay for the goods, to pay rent, but at least this was a start.

"I'm working again, at the same place," Jack said. "I left because I was told I had to work on Shabbos. Now the man says I don't have to work then. What do you think of that?"

"In time the shop will do better, but your wages will come in useful," Fay said. "We'll use your wages to pay for the Shabbos food, and this money can be put aside to start paying for all these goods."

Jack wondered what she would have said if he hadn't been working once again.

"Soon the shop will be doing a good trade and then you can go back to school," Fay said. "Such a shame for you to be missing school! But what can I do?"

Jack was less upset than his mother at the thought. True, he had enjoyed school. But he also enjoyed working. Every day was different. Such a variety of people came into the shop. Mr. Grocott was good to work for, rarely criticizing, often praising.

Just then Pinchas walked into the shop. He had woken late, davened at home and then tried to learn for a while. He had given up and gone back to bed. Now he walked into the shop and heard his wife discussing financial matters with his son. Humiliation overtook him. He must get well. He must find work. This could not continue.

His wife and son hadn't noticed him entering, and he silently left the shop and went back to the bedroom.

He had become irrelevant to his wife, irrelevant to his family. He was simply a burden to them. Why had he ever left the shtetl?

Letters from home showed their families were leading a peaceful existence. What foolishness had made him heed the words of his old friend in faraway London, and not those of his dear wife?

He must get well. He must get strong again. He was the head of the family. He must provide for them. All decisions should be made by him.

How foolish he had been, and now he was paying for his stupidity.

Chapter 17

"One of the first factories in South Africa had its origins in 1876.
The founders were two Jews who traded as D. Isaacs and Co. At first
it was but a workshop to make furniture for their shop in Cape Town.
Later, when it became a very large factory, they supplied other dealers."
— Mendel Kaplan, *Jewish Roots in the South African Economy*, p. 150

Exactly a fortnight after landing in Cape Town, Pinchas woke up
with a feeling of well-being. Gradually, each day, he had felt his health
return. On that first day, when the boys had told him about a shul nearby,
he had forced himself up, feeling the need to resume his daily routine.
However, that first walk to the shul had tired him more than he liked
to admit. Not only that, the place felt strange to him, nothing like his
familiar *shtiebel* in London, and certainly nothing like the little shul of
his youth, in the shtetl.

Pinchas had felt looked down upon there, in that large fancy shul.
When he was well again, he would go there. He would get used to it. But
for now, he lacked the energy.

Each morning, Pinchas davened alone at home. His thoughts were
filled with longing for the shul he had left behind, the friends who had
davened by his side, the worn *sefarim* that he had learned from before
and after work. Why had he ever left the shtetl? Why had he persuaded
his Faigy to leave? He remembered her tears as she sat on the cart with
the children and their few belongings. If she had refused to go, would
he indeed have gone alone, without her?

It was too late now for regrets. They were so far from home now that
thoughts of return were worthless. He must get well. He must find work.

He must make a success of their life in this new land. Faigy must give up the idea of running a shop. She was working too hard, seeing to the shop and to the family. It was too much.

Jack had to return to learning. He was a clever boy. The headmaster at his school in England had said that if he continued his studies he could go far. Had not his *rebbi* back home in the shtetl said the same thing? True, the headmaster in England had spoken of university while the *rebbi* had spoken of great yeshivos. Neither had spoken of a boy spending his days selling groceries.

Pinchas had tried each morning to offer his help in the shop, but Faigy had laughed and said, "Oh, there are so few customers. I spend most of my day sitting here and doing crochet work."

In fact, Fay was spending every spare moment learning to read and write English. When they had unpacked the goods together, she had asked David what each item was. As she placed it on the shelf, he wrote out a card with the name of the item and its price. Daily, she would write out the words printed on the cards. She had been terrified that a customer would ask for an item and she wouldn't be able to find it on the list. Now, with much practice, she knew each item and its price. She could write everything down, so she could re-order items when they were sold.

What was the use, though, when there were so few customers? Faigy put her crochet skills to good use. She sat there, waiting, hoping to hear the little bell by the door announce that a customer was entering.

Pinchas was aware of the lack of customers. If the shop was not going to provide for his family, then he must get fit. He must find work. Where could he find work as a carpenter?

Each day after davening at home, he walked a little way down Long Street, toward the docks, and then back home again. Each day he increased the distance very slightly, returning home in a weak state and knowing that he was not yet fit for work.

This morning was different. This morning he had felt as if he could walk for miles without tiring. After davening and eating, after asking once again if he could help in the shop and being refused, he set out down Long Street.

He arrived at the docks, feeling amazed at his achievement. Instead of returning home immediately, he went to watch a ship that was just docking. He perched himself on some crates, wondering at the great distance they had all traveled.

Slowly, the ship came alongside the harbor wall, and the gangplank was pulled up to the ship and secured. People started coming down, a few at a time, then more and more. Pinchas, a sociable man, had not spoken to anyone except his family for days — no, for weeks — and he felt content now, sitting and listening to the people around him.

A group of young men were talking.

"Looks good! What do you say? You think this chap Isaacs will be there to meet us?"

"Well, he brought us out to here, didn't he? He wants us, skilled mechanics to work that new carpentry machinery he bought for his new factory, so here we are. Course he'll be waiting for us."

"But what if he's not?"

"Well, we have the name and address — D. Isaacs and Co., Barrack Street. How difficult can that be to find?"

Pinchas concentrated now on what they were saying. What was all this talk of machinery? Isaacs, they had said. That sounded like a Jewish name. Then he remembered that first morning in the shul. Was the man who had welcomed him the same Mr. Isaacs?

Well, he was a carpenter. He had regained his health. Just look how far he had walked that morning. At last he would be able to once again take up his rightful place as the head of the family, as the family breadwinner. What had they been living on until now? Jack's money? That couldn't continue. No, he would get a job at that carpentry place these men were talking about. What exactly was a factory? No matter, carpentry was what he did.

Just then, a well-dressed, distinguished-looking man arrived, and Pinchas recognized him at once. How could such a man not be remembered, with his stately bearing and long whiskers parted in the middle and hanging down onto the lapels of his suit? The man was not only the president of the shul, but he must also be the factory owner, the "D. Isaacs" the men had spoken of.

Pinchas watched as David Isaacs walked up to the group of arrivals and said loudly, "Well, fellows, you must be my new men. I hope the journey was a good one, and that you are fit and well and ready for some hard work."

It was now or never. Pinchas went up to the man and said, "I see you are bringing carpenters from England. Well, I am a carpenter, and I already live here." There was silence. Everyone stared at this man, this man who spoke accented English, who was standing there in front of everyone and asking for a job.

David Isaacs hesitated. His old workplace on Mostert Street had burnt down. He had decided to turn the disaster into an advantage by transitioning from an old-fashioned workshop to the new factory system of producing goods. He already had a suitable property on Barrack Street. He had bought fancy, complicated machinery from England. He had paid the passage from England of these unmarried men, who were experienced at working these wondrous machines.

Now, before him stood a middle-aged Jew! His *arba kanfos* were sticking out. He had a long beard and was wearing an old-fashioned suit, and he was asking for work. What could he say to a carpenter who had learned his trade in the shtetl?

On the other hand, how could he embarrass this man publicly by rejecting him?

"Now I must take these men to their lodgings," he said, his voice strained. "Come tomorrow to 30 Barrack Street at ten in the morning. We'll talk then."

He had chosen his words carefully. Talk — that's what he would do.

He would explain to the man the nature of the work, and the fact that he was looking for men skilled in this new way of manufacturing furniture.

True, he did employ Jewish carpenters, but they were young and fit. Some were from England, where they had worked in factories. This man had obviously lived in England after leaving the shtetl. Had he worked in a factory, or in one of those tiny workrooms that made everything by hand? It seemed to him the latter. How could such a man adapt to working in what would be the most modern factory the country had yet seen?

No, this man could not work for him. He would explain this to him and give him some money to tide him over. Perhaps he could find something else for him to do, maybe help him buy a barrow to sell goods. Now he had to see to these new workmen of his.

Pinchas, however, accepted these words in quite a different way. The man was giving him a job. What news he had to tell Faigy! He repeated to himself the address, again and again, so he wouldn't forget. 30 Barrack Street. Where was that? Jack would know. Jack seemed to know his way around this new place.

Meanwhile, David Isaacs was thinking about Abba Samuel Ginzberg from the shul. He not only allowed new immigrants to stay in his home, but he also helped them find a livelihood. In the last number of years the small Jewish community in Cape Town had increased to over a thousand. How amazing. Most of these immigrants were poor young men from Eastern Europe, and Abba Samuel had made it his business to help them. Before tomorrow, he must speak to his friend and see how he could help this man. Maybe there was some other place where an old-fashioned carpenter could find work.

An hour later Pinchas arrived home. "Faigy, I have a job," he said. "I begin tomorrow. Jack can go back to school. We can have a fine *kiddush* for Jack, for his bar mitzvah. I have a job. Now everything will be fine."

Pinchas saw the look that Fay gave him. Did she not believe what he had said?

It seemed not.

"Where did you go to find work?" she said. "Are you well enough? Why the rush?"

Pinchas was not happy with her questions.

"I went to the docks," he said, almost defensively. "I walked all the way and felt fine. Mr. Isaacs was there, the man from the big shul—I told you about him, didn't I? Well, he was meeting new men for his factory. They came off the ship, all the way from England. He has a carpentry factory and he will give me a job."

"You met him at the docks, and there he gave you a job?"

She looked less than excited. Didn't she believe him? Her next words were like cold water thrown at him.

"You've been away a long time," she said. "Maybe you'd like a cup of tea?"

Had she lost all faith in him? He shook his head.

"No, not necessary! I'm fine."

In fact, he was terribly thirsty and tiredness was beginning to overtake him. Well, he would show her. He would become the wage earner again. Faigy would not have to sit, waiting hopelessly for customers. Jack would continue his schooling. Pinchas was not a man to give up. He would once again be the head of the household. Soon everything would be good once again.

How could he know that David Isaacs, who was at that moment showing the new men around the factory, had already forgotten about the earlier encounter at the docks?

Pinchas fell asleep just as Fay walked into his room with a cup of sweet tea. She placed the tea beside him but didn't wake him up. What a dreamer her husband was. What had really happened? Had a job truly been offered? What type of work was it? Was he fit enough to start working? Would she ever really trust him again?

All his decisions had been bad ones. She should never have listened to him or to her mother. She should have remained in the beautiful little shtetl. Would he have left her there? She thought not. Now it was too late for such thoughts, but one thing was clear to her: She would be the one to make decisions in the future. She would make a success of the new shop. She would succeed in this new land. The days of meekly doing what others told her were over.

Chapter 18

"It must be remembered that timber-dealing and carpentry or cabinet making were occupations that Jews had followed in Lithuania before immigration to South Africa."
— Mendel Kaplan, *Jewish Roots in the Economy of South Africa*

"District Six was once home to thousands of immigrant Jews who were escaping poverty and Tsarist oppression. Mainly from Lithuania, they established a vibrant community within the multiethnic neighbourhood in the early twentieth century Cape Town…"
— *Kaplan Centre for Jewish Studies, University of Cape Town, Exhibition on The Jews of District Six, 2012*

Pinchas woke early the next morning. He thought of the day ahead. He was to go to Mr. Isaac's factory at ten. Now it was time for Shacharis. How could he begin such a momentous day without davening with a *minyan*? The shul was a bit different, but it was still a shul. It had a *minyan* and a *chazzan*, and the words were the same. Well, the pronunciation was a little different, and the men stood as if any movement would cause them to break. Still, it was a shul, and it wasn't that far of a walk. Had he not walked three times that distance to the docks the day before? Besides, a man from the shul was giving him a job. He shouldn't judge people unfavorably just because they davened a bit differently.

Pinchas dressed in his Shabbos suit. He would have to change before going to work, but he remembered how the men had been dressed the first time he went to shul.

Pinchas called out to Jack, and soon the two of them were walking down Government Avenue, toward the shul. As they entered, Pinchas saw his new employer talking to a tall man. He went up to them.

"Meet my son Jack, Mr. Isaacs," he said. "Jack, Mr. Isaacs is going to give me a job. I begin work today." He beamed at the men and at Jack. He didn't notice how Mr. Isaacs's face had turned white.

Pinchas and Jack walked off to find a seat, and Abba Ginzberg turned to David Isaacs.

"It's the highest form of charity, giving someone a job," he said. "Me, I help where I can, but this is really wonderful what you're doing."

All the words that had been about to tumble from David Isaacs's mouth dried up. Oh no, now he was committed. Otherwise he would look foolish. What could he find for this man to do in his brand-new factory?

After davening, Pinchas walked home with Jack, feeling like a new man.

"We must talk to the *rav* tomorrow and see when you can be called up to the *bimah*," he said. "I'll teach you how to *lein* the *parshah*."

Jack listened but said nothing. Unlike his father, he had been to shul on Shabbos. He had seen everyone, especially the women and girls, dressed up like princesses. How could he have a bar mitzvah in this place? Where would the money come from, to buy fine clothes and make a *kiddush*? No, this must be avoided.

Jack ate his breakfast hurriedly. He hadn't really planned on going to shul this morning. He usually davened quickly at home and then rushed off to the grocery shop. Pinchas changed into work clothes, took his tool kit and food for the midday break, and put the map Jack had drawn for him in his pocket. He said farewell to the children, just as Fay called them into the kitchen to eat.

He walked toward the Gardens, as he had done earlier with Jack, then turned left and found himself walking down a wondrous avenue of oak trees. The early morning sun filtered between the leaves, creating a patchwork effect.

This was a fine way to go to work, Pinchas thought. The bad years, hopefully, were behind them. Had he been wrong to take his family away from their beloved shtetl? London had been a nightmare. Why had he not simply returned home? Was he too proud to admit he'd been wrong? Was it lack of money for the trip? He tried to think back to those early years, but all he could think of was the past few months, those weeks when he'd thought he was dying, and he'd wondered what would be with Faigy and the children.

Yet here he was, walking down this beautiful place, the trees overhead providing shade. Surely now the bad times had passed and only good lay ahead.

Pinchas reached Adderley Street, a fine-looking street. On the right was a large, impressive white building. According to the map, it was the courthouse.

Pinchas turned right, walked past the building, then down one street and past another until he was on Plein Street. He gave a sigh of relief and turned right. He was nearly there. The next street on the right would be Barrack Street, his destination.

He made a sharp right turn and felt as if he had entered a different world. He had entered District Six, one of the few areas where the many different people of Cape Town, people of all colors and religious denominations, lived together. Because accommodation was cheaper, new Jewish immigrants, who were lacking in resources, were generally directed there. Pinchas was ignorant of such things. He only knew that he must find the place where he was to work.

The street was narrower than the others he had been walking through. Many people were hurrying up and down, all dressed slightly differently. The hues of their skin were varied and the languages that rang out were a jumble of different tongues. He heard guttural sounds, almost like German, then English, and then Yiddish. A man with his *tzitzis* hanging out and holding two small boys by their hands hurried past. There was a fleeting impression of *peyos*, and then they were lost in the crowd.

The place had the buzzing energy of the shtetl on market day, but the style of dress and the appearance of the people was far more exotic.

This place was certainly different from where his family had set up their new home. Were there more Jews here who spoke Yiddish? Where did they *daven*? He hadn't seen anyone like that in the Gardens shul.

Then Pinchas saw the large sign that he sought. The walk had taken him far less than the hour he had allowed himself.

He gazed at the building. So large! Could this be correct? But there was the name over the door: D. Isaacs and Co. He entered the building and saw a great mound-like structure of steel machinery. Was this a carpenter shop? In his hands he clutched his toolbag. Where were the workbenches?

His feeling of joy evaporated. What work could he do in this strange place? Meanwhile, Mr. Isaacs was thinking along those same lines.

The men who had arrived the previous day walked together from machine to machine, looking, touching, and talking among themselves. Then, quite suddenly, there was a loud noise. One of the men held a piece of wood to the great steel monster, and in two seconds it had been cut in half. Pinchas stood there gaping.

Then he heard the urbane voice of his employer.

"Right men, very good! Now here are the plans for the furniture. Here is what the finished product must look like. Let's get organized. Oh, Mr. . . . . um, oh, so you have arrived. Good, good. I will be with you in a moment."

Well, it turned out to be a very long moment. Pinchas had no choice but to wait patiently. In the end, however, the problem of what he was to do was solved. The machinery could make the basic shapes, but the little touches, the carving to make the furniture look special, could only be done by hand. A small space was found for Pinchas and a workbench was constructed, and he was given a piece of wood to practice the designs he would have to make once the factory was in full swing.

Pinchas was tired at the end of the day, but as he walked into his new home he felt satisfaction. Once again, he was the breadwinner. True, there was a slight tightening of his chest, a slight difficulty in breathing, but as he walked, the sensation eased. He was pleased with himself, proud that he had succeeded in making a place for himself in this new land.

Unfortunately, as he walked into the house, Faigy soon put an end to his good feelings.

"Go into the kitchen," she said. "I'll be with you in a moment. Sit down, I have hot food waiting for you."

Moments later she was standing beside him, dishing out the food.

Pinchas was hungry, but more important to him than food was the need to talk to his wife.

"Sit down, Faigy, we must talk about a bar mitzvah in shul for Jack."

"No, I can't leave the shop," she said. "Later, when the shop closes we can talk. Jack already spoke to me about the shul. He says he isn't ready for his bar mitzvah *kiddush* yet. He says, well, the expense…"

Pinchas was amazed at his wife. Since when was this for women to decide?

"Faigy, he is well past the time when he should have made his *aliyah* to the Torah."

"Yes, but here it's a big thing with fancy clothing and a fancy *kiddush*. We can't afford that yet. It will have to wait. Besides, once a young man is thirteen he's a bar mitzvah, whether he's called up to the *bimah* or not. Correct?"

Pinchas suddenly felt all the tiredness of the workday seep through him. His feelings of optimism and pride left him. So now his wife made decisions not only in the home, but also about shul matters. What was the world coming to?

Did Faigy realize how she had overstepped her role? It seemed not, since she continued talking.

"What was the work like? What are they paying you?"

Too tired now to even think, too tired to explain that he hadn't even thought to ask, he muttered, "Don't worry. At the end of the week you will get it all."

If his wife even noticed that he was upset, he would never know, since just then the bell on the front door jingled as a customer walked in. Pinchas was left alone with his thoughts.

The next day, as Pinchas walked to work and entered the narrow streets and the mass of humanity, he looked around, searching for the man with *peyos*, someone who could tell him if there were other Yidden here and a proper shul. However, though he saw many different people and heard many different languages, he saw no man with *tzitzis* hanging out, no little boys with *peyos*, no Yidden.

Each day, Pinchas davened as quietly as he could in the Gardens shul with Jack by his side, ready to tug at him if he became lost in prayer, if he began to sway or mouth the words of prayer too loudly.

Sometimes he noticed men dressed like him, and sometimes during the service he would hear their loud, heartfelt davening. He wanted to talk to them, to get to know them, but they left quickly as the davening ended. Clearly, they were no more at ease in this place than he was.

After breakfast, he would change into work clothes and walk to work, looking out for a proper Jew with *peyos* and *arba kanfos* hanging out, even though his were now discreetly tucked in. On some days, as he entered District Six, he thought he heard Yiddish, but somehow, he never saw another Jew and he began to think he had imagined it.

Once the workday began, Pinchas sat at his bench, carving with great concentration. The fine dust from the machines began to slowly fill the room. As the day wore on, Pinchas felt his breathing become more labored. By the end of the day, he barely had enough energy to walk home.

Here, in this new land, he davened Minchah and Maariv without a *minyan*. Guilt gnawed at him, yet what could he do? He barely had the energy to eat his evening meal. The walk to the Gardens shul was impossible to contemplate.

So the week passed. Each day Pinchas trudged to the factory. In the morning he felt fit. By the end of the day he could barely find the strength to walk to the door and leave. By the time he arrived home, after breathing in the clean, pure air of the Gardens, he felt a bit better, enough to hide his lack of well-being from Faigy.

Pinchas began to think of Rosh Hashanah.

They had come all this way so his health would improve. Now he was once again struggling for breath as the workday ended. He was not as ill as he was in London, but he didn't feel well nevertheless. Would be merit another year? There were some days when he doubted it. On Rosh Hashanah, and then Yom Kippur, could he stand stock-still in that vast fancy shul and *daven* with feeling? He doubted it. But what option did he have?

His thoughts wandered to Sukkos. In the shtetl they had built their own *sukkah*. In London, he had used the *sukkah* in the small *shtiebel*. Here he had space to build his own *sukkah*—but with what? How much would wood cost? When would he have time to build it? After work he barely had enough energy to eat and then go to sleep. His health was deteriorating. The moment he walked into the factory he could feel his breathing grow labored.

Pinchas tried his best to put away his weekday worries over Shabbos. The children spoke about their week, their schoolwork, and their teachers. They said nothing about making new friends, something they had spoken about often in London. Still, they seemed happy enough and it was yet early days.

The following day was Sunday, and Pinchas had been told that Sunday was not a workday. In London he had worked in a *frum* carpenter shop. They had not worked on Shabbos, but on Sunday they returned to work. For that reason his pay had not been good. Many other workshops, even though they were run by Jews, worked on Shabbos. Here, after Shabbos, there was another day of rest. This was a great relief. After another day of rest he would be able to return to work—or at least he hoped he would.

On Monday morning, Pinchas arrived at work and sat at his workbench. The sawdust from the machine flew in the air and he could feel his chest tighten. He fought to keep his breathing even.

Two other men also worked on the carvings of the finished products. Their workbenches were a bit further away from the machines. Perhaps, Pinchas thought, he could ask for his workbench to be moved further away.

He looked and saw there was little space there. What was he to do? Day by day he felt he was getting sicker, taking longer to recover at the end of each day. If he continued like this he would soon be ill again. That would be disastrous. He must stay well. He must work and bring in money.

Could he simply leave? But he had only just begun to work again. How could he tell Faigy of the way his chest tightened up as the day wore on? Where would he find other work? Did all the carpenters in this new land work in places with such machines?

Sitting at his work bench, working on the carving, Pinchas thought back to the previous Shabbos. He had gone with the older boys to the Gardens shul, where everything was so stiff, so unlike everything familiar to him. It was so quiet, so restrained, almost as if they were in the office of the Czarist army recruiting center, rather than the joyful confines of a shul.

In the afternoon, there were no men sitting in the shul and learning, no *chavrusa*. Was this a way to spend Shabbos?

True, he had learned with Jack and David, but the way they had learned in London was so different from the way they would have learned in the shtetl's *cheder*.

What would he do for the upcoming *chagim*? Surely it was past time to discuss these matters with Faigy. Yet he remained silent.

Although Sunday gave him a chance to rest, there was no getting away from the fact that working had weakened him. Each day the fine dust affected him just a bit more. He returned home each evening, trying to look cheerful and appear fit, but the effort was becoming too much for him. What could he do? This place was as bad as London for his chest, but how could he find other work?

A feeling of despair overtook Pinchas as he sat by his workbench. He had only another hour to go before the lunch break. Then he could go outside and walk about, get some fresh air. The dust swirling around the workroom seemed to fill every crevice. His breathing became more labored.

At this rate, it didn't seem likely that he would last out the day.

Chapter 19

"It is of interest that D. Isaacs and Co. was one of the first companies in South Africa to use large, illustrated advertisements in the press."
— Mendel Kaplan, *Jewish Roots in the Economy of South Africa*, p. 157

Pinchas was deep in thought. How would he tell Faigy that he could no longer continue to work? Just then, Mr. Isaacs and a man in a smart suit walked by.

"Jan is bringing the cart here from the shop as soon as the order is loaded up," the man said. "The customers are in a hurry for their goods, so we'll leave as soon he gets here."

Pinchas looked at the stranger. He'd never seen him before. He had heard about him, the salesman who went far beyond Cape Town to sell furniture. He took with him drawings of the furniture they made, so it was quite clear what the product looked like.

Pinchas knew that those sales were almost as important as the sales in the shop, a little closer to Adderley Street. He'd known that the man would be arriving today, since he'd been told the previous day, "Please finish up that carving today. It must be attached to the wardrobe early tomorrow morning so it can go with our traveler and be delivered."

Suddenly, the salesman tripped on some planking. There was a horrified moan, then, "Oy, I can't stand on my foot. Oy, I think something is broken. Oh ... the pain ..."

A doctor was called. He came hurrying into the factory, carrying a black bag.

"It's a break, all right," he said. "All I can do is splint it up and give him some laudanum for the pain. Then you had better see he gets home. I'll call on him this afternoon."

Somehow, during this episode, the work went on. The machines roared and the men went about their tasks, as the air filled more and more with fine dust.

Pinchas was unable to concentrate on his carving as he watched the doctor tend to his patient. Now he saw Mr. Isaacs come into the shop. He was talking to a man, another stranger. He was dressed differently, though, in rough workman's clothes, rather than the smart suit and sparkling white shirt of the injured salesman.

"Jan, I don't know what to tell you," Mr. Isaacs said. "Your wagon is loaded up. The people want the furniture, but who will go with you now?"

The idea came suddenly to Pinchas. Maybe there was a way he could escape from this place, even if only for a short time. He got up from his workbench and, shouting to be heard above the noise of the machinery, said, "I can go." He was amazed at himself. "I can go," he repeated, more loudly.

Mr. Isaacs looked at him in amazement. "You?"

"Why not?" Jan said. "Is there anyone else who can travel with me? I know everything—where to go, what everything costs—only the people won't be happy if a colored man comes. Let the white man come. I'll see that he knows what to do."

Pinchas realized that the expression on Mr. Isaacs's face did not bode well.

"But your wife! What will she say?" Mr. Isaacs had been less than impressed with the social skills displayed by Pinchas and was looking for an excuse to turn down his offer.

Pinchas could think only of getting out of the shop. He had to escape the dust. He would be far away if he was traveling. Where would he go? He wasn't sure, but he had to convince the man and take this opportunity.

"Oh, she will manage," he said. "I know she won't mind, only I must go now and tell her. I'll be back here within an hour."

Jan spoke up again. "Is there anyone else you can send? We must leave soon. The first part of the journey is long."

Pinchas watched when, after a few moments, Mr. Isaacs shrugged his shoulders, sighed, and said, "You will go with Jan. There is no time to walk home and return here. Tell Jan where you live. You can drive there with him and collect clothing for the journey. There is already food in the wagon. And . . . and . . ."

Immediately, Pinchas realized that his clothing was being scrutinized.

"Oh . . . yes . . . I will wear the suit I wear to shul, not these clothes," he said to Mr. Isaacs.

Pinchas looked at Jan, the man who had spoken up for him. Together they left the factory and began the journey to the house on Kloof Street.

When they arrived at home, Pinchas quickly explained what had happened.

Fay was not happy with the news. "But you are not yet fit. You return from work each day exhausted. How can you go off in a wagon, traveling in the wild county? What has this to do with being a carpenter? Did they not employ you to be a carpenter?"

"Tell me," Pinchas said. "Does the shop bring in sufficient money for food? Do you want me to lose the job? It's only this one trip, and then I'll return to the workshop. Now, go and prepare food for me." He turned to Jan. "How long will we be away?"

"We'll return lunchtime on Friday," Jan said. "But we have food, Baas. It was already in the wagon when I came to the shop. The other Baas is also a Jew. He takes with him special food."

Pinchas was taken aback to be called by such a title. Why would the man call him his boss if they were both working for Mr. Isaacs?

Faigy had already gone to the kitchen. She returned with two loaves of bread, a pot containing bread pudding she had made from leftover *challah*, still hot from the stove, and a bottle of water. "Such short notice! It's all that I have. If only you would wait a short time. How can they do this to you, to suddenly send you off like this?"

Pinchas didn't he say that he had volunteered to go. He wasn't too concerned about food at that moment. He simply wanted to leave, before Mr. Isaacs decided this was all a mistake and sent a fast horse and cart after him, calling him back.

Soon they were off, and as he looked back, he saw his Faigy staring after the cart as it traveled into the unknown.

After she could no longer see the wagon, Fay returned to the shop and sat down. Had she really gone and given practically all the food in the house to her husband so that he could travel on a wagon with a stranger, far into Africa? Why hadn't she stopped him?

Besides, he wasn't well enough for such a trip. Since starting work he had once again begun to breathe heavily. Once or twice she had raised the issue with him, but he had angrily denied that he wasn't well.

The doctor in London had told the truth. This new land did indeed cure—but the cure hadn't been total. Going back to work was bringing on illness once again. And now, all the effort to make a good new life, to cure Pinchas, would be thrown away.

It was bad enough seeing him come home each day from work, white and exhausted and breathing almost like old times. But to go off in that little wagon, inland, with all the dangers that entailed—it was madness!

Why was he going? What did this mean? Pinchas had been hired as a carpenter. Why was he going on this madcap trip? Why hadn't she stopped him?

When the *shidduch* between her and Pinchas had been suggested, how could she have known that she would end up living here, far away from her family? If she had known, would she have done things differently? No, she thought not.

Pinchas was a good man. She had no regrets marrying a carpenter instead of someone who was learning in a yeshiva. Looking back . . . well, it was better not to look back. Life in the shtetl had been good. Pinchas had provided for his family and was well respected in the little community. He was a truly good, kind husband. Marrying him had been a good decision.

London had been a mistake, but what could she say? Mistakes happened. Those awful, gloomy years in London, Pinchas coughing, Pinchas gasping for breath — it was all a bad memory that could be forgotten.

Until now, she had been pleased to be in this new land. Pinchas had recovered, just as the doctor had said. True, lately she had felt that working was bad for him, and she'd been planning to speak to him about it. But with a little more time, he would surely continue to improve.

The children were happy in their new school. Jack seemed satisfied to be working.

The little shop was not yet making sufficient money to care for the family and to repay Mr. Davidoff, but she was sure that in time, she would succeed.

For the first time, since that terrible day when she had left behind all that was familiar to her, family, friends, and her sweet little home, she had been feeling in control of her life. In this beautiful town, in this fine house, it was a pleasure to wake up each day. But now, with the worry about Pinchas, she felt as if the world was tumbling about her. It seemed that disaster was threatening.

Foolishness! This journey, this dangerous journey! Why had she simply gone to fetch food and watched as the wagon pulled away?

The bell above the door rang and a customer entered. Fay forced her thoughts away from Pinchas, from the dangers that he faced, and concentrated on the woman who wanted a few small items.

When the children came home from school, Fay put on a false smile.

"Your *tatte* has been asked to do some important work for Mr. Isaacs," she said. "He is traveling to country villages to deliver furniture for him."

It was bad enough that she would worry until he returned, but if the children were worried and constantly asked questions, she didn't think she could cope.

One thing was for sure: Pinchas would not do this again. She had been taken by surprise, but now she was prepared. She would not allow this to happen again.

The children seemed to accept her explanation without any problems. They sat down at the kitchen table and ate the soup she dished out. There was no bread. She had given it all to Pinchas. Later, when the shop was closed, she would have to bake. In London there had been a kosher bakery. Was there one here?

A few customers came in the afternoon and bought small items that they had clearly just run out of or forgotten to purchase at their usual shop. Fay was extra polite and helpful, hoping they would return for larger purchases in the future.

As she was closing the shop, Jack arrived home. He ran to the kitchen.

"Tatte?" he called. "Where is Tatte? Is he sleeping?"

Fay followed him into the kitchen. "Wash your hands and sit down. I have soup for you. Your *tatte* will be away until Friday. He has gone to deliver furniture that the factory made."

"Where did he go?"

Fay shrugged. She hadn't thought to ask.

"You don't know!" Jack looked aghast.

"Listen, my son! Your father arrived here this morning. He asked for food to take with him on his journey. I gave him what I had and then he left."

At work that day, Jack had heard a story about a man who lost his way while traveling upcountry. He had driven around in circles and had been found just in time.

"How was he traveling?" Jack asked.

"On a big wagon, covered like a tent and packed with furniture. Another man was driving the wagon and said they would be back by lunchtime on Friday."

Jack was hungry after working all day. He went to the bread bin. It was empty.

"Your father needed all the bread I had for his journey," his mother said. "But I made some extra potatoes. Wait, I'll get them from the stove for you."

Fay took some soup for herself. She didn't feel like eating, but she had to keep up her strength. What if . . . ? No, she couldn't allow herself to think like that. Once her husband returned and had rested, they would talk. She must find out more about how the trip had come about and if it would be repeated. No, it would not be repeated. Impossible!

Chapter 20

"The little Jewish community of Uppington, at the edge of the Kalahari ... at Rosh Hashona ... numbered more than two *minyanim*, (and) consisted of the local Jewish residents and their friends from the neighbouring districts of Draghoender, Grootdrink, Ratedraai and Zwartmoeder."

— Saron and Hotz, *The Jews in South Africa*, p. 40

Pinchas watched as they traveled through the streets of the town at a sedate speed. Jan drove carefully, concentrating fiercely and saying little.

After a while they were out of the town, making their way through the open countryside. Jan flicked his great whip and the horses went faster.

By now, they had been away from the factory for a few hours. Pinchas was once again breathing easily. For a while, nothing else seemed important. Now he began to think about the task he had undertaken.

"I heard you say that you know exactly what had to be done," he said. "Tell me, then, what I should do."

Jan was only too happy to oblige. For years he had driven salesmen around from place to place. Now he was only too happy to display his knowledge.

"First we'll go to a farmhouse, not too far from here," he said. "They grow grapes and make wine there. They want a new bed—it's here, but in three pieces. I will put it together and you will collect the money. The money is stored in a special place in the wagon—I'll show you. Then we'll go toward Swellendam, but we'll make other stops on the way."

They reached the farmhouse after several hours. It was a place of incredible beauty, with tall gables above the entrance of the large white house. The transaction went smoothly. Jan acted as though he was taking orders from Pinchas, but in fact he organized everything. Pinchas was grateful and felt slightly more confident as they drove away from the farmhouse.

Jan pulled out of the large gates, facing the open road, and said to Pinchas, "Now we'll go toward Swellendam, and we'll return through Stellenbosch. Sometimes I go to Bredasdorp and Caledon, but not this time, because we have no orders to deliver there. After that, the trip is far north, in the direction of Piketberg."

Pinchas noticed that Jan hadn't said "*we* go," but "the trip *is* far north." Clearly, there was doubt in the driver's mind as to whether Pinchas would be going on that trip. Pinchas looked around at the countryside they were passing through. It was lush and green, covered with vineyards and dotted with solid white gabled farmhouses.

He must prove himself capable. He must do well. How could sitting in that terrible dusty workshop, that horrible factory, compare with the joy of a day like this?

Pinchas wanted to know more, and with his encouragement, Jan began telling stories about other places. He spoke about Klapmuts, Riversdale, Robertson, and Montague. Pinchas listened in fascination to the unintended dramas that travel brought about, to accounts of the variety of people he would have to deal with. From each story he learned something of what lay ahead.

Pinchas wondered why it was necessary for him to accompany Jan if he knew so much and Pinchas knew so little. But then he thought about the heavy furniture that would need to be taken off the wagon and reassembled. Of course, one man alone couldn't do the job.

As a newcomer to the Cape Colony, Pinchas was new to the concept of racial prejudice. He couldn't understand that some people would only deal with a man of light complexion. Later, he would realize why Jan could not travel alone, though he would never approve of this prejudice.

But on this happy day, he was simply eager to learn everything that Jan could teach him.

Pinchas found himself in small villages, mostly with one dusty main street. Sometimes there were only a few houses, and sometimes a few hundred. Upon arriving at their destination, the furniture had to be delivered. Sometimes there was a new order. Then the horses had to be watered and rested, and they had to find a place to stay overnight.

To Pinchas's amazement, there were some Jews in each place. What were they doing here, so far away from everything that was familiar?

Somehow, they always knew of his arrival, even when he wasn't delivering furniture to them. How pleased they were to meet him and learn with him. They were happy to invite him to their homes, to their shul, to talk business with him, and introduce him to anyone who needed furniture.

Pinchas couldn't realize then how isolated these Jews felt. He didn't know that any Jew, particularly someone from Lithuania, was made welcome. When the men discovered that he had spent a few years in a yeshiva and could talk in learning with them, they were overjoyed.

Always, when there were Jews in the village, Pinchas was royally entertained. The simple fare he had brought with him was not needed.

His battered feelings of inadequacy began to recover. For too long he had felt himself to be a failure. He had foolishly believed his old friend, Avraham Cohen, and had brought his family to a place of poverty and squalor.

Years before, when he rejoiced that Faigy had become his bride, he had vowed to himself to give her a good life, a life that would make her forget anything bad that had ever happened to her. Instead, he had brought her hardship.

She had brought them all to this new land. She had always yearned to return home, and now they were farther from it than ever.

Not only that, but in this new land, it was Faigy who was running the family, Faigy who was trying to make a living. Now, miles away from his family, he was being fussed over. His confidence was boosted, and he resolved to somehow persuade Mr. Isaacs to let him keep this job, since sitting in that stuffy, dusty, wood-filled room was no longer possible.

In the evening, wherever possible, Pinchas attended the Maariv service in a private house. In these small *minyanim* it was permitted to sway, to cry out one's prayers.

Pinchas felt as if he had left behind a nightmare and entered a familiar, comfortable world. He dreaded his return. Once again, he would have to *daven* in the unfriendly Gardens shul on Shabbos. He would have to sit in the factory, with the dust from the wood flying through the air, clogging up his lungs, causing such terrible tightness in his chest. Here, in the clear dry air and the wide-open spaces, he felt young and fit again.

The trip was almost over. He was at the last town before they would make the journey home.

"Going back to Cape Town tomorrow," he told a Jewish customer.

"Lucky you, not to be stuck out here, behind a counter, far from all things Jewish," the man said.

Pinchas felt an urge to shout that he had no desire to return, that he would gladly stay as the man's assistant, that he would go and fetch his family and bring them here.

But he said nothing. Would Faigy agree to such a thing, his Faigy, who had found a fine house and was running a shop? What kind of school was there here? Would his Faigy take the children out of a fine school and bring them to this small, faraway place? He thought not.

So he sighed and replied, "Why complain? It's a good life here. You're never short of food. The weather is fine. You don't fear your neighbors as you did in *der heim*. You don't yet have a shul, but you have a *minyan* and a *sefer Torah*, and the Yidden here are such fine people. Nu, be satisfied."

"You know, you should be the *rav* here, not selling furniture from pictures," the man said. "Such a clever man you are. Those words are such a comfort to me. I feel so far away from my family and friends in the shtetl, but there we sometimes lacked food. Here, food is plentiful. I can clothe my children properly. There's no *cheder* here, but there is a school, and the boys and girls go. My wife and my children don't complain. It seems they're satisfied, with no longing for the shtetl. Yes, I should be satisfied. You're correct…I have everything that I need here—a good living, sufficient Jews for a *minyan*. Yes, those are wise words you have spoken. "

The words were a balm to Pinchas, making him feel worthwhile and enabling him to contemplate his return to Cape Town, where he hoped to ask Mr. Isaacs to let him go on another trip. If he was refused, he would tell Faigy of these small villages, where there were Jews like them, where a man could make a living from a small shop.

Meanwhile, his chest gave him no trouble. The money he contributed to his family was good. For the moment, anyway, he had nothing to complain about.

So he would go to that fancy shul for the *chagim*. A man could learn to stand still and yet *daven* with *kavanah*. When Rosh Hashanah arrived, if all went well, there would be money for new clothes and food. Sukkos, too, would be no problem. They had their own little yard, and he could buy wood from Mr. Isaacs. The boys would help build a *sukkah*. Why had he ever doubted that this country would be good for them? It was simply a matter of adapting to new circumstances.

Little did he realize that plans don't always fall so easily into place.

Pinchas arrived in Cape Town on Friday, late in the afternoon. Jan dropped him off at his home and took the empty wagon back to the factory. Pinchas took the money in the small tin box and brought it into the house. It was a vast sum. He would have to take it to Mr. Isaacs on Monday.

He saw that at home, life had proceeded smoothly. Although the children expressed pleasure at seeing him again, they seemed self-sufficient, without any feelings of sadness that he had been away for the whole week.

If his Faigy had been pining for him, her greeting didn't display any signs of loneliness or worry about him.

"Right, so you're back just when the man said you would be," she said. "Now we can enjoy Shabbos together, but first I must stay a little longer in the shop. There's plenty of hot water. I told the children to wait to bathe until you got home."

Well, that was better than nothing, he thought. There were no warm words, but there *was* mention of hot water.

Fay didn't say how she had stayed up late the previous night, when the children were asleep, making all his favorite dishes. Only by doing this could she keep her fears at bay. On the stove she had vegetable soup, potato kugel, carrot kugel and fish made the South African way, fried in batter. In the pantry, besides perfect *challah*s, there was apple compote and sweet biscuits sprinkled with sugar. The tea essence was prepared and the samovar had hot water. Everything was ready, but she suddenly felt terribly tired.

The week had been difficult. She had hardly slept because of her worry over Pinchas. The money he had given her the previous Friday had disappeared at an alarming rate. The girls needed new exercise books for school. Would the financial demands from this new school never end? There hadn't been money to buy chicken, so there was no chicken soup and no roast chicken. Just when she had wanted the meal to be special, she had to skimp. But the fish was cheap, and it looked good once it was fried in batter.

When Pinchas came through the door, she had almost cried with relief. But as he walked in, she saw a customer approaching the shop door. Every customer was important. Good service would hopefully mean another visit.

Fay was determined to make a success of the shop. True, Pinchas had a job, but he had just been ill. Was he truly better? Would he get ill again?

What kind of job was this, traveling so far away and for so many days? What dangers had he faced on the journey? Would they send him again?

It was all one big worry, but her role, from now on, was to provide a stable income for the family. Only then could she properly care for her children—and yes, also for her husband. The shop must come first. They were still relying on Jack. That had to end. He must resume his schooling.

Fay forced back her desire to follow her husband and ask how he felt after the long journey. Instead, she focused on the customer.

Pinchas had expected a warmer welcome. Had his Faigy not missed him as much as he missed her and his family?

He went to run the bath water. What a delight this was, not to have to go to a crowded, gloomy London bathhouse. So the greetings hadn't been effusive. No matter. They would enjoy Shabbos together. He was home with his own family, not sitting at a strangers' table, even though the Jews he had met had been most hospitable.

But Faigy's cool welcome affected him. He lost some of the confidence he had gained on the trip.

Now he began to worry about what would be when he went to the factory on Monday morning. Everything had gone so smoothly during the trip. Jan had delivered the furniture and they'd taken many new orders. Everywhere Pinchas went he felt welcome. Jan had assured him the trip was going well.

Now, however, as he prepared for Shabbos, unpleasant thoughts flitted into his head. What if he had not taken sufficient orders? What if he had incorrectly counted the amounts of money he had collected and carefully stored in the small tin box?

During those long years in England he had taught himself to write. What if his receipts were written incorrectly?

Even if everything was satisfactory, what if another salesman had been hired? Would he still be employed by the factory? It all came back to him—the loud machines, the terrible air that made breathing so difficult.

He forced these thoughts away. He brushed out his Shabbos suit, since it looked a bit worse for wear after being worn so many times. He heard as one child after another called through the bathroom door, "Hurry, it's my turn now. Don't use all the hot water." He thought back with longing to Shabbos in the shtetl, and then slowly began to focus on the peace and serenity of the coming Shabbos.

They were in a new land filled with promise. They were in a fine house. The children were in a fine school. He had work. It was up to him to make Shabbos special.

Jack came running into the house.

"Cold water!" he shouted. "Couldn't you leave just a little bit for me?" A few minutes later, there was a knock on the door. "Welcome home, Tatte!"

Pinchas walked with his two older boys to shul. He davened fervently that he should be asked to go on another trip. How could he know that back at home, his wife was davening just as hard that he should not be asked to go again?

As they walked home through the beautiful avenue of trees, the boys asked about his adventures.

"No," he said. "We will not talk now of weekday things. Do you know the *parshah* of the week? Well, let me tell you." He began to recite the ancient words learned long ago as a *cheder* boy, giving some explanations from his pleasant days of study at the yeshiva.

They returned home to a family seated around the kitchen table, which was covered by a white cloth. The Kiddush cup gleamed. It was a miracle that throughout those years of terrible poverty they had managed to keep this precious silver cup. The *challahs* were covered with an embroidered cloth. The lights of the Shabbos candles were reflected on the gleaming brass candlesticks.

Pinchas looked at Fay. She smiled at him. This was good, like old times.

Then they began to sing the words of greeting to the two Shabbos angels. "*Shalom aleichem . . .*" Slowly, weekday cares drifted away as the words resounded loudly in the room.

Pinchas said *Eishes Chayil*, the words of praise to his wife, with feeling. He thought of everything she had accomplished, of how she had brought them to this new land, where surely they would prosper. He moved around the table, blessing each child.

Fay listened to the words, warmed by them, feeling once again relaxed and valued. Her husband was a good man, a learned man. She had chosen well when she had agreed to the match.

As Pinchas said the last words, she saw him glance at her, and she knew that her feelings were reciprocated. It had been a difficult, worrying week, but now Pinchas was back, safe and sound. Her prayers had been answered.

The following day, after shul, the family ate a cold meal, with only the water from the samovar providing some hot tea.

So Shabbos passed. Pinchas felt a deep contentment, and all was well in the Levine family.

As Pinchas was about to make Havdalah, he suddenly remembered the starry sky, the night he and Jan had been forced to sleep out in the open countryside. He remembered then how in the shtetl, before Havdalah, he used to take his family outside to count three stars, the sign that Shabbos was over. It was time to renew this old custom. Instead of lighting the candle, he said, "Come, we will count the stars."

The younger children looked up at him with worry in their eyes, but Jack said, "Yes, just like we did before we left home." So the child still thought of the shtetl as home. Pinchas had thought that he was the only one who felt that way.

"No, this is home now, and we will go and count the stars before we make Havdalah," Pinchas said. He walked out of the back door into the yard. The children and Fay followed him, and they gazed upwards at the clear sky with the twinkling stars.

"Look," Fay said. "There are many stars."

They all trooped inside and Pinchas lit the candle, took the Kiddush cup in his hand, and chanted the words that ended the Shabbos.

On Sunday, Pinchas hoped to spend time with Fay. Instead, Fay and the older girls were out in the backyard, busy with laundry. The older boys took the younger children to the park across the road.

Pinchas felt superfluous. He took his *sefarim* and sat and learned.

There was a hurried lunch, leftovers from Shabbos, and then Fay and the children started to clean the house. Pinchas was unsure of what to do. Such domestic happenings had usually taken place while he slept the day away.

He made a half-hearted offer to help.

"No, you have been away all week," Fay said. "You had a hard time. Rest now!"

At first Pinchas felt alone, distant from his family, while all around him the place buzzed with activity. Then the words he was learning overtook him and filled him, and he was lost in the joy of learning.

As evening approached, the dry laundry was brought inside and the whole house sparkled. The family sat down to a leisurely meal, and Pinchas finally told them about his week.

He didn't tell of the time he and Jan had misjudged how long they had remained in one shop, so by the time darkness came they were far from the next village. Jan had cleared a small area and made a fire. He had tethered the horses and surrounded them with thorn bushes for protection against wild animals. At first Pinchas had felt fear, but then, seeing how relaxed Jan was, he too began to relax. He slept that night in the wagon and Jan slept by the fire, replenishing it as it burned low.

He didn't tell them of the big snake Jan had killed one day, just as he was about to step out of the wagon.

Instead, he told them of the beautiful vineyards, and the large white houses with fancy gables. He spoke about the little towns and their shops and the Jewish families that owned them. He told of meeting *landsleit*—not quite from his shtetl, but from places not too far away.

It wasn't until the children were asleep and the day had ended that he began to think of the following day, when he would go to the factory. Suddenly, his feeling of euphoria left as worry overtook him.

Fay was relaxed after a day of hard work, and she wanted to talk to her husband.

"Your trip was a success," she said. "I'm pleased, but I'm more pleased that you're back safely. You must make sure never to do such a thing again."

"Oh, don't worry about that. I'm sure by now Mr. Isaacs has found someone to do the work while the salesman's leg heals."

What he wanted to say was, *Oh, if only I could always do this. The air was so fresh and the people so friendly.*

He was pulled back to the present when Fay continued speaking. "In any case, you'll have to leave this work. I've noticed that it doesn't suit you. At night you breathe like you did in London, before we left."

Although Pinchas himself had been worried about his deteriorating condition, he was now annoyed. His voice took on a harsh tone, new to both him and Fay.

"What? Jobs are so easy to come by, I suppose. Besides, why should another job be any different?"

Fay seemed not to notice his anger. "I now have a shop. You can take time looking for something suitable. There's no rush."

"Hah, so for this shop you earn sufficient! I see how few times that little bell rings. If not for Jack would we even have enough money for food?"

Fay knew that he spoke the truth, but now she too was angered. "Have you starved since we came here? Have I not survived weeks without you going to work?"

Pinchas was dismayed. His wife spoke the truth. For weeks he had simply let the world go by, not even inquiring where the money came from. But now it was different. He could work. He *would* work. He would get used to the factory, and he would not allow himself to get ill again.

There was more that Fay wanted to say, more that Pinchas wanted to say. But, as if by mutual consent, the conversation ended. Yet the bad feelings that had sprouted between them didn't go away so easily.

Chapter 21

"Malays, Cape: Community of Eastern, mostly Malay origin, in and around Cape Town, where a large section occupies the 'Malay Quarter' on the slopes of Signal Hill. Their ancestors were brought to the Cape as slaves by the Dutch East India Company, the first arrivals being recorded in 1667."

— Eric Rosenberg, *Encyclopedia of Southern Africa*, p. 330

When Pinchas left to work on Monday morning, Fay was already in the shop.

Their angry words of the previous night echoed in her ears.

"You have your food for work?" she asked.

She received only a nod in assent.

The week that Pinchas had been away had been so difficult. She had kept a brave front in front of the children. She had pasted a bright smile on her face for the customers, but at night, alone, she wept. Had she brought her beloved husband to the warm, pleasant Cape, only for him to be lost to her on this dangerous task that took him into the wild interior of Africa?

Surely he would not have to go again!

Pinchas had not told her that he had requested to go. She had assumed that he was forced to embark on this foolish trip. Now, surely, the regular salesman would resume his role, and Pinchas would be safe in Cape Town once again.

She would not have another week of worry, of crying herself to sleep. The trip was over. Pinchas had returned safely. That was all that mattered. Somehow, she would persuade him to find work in another place where he would not get ill.

Pinchas didn't know how to tell Faigy how much he wanted to continue traveling. Travel meant he would not have to sit in the sawdust-laden workshop. It meant freedom from being under the control of the foreman. It meant clear open skies, an interesting travel companion, and respect from those he dealt with. It was a good feeling.

He hadn't told Faigy of the clear pure air that made him feel young and fit again, of the beauty of the never-ending landscape. The open country raised his spirits and caused him to praise the Creator. How could he speak of such things when they could be snatched away from him?

During the night, Pinchas had been plagued with terrible dreams. In the darkness of the night he had seen himself handing the tin box to Mr. Isaacs, and then the money had been scattered on the floor as Mr. Isaacs grew and grew, until he towered above him, roaring in a voice of thunder, "*Gonif!* Where's the rest of the money?" Next, the book of furniture orders was flung at him. "The orders, why are there so few orders? What were you doing all this time?"

When Pinchas awoke in the morning, he was no longer the confident man who had traveled alongside Jan, who spoke so assuredly to customers. He was a man in need of a kind word of encouragement from his wife. But Fay was still upset about their conversation the previous night.

Pinchas was upset at her curt farewell. He took the packet of food for lunch and gave Fay a dismayed look that she totally missed, as she watched a customer enter the shop.

Now, as Pinchas began the long walk to the factory, he forgot about his disappointment with his wife and her angry words. He forgot about the lonely Sunday, with his family so occupied that they had no need for him.

Instead, his mind was filled with worries about how Mr. Isaacs would react to the trip. Pinchas walked to the Gardens and then down the beautiful avenue, hardly noticing the surroundings that normally gave him so much pleasure.

In his hand he clutched the order book and the box with the money. He had only made a few dozen sales, though he had been away for a full week. By now, a new salesman would have been found. He would have to sit at his workbench, carving, while all around him the fine dust from the machines swirled in the air, making the simple act of breathing more and more difficult. His wife was correct. The place made him ill, but he couldn't leave. Where could he find other work?

If only he could find something different to do. If only he could live in one of those small villages that he had visited these past weeks, with Jews like himself, Jews from Lithuania, Jews who dressed and spoke and davened like him, loudly and with fervor, not like the stiff Englishmen in the Gardens shul.

Pinchas trudged down the now familiar streets thinking gloomy thoughts, until he found himself at Barrack Street. With a deep sigh, he went into the factory. First, he must give the money and the order book to Mr. Isaacs. Then he must try and explain why he had so few orders, and then he would have to go to his workbench. His idyll in the countryside was over.

Pinchas walked straight to the office. The unpleasant task would soon be over. He was greeted warmly by Mr. Isaacs and told to make himself comfortable on the chair. Pinchas drew in his breath as the money was counted. Mr. Isaacs smiled at him.

"All in order, I see."

Then he took the order book. Pinchas shifted from foot to foot, hardly wanting to look at Mr. Isaacs. Quickly, page after page was flicked through.

"My goodness, but you have done well," Mr. Isaacs said. "So many orders! How did you do it?"

Pinchas almost gasped with surprise. Words eluded him.

"Look, we haven't managed to find another salesman," Mr. Isaacs said.

"Do you think you could carry on for a while? Does your wife mind that you are away?"

Now Pinchas found his voice returning. "My wife is a capable woman." Well, *that* was true. Faigy would definitely mind, but he wasn't going to let this opportunity pass. "My wife will manage. She managed everything while I was away last week and she'll do the same in the future."

He was the husband. He would make these decisions. Besides, what other option was there? The shop was clearly not doing well. There had only been a trickle of customers since he arrived home. Not only that, but it seemed that no one had missed him, not his wife and not his children.

Then Pinchas remembered something else that had been worrying him. How to explain it? Would it ruin his newfound luck?

"Er . . . well . . . a few people asked for favors," he said. "It's difficult for them to find everything they need. Mrs. Tanzer asked me to buy for her some new cutlery. She wanted to give me money for it, but I said it could be collected when she received the new set.

"Mr. Gershowitz asked if there was anywhere to buy a new *siddur*. The Stollers asked if our salesman could bring up a few rolls of fabric."

There was silence as Mr. Isaacs took this in. Pinchas felt disconcerted.

"I know that furniture is what we do, but it was so difficult to refuse," he said.

Mr. Isaacs gave a hearty laugh. "Well, now I see why you got these orders. These people really like you and trust you, if they feel comfortable enough to ask these favors. Right then, while we assemble these furniture orders, you go ahead and purchase these things for them."

Mr. Isaacs paused. "Fabric, cutlery — that's something women would know of better than us men. I think I'll ask my wife to take care of that. But you should buy the *siddur*. Just charge it to the firm. They know they'll be paid."

Mr. Isaacs wrote down an address and handed it to Pinchas.

Pinchas felt relieved. He had been wondering how he was going to know which cutlery and fabric to choose, and how he would find the money to pay for them, even though he knew he would be paid back as soon as he delivered the items.

"Oh," Mr. Isaacs suddenly added, "if you are to be our new salesman, a new suit will be in order."

Pinchas quaked. How could he take money from his salary for a new suit?

"But when I call on customers, I wear my Shabbos suit. Today, I'm in my work clothes, but…"

Mr. Isaacs didn't know how to tell the man that even his Shabbos suit looked worn and old-fashioned. Of course, the man was worrying about the price, but he really couldn't represent the firm unless he was suitably clothed.

"Of course, the firm will pay for it. Just go to my tailor, and he'll see to it. You know where the Malay Quarter is? No? Well, go through the Gardens to where Long Street begins, then up the steep hill. At the top you'll see the Malay Quarter. Here, I'll write the address for you. Best tailor in all of Cape Town. These people were brought here as slaves — just think about that. It's a good thing the British took over the country, or they would still be slaves.

"Go to my clerk in the next room. He'll write a note for you so the account will be sent to the firm. Oh, I meant to tell you that young Smith has been doing your carving work while you were away. He's not bad. Not as good as you, but not bad at all. Tell the tailor you also need three white shirts. "

It appeared to Pinchas that he would be going on another trip, maybe a few more. Then what? Broken legs heal. Young men learn quickly. Would he find himself jobless in a few months? Pinchas coughed nervously.

"I…well…what I want to say is…" He wanted to ask how long he would be doing this work.

Mr. Isaacs assumed that the man before him wanted to discuss a salary raise. That was understood, of course, but he had forgotten to mention it.

"As a salesman, your salary will be increased," he said. "That goes without saying."

Mr. Isaacs set pen to paper and wrote for a few minutes. "Take this to the office two doors from here. They'll pay you what we owe—your salary for the week, and, of course, the commission on your sales."

Pinchas felt relief course though him. He would be working as a salesman in the clean country air. He would have money to take to Faigy.

"It will take some time to fill out these orders," Mr. Isaacs said. "Some things are in our furniture shop, but some items will have to be made specially. Take this week off to spend time with your family. The next trip will be longer—you'll be away for two weeks.

"Use the week to get over the last trip, and be fresh and ready to leave on Monday morning. On Friday I'll send Jan to your house with this week's salary. He'll tell you exactly what your route will be and what time you will leave. By then your new suit should be ready."

"I don't understand," Pinchas said. "Next week I must stay home, yet you will send Jan with my money?"

"Well, that was the arrangement we made when a salesman had to go on a long trip. Does it not suit you?"

"Oh, yes, yes, of course," Pinchas answered.

Pinchas collected his money, amazed at the sum he was given. How was it possible to be paid so much for work that seemed to him more like a holiday?

He left the building in a dazed state, and not only because of the money, now firmly placed in his inside jacket pocket.

Mr. Isaacs's words were echoing in his head.

Such a large order! To think he had worried that not everyone he called on had given him an order. Then he thought of a week off from work, and yet he would still receive a salary! Would wonders never cease?

Another trip lay ahead of him, so there would be yet another few weeks of respite from that dust-filled workshop. It all seemed too good to be true.

He had two stops to make on the way home, the tailor and the bookshop. Pinchas found the bookshop near the shul and chose a *siddur* with care. Then he looked at the slip of paper with the tailor's address. He asked a passerby to point him in the right direction, and he was soon making his way past his home, up a steep incline, to the area known as the Malay Quarter.

He entered an area quite unlike any other he had seen thus far. The streets were cobbled and dust free. Solid one-story houses came up almost to the street. A few women, their heads covered with scarves, moved between the houses. Young boys, their heads covered with caps resembling yarmulkes, came pouring out of a large building.

Pinchas showed one of the boys the paper with the address and was taken there. He was welcomed in by a small, alert man with light brown skin. Pinchas was treated with a deference he was unaccustomed to.

"So you were sent here by Mr. Isaacs, a fine man, a good customer," the man said. "Now, let's see what he writes—a suit, a good suit from strong material, suitable for traveling. Right then, measurements first. After that you can choose the fabric and style."

In fact, the tailor did the choosing, imperceptibly almost, pushing Pinchas to make suitable decisions. The suit wasn't quite what either man had in mind. It was a subtle compromise between the style of the shtetl and the more modern style of the Colony.

Pinchas walked home buoyed with confidence. He would not be told to leave the firm. Mr. Isaacs was pleased with him. He could return home and tell his Faigy that she needn't worry about her shop. She could return the goods to the wholesaler. From now on he could provide for all of his family's needs.

Of course, she had said that she didn't want him to travel again, but he would explain to her that Jan was very capable. He had been doing this for many years, without any harm befalling him or his passenger. And of course, the salary was good, really good, even without the bonus he would receive for sales. He would explain carefully and Faigy would understand.

———

Fortunately for his buoyant mood, he didn't realize that the wife who had endured the poor conditions of England so silently had weathered problems that had changed her forever.

In England, Fay had remained silent out of desperation. Until they had money to return home there was nothing to be done, so complaining was of little use. She had been wrong to agree to leave with Pinchas, but what would it help if she spoke bitter words?

Only when she had been forced to make decisions on her own, to make the long journey across the ocean, had her old stubborn nature begun to reassert itself.

By the time the family had settled into their new home, and the shop had been filled with supplies, she was quite determined to rely only on herself in the future.

Pinchas was well. He was working again. She had davened for this. But she had also davened that her new venture would succeed, that she would never again be in a position to follow the dictates of others. She would depend on her own ability. If Pinchas could work and earn, well and good! But never again would she depend on him, not for money, and not for any major decisions.

Pinchas returned home, determined to put an end to his wife running a shop. Once again, he would be the wage earner and his wife would devote herself to the house and the children. The past weeks had been hard for her. Now, at last, he was in a position to care for her needs.

How could he know that his wife would be horrified at such an idea? In his light-hearted mood, how could he realize that his wife was determined to make a success of her new venture? Only then would she feel a sense of stability. The years of poverty in London had left her with an abiding fear of destitution. Now, here, they were living a good life and she intended to improve it and keep it that way.

Did she for one moment think that Pinchas would view this as a loss of respect for him? It didn't occur to her. He had done his best. She could not fault him. But now he needed a true helpmate, just like those learned men who studied all day while their wives ran a small business to provide a livelihood.

Her shop would do well. Jack would return to school. Her husband would find another job, something where he would not get ill. All would be well.

"...the material impoverishment of the Lithuanian Jews encouraged the
development of Talmudical colleges—often situated in the smallest
of villages—and the rise of great Rabbis and scholars."
— Saron and Hotz, *The Jews in South Africa*, p. 64

While Pinchas was happily planning how to tell Fay that she
could give up the shop, Fay was thinking about Jack.

He wasn't in school. There were no yeshivas here, just as there had
been none in London. Back home, she had been told that her Jack was
a clever boy, that he would one day go to a prestigious yeshiva. She had
been determined then that her boy would be able to learn for many years.
One day, he would be a rabbi like her father.

But that was long ago and far away. Here, everything was so different.
The shul rabbi was chosen in faraway England by a man called the Chief
Rabbi. That man had so many powers. He chose the rabbis for all the
places ruled by the British.

Not only that, but he had ruled that only he could have the title of
Rabbi. All the other *rabbanim* would be known as Reverend. What was
even stranger was the type of education they received. There seemed to
be no great yeshivas in England, no system of great rabbis testing and
giving *semichah*.

Some sort of English education sufficed, so it seemed. All this she
had learned from her husband, and also from Jack. It was no use thinking
any longer that Jack would become a *rav*.

Here, a different type of education was considered important.
University education led to professional qualifications that meant both

prestige and good earning power. She had learned that in London, and here, in a British colony, the same rules must apply.

Fay thought back to that day in London when she had been summoned to the office of Mr. Angel, the headmaster.

"Your boy Jack, he learns well," Mr. Angel had said. "He should continue his education and gain a profession. I will try to get him a scholarship for university, when the time is right. That means he won't be able to earn for many years. Are you agreeable? If you are, then I will keep an eye on him and watch carefully how he progresses in his studies."

Well, of course she had agreed. But in this country, there was no Mr. Angel to help pave the way. Here she must do everything herself — like finding a good school.

Was there a university here? How did one go about finding a scholarship here? Was there even a way? She must begin setting aside money each day to pay for education, so Jack could learn a profession.

The younger children were all at school. In time they could take advantage of further education. But Jack was working in a shop, his education at an end. What would become of him? Jack must return to school.

For the moment they still depended on Jack's earnings. Who knew how long her husband would continue to work for the Isaacs firm? Would he once again be asked to travel inland? No, it was unthinkable. Who knew what dangers he faced in the wild countryside? She must earn enough profit so her husband could take time off to find another job.

Now that she had this little shop, she felt she had some control over her life, over the well-being of her family. True, at the moment she wasn't earning much. The customers came in dribs and drabs, and then only for small items. But she was determined to succeed. Each customer was treated politely. Every night before she went to sleep, she said *Tehillim* with fervor. Very slowly, more people were coming in. Mr. Davidoff had encouraged her, saying that the position was a good one and that all would be well.

The children looked well, better than they had ever looked in London.

Their cheeks were red and rosy. True, they weren't at a Jewish school and she hadn't yet found a *cheder* for the boys, but the children were blooming in the wonderful climate. She would make the shop work so they could all remain here in this beautiful house.

At last, after those dreadful poverty-stricken years in the gloomy rooms in London, she felt a sense of stability and optimism.

Pinchas returned, a bounce in his step. He wanted to discuss his good fortune and tell Faigy that she could close the shop, return the goods, and he would once again support his family.

The shop was unusually busy. Customers came in, one after another, to make small purchases. There was no time to talk to Faigy. Although the purchases weren't large, the very fact that the little bell over the door kept ringing merrily as each person walked in lifted Fay's spirits.

Fay was unaware that Pinchas was in the bedroom, counting money, laying it carefully in the small drawer and waiting to give her the good news that she could relinquish the shop.

Fay heard the children as they came into the kitchen. They had been told to always use the back entrance, never the shop entrance. She handed two reels of white cotton to a woman and took the few coins. As the woman left the shop, she called out, "Frieda, see that the children wash their hands and sit at the table. Look in the pantry. You'll find bread, freshly baked this morning, and boiled eggs and pickled cucumber. The boiled water should be cool by now, so put that on the table."

In London, she had always boiled and strained the murky water through a muslin cloth. Although the water here was clear, she had continued the practice.

Frieda came into the shop. "Mother, you know, they don't boil the water at school. Maybe..."

The bell rang.

"Listen, just do as I tell you and see that the children eat and *bentch* and then do their homework. And Frieda, no noise. I can't be disturbed. Understand? Oh, and call your father and serve him lunch."

Pinchas heard the exchange from his room. How tense his wife sounded. How pleased she would be to give up the shop.

It was many hours before Fay was free. Pinchas ate lunch and then took out his *gemara*.

"David, come learn with me," he said.

"But Tatte, first I must do my homework," the boy answered.

While the children sat at the kitchen table preparing for the following day, Pinchas learned alone.

By the time David had completed his homework, Pinchas had fallen asleep. The tensions of the day had tired him. He woke up to hear Jack return from work and the sound of children playing in the backyard. He heard Fay close the shop doors and say to Jack, "Just soup for supper. I used up all the money for Shabbos."

It pained Pinchas that his wife discussed this with his son and not with him. Still, there would be no need for such talk in the future. He would provide for his family. He was feeling much more confident now that he would be continuing his job as a traveling salesman.

Even if the other salesman returned when he was healed, there would be time to familiarize himself with the new country and find other similar, satisfying work.

Pinchas got up and went to the kitchen. He praised the soup, and, like the rest of the family, filled up on the bread that Fay had baked. When at last the children were in their own rooms, he brought the money to the kitchen table. Fay was just about to turn off the gas lamps.

"Sit, please," he said. "We must talk."

Poor Pinchas! How could he know that Fay was tired beyond endurance, and that the last thing she wanted to do was talk?

"This is my salary for last week," Pinchas said. "It's more than double what I earned before."

"Good, so they paid you for last week."

"Not only that, but I am to travel again."

Tiredness fled from Fay. "No, surely not!"

Pinchas was so confident that she would be pleased with the news, he didn't hear the alarm in her voice.

"Yes, and I think there will be many more trips," he said. "Today Mr. Isaacs sent me to have a new suit made, paid for by him. He wants his salesman to look good. Would he do that if he wasn't going to send me many more times?"

Fay was stunned, silent, as Pinchas continued happily.

"You can send back the things in the shop and pay for the ones that are gone, and from now on I will supply money for us to live on."

Now anger overtook Fay. "What, give up the shop? Does my word to Mr. Davidoff mean nothing—and after all he has done for us? He said he wanted me to run the shop, and run the shop I will."

Pinchas was astounded. Surely *he* should make such decisions, not his wife. But Fay wasn't finished.

"You agreed to go off again! You didn't think to first discuss it with me? Do you think I came all the way here so my husband could go away for weeks at a time, to dangerous places?"

"But Faigy, my Faigy, I thought..."

"Well, you thought wrong. I will not give up the shop, and you will tell this man that you have a wife and children and cannot go off on mad adventures."

"I cannot tell him that," Pinchas said. "The terms are good. I can't give it up."

"I will not give up the shop. Go if you like. The children and I will manage all week without you."

Pinchas hesitated. He had to tell Faigy that he would be away for Shabbos.

"Well..." He coughed. "Next Shabbos I'll be away, but the Friday after than I will be home again."

Fay had heard enough. She could not deal with anything else. Soon she would be too tired even to walk from the kitchen. What was her husband talking about? He had casually mentioned he would be away for Shabbos. For this she had left her family and endured those terrible years in London? For this she had traveled for weeks on the ocean, so she could sit alone with her children on Shabbos?

"Goodnight," she said, and left Pinchas sitting stunned at the kitchen table.

Chapter 23

"The small inlet which marks the end of Sea Point is known as Three Anchor Bay and is named after the three anchors originally used to hold a defensive chain across the inlet."

— T.V. Bulpin, *Discovering Southern Africa*, p. 56

The blinds were just being pulled up from the shop window and the owner was rolling up his shirt when Jack entered the shop.

Jack always enjoyed Shabbos, but this last Shabbos had been strange. His father had been away, and his mother had spoken in a bright, tight voice.

"Children," she had said. "Your father has a new job. He travels too far away to come home every Shabbos, but next Shabbos he'll be back. Jack will say Kiddush on the wine and *Hamotzi* on the *challah*."

There was a stunned silence, and then little Joseph spoke up.

"Shabbos with no Tatte? How can that be?"

"We'll have a regular Shabbos, just as we always do," Fay said. "Next Shabbos, we'll tell Tatte all about our Shabbos and hear about his Shabbos."

"But how can Tatte make Shabbos all alone without us?" Joseph persisted.

"There are Jews who live in these places that your Tatte must travel to," Fay said. "He will be their Shabbos guest."

She hoped she was correct. Pinchas had said something to that effect, but in her anger she had hardly been aware of what he was saying.

Only Jack and Frieda had been aware that their mother was not as upbeat as she appeared. Since there didn't seem to be any point in asking more questions, Jack, Frieda, and the other children had gone along with Fay's instructions and attempted to make the Shabbos as normal as possible. But Jack missed walking to shul with his father. He missed his father's discussion of the *parshah*. He felt odd saying Kiddush and *Hamotzi*. Without his father, he felt the family was lacking their usual Shabbos joy.

Jack had been relieved when it was time to make Havdalah, when the long, difficult Shabbos was finally over. The following Shabbos his father would be back. What a relief! Now he must concentrate on his work. It was good that his father was working, but past experience with his father's illness had made him wary of anything lasting forever. He must work hard. He must keep this job.

Later in the day, Mr. Grocott called him over.

"My boy, one of my customers has moved out of this area, to Three Anchor Bay—the area just before Sea Point," he said. "She wants to be by the sea, she says. They used to live in Plymouth, in England, before they came here. Their house there faced the sea.

"It's quite a distance, so it will take too much time for Piet to take the horse and cart all the way there. Well, I was thinking. There's a tram out that way, and the last stop is not all that far from her house. You're a strong lad. I've packed the order into two large baskets. Piet will take you to the tram stop near here.

"Get off at the stop marked 'Three Anchor Bay.' The road above the station is called Beach Road, and above that you'll find High Level Road. Just look for number 14."

One hour later Jack had carefully emptied out the order onto the customer's kitchen table. As he left, he stared into the distance at the sea. Beyond some rough patches of ground he could see a small stretch of sand, with waves washing up on it.

He left the house and walked down a little path, going toward the sea. He stood and gazed at the seashore. He saw a woman watching three small children. They were barefoot and paddling in the water. Moments later he joined them. The water was icy, stinging his feet, and he hopped in and out. The children laughed at him.

"No, stay in," they said. "Then the water doesn't feel cold anymore."

Jack followed their instructions, and to his delight found that the water was icy cold, but just bearable. It gave a pleasant, tingling sensation.

Suddenly, he realized that time was passing. It wouldn't do now to get the sack. He dried his feet as best as he could and hurriedly put on his socks and shoes. Then he ran back to the tram stop. He kept thinking of his brothers and sisters, and the small backyard. Wouldn't it be marvelous if he could bring them to this place?

But how? It was too far for the little ones to walk all the way from the tram station. Besides, the tickets cost so much. Every penny Jack earned he gave to his mother. Now his father was working, but just because there was enough money now didn't mean they should indulge in unnecessary extravagances. Oh, but how the children would enjoy the beach!

Jack returned to find the shop crowded with customers.

"A picnic on the beach is a great idea," a young man was saying to a young woman next to him. "Since we moved to Sea Point it's a pity not to make use of the beach. Mother will ask the servants to pack everything in the picnic hampers, and then we'll carry it down the road, to the beach."

The words "beach" and "carry" caught Jack's ear. He went quietly to the owner and suggested a way to keep his customers happy.

"Are you sure you don't mind working on Sunday?" said the man. "Are you sure you can manage the horse and cart?"

"Ask Piet about the horse and cart," Jack said. "Sometimes, when I carry the orders out to the shed, I help him harness the horses. I did it often in London. And I don't mind working on Sunday, but I'm supposed to help my mother with the younger children then. Perhaps I could take them with me? I'll drop them off first at the beach, then go on to the house and pick up the people. Later, I'll go and fetch them."

"Well, yes, that's an idea. They're good customers. I wouldn't like to lose their business just because they moved."

The grocer went over to the young man and woman and told them of the plan.

"I must first make sure that my young man can handle my horses properly," he added. "Later I will test him. If he's as capable as he says, then we'll confirm the arrangement later today when he delivers your order."

It was tentatively arranged that a cart would collect the young people at midday on Sunday, take them to the beach, and collect them again later, to take them home.

"Piet, come here," Mr. Grocott said. "Take young Jack with you. Let him do everything himself, from harnessing the horse, to taking the deliveries, and caring for the horses properly when he returns, then tell me if he can be trusted to do this alone on Sunday."

When Jack returned with a positive report from Piet, he went again by tram to deliver the extra order to the house near the sea. He also confirmed the time he would be collecting them on Sunday.

Jack spent the rest of the day serving customers. At the end of the day he received the fruit and bread that was about to be discarded and took them down to the entrance of the docks to sell for a drastically reduced price.

At last, he was able to go home and share his exciting news with his mother. To his dismay, his mother was less than enthusiastic.

"What, sit on the sand and eat food? What an idea! Paddle in icy cold water? Now what fun is that? Besides, sitting all day in the hot sun! No, everyone will become ill."

"But this Shabbos Tatte will be home again. He'll be tired after being away for so long. On Sunday, if I take all the children, the house will be quiet. He can rest."

Fay thought for a moment. She thought about a quiet house, no children. She could use the time to talk to her husband, explain why she didn't want him to continue these dangerous travels. She wouldn't be tired then. She would be able to speak calmly.

Surely they would come to an understanding. He would see that this work was not for him and he would find something else. She gave her consent, and Jack ran to tell the others of their upcoming trip to the beach.

<hr/>

Fay spent all week preparing for Shabbos. Pinchas would be home again. He had left enough money so she wouldn't have to stint. She prepared a feast with many courses—fish followed by chicken soup with *kneidlach*, and then roast chicken with *tzimmes*, and potato kugel, and finally a compote of apples and red plums.

On Friday afternoon she kept going to the shop door and looking out. No wagon appeared, no Pinchas. The children kept running into the shop, though they knew this was forbidden.

"Is Tatte here yet? He wasn't here last Shabbos. You said he would be home this Shabbos."

Yet Pinchas didn't come. It was a difficult Shabbos.

"Now children," Fay said, "your father is only delayed. He'll be home after Shabbos, never fear. We must have a nice Shabbos and tell him all about it."

However, this was easier said than done. Even the younger children were worried and upset. Somehow the day passed, followed by a sleepless night.

Sunday dawned bright and clear. Fay was quiet as the children rushed around getting ready for the trip with Jack. The clouds that sometimes appeared over Lion's Head, the mountain that lay next to Table Mountain, and the augur of wet weather, was absent. The tablecloth, the layer of cloud that sometimes covered Table Mountain, bringing advance notice of a wild southeaster rushing down the mountain to the town, was absent.

The children, wearing their oldest clothes, got into the cart that Jack had fetched from the shed behind the shop. The horse was a fine specimen. Jack was happy to be in control of a horse and cart once again.

Then suddenly, there was an extra passenger.

Fay was in an irritable mood. What had happened to Pinchas? Why had he not arrived home for Shabbos? She had spent Shabbos pretending that everything was fine, but the pretense had taken its toll. Now tension enveloped her. On Sunday she usually did the laundry, with the older girls helping her. How would she do it alone? Impossible! They could wash the clothes in the afternoon. She would leave the sheets on the beds for another week.

Besides, how safe would the children be alone on the beach? How could she have agreed?

Well, since it wasn't doing any good sitting and worrying about Pinchas, she would go with them. She couldn't risk her children being alone in such a strange place.

"I'm coming," she suddenly cried out, just as they were about to drive off. She locked the door and got into the cart. She had prepared food and bottles of water. Now, with the extra passenger, there was hardly room to move.

Jack feared that the load was too much, but the horse was made of stern stuff and soon they were moving down Long Street, toward the sea, then along the sea front, until they reached Three Anchor Bay. There Jack led the way to the beach, assured them he would be back within the hour, and watched as they settled themselves on a large smooth boulder, a little distance from the sea.

There was another family already on the beach, a father with three little boys. They were dressed in their Sunday best and didn't run into the water, but stood on the pebbles, staring at the sea. Jack heard the man say, "Right, boys, let's go home now for lunch. Maybe later, we'll change, do a bit of fishing from the rocks. But now, it's time to go home."

Jack had seen the effect of too much sun on the skin of newcomers, who had stayed out too long. Sometimes they came into the shop, asking for a cure for their red stinging skin. Jack warned his family not to stay in the sun too long, but to sit under the large black umbrella he had brought along. Then he made his way to collect the picnickers.

The young man was standing on the steps of the house, waiting, and three young women were called out. The man was wearing a panama hat, white and broad brimmed. The girls were wearing straw hats with wide, slightly floppy brims.

Jack wondered where they had bought them and how much they cost. The hats shaded their faces from the sun. That would be better for the children than sitting under a black umbrella. Perhaps he could get that type of hat at the market at the Parade, or at Green market square.

Two maids brought out hampers. Jack helped them load everything onto the cart, and the three women clambered on. The man laughingly said he would rather walk, and about twenty minutes later, Jack left them all at a long pebbly beach and made his way back to his family.

He found his mother sitting in the shade of the umbrella, and his brothers and sisters clustered around her. They had been on the sea for many weeks as they traveled to the Cape, but this experience of seeing the waves fall upon the sands was new to them. Slowly, Jack tempted them to remove their shoes and socks, first the boys and then the girls.

Fay sat, disapproving but saying nothing, wondering how she had been talked into this foolishness. Then Jack went to the water's edge.

Slowly, one by one, the children followed him. Soon they were squealing with delight, running in and out of the icy water.

Fay called, "Food!" and soon they were all sitting under the large umbrella, eating bread and cheese and sweet green Cape grapes, which even the common folk could afford in this amazing land.

Jack had been told to collect his passengers a short time after the great cannon sounded at midday on Signal Hill. He heard the loud boom soon after they finished eating. Reluctantly, he left his family, smoothed his unruly hair, and off he went to collect the picnic party.

It seemed to Jack that he carried more food off the beach and into the cart, than he had carried on. But then, they had brought with them three large hampers, so clearly they had brought too much. Once again the young ladies rode, while the man walked beside the cart.

They thanked him with gusto once they disembarked, and the young man handed Jack a sovereign.

"Wonderful idea of yours," he said. "Would you do it again another time?"

Jack nodded. "I don't mind, but it's not up to me."

The young man immediately understood.

"Right then, we'll be in midweek with a large order and see what can be done."

Jack returned to his family waiting on the beach. The horses trotted back to Kloof Street, and Fay and the children got off. Then Jack took the cart and horse to the small shed behind the shop. He took off the harness, brushed the horse down, and prepared food and water. Once the horse had cooled down, Jack brought water and food and watched as the horse ate and drank its fill.

After making sure that everything was in order, Jack went out and locked the door carefully behind him. He was troubled as he walked home. Where was his father? He was supposed to return in time for Shabbos. There had been no word from him. Had something gone wrong? Jack had heard talk in the shop about the wild, untamed land that lay behind Cape Town.

Momentarily, fear overtook him. Then he thought of his mother, and how calmly she had sat under that big umbrella. She had smiled as the children ran in and out of the water. She had supervised their lunch, making sure that they washed their hands and bentched. No, there could be nothing to fear.

Little did he know that while Fay had shown an outer calm, inside she was very worried.

Chapter 24

"The first to go were always the menfolk . . . sometimes a bride would
be sent out to a South African immigrant whom she had not met
before . . . It was the strong family ties existing between the closely com-
pact Lithuanian community that brought the majority to this country."
— Saron and Hotz, *The Jews in South Africa*, p. 75

Earlier that week, just as Jack was making arrangements in the shop
to take the young people to the beach, Pinchas was getting ready for the
trip back home.

The weeks had gone well. Soon he would begin the journey home,
stopping on the way at smaller places, some with just a scattering of
houses and maybe one general dealer shop. Surprisingly, in most places
there was at least one Jewish family. Usually they owned the shop in the
village.

Pinchas felt fit and well and full of confidence. Sometimes, in that
little house on Kloof Street, when the soft rain fell from the skies, clos-
eting the house in dampness, he felt the old tightness in his chest. True,
it didn't rain all that often, nothing like London, and he recovered when
the sun came out. Nevertheless, here, in the dry, pure air, he felt like a
young man again.

The hotel owners in this village, and in fact in a few other villages,
were Jewish. Pinchas had eaten with them in their private dining room.
He remembered the inns back home, mostly run by Jews. There was no
comparison to these hotels, these fine buildings where each guest had
his own large room.

Besides Jewish shopkeepers and hotel owners in these areas, there were also Jewish farmers. Of course, back home Jews had also farmed the land, but always on property they had rented from non-Jews.

Here there was no law to prevent a Jew from buying vast tracts of land. Pinchas had met some of these farmers. Some had bought land because they already knew how to farm. Others had no previous farming experience but knew that on a farm they could keep Shabbos without compromise. All the Jews Pinchas had met appeared to be successful.

On Friday evening the Jewish men of the little community gathered together in the front room of a house. There was often a *minyan*. Sometimes there was even a *sefer Torah*.

In these small *minyanim*, the davening was loud and fervent. The men moved back and forth as they davened. No one said in an embarrassed whisper, "Tatte, see the other men. They stand still when they *daven*."

Here the other Jews made a fuss over him. They wanted to know the latest news of Cape Town. They wanted to talk about their problems.

"Should I bring out my younger brother? Does it matter that there is no yeshiva here?"

"Do you think I should add fabric to my stock? What is the cost of a roll of calico? A traveler last week gave me a price that seems so high. Can I trust him?"

Then, of course, there was the furniture. Pinchas carried with him not only leaflets with pictures of everything they sold, but also small blocks of wood, to show the grain and color of the finished product. Years of carpentry had made him an expert in this field. Here, he could answer questions with confidence.

Pinchas was too honest a man to say a product was good for a certain purpose when it was not. When asked if a fancy wardrobe would be strong enough to place in a shop and store heavy rolls of fabric, he said that he didn't think so. When he did approve a piece of furniture, his word was accepted. The little order book was filling up rapidly.

Now, sitting in the sun, waiting to be collected by the children of the shopkeeper's family so they could go to his house and learn a little, Pinchas thought with longing of his own fine family. He must arrange for Jack to return to school. Was there an afternoon *cheder* in Cape Town? He must make inquiries.

David was rapidly approaching his bar mitzvah. Pinchas wanted to begin learning with him on the weekends when he was home.

For so long, he had been too ill to see to his children's education. He had left everything to Faigy. Now he was well again and earning again. He must take control of his boys' learning.

His dear wife had been so brave. She had taken him from a place of grey misery and ill health, to this wonderful country. It was only because of her that he was once again healthy.

He had not been tactful when he told her to close the shop. Besides, if he was away so much, perhaps it was a good thing she had the shop to keep her busy. She would hardly miss him. Who knew? Maybe more customers would yet come. These things took time.

Pinchas was so looking forward to being at home again for Shabbos. True, this past Shabbos, the first time he had ever been away from his family, there had been wonderful Jewish hospitality, but that couldn't compare to sitting at his own Shabbos table.

In his suitcase he had presents: flutes carved out of wood for the boys and sweet little baskets for the girls. They had been made by farm laborers and sold at the roadside as he left Cape Town. Even from the time he left, his thoughts had been on his return.

At the beginning of the trip, Pinchas had hoped that the weeks ahead would be as successful as the trip that had just passed. However, he could not know that the very success of this trip would bring in its wake disappointment.

———

Looking back, the way it came about was so unexpected.

Jan had been doing this route for years and knew the meandering dirt roads that wound from one farm to another and from one small village to the next.

This was a well-settled area, with farmers living in large, Cape Dutch style farmhouses. These houses needed furniture from time to time, and Jan knew just which farms to stop at.

Twice on the trip dusk had come suddenly, when they were far from any town or farm. Jan had built up a fire and taken out the kosher utensils, and with Pinchas assisting, a hot vegetable stew was cooked out in the open, under the stars. On these nights Pinchas felt at peace with himself and the world.

The small fire burned throughout the night. Jan slept next to it and kept it going. Pinchas slept in the wagon, wrapped in blankets, with an animal skin on top to keep him snug and warm. He could hear the night sounds of animals, but they sounded far away, not at all threatening.

At night, beneath the vast African sky, everything seemed unreal. His family in the faraway shtetl and his longing for them, his miserable years in London and the regret that he had ever gone there — it all seemed so far away, unreal even.

On those nights he slept soundly and woke up refreshed and eager to begin the day. As he davened at sunrise, with his *tallis* wrapped around him and nothing at all visible except grass and shrub, and the horizon stretching out far beyond, Pinchas felt an overpowering closeness to his Creator.

On the last day of the trip, after all the furniture had been delivered, Jan informed him that they were now ready for the last stage of the journey back to Cape Town and his family.

There was only one more quick detour to be made.

They stopped, as planned, at a small cluster of houses, not even sufficient to be called a village. A Jewish shop owner welcomed him with unusual fervor. The reason soon became clear.

"It's my son's bar mitzvah this Shabbos," the man said. "My family was supposed to come, just enough for a *minyan*. Now one of my brothers can't make it. We have everything—a Torah, *siddurim*, and plenty of good food—but no *minyan*. Would you agree to stay over for Shabbos?"

Pinchas thought of his family. They were expecting him, and he longed to see them. No, he couldn't stay. Perhaps they could find another Jew at a nearby village or farm.

It was the woman of the household who finally swung the balance. As he walked into the house, she came forward, her eyes red and puffy.

"A Yid," she said. "My prayers have been answered. You will stay here for our only son's bar mitzvah."

Pinchas went outside and spoke to Jan. The man also had family. They too were expecting him home.

Jan was more than surprised to be asked what he thought. White men gave orders; they didn't ask colored men what to do.

"Of course, if that is what Baas wants, then that is what we will do," he said.

And that's how, while Fay wore a bright, false smile and sat at the table when Jack made Kiddush, Pinchas was far away, in a small village, sitting at a large table with men who had traveled many miles to be with the beaming bar mitzvah boy.

"So good of you to stay over for the bar mitzvah!" one of the men said. "My brother would have been so disappointed if there was no *minyan*."

"Next time you travel you must come our way," another man said. "I found my place about a year ago. There was no shop there, and people were used to buying from the *smous*. Now things are better. Yes, next time, come my way."

There were four brothers. They had all been brought out of Lithuania by their youngest brother, who had fled somewhat precipitously, after a run-in with a gentile neighbor had threatened to turn unpleasant. Anywhere else, it would have been considered simple boyish exuberance, but in that place and at that time, when Pesach fell around the non-Jewish holiday, the whole community was in danger.

Later, Pinchas heard the story from the woman who had asked him to remain.

"My husband, he came here alone as a young boy, bar mitzvah age, with only a shilling in his pocket. Would you believe it, but after a year he was beginning to make money by working for a shopkeeper in Cape Town? Not only that, but he was also able to save a bit, until after a few years he sent for me. Together we saved, until we were able to buy a small house in a village that had no shop.

"After some years we were able to bring over my husband's other two brothers. We thought then of my sister, alone with our old parents, and what do you know? A fine young man living on a nearby farm came to us and said how lonely he is, and how he wished he could get married. You know how many Jewish men there are here and so few women. So when I suggested my sister, he was happy with the idea. After all, he knew we were honest people. He paid her fare, and just look at them. Look at her fine children. Such a good, happy family! It's a blessing, to be sure."

After Shabbos, Pinchas was repaid in some measure for his good deed. Once Havdalah had been made, the women in the room admired the furniture. It had all come from the Isaacs factory, and Pinchas was sitting there with his catalogues. Soon each member of the family had ordered a piece of furniture.

When Sunday morning came, Pinchas had a full order book and produce from the garden surrounding the shop. He was feeling good. True, he had not been at home for Shabbos as he had planned. However, he had done a mitzvah by making up the *minyan*, and if the journey went well he would arrive back home in the afternoon.

Jan sat in the driver's seat, and Pinchas sat beside him. It was very early Sunday morning, before the sun had fully risen, since both men were keen to be with their families.

They arrived at Kloof Street mid-afternoon. Pinchas bounded up the steps, only to find the door locked and the house silent.

Fortunately, he always traveled with the house key, in case he arrived in the middle of the night. But entering an empty house after so many days away was shattering.

Didn't his family care about his arrival? Weren't they worried when he hadn't arrived home for Shabbos?

Pinchas smiled at Jan, so that the man wouldn't see his disappointment, and waved him off. The house was cool after the heat of the journey. He walked around the rooms. Everything was just as he had left it. There seemed to be no cause for alarm. But where was everyone?

Sitting in the empty house, he began to worry about his family. What if something bad had happened because he was away? Just as he was about to go to the neighbors and ask if they knew anything, he could hear children chattering and rushing in.

"Now straight into the yard, and shake off all the sand," Faigy shouted. "Then go to the kitchen and wash your hands, and I'll give you cookies and a drink."

Pinchas gave a sigh of relief. His family was home, safe. However, his reception wasn't exactly what he had anticipated.

Pinchas came out to greet them. "I was just beginning to worry."

"What, *you* were worrying?" Faigy said, her voice shrill. "What about us? Didn't you say you would be back for Shabbos? Then the sun set and the sun rose, and set again—and no word from you. What was I to think?"

Faigy wasn't pleased to see him, it appeared. She was angry with him.

"Let me just explain," he began, but Faigy glared at him and stalked away.

Pinchas hurried after Fay to explain what had caused the delay. He found her sitting on a chair, staring out the bedroom window.

"I'm sorry you were worried," he said. "But listen to what happened. Please try to understand."

Fay sat unmoving. Pinchas sighed and told her about the bar mitzvah that was short one man for a *minyan*.

"They pleaded with me to stay," he said. "How could I refuse?"

"Very easily, by saying your wife and children were expecting you home for Shabbos."

Pinchas remembered how the woman had pleaded with him, and wondered if he could have found those words. He sighed again. How could he explain just how difficult it had been to refuse the request?

"What if I say I won't do such a thing again?" he said.

"No, next time it will be a different excuse. Clearly, others are more important to you than your family."

"We're all clean now!" the children called. "We're going to the kitchen."

Fay got up. "The children must have something to eat and drink."

Pinchas was left alone. Now what was he to do?

He had eaten very little that day in his haste to get home. They had left quietly, not wishing to disturb the family. As the sun rose, Jan had stopped the wagon and pulled to the side and made coffee. They ate the sandwiches that had been prepared for them by their hostess the night before. Later, midmorning, they stopped again for coffee and some leftover cake from the bar mitzvah. Now it was lunchtime and Pinchas was hungry. Hesitantly, he approached the kitchen.

The children smiled and erupted in a babble of voices.

"Sit down, Tatte!"

"Why didn't you come home for Shabbos?"

"We had such a nice morning. The sea is so wonderful."

It was Frieda who said, "We ate lunch on the beach. Did you eat lunch?"

Pinchas looked at his wife. His Faigy wouldn't let him go hungry. She was angry, true, but . . .

"Frieda, go to the pantry," Fay said. "There's some cold chicken left over from Shabbos and also some potato kugel and pickled cucumber. Bring it to the table."

Pinchas asked for bread, and he washed and ate. He listened as the children spoke of the beach and the people they had seen, and what fun it had been to ride behind the trotting horse.

When the children had finished eating, Fay said, "Leave your father to finish his meal. You know we didn't do the laundry this morning, so we had better get started." The girls groaned. "Now, do you think everything is going to get clean by itself? Boys, you know what to do. We want the house spic and span."

Pinchas watched as the children busied themselves with their tasks. Somehow, he had never been fully aware of the hard work that went into keeping house. He had always been at work or learning in the *shtiebel*, both back in the shtetl and in London.

Now he watched as clothes were hauled out, soaked, and scrubbed. He saw how they were hauled onto the washing lines in the backyard.

Faigy was doing all this work, as well as cooking and looking after the shop. No wonder she was dismayed that he hadn't arrived home on time. She had to cope with so much, and she'd been on her own for two weeks.

Yet how could he have refused to stay? What would have been the right thing to do?

The day passed with Fay saying little to Pinchas. The laundry dried quickly in the sun and was taken down. Supper was served, a simple meal of soup, and the children went to sleep. Then Fay took out the heavy iron, heated it on the stove, and began to go through the huge pile of creased, dry laundry. She tackled the children's clothing first and then took the clean clothes into the bedrooms.

Pinchas tried to talk to her, but her replies were monosyllabic. When she came back into the kitchen Pinchas said, "Sit down now. Rest for a while. Can I make some tea for you?"

"Oh, what's the use? Now you'll make tea for me. Then suddenly you'll be gone again, and return who knows when. Why did we ever leave home?"

Pinchas was at a loss. What could he say? London had been a terrible mistake, but now they were in this fine house. He was well again and enjoying this new experience of traveling through the beautiful countryside.

The children appeared to have settled down well. He thought that his wife was happy in this new land, yet now it seemed she longed for home, for the shtetl. How could they ever return?

"Do you wish we could go back home?" he asked.

"We should never have left. But to return? Foolishness! Why should I even think about it?"

Pinchas decided that the less said the better. Whatever he said only seemed to anger his wife. She bustled around the kitchen, making quick, jerky movements.

He stood up slowly and made his way to his room. He was tired after the day's journey—but somehow, he didn't think he'd be able to sleep.

Chapter 25

"Kingklip, sole, snoek . . . are also main local varieties . . . providing particularly delicious eating for those who are prepared to go to the harbor personally and purchase the fish absolutely fresh."

— T.V. Bulpin, *Discovering Southern Africa*, p. 13

The next morning Fay woke to a grey predawn. She tossed and turned, but sleep eluded her. As she stared at the ceiling, she remembered a conversation she'd had during the week with a customer.

"Oh, listen, I hear the wagon selling fish," the woman had said. "But I never buy from them. My husband goes out just as the sun is rising, when the fishing boats are just coming in. The prices are so cheap and the fish so fresh."

Pinchas and the children were asleep. Fay dressed and took a basket, then walked down a still, quiet Long Street to the docks.

She found the returning fishermen easily. The fish catch was being sold quickly to other early purchasers. Returning home, Fay found her family beginning to wake up. She placed the fish in the cool pantry and went through the usual morning routine, seeing the children had a good breakfast, checking their clothes, making sure they had food for the break.

By the time Pinchas and Jack returned from shul, she was already in the shop. It was beginning to get depressing, this sitting, waiting, hoping and serving just a trickle of customers. Still, she persevered.

Fay left the shop for a short while to serve her husband and son breakfast, and then she was once again back in the shop. By midday she had tired of sitting and waiting, and she thought of the fish in the pantry.

She would be able to hear the shop bell from the kitchen if anyone came while she was preparing the fish.

She had just finished frying the fish, when the shop bell rang. Without thinking, she hurried into the shop while holding the plate of fish in her hands.

A youth looked at the plate. "Oh, do you sell fried fish?" he asked. "Do you also sell chips? I remember how we used to eat fish and chips in London. How much?"

Fay was shocked when she realized that she was still holding the plate. The fish was for her family. She didn't know what to answer. She named a price that seemed exorbitant to her, so that the young man wouldn't want to buy it.

"Tuppence a slice," she said.

To her surprise, he bought not only a box of matches, but also two slices of fish.

Some time later two young men arrived, both wanting to buy a slice of fish. While they were there, they also made other small purchases. It seemed that news of the food was bringing young men from the nearby offices to the shop. Fay realized that at last she had found a way to entice customers.

She would have to continue selling fried fish. This would mean a long, early morning walk to the docks and back, and then all the work to prepare the fish. But she had no choice. She had to do this.

Early that same morning, Pinchas had gone to the factory filled with worry. He had happily taken the extra orders after the bar mitzvah, but these people were not on his route. Had it been wrong to accept their orders? Maybe another salesman traveled that route.

He went to the office and handed Mr. Isaacs the money and order book.

There was a long silence, then, "But these orders, these places weren't on your itinerary. How did you get them?"

Now what?

With trepidation, Pinchas told the story of how he had stayed on for the bar mitzvah.

"Well, I never," Mr. Isaacs said. "That is good. You received orders without even having to travel there!"

Pinchas gave a sigh of relief. What followed was even better.

"How would you like to continue with this work? It seems that although his leg will heal, my salesman no longer wants to travel. If you take on this work, he can work in our furniture shop down the road."

Pinchas could hardly agree fast enough. He sat as different routes were discussed. He listened to facts and figures, commissions on sales, times when it was best to travel, and best not to. When he was in town, he would visit the new suburbs that had sprouted up beside the railway line. Pinchas did his best to take it all in, marveling over the fact that his days in the dusty factory appeared to be permanently over.

Pinchas returned home in a buoyant mood. He couldn't wait to give Faigy the good news.

As he entered the house through the front door, Pinchas was surprised to see the shop was full of customers. He offered to help but was refused, so he went to the kitchen. The children were already home from school and eating.

"Oh, Tatte," little Samuel said, "we were told to always come in through the side gate and then into the kitchen, never through the shop."

"But of course that doesn't apply to you," David said to his father, giving his younger brother an angry look.

Frieda got up and put some leftover chicken and hot mashed potatoes on a dish.

"Your lunch, Tatte. I was told to give you lunch when you came in."

Pinchas ate, wondering at the sudden influx of customers. How had it happened?

By mid-afternoon the shop was quiet. Pinchas walked in, bursting with his news. To his dismay, Faigy's response was not what he had expected.

"What?" Fay cried. "You accepted this job, this constant travel, without even discussing it with me! I thought you were only going a few times! How many times must I be forced to sit alone at the Shabbos table, worrying about you? What about the children? Have you given any thought to the children?"

"But Faigy, it's not dangerous. Jan has been driving this route for many years. He knows the country well."

Pinchas was dismayed. All these years, his Faigy had been so amenable. She had even left the shtetl for him. Yes, there had been some arguments, but in the end she had agreed. Well, maybe it would have been better had she not agreed. Would he have gone on alone, intending to send for her? Would he have remained in London? Now, all these years later, he didn't know.

"I will keep traveling," Pinchas said firmly. "That's how it will be."

He had been so sure she would be happy that Mr. Isaacs trusted him enough to give him this position on a permanent basis. He felt diminished that his role as a wage earner was unappreciated.

Fay was furious that her future family life was going to revolve around the worry of her husband's long journeys. How could he have agreed to such a thing without first discussing it with her? First he had accepted that one trip. Then she had accepted that he would travel just until the previous salesman returned. It was difficult, but she could endure it. After all, what choice did she have? But now, this! It would be permanent, forever! She couldn't do this.

Did he really think, after all she had done for him, that she should be alone, worrying, week after week, while his life was in danger as he traveled to faraway places?

As if by mutual consent, no further discussion took place, but the anger remained.

Throughout that week, they spoke to each other only when necessary.

The children were too busy adapting to their new way of life to notice. They went to school. They walked home together, ate, did homework, and then played in the backyard, reveling in their own little patch of greenery.

Fay was worried about the shop. Though at lunch time the little shop was crowded with office workers buying not only fresh fried fish, but also tobacco and even groceries to carry home at the end of the day, the rest of the time the shop was mostly empty.

True, Pinchas had said he would be earning nicely, but life had taught her not to rely on him. She had done so in the past, and the results had not been good. Now, though, it was even worse. He would constantly be traveling, constantly facing danger. She must find a way to make the shop a busy place.

One of her Jewish customers had said to her, "Mrs. Levine, I notice that you close your shop on Shabbos. I don't like to interfere, but here, things are different. Here the shops are open on Shabbos. That's the busiest day of the week. My husband, he would never have done this back home, but here, he goes to his shop on Shabbos morning. He makes in that one morning more than he does the rest of the week."

Another customer had walked in and the conversation had ended, but Fay kept thinking about it. She wished she could discuss this with Pinchas, but a simmering anger prevented her from speaking to him.

She, who had grown up as the *rav*'s oldest daughter, who had always loved Shabbos—could she really violate Shabbos in such a way? Could she do such a thing after all the miracles that Hashem had done for her?

She thought of Jack's stamps, of the empty cabins on the ship, of Mr. Davidoff finding them at the docks. One after another, Hashem had brought about these events. Now, after so many miracles, to violate Shabbos! Besides, her dear husband would be far away, facing danger. How could she even think of breaking these precious laws while davening fervently for his safety? Impossible! Yet, despite the ludicrousness of the woman's words, they continued to trouble her.

Of course, she would never violate Shabbos. This morning, more customers had entered her shop than ever before. She would earn whatever she could the rest of the week, and she would never tell her husband that she had considered following this woman's advice, even for just a moment. How could she have harbored such thoughts? Shame overtook her.

Fay wondered if her husband knew just how much he owed their oldest son. Had she told him about selling the stamps? She couldn't remember. Those days of preparing to leave England were a blurred jumble of images. Pinchas had been so ill and she had been so worried about the voyage, wondering all the time if instead of traveling yet further from her family she should simply return to the shtetl and all that was familiar to her.

Looking back, if she had only realized then how well everything would turn out, she would not have worried so. But without Jack none of this would have happened. They would not have had money to leave. Besides, even if they had managed to leave, their belongings would have been stolen upon arrival if not for Jack's quick thinking.

The commotion Jack had caused by loosening the horse's harness had brought them to Mr. Davidoff's attention, and so they had been led to this house. Where else would they have stayed?

Fay thought hard. She had a debt to her oldest son, and all debts must be repaid.

Once she would have confided her worries to her husband. Now, so many months later, she was a different person. Adversity had toughened her. She would work something out.

But first, she had to make peace with Pinchas. How could she allow him to leave on a dangerous journey when there was so much tension between them?

When the shop was quiet, she went to their room, where he was sitting and learning. She hoped she would hear the shop bell.

"I'm sorry I spoke in haste," she said. "It's true I fear for you when you travel. I would prefer for you to remain here, with us. But if this is how it's meant to be, so be it."

Pinchas gave a sigh of relief. His old, gentle Faigy was back.

"I wouldn't do this if there was risk," he said. "I care too much for you. I care too much for the children. Please believe me when I say that I take every precaution."

"But your health!"

"Do I seem ill to you? Do you not see that the travel is good for me?"

Fay looked carefully at him. His cheeks were rosy and he had even put on some weight. Slowly, she felt herself reassess the situation. For some strange reason, this travel was good for him, although she couldn't fathom why.

"We'll manage while you are away," she said. "But please, remember always that each day I pray for your safe return. Do nothing that is risky."

A few days later the cart with the furniture to be transported up country arrived. Pinchas wore his old work clothes for the long, dusty journey. As they approached the village where his first customer lived, he would change into his new suit.

Jan waited patiently as each child said a solemn goodbye and Fay handed over a package of food for the journey. Then Pinchas was off, his heart full of joy, to be traveling again to the marvelous freedom of the hinterland.

Fay returned with the children to the house and looked them over carefully before sending them off to school. She wanted to talk to Jack, but by the time the last child had left for school, he was also gone.

She went to the shop, expecting the day to proceed as usual. But that day only brought fresh troubles of an unexpected nature.

Chapter 26

"Written in 1891: Our brethren generally live in peace and tranquility, and enjoy the light of freedom and liberty undisturbed. The English flag upon which freedom and equality for each man, irrespective of faith and religion, is boldly inscribed flies everywhere in the Cape Colony."
— Gideon Shimoni, *Jews and Zionism*, p. 8

Samuel was a quiet boy. As he slowly adapted to the new school, he became more confident. That day, he was proud of his father for going off so boldly into the vast interior that they had learned about in school. His hand shot up as every question was asked. The teacher was pleased. The boys in his class were less so.

"Showoff, little Jew boy," said a boy who until then had been the star pupil.

When they left the classroom, the boy grabbed Samuel by his shirt and punched him fiercely.

Samuel ran to his family at the gate. He had a bruised eye, a bleeding lip, and a torn shirt.

The Levine children were shocked when they saw him.

"What happened? Does it hurt?"

Samuel wanted only to get away from the school, to the safety of his home.

"Later, I'll tell you later," he said. "Let's go now."

As soon as the children arrived home, Frieda went to the shop to call her mother. Normally, she knew her mother shouldn't be disturbed, but this was urgent.

Fay saw the expression on Frieda's face even before she spoke, and hurried toward her.

"Samuel is hurt!" Frieda said.

Fay gasped when she saw Samuel. She quickly sat him down and gave him water.

"Sip this slowly," she said. "I'll put cream on to make you feel better. Soon you'll be feeling fine."

Fay gently took off the torn shirt and dressed her small son in a warm sweater.

"Frieda, make some tea for all of us," she said. "Now Samuel, tell me what happened."

"It happened when we were leaving school, just when we came outside.

A boy said, 'So you think you're so clever, Jew boy?' He pulled my shirt so hard it tore. Then he hit me twice. I saw everyone at the gate waiting for me, and I ran to them. I thought he was my friend. Why did he do that to me?"

Frieda was crying. "What could I do? I didn't know what to do. So I thought we better just come home."

Fay wished Pinchas was home. She had no idea how to deal with this. Should she take her children out of that school? Was there truly no Jewish school in this place? If the Jews here had such a fine shul, surely they also had a fine Jewish school.

Her sweet Samuel hurt so. Had not Pinchas left the shtetl because he feared violence from the peasants? Avraham Cohen had written that there had never been a pogrom in England, yet here, in a British colony, there was violence? Had Pinchas really wanted to leave because he feared violence? Was there not a quite different reason?

His pride had been hurt when he overheard gossip in shul about her sister and the yeshiva *bachur* who had really been intended for Faigy. He didn't want to be thought of as the man who had married the bride who had been spurned.

The old anger, which had never truly left her, welled up once again inside her. Then she pulled herself together. This was not the time for such thoughts. Samuel needed her.

As she went to collect water from the tap, she called to Frieda, "Go to my room. You'll see a small calico bag on the chest of drawers. Bring it to me."

Frieda rushed to get it. Fay took a soft, clean cloth, dipped it in water, and softly bathed the torn lip. From the bag she took a salve and carefully smoothed it over the injured lips and around the bruised eye.

"Well, tell me," she said. "Did such things happen before? Were there bad words about Jews and you kept it from me?"

"No, never!" Joseph said. "I'm the only Jewish boy in my class, but everyone has been friendly."

Frieda spoke up. "I don't like standing outside while they learn scriptures each morning, but otherwise I like the school. The girls are friendly."

"I don't want to go back," Samuel cried. "Why didn't the other boys stop him? They just watched and laughed."

"In London, some boys threw stones at us," Frieda said. "Jack punched one of the boys and they ran away. We were never bothered again. Jack will know what to do."

Fay was horrified. Why hadn't she known of this? Pinchas had said the peasants back home would make trouble for the Jews. Yet, from what she had gathered from her mother's letters, they had not made trouble, while here, under English rule, her children had been attacked. Here, where the flag of England flew on flagpoles, her little Samuel had returned home with a torn and bloody shirt and an eye that was rapidly turning blue and black.

"Jack will know what to do," Frieda had said. How could he?

Well, she certainly hoped that Jack would know what to do, since she was reluctant to speak to her Jewish neighbor, who was apparently satisfied with the school.

Jack's reaction, when Fay discussed the matter with him, was unexpected.

"Send them to a Jewish school?" he said. "If there is one, why does our Jewish neighbor send her children to this school?"

"But look at poor Samuel. He can't go back there. What can we do?"

"Look, do you think such things never happened in London—not in school, but on the streets, on the way home from school? We knew how to put a stop to it. I'll talk to David and Joseph and we'll come up with a plan. I think you should give each of them extra food for the break, and they'll say that their little brother forgot it at home and they must take it to him."

Fay nodded apprehensively, and Jack went to speak to his brothers. "Tomorrow, Mother will give each of you an extra packet of food. When it's break time for the little ones, tell the teacher that Samuel forgot his package and you must give it to him. I don't think they'll refuse. Then find him and find the boy who hurt him. Remember how I protected you from the boys in London who hurt you? Now you must protect Samuel. Don't hurt the boy, or you'll be in trouble, but scare him. Understand?"

They understood only too well. Jack hoped they would succeed. He hoped that this bully would be as easily cowed into submission as those rough boys had been in London.

If not, he would have to ask for time off from work, and he was reluctant to do that. He enjoyed work and the increasing responsibility he was being given. Most of all, he enjoyed the money he was able to bring home.

Next, he spoke to his little brother. "Samuel, listen to me. You must be brave and go to school tomorrow. You'll be safe in the classroom. The teacher won't allow any nonsense in the room. Right?"

"But afterwards, in the playground . . ."

"Don't worry. As soon as the bell rings for your break time, David and Joseph will be there. They'll look after you. You can't stay away, or the other boys will think Jews are always afraid. They must learn that it isn't so."

The following day, Samuel went to school, although somewhat reluctantly. It was a quiet journey to school, with each child deep in thought.

When Jack returned home, he went right away into the bedroom where his brothers were sitting and doing their homework.

Before he could ask what had happened, Samuel ran up to him.

"David and Joseph came," he said. "They said, 'Hey, boy, yesterday you called our little brother 'a showoff Jew boy,' and you hit him with fists. Come now and see what it feels like to have a Jew boy hit you with his fists.' Well, he ran away so fast. You just can't believe how he ran. Now he leaves me alone."

Jack felt pleased with himself. Without even going to the school he had solved that problem.

David and Joseph were beaming.

"It worked just like you said," David said. "We didn't even have to touch him."

"Did anyone ask about Samuel and his black eye?"

"You know Mr. Thorner, the headmaster?" Joseph said. "Well, he teaches our class history. At the end of class he called me to stay behind and said, 'Yesterday I saw a little problem after school. I was going to see to it later today, but I was just about to go into the playground when I saw how you and your brother solved it. So for now, I think, unless there's trouble again, we'll leave things as they are. More effective, I think.' And you know what? I think he's right."

Jack thought about bullies and how scared they became if anyone challenged them. "I don't think that boy, or anyone else, will try anything like that again. But if anything happens again, come straight to me. I'll deal with it. Even if they only use bad words, come to me. Bad words lead to bad deeds."

Jack thought back to his days at school in London. He remembered the headmaster telling him that he was heading for a university scholarship.

Well, that was all over now. He had to work and earn money. He would never go to university. Besides, *was* there a university here, in this faraway place?

Oh, well. That was all in the past. Right now, the main thing was that Samuel was safe.

Chapter 27

"The old-fashioned way of acquiring clothes was to purchase material and make them at home or patronise a tailor or dressmaker. Both tailors and dressmakers were often employed in shops to make what we call 'custom made' garments ... but there was no mass production of identical garments."

— Mendel Kaplan, *Jewish Roots in the South African Economy*, p. 226

After delivering the furniture that had been ordered, Pinchas and Jan covered new territory, traveling to Lindeshof, Greyton, and Bereaville. The journey was arduous. The distance between villages was greater, sometimes necessitating sleeping outside in vast, empty spaces. Pinchas had found it frightening the first time he had to sleep in the wagon, but as Jan kept the fire going throughout the night to keep away wild animals, and the clear air around him allowed him to breathe easily, he came to enjoy the experience.

He kept thinking about his family. What had Faigy done about finding Jack a Jewish school? How was she managing on Shabbos without him? How were the little ones doing at school?

As soon as he returned home, his first question was about Jack. Fay parried the question.

"Soon it will be Rosh Hashanah," she said. "Now is not the time to make inquiries about such things. Things are different here. They don't begin school after our new year, like they did in London. The time to inquire here is when the non-Jewish New Year falls out."

The truth was, she hadn't been able to find out if there was a Jewish school. Yet she was sure there must be one.

Pinchas wanted to argue that surely now, well before the non-Jewish New Year, was the time to make inquiries, but he had too much to do. He had to go to the office and deliver the money, and then discuss the new orders. He stifled his comments for the time being and hurried to the office.

Mr. Isaacs received him in his office and once again seemed more than satisfied with the trip's outcome. He paid Pinchas the money he owed him, and they discussed the upcoming *yamim tovim* and how to time the trips so Pinchas would be home in time.

As Pinchas left the office he thought about the money he had been paid. He was delighted when he realized that he had sufficient money to pay for new clothes for Faigy and the children. They would all have new outfits, really special outfits, smart enough for that fancy Gardens shul.

As soon as Pinchas arrived home, he gave the money to Fay, holding onto enough to pay for new suits for the boys. As soon as Jack returned from work, Pinchas and his boys made their way to the tailor whom Mr. Isaacs had used for his suit.

Pinchas wondered why Mr. Isaacs had sent him to a Malay tailor. Were there no Jewish tailors here? In the shtetl, there had always been at least one Jewish tailor. In London there had been many, but even their low prices had been too much for Pinchas. He had made good use of the second-hand stalls when he needed anything. But he had been pleased with the suit the tailor here had made for him, and so he would take his sons there as well.

As they walked up the hill together, David looked around.

"You know, this is where that loud chanting comes from every evening," he said.

Jan had explained the reason for the chanting to Pinchas.

"It's the call to prayers," he said. "You can't really hear it during the day, but at night, when all is quiet, the sound travels as far as our street."

The streets were quiet when they entered. Then quite suddenly, the street was filled with boys of all sizes, some walking and others running.

"Reminds me of when we finished *cheder* for the day," Jack said.

Soon they were at the tailor's rooms.

"My boys need new suits," Pinchas said.

"Ah, so this time you pay," the man said. He wondered if Pinchas knew how much this would cost. As he showed them different materials, he told them how much each suit would cost.

The boys had never had a suit specially made for them. In London, the family had made judicious use of the market and its second-hand clothing stall. They had also received free suits every year at school. They were awed by the tailor and the rolls of fabric in the shop, by the many choices he offered them and the way he measured them as they stood still.

The tailor knew that this man was clearly a newcomer to Cape Town. The boys looked ill at ease, as if they had no idea what to choose. So he guided the boys gently to sensible choices, just as he had done for their father only a short while before.

Surely the man had a wife and daughters, the tailor thought.

"My wife is a fine dressmaker," he said. "The ladies do not like to travel about, so my wife goes to their homes with swatches of material and drawings of the latest styles. Maybe your wife would like her to visit? Do you also have daughters? Would they not like new dresses?"

Pinchas knew better than to make such a decision without consulting Faigy.

"I'll talk to her," he said. "If she is agreeable, I will come to you and we can make arrangements."

Pinchas waited until he could find time when he was alone with Fay, but it wasn't easy. The next day, he hoped to talk to her at lunchtime, but then he heard his wife say to Frieda, "Stand at the door, just inside the shop. Call me as soon as anyone comes in."

He sat with the children and watched as Fay hurriedly ate her meal, and then quickly bentched and returned to the shop, sending Frieda to continue with her meal.

Oh, my Faigy, do you never rest? he thought to himself.

It was only late in the evening, when the last child had left the kitchen, that he had a chance to talk about the dressmaker.

Fay was relieved, but was silent for a moment. She'd had absolutely no idea how to get new clothes in this strange place. She knew the ins and outs of her shop, she knew about the children's school, and she knew where the fishermen brought their catch at the docks down the road.

Yet she knew nothing about where to purchase clothes.

In the shtetl, she'd had plenty of time to make everything she needed. Her mother had taught her not only how to cook and clean, but also how to sew. In London, tired from the arduous cleaning needed each day, from drying clothes in the small, confined space and caring for her children, she had no time nor energy to sew. She had bought clothes at the market in Petticoat Lane, at the secondhand stall, then washed and ironed and mended everything so that they looked new — well, nearly new.

Here she was in the shop all day. She dared not leave. What if someone came in while she was away? She needed every customer.

There were offices nearby, and shops, and it seemed that the fame of her fried fish had spread. Workers came at lunchtime; they bought fish and a few other things.

In the morning and afternoons it was quieter, but people in the neighborhood could see people streaming in and out of the little house at lunchtime, and they were starting to realize how convenient it was to shop nearby.

Each day Fay walked to the docks before sunrise to purchase fish, and then returned home to fry the fresh fish in batter, even before the rest of her household was awake. Her days were long, but slowly, as more and more customers came, she began to hope that soon she would be able to pay off her debt to Mr. Davidoff. At least they were now paying rent for the house. Bit by bit, life was improving.

Pinchas watched as Fay sat, stock-still. Was she annoyed that he had interfered with what was normally her domain? It was difficult to know these days what would please his wife and what would cause her annoyance, even anger!

Fay was thinking. The girls needed new clothes. In this land, with its plentiful food and sunshine, their dresses were getting too small. Even she needed new clothes.

At last, Fay came out of here reverie.

"What a good idea! She will come right here to our home? How good of her!"

Pinchas was relieved. Life was resuming its old patterns, where he made the decisions.

◁═

The dressmaker came late one afternoon. Her hair was covered with a brightly colored scarf.

Fay, standing at the entrance, saw a small cart. A young girl was holding the reins. Her hair too was covered by a scarf. Fay remembered how back home, many women covered their hair with a scarf. She immediately felt relaxed and at ease.

Before Fay could say anything, the dressmaker said, "My daughter has come to help me bring everything inside. Then she will stay with the horse and cart, to keep it safe. A good girl, my daughter!"

Fay looked at the cart. "Did you come from far away?"

"Oh no, we live just up the road, in the Malay quarter." She pointed toward the conical mountain. "There, on the slopes of Signal Hill, just up the road! Easy coming down! A bit more effort needed going up that slope, I can tell you!"

Samples of materials were brought into the house and then heavy books of fashion pictures were brought up the steps, through the shop and into the girls' room.

The young girl returned to the cart, and now the dressmaker began to show Fay different materials. There was stiff cotton, striped pink and white, soft cotton with small bunches of flowers on a white background, and a delicate blue material with feather-like swirls.

Fay worried about stains showing up on such pale materials.

"Do you have anything in darker colors? It would be more serviceable, I think."

"Oh no, Mother," Bertha said. "These are so pretty."

"We will be so careful," Frieda said.

Even little Ethel and Rose joined in. "So pretty. Yes, so pretty!"

"Just like the other girls at school wear," Frieda added.

It seemed that the quiet children from London had become independent minded. Well, what could she say? This was where they now lived. If that was the way things were, who was she to fight it?

Frieda chose the blue material. "So soft," she said, stroking it.

Bertha liked the crisp striped cotton. Ethel and Rose both liked the small flowers on the white background. Ethel chose the sample with lavender flowers, and Rose the deep pink.

Once the material had been chosen, a large book with various designs was opened.

The pictures showed huge, puffed sleeves ending in a tight long cuff, with dainty white collars of different designs. Fay thought those huge puffy sleeves were a waste of material, but Frieda spoke up once again.

"Oh, please, Mother, that's what the other girls wear at school."

When the dressmaker showed where the hem would be, a good few inches above their ankles, Fay was about to object, but once again there was a chorus of "Oh, please, that's what the other girls wear at school."

Only then did Fay realize she had paid no attention to their clothing, only that it should be clean and ironed. Did her children feel strange, different from everyone else? She must pay more attention in the future to such matters.

Fay herself was persuaded to choose a silky black material, with even more puffy sleeves but a narrow cuff. The large collar of lace-edged silk caused a moment of concern.

"That collar, the lace, what will it add to the cost?" she asked.

"Now don't worry," the dressmaker said. "Instead of that lace, I'll make a little frill, with the same material. It looks just as fine."

The skirt was long and full, to the ground, and for that Fay gave a sigh of relief. What would she have done if she had been told that the new fashion was shorter now for adults too? She nodded her agreement.

"You wear that in the shop?" The dressmaker pointed to the simple dress Fay was wearing.

"Why, is there something wrong with it?" Fay was hurt.

"No, but you need something different, something more like we wear here."

Fay found herself agreeing to a dress of dark navy cotton and a narrow white cotton collar.

Then the dressmaker looked at the girls. "Those dresses they wear now — they wear them to school?"

The girls nodded. She looked at them.

"The other girls, their dresses are different?"

Once again, the girls nodded.

"No, that is not good. I will make another dress for each one, with special material, not so expensive."

Yet another batch of fabric samples was pulled out from the pile on the bed.

"See, this is good material for every day — strong and good for washing. Look at this, a nice dark blue, pretty, but not so dark as the dresses they now wear."

Fay was upset. Why had she not thought of that? Had her girls been ashamed?

"Yes, they should each have a dress for school," she said. She hoped there was sufficient money for all these purchases.

When it was all added up, she was relieved to see that Pinchas had left her with more than enough money.

"You have gloves?" the dressmaker asked. When Fay looked quizzically at her, she said, "For the synagogue, for your new year, the women and girls wear gloves."

So the delighted girls found themselves awaiting the imminent arrival of two new dresses each, as well as the promise of fine white gloves.

When Pinchas arrived home some time later, he was met by a gaggle of excited girls.

"She came, and she brought..."

"Pink flowers, so pretty, and also..."

"Gloves... white gloves from the shop on Adderley Street..."

"Tatte, thank you. Mother said that you..."

Pinchas was happy. He was spending these few weeks delivering furniture in the Cape Town area, to the new suburbs that had grown up along the railway line. He enjoyed seeing the little villages by the seaside. Fay was more relaxed now that he was home every night and she didn't have to worry about him. For the moment, there were no sleepless nights or the terrible dreams when she finally did fall asleep.

That Sunday, Pinchas took the family by train to Muizenberg, where the warm sea met the pure white sands. Even Faigy came.

It hadn't been easy getting her to join them.

Pinchas had planned the day as a surprise. On Thursday, when returning to town, he had brought fruit. When he came home, he had quietly placed the package in the far corner of the pantry.

He also carried a large package. Inside it were hats. He had seen a young boy standing by the roadside, selling hats woven from straw. He had carefully selected one for each child, so that they would not burn when sitting in the sun for so long. He took the package into the bedroom and placed it in his drawer.

On Friday afternoon he returned from the final delivery later than usual. This delivery had proved troublesome. The wardrobe they had delivered wobbled when they stood it in the bedroom. Since Pinchas always traveled with his carpentry tools, he spent some time adjusting the base, until it was perfect.

Since he had to get ready hurriedly for Shabbos, there was no time to discuss his plans for Sunday with Fay. After Havdalah would be a good time, he told himself.

How was he to know that by the time the kitchen was cleared, Fay would disappear into the shop and tell everyone she was not to be disturbed? She needed to do some accounting, to make sure she had enough stock. Thankfully, the week had been so busy that there had been no time to do this before.

By the time she had finished, Pinchas, who had been trying to stay awake, was fast asleep.

Early Sunday morning, he awoke to find Fay already in the kitchen, with the children seated around the table.

"I have a big surprise for you today," he said. "I found a beautiful place, where the land meets the sea. There are miles of soft white sand, and a few houses and shops, and in the summer it's filled with people swimming in the sea. It's called Muizenberg.

"It's warm enough for us to sit on the sand even though it's too cold to swim. Right near the sea, there's a railway station. We can go by train from the station near here, right to the sea. We can spend all day there."

He expected a chorus of excitement, and that he received. Faigy's response, however, was quite different from what he'd expected.

"Impossible. What will you eat, out on the sands all day?"

"I bought plenty of fruit, and you always have *challah* left over from Shabbos. I also bought special hats, to shade against the sun. Wait, I will fetch them."

Fay looked even angrier now. "So you'll all go off and leave me to do the laundry alone?"

"Laundry?" Pinchas suddenly looked bemused.

How selfish he was, Fay thought to herself. Hadn't he noticed that on Sunday, when he sat immersed in learning, the older girls helped with the laundry, while Jack and the other children cleaned the house and then went to the Gardens?

"Yes, the sheets and towels and clothing must be done. When else do I have the time? Today you'll all go off and I'll have to do everything by myself!"

There was a heavy silence in the room. Then Frieda spoke up.

"Mother, of course we won't go with the others. We'll stay and help like always. Won't we?" She looked across the table at Bertha.

Fay heard the sad resignation in her daughter's voice. She saw as Bertha, her eyes beginning to fill with tears, murmured, "Yes."

It was more than Fay could bear. She could not let the two girls give up this pleasure. "Very well. We will all go. I can't have you two miss out on what your Tatte planned for you. The laundry, well . . . well, we'll do it during the week."

Even as Fay spoke, she knew this was foolish. When would there be time during the week? But the excited babble of her children's voices surrounded her, and she hastily sliced the leftover *challah*, filled two bottles with freshly boiled water, and carefully checked that windows were closed and doors were locked before they set out for the train station.

Pinchas was kept busy, getting the family to the station, buying tickets, seating everyone, keeping a lookout as one station followed another, supervising everyone as they got off the train, and finally, leading the way to the soft white sands.

As the children frolicked near the water, he looked at his Faigy, sitting on a blanket on the sand, surrounded by children's discarded socks and shoes. She looked less than happy. Why?

He left his place near the water's edge, seeing the children were in no danger, and went to sit beside his wife. "Faigy, why are you not happy?"

"Me, not happy? What a question! Of course I'm exceptionally pleased with the way this day has gone! Of course, there will be no clean sheets this week, and what will the children wear to school, with the laundry still waiting to be done? But of course, by tomorrow you'll be far away, so this can't bother you."

Pinchas was taken aback. "But you said you would come with us, that the girls needn't stay home. They said they would stay and help, if you wanted."

"Oh, and then they would work all day, and everyone would come back home and they would have to hear about the marvelous time! How could I do that to them?"

"Now that I travel, I earn enough money. Can you not see that? Was there not sufficient money for fine new clothing? Why must you continue with the shop? It's too much for you, with all the work in the house."

"Oh, such a clever solution! What about my commitment to Mr. Davidoff to run the shop? What about the dangers every time you travel? During the day, I'm too busy to think, but at night . . ." Fay paused for a moment, then continued. "Do you remember London? There I depended only on you. Now your money is good, true, but so is the money from the shop."

Pinchas was too taken aback to answer. He hadn't thought about the laundry. He only knew that everything was always clean and crisp, from tablecloths to clothing. But there was more to this outburst. He felt safe on his travels. Jan was so competent. He'd been taking these trips for so many years. It had never occurred to him that to Faigy, he was in danger every time he left home.

For some time he sat silently by her side, thinking. Eventually he said, "About the sheets and towels — we can use them as they are another week. How can that hurt us? About the clothes for the children, well, you told me that the first dresses arrived, the ones for the girls to wear for school. Let them wear them this week. Why wait until after Rosh Hashanah like you planned? I don't know about the boys. Do they not have even one spare shirt? Don't worry about my shirts. The hotels we stay at will do laundry if you pay them."

Fay was annoyed. Didn't this husband of hers realize that somehow, during the week, the laundry would have to be done? Everything dried quickly in the sunny backyard, but when would she wash it?

"Oh, that's all so easy. So everyone has something to wear for the next few days. But still, everything must be washed this week. When can I do that? I get up before dawn to go to the docks. I must fry the fish and get food for the children before I open the shop. By the time the shop closes it's already dark. Please, don't give me any more surprises like this one."

"I never thought. I . . . I . . . isn't there anyone who can come and help?"

"Who can I ask? Back home, there was always someone to help. Family, friends, even my mother, though she was always busy herself. Who can I ask here?"

Pinchas was flummoxed. He thought of the houses where he was a guest during Shabbos. He knew that the womenfolk helped in their husband's shops. How did they manage with the home and the shop? But they were only helping out in the shops, he realized. They weren't the only person in charge.

"We could pay someone to help," he said. "There is spare money."

Fay realized that at least Pinchas now realized the problem and was doing his best to find a solution. Yet where was she to find such a person?

"Oh, that's wonderful. Someone will appear miraculously and do all my laundry for me! I won't have laundry to worry about, only your safety. Just marvelous!"

"You worry about me, but why? Did I not tell you how capable my driver is?"

"You think I'm a fool to believe that? Why do they pay you so much, just to deliver a few bits and pieces? It must be because the work is dangerous and no one else will do it."

Now, for the first time, Pinchas took the trouble to explain how he took orders, big orders that were important. He was not only paid a good weekly salary, but also some extra money for every order.

"But the danger, is it worth it?" was the response.

"Many people send their children here to the Cape to be educated, once they're a bit older. The schools inland are only for the younger children. Would they send away their children, who have to travel back and forth at least three times a year, if it was so dangerous?"

"Yidden also do this?" Fay was not convinced.

"Of course! They want their children to be well educated. Do we not want that for our children? Why should they be any different just because they live far away from this large town?"

Pinchas began to talk about his travels, about the people he met, about the wondrous land and its beauty.

Fay spoke about the shop, and how the fish she fried brought in new customers.

They watched the children run in and out of the waves, shrieking. After a while, they called the children and sat them around the blanket. As they passed food around, they warned, "Careful, don't let the sand get in your food."

Then they bentched loudly and clearly, alone on the endless sands, with the blue sea and the white foamy waves, before making their way home.

Another long trip lay ahead for Pinchas. Fay would once again be alone, yet after that day by the seaside, their relationship was once again firm.

There were problems, to be sure, but somehow they would be overcome.

How could they have known that new challenges would come, once again bringing turmoil and bad feelings?

Chapter 28

"The coloured population increases year by year ... the vast majority
being in the Cape Province. Their grievances are their low economic
income and the political discrimination which they suffer."

— C. Ziervogel, *Brown South Africa*, p. 19

Pinchas returned on Wednesday, just days before Rosh
Hashanah, which fell out on Shabbos and Sunday. That meant he could
take the money and new orders to the factory on Thursday, and spend
Friday preparing for Yom Tov.

He realized now that for the Yamim Noraim, he would have to go
to the Gardens shul. He would have to endure the quietly restraining
hands that his sons occasionally put on his arm, when his thoughts and
prayers overtook his body and he began to sway as he prayed with fervor.

However, as he walked down the avenue, on the first day of the new
year, his Faigy seemed more like her old self, preening in her new clothes.
Like him, she was watching their children with pride. The girls wore
dresses with white collars. They had ribbons in their hair and white gloves.

The older boys had suits similar to his. The younger boys wore
slightly shorter trousers, and suits with a sailor collar. As they walked
up the avenue to shul, they looked quite different from the family that
had walked just one year ago to the small *shtiebel* in London.

Although Pinchas had been at the Gardens shul many times with
Jack and David, this was the first time he would be there with his
whole family. He was determined to concentrate on standing still and
davening quietly. He didn't want to disgrace himself in front of Faigy
and the girls, and in front of his younger boys who now walked into

the men's section with him and their older brothers.

By the time the service was halfway through, this discipline had become almost automatic, and he was able to concentrate properly on his prayers.

After the service, as they walked home under the large oak trees, the girls were ecstatic.

"We could see everything," Frieda told him. "Here the ladies sit upstairs and look down. They don't sit behind a curtain."

He heard them talking among themselves. "Did you see how those girls looked at our dresses? Huh, I bet they thought we would wear the same dresses we wear to school!"

"Yes, and don't you think ours were the prettiest by far?" Bertha said.

Pinchas gave Faigy an amused glance. Oh, there was plenty of time for them to realize that shul was for davening, not for admiring clothes. He was earning enough money to make his family happy. That was all that was important to him.

Right after Yom Kippur, Pinchas and his sons began building a *sukkah* with wood that Mr. Isaacs had given them. Pinchas had asked to buy some, but Mr. Isaacs had shaken his head.

"Oh, it's only discards," he said. "You may as well have them. I'll have Jan deliver them to your house."

Of the children, only Jack could remember a time when they had their very own *sukkah*. In London, Pinchas had used the shul *sukkah*. Now, the children watched in amazement as the *sukkah* was built.

Pinchas had been a bit worried about being required to work over Chol Hamoed. He was very relieved when he was given those days as a holiday.

The days of Sukkos were a delight. True, although Pinchas had wanted Faigy to close her shop it had remained open during Chol Hamoed, but Pinchas and the children ate all their meals in the *sukkah*. Pinchas and the older boys even slept in the *sukkah*, in spite of Faigy's voluble complaints that Pinchas would make himself ill again. But he stayed well, and eventually she stopped nagging.

For Fay, too, Sukkos was a delight. After the difficult years of trying to feed her family with the pittance that Pinchas had brought home, she reveled in the marvels she was able to provide.

Fish and meat were more than affordable. Exotic fruits they had never seen before—papaya, peaches, and grapes—were so cheap that they seemed to be everyday fare. They supplemented Faigy's marvelous fish, chicken soup, chopped liver, steaming potato kugels, and carrot puddings. Fay outdid herself, and the family, following their father's lead, praised her. Meanwhile, sitting in his own *sukkah*, surrounded by his family, Pinchas once again became expansive as he sang *zemiros* and told stories.

He felt fitter than ever. Unlike the shtetl, where Sukkos heralded winter and snow, or England, where the rain became more persistent, here, in this new land, it was getting warmer, not colder. Winter, with its occasional rain, was behind them. The sun shone. The *sukkah* was a warm and pleasant place to be in.

Early one morning, right after the *chagim*, Pinchas left again with Jan. He was happy with the way the family had celebrated together, but troubled because he could see that for his wife, it had not been a holiday at all. She had to cook extra dishes and serve them in the *sukkah*, and she was busy with the shop as well. She looked tired. Had she lost weight?

Pinchas remembered the conversation they'd had about the laundry, weeks before. Sundays were for laundry. Yet the second day of Rosh Hashanah had been on a Sunday, and so had Simchas Torah. How had she managed? She must have worked from early in the morning to late at night. How had he not noticed? No wonder she was not quite looking her usual self.

The problem of getting help had not been solved. He had left it to her to find someone, but where would she find time for such a task? Every hour of her day seemed to be taken up.

Now he had to concentrate on his customers and take back a full book of orders. When he returned, he would set his mind to solving the problem.

Pinchas greeted Jan with as much of a smile as he could muster, but Jan saw through it.

"Your festivals were not good? You are troubled?"

Suddenly, Pinchas wanted to share his woes with someone.

"My wife works so hard, in the shop, in the house, and there is so little I can do to help her," he said.

Jan also had problems. His daughter Lettie had begun to work for wealthy people newly arrived from England. She was unhappy.

"I do their laundry, I wash all their dishes, and then, what do they do?" she had said. "They give me a special cup and plate and cutlery to use. If I'm clean enough to wash their dishes, why am I not clean enough to eat from them? I'm the only worker there. All day I'm alone—no one to talk to, just work, work, work!"

"Who cleans your house?" Jan asked Pinchas. "Who lays the fire? Who prepares the food? Who does your laundry and ironing?"

"Why do you ask? My wife, of course, and the older girls sometimes help her."

"All those children to care for, and the house to clean and the cooking and the laundry and the shop, and your wife has no one to help her? No, surely not."

Jan thought momentarily of his daughter. Since Pinchas treated him as an equal, he felt that in Pinchas's home, his daughter too would be treated with respect.

"My daughter, she's a good girl ... she could do all that work for you."

"What? But we are not a family with much money. Does she work now? What is she paid?"

Pinchas was amazed to learn that with his salary he could indeed afford to hire someone to help. But would Faigy agree?

They had only traveled a very short distance, so Jan stopped the cart and said, "Go now, ask your wife if my Lettie can work for her."

Fay was astounded when Pinchas entered the shop, only a few moments after he had left. When he told her about Lettie, Fay wanted to say no, to stop her husband from interfering, but the thought of all the laundry that would have to be done by the end of the week made her pause.

"Tell Jan I would be happy if his daughter could help with the laundry," she said.

Pinchas didn't want to force her to agree to let the girl do all the housework, like she did in the other house she worked in. Maybe the girl would agree to do just the laundry. He ran back to the cart and repeated his wife's words.

Jan was disappointed, but then he said, "That's good for a start. When she sees how well my Lettie works, she'll take her for more than just laundry. We'll pass District Six on our way out. Lettie is home. She refused to go to work today. I'll run and tell her to go to your house. It will only cause a very small delay."

An hour later, Lettie entered the lives of the Levine family.

She entered the shop dressed in her Sunday best and carrying her work clothes in a bag.

Fay saw her enter and thought she was a customer. "How can I help you?"

Lettie smiled. "No, I have come to help *you*, to do the laundry. My father sent me. He says Mr. Levine, whom he drives, has given him money for me."

"You know how to do laundry, all by yourself?" Fay had been expecting an older woman.

"Oh, yes! With five younger brothers and sisters, there is much to do. Every Wednesday, I do all the laundry. I can work for you today and tomorrow. Today I will wash and tomorrow I will iron."

How much had Pinchas paid? Fay didn't want to look ignorant and foolish by asking. She felt as if a burden was being lifted from her, so she agreed. "Right, then. When can you begin?"

Lettie had earned a good salary by working every day. Her family needed the money. Here she was being offered work for only two days a week.

"Could I not also help in the kitchen?" she said. "I'm a good cook, so my mother says."

"It's kind of you to offer, but you see, well, we have special rules we follow for food. Though I am sure you're very capable, it's only the laundry I need help with."

"Oh, yes, you are Jews. I forgot. We have Jewish neighbors where I live in District Six, and my brother goes there every Saturday morning to light the fire in their stove. They wanted to pay him for this, but my father wouldn't allow him to take money for helping out a neighbor. They give him a sweet, twisted loaf they call a *challah*, and sometimes also a carrot pudding they call kugel, and even better, if it's a festival they give him a sweet, sticky confection they call *teiglach*."

"You live in District Six? That's where the furniture factory is."

"Yes, it's very convenient for my father, and for my mother. Next to us is a family that came here from India. They have a grocery shop, and my mother works there on Friday, when it's their religious day." She hesitated. "Maybe you could teach me about your kind of cooking and then I can help in the kitchen?"

To Fay, this was unthinkable. "No, my dear, cooking for my family is my pleasure, not work."

Lettie was disappointed. She was giving up a full-time job to work only two days a week. What would she do the rest of the week?

Fay went to the front door and locked it. She placed a notice on the window that said, "Back in five minutes."

"Come, I'll show you where everything is. You're sure you can manage alone? I usually have my two older girls to help me."

They walked through the kitchen and down the steps into the backyard. Three large bundles lay there.

"Sheets and towels, clothing, whites and coloreds," Fay said, pointing at the bundles.

Beside them lay a washtub and inside it a scrubbing board and soap.

"I see you have plenty of washing lines," Lettie said. "That's good. It's a fine day. Everything will be ready to take in by this afternoon."

"It's such a hot day, and you walked so far," Fay said. "First come inside and sit down. I'll pour you some cold water. Try my cookies, my special recipe."

Lettie was served cool water from the pantry in a fine glass and cookies on a delicate plate. Here she would not be served food on separate plates.

Fay also sat down with a glass of water and quickly drank it. "I must go back to the shop. Come to me if there is anything you need."

Lettie finished eating. She changed into her work clothes, carefully folding her Sunday best.

Lettie now felt that her father had been correct. This was a good family to work for. Here she would be treated well. But to work just two days a week? The house needed to be cleaned. The woman couldn't leave the shop. Yet no dust lay upon the surfaces, in spite of the dusty streets and the wind. Did the woman clean after she had been in the shop all day? Did the children clean the house? She would ask if she could also do the cleaning.

If the woman didn't agree, maybe she could find other places to work where they also wanted her for only one or two days. Anything was better than that big house on the mountain slopes, where she ate alone, in a small back room, using separate utensils. Yes, this was a good place to work.

By noon the washing was almost done. Only the white shirts remained.

Children came rushing through the side gate, and then stopped and stared at her.

Before they could ask questions, she said, "I am Lettie. I have come to help your mother."

The children looked at her in amazement. Someone doing their laundry? Things were getting stranger and stranger!

"You must have been working all morning!" Frieda said. "What about lunch?"

Just then David, who had run ahead, shouted from the kitchen door, "Mother says we are all to come in straight away. The food is on the table. She said to tell Lettie that an extra place has been set for her. Hurry now, before it all gets cold."

Lettie had never before eaten with the family she worked for. Now she ate quickly, said little, and went back to her work. The food had been good, not as spicy as her mother's food, but good nonetheless.

With renewed vigor she tackled the shirts. The first washing lines were now quite dry, so there was room for the shirts. By late afternoon everything was neatly folded, ready for ironing the following day.

Lettie was too tired to change back into her Sunday best. She rolled down her sleeves and walked into the kitchen.

From the passage came the sound of children's voices. "This homework is difficult."

"Come here, then, let me help you."

"Who is that lady working so hard with the washing?"

"Didn't you learn in school in London that curiosity killed the cat?"

"Well, so what! I'm not a cat!"

Lettie walked into the shop. There were no customers. Without meaning to voice her opinion, Lettie said, "There's no sign on the window, like in other shops. Why not?"

"Oh, I never thought of that!" Fay said. "Yes, maybe I will see to it. Are you leaving now?"

"Yes, the washing is folded, on two chairs in the kitchen. I wasn't sure where to place it. Tomorrow I'll be here early to do the ironing." Then she added, one sentence running into another, "On Wednesday I do the washing and ironing at home, but on Thursday and Friday I can return and clean the house. If you're in the shop all day, when do you clean? I see everything is so shiny, but when do you do it?"

Now Fay was no longer smiling.

Oh no! Lettie thought. *I should have listened to my father and just worked for two days. Now I have ruined everything!*

Fay was thinking of how tired she was at the end of each day. She looked at the girl.

"At night, when everyone is asleep, that's when I clean the house. Yes, maybe you could clean on Thursday and Friday. We'll talk about it tomorrow."

Maybe they could afford four days of help. What had Pinchas paid the girl? Not to have to start cleaning after the long day in the shop, after cooking and seeing to the children . . . Could it be possible that there was enough money for that?

"My father told me that he was paid enough money for as many days as I work here," Lettie said. "I can work those extra days."

Fay simply nodded. Lettie felt she had said more than enough and walked rapidly out of the shop.

—

Far away, both Pinchas and Jan were thinking about Lettie. Was everything working out satisfactorily? As if by mutual consent, they refrained from discussing the matter.

This was to be a long journey, two full weeks. They spoke of the coming trip as they went north, heading toward Malmesbury.

This was new territory for Pinchas. Jan had told him that the Boer farmers spoke with a strange rolling guttural "r," called a "*brei.*" While Jan demonstrated, Pinchas wondered if he was being teased or if the people really spoke that way. On the way up, they would stop at smaller villages and at farmhouses. Then they would go west to Mamre, and on the return trip down through Philadelphia and Kuilsriveir and then home.

By now, Jan had developed a friendship with Pinchas and was happy to travel with him. He wanted to carry on traveling with this man who treated him so kindly, without condescension. He went out of his way to talk about the area they would cover, the type of customers they would find, and what would be expected of Pinchas.

Jan and Pinchas sat side by side, as the wagon carried them both away from their homes and their families. Now, at the beginning of summer, wildflowers that had lain dormant during the winter were springing up between patches of grass and small thorny bushes. In the distance, a small buck would suddenly appear, or even a whole herd. It seemed to Pinchas as if they were alone in the world, surrounded by the beauty that Hashem had created for man.

Pinchas felt happy, satisfied with this new life. Yet one thought troubled him: his son Jack. He was such a clever boy, but he wasn't learning Torah. He also wasn't learning in school like his younger children. What would become of him?

He had spoken briefly to Faigy about Jack before he left.

"When I return, we must see that our oldest son returns to learning."

Had his Faigy listened to him? She had merely nodded and then gone off to attend to something in the shop.

When they returned from this long trip, he must make sure to take care of Jack. His oldest son, who had done so much for the family, must resume his studies, both in Torah and in the secular realm.

As his father, he would make sure this happened.

Chapter 29

"[Rev. Ornstein] ... had established a 'collegiate' school for Jewish
boys with properly qualified staff for secular and religious learning,
the first of its kind in South Africa."

— Dr. Louis Herrman, *A Centenary History*, p. 47

It was during the second week of Pinchas's absence that Fay
remembered his words.

"When I return from this trip I must see to Jack's education," he had
said. "He has not been to school. He has not been to *cheder*. What will
become of him? It is not sufficient that he goes to shul each day. He
must learn. When I return, I'll make inquiries. If they have such a fine
building for a shul, there must be a place for Torah learning."

Fay realized that she could put things off no longer. She had run
out of excuses. Had Pinchas not provided them with their every need
and more over this past week? Lettie had taken hours of tiring work off
her shoulders, and her shop was slowly doing better since Lettie had
suggested she put up a sign.

David was good at drawing. He had made a sign, a nice sign with
fancy lettering. He had been proud that he had been asked to make the
sign and had worked carefully, with pen and ink, on his drawing book
from school.

What a difference it made having Lettie! That week the girls no longer
had to help with the laundry. On Friday night the house was sparkling,
and the terrible fatigue that had begun plaguing Fay had quite disappeared.

On Sunday morning, for the first time ever, Fay and all the children
went together to the Gardens.

"There's time now to go to the park," Jack had said after breakfast. "Come, boys, hurry. You know this is the best time to get there—early, before everyone starts coming."

"The laundry is all done," Frieda piped up. "The house is clean. We can all go!"

Fay heard her and thought, *The girl is right.*

"Quickly then, clear up, and we'll all go together," she said.

A short time later, Fay sat on a bench and relaxed in the warm sunshine. She watched as the boys ran around and the girls walked sedately up and down the little paths.

Her thoughts returned to Jack.

When Jewish women had walked into the shop that past week, she had made inquiries. The first few women only had very young children, and they all went to Mr. Thorner's school. Then, at last, on Friday afternoon, just before it was time to close the shop, she received the information she wanted.

"My dear, Rev. Ornstien's school is where my sons go," the customer had said. "It's a fine school. The boys are taught both secular and religious subjects. No need for the old-fashioned *cheder* here, my dear, when the boys learn so well. This year our dear Rev. Ornstien is away in London, but soon he will return. His deputy is running the school well, but still, the boys are looking forward to his return. Next week, I believe, he'll be back."

Well, Fay thought, that sounded just like the Jews' Free School in London. Yes, Jack must stop working and go to this school. She had been too shy to ask how much it cost, but surely, if the younger children had to pay for their schooling, Jack would also have to pay. Did the *rebbeim* in *cheder* not take money?

How much, then, was the question. She was reluctant to ask the woman. For some time already she had been putting away a small sum at the end of each day, for an emergency. Had life not taught her about sudden mishaps? Now she thought of that money. Would it be sufficient to pay for this school?

Life proceeded smoothly for Jack as the summer sun in the Cape shone brightly. He was happy. He was taking on more responsibility in the shop and his salary had been slightly raised. He was quite unaware of his mother's plans for his future.

Now, after the *chagim*, when he'd missed so many days of work and was always fearful that a replacement had been found, everything was back to normal. His father was away. His brothers and sisters were back at school, and his mother was once again behind the counter.

So on this day, as the year 1891 was drawing to a close, Jack was content.

The next night, after his mother had given him supper and checked on the younger children, she beckoned to Jack.

"Come here, I need to talk to you."

Fay had rehearsed what she would say, but the words burst out from her. "You're a good boy to help us, working so hard for us, but what is to become of you? You can't work in a shop forever. Now that your father and I earn sufficient money, you must go back to school."

Jack was horrified at the thought. He recalled sitting on uncomfortable benches and cramming for exams. No, impossible. He enjoyed work. He brought in much-needed money. There was no way he was going to become a bored schoolboy once more.

His mother continued, unaware of his thoughts. "Rev. Ornstein has returned from England. We're going to see him tonight. He has a school, a fine school for Jewish boys. Go change and put on your Shabbos suit."

David, Joseph, and Frieda were sternly admonished to keep order, and Jack and his mother set off, down Kloof Street, into the Gardens, down through Government Avenue, to speak to Rev. Ornstien, who Fay believed would solve her problems.

Jack banged on the large brass knocker on the imposing front door.

A servant answered, took them into a book-lined room, and told them to wait. Shortly after, Rev. Ornstien came into the room.

Immediately, Fay said, "I want my son to learn at your school."

"What school are you attending now?"

Jack thought he saw a chance to avoid leaving work. If Rev. Ornstien knew he had spent the past months working in a grocer shop, he would not be inclined to accept him.

"Well, I haven't been to school since we arrived," Jack said. "I'm working at Grocotts, the grocer a little way down Long Street. We need the money my work brings in."

Fay interrupted Jack. "We no longer need that extra money. It's time for my son to return to learning."

Jack tried another tactic. "What are the fees?"

Rev. Ornstien looked disconcerted for a moment, and Jack felt himself become a tad more optimistic.

"Well, you see, it may sound a lot, but I wanted a school for Jewish children," the rabbi said. "I wanted the fees to be low, so it would be manageable for everyone. But no, the parents didn't want that. They mostly send their children to non-Jewish schools, fine schools, but not Jewish schools. The few parents who want a Jewish school for their boys send their children to me. Their sisters go to the local schools. The mothers say they can give their girls whatever Jewish learning they need. Did they not learn from their own mothers?"

He paused, and then named the fee. Jack gasped.

"Well, that is for the full year, not each term," the rabbi added.

Jack had heard enough. "Come, we must go," he told his mother. "The children will be getting restless. You can't afford to pay fees for the children and for me. Thank you, Rev. Ornstien, for seeing us."

"What a gentleman your son is. What a good, polite boy. I surely would like to have him in my school. But you see, I must charge everyone equal fees. I can't have charges of favoritism."

"Jack, sit down," his mother said.

The amount had surprised both of them, and Jack had been sure they would leave. Instead he sat and heard his mother say, "Right then, when can he begin?"

The rabbi looked at the woman before him, plainly but neatly dressed. He knew that the family had recently arrived.

He had only been back at shul for a few days, but he had seen the youngster there and had spoken to him. When asked why his father was absent, the boy had said his father had gone to the country, selling. He was probably working as a *smous*, going from farm to farm with a pack on his back. What, then, could he make? How could this family afford his fees? What was he to say? How could he accept one boy without payment, and yet charge the other boys?

"We begin this year, on the fifteenth of January," Rev. Ornstien said. "The fees for the term must be paid in advance. If you would like your son to attend, come with him on the fifteenth and bring the fees at that time."

He felt pleased with himself. He had handled that well. He hadn't insulted the woman, hadn't refused to take her son, and by the time she had walked halfway home she would realize how impractical the idea was.

Jack felt equally relieved. His mother would forget all about school, especially that school.

But neither the man nor the boy understood Fay. She was determined that all her boys would go to this school, starting with Jack.

Fay reached for her purse. She had brought with her what she felt was a vast sum of money, just to be sure. Now she realized she had enough money with her, but this school certainly wasn't cheap. Yet this was the only Jewish school here. This was where her Jack would go.

Jack watched, stunned, as his mother handed over the money. He didn't want to go to this school, but what could he do?

As she handed over the money, Fay wondered how she would manage each succeeding year. So much money gone! She felt a bit shaky but tried to hide her feelings.

This was the only Jewish school. This was where her Jack would go.

Jack watched the money pass over the desk. In the old days, in London, he had been in control. His mother had quietly worked in the home, not interfering.

Here, it seemed as if his mother was a different person. It was as if they had left behind in London a sweet, tired lady, and brought in her stead a fierce woman who could not be fooled or bested.

The rabbi looked at the money, amazed. What could he do, but tally it up and hand over a receipt and welcome the boy to the school? Where had this money come from? The boy himself looked less than happy.

"So, next year you will be a pupil here," Rev. Ornstien said.

"Yes, it looks that way," Jack mumbled.

"Oh, I nearly forgot," Fay said. She pulled from her bag the report that Jack had obtained from his old school.

"Ah, so you went to the Jews' Free School. So did I. In fact, I taught there too.

Mr. Angel helped me obtain my first position as the rabbi at Portsmouth. Oh, you have a fine report. You will do well here."

Fay walked home, down the avenue, with a determined step. "It's a good school. Soon your brothers will also go there. It's only a small school, not like the one you went to in London, but I have heard good reports about it."

For once in his life, Jack was at a loss for words. He plodded silently beside her.

How would they manage without his contribution? True, his father was earning nicely now, but in the past his father had worked and then suddenly had to stop. What if that happened again?

Not only that, but the other boys would know so much more than he did. How would they treat him?

How on earth had this happened? He had walked into his home only a few hours before, happy as a lark, and now everything had changed so quickly.

Fay, for her part, was elated. At last she could help her son. She could finally begin to repay him for all he had done to help them come to this new land.

"It's a fine school," she said again. "You will do well there. Remember how Mr. Angel spoke to you about university? Well, now we can think about that again."

"Oh, such dreams. How can that be possible? The school costs so much money. How much would university cost? Besides, do they even have a university here?"

Fay wasn't sure. Buoyed by the success of that night's visit, she said, "There are doctors and lawyers, and teachers. Where did they study? You'll study wherever they did. Now just be a good boy and learn well. When the time comes, we'll see where you can learn a good profession."

Jack walked up the avenue, his thoughts swirling. Maybe everything his mother said was true. Or maybe they were simply hopes, pipe dreams, never to be attained. Who could tell?

The money — a vast sum — had been paid. What could he do but fall in with his mother's dictates?

Chapter 30

"The third minister appointed to the Cape Town Hebrew Congregation was the Rev. Abraham Frederick Ornstien... Yet as time was to show, his essentially English outlook was not altogether suited to local conditions. It brought him into conflict with the new immigrant element, which was becoming increasingly dominant in the changing structure of the South African Jewish community."
— Israel Abrahams, *The Birth of a Community*, p. 47

In the month of December, in the mid-summer heat, Pinchas sat beside Jan as the cart headed toward Cape Town. Due to the excruciating heat, they had traveled mostly in the early dawn hours.

Never had Pinchas been more pleased with the expertise that his driver showed over those weeks. By the time the sun was high in the sky they were already in a little village. The shops and houses were built for this climate and were cool indoors. The days passed pleasantly.

Now they were traveling in the midday heat, in their eagerness to reach home.

Pinchas was thinking about something he had heard a few days before from one of the Jews he'd met.

"My son goes to Rev. Ornstien's school in Cape Town," the man had said. "It costs plenty, but it's worth it. They have good teachers. They learn everything that the ordinary school teaches, and also *limudei kodesh*. This last year Rev. Ornstien was in England, but they still had school. It's good that he is back again. He's a good man."

Pinchas was pleased that his problem was now solved. He would arrange for Jack to begin attending this school on the English New Year.

Since he was returning from a long trip, he would have a full week at home. Besides, Jan had told him that because of the December festivals, all factories would be closed for a week. That meant two full weeks at home—plenty of time to arrange for Jack's schooling.

Full of hope in the future, Pinchas returned home.

As the wagon drew up beside his home, he thought of Jan's daughter. Had she gone to work at his house as instructed by her father? What had been Faigy's reaction?

Jan, too, was thinking of his daughter. Had she succeeded in persuading Pinchas's wife to let her help? Was the arrangement working out well?

The answer became clear when a small figure ran down the steps.

"You have returned, Pa!" Lettie shouted. "I saw you from the bedroom window. I was busy there, cleaning. I work here now four days a week—two days washing and ironing, and two days cleaning."

Jan beamed at his daughter. "So you obeyed me?"

"Of course!" a beaming Lettie replied. "When did I not listen to you? You were correct. This is a good place to be."

Fay walked down the steps a few moments later.

"What a lovely young girl, your daughter!" she said. "Such a difference she makes. She's a pleasure to have around the house."

"She works here four days a week?" Pinchas asked.

"Yes, she said she could also come on Thursday and Friday and help with the cleaning," Fay said. "Such a difference it makes for me—no laundry and no cleaning."

Pinchas made a rapid calculation. He had left enough money to pay for only two days of help each week. He reached into his jacket pocket, counted out some coins, and handed them to Lettie. She reached up to her father, who was still on the wagon, and gave them to him.

"Tell Ma I'll be home soon," she said. "I'm almost finished."

"No, it's such a long walk home," Fay said. "Go with your father. The girls can finish up. Quickly, run and get your things."

In no time at all Lettie was sitting beside her father, and the wagon was on its way.

Filled with confidence now that his plans to help Fay had been so successful, Pinchas waited until the children were in bed before raising the subject of Jack's education.

"About Jack," he said. "I've been thinking—"

"Oh, yes, it's time he returned to school," Fay interrupted. "It's all arranged. When the new school year begins in January, he'll go to Rev. Ornstien's school."

Pinchas was taken aback. "What, you did this without me?"

"Well, what was I to do? Wait until you arrived home, before arranging with Rev. Ornstien for the boy to attend his school? Absurd! What if I had waited and someone else applied, and the slot would have been filled?"

"But surely this was something we should have discussed."

"You're not happy that Jack will be learning with Jewish boys?"

"Listen, I'm the father. These decisions should be mine. If the school is so good, fine, but I should have gone there myself. I should have made the decision about my son's education."

Instead of giving the good news to his wife about the school and taking his son there himself, his wife had arranged everything. Pinchas felt cheated.

Fay was more than annoyed. "Fine, next time I'll send a carrier pigeon to ask if the boys can go to shul that day."

"You think it's good for me, to be away from my family like this?"

"So it's my fault? *I* told you to leave us, and for weeks at a time?"

"There was no urgency to arrange Jack's schooling. The decision about the boys' education is mine to make."

"Oh, so I'm not capable of making decisions? Who decided we should travel here? Was that a good or bad decision? I went with Jack to Rev. Ornstien. He's a fine man. Do you know he too went to the Jews' Free

School in London? When the others are older, they too will go to his school. Our boys will do well there."

Pinchas was astounded. He was welcomed in the small Jewish communities he traveled to. He was asked to *daven* in shul and give *shiurim*. He was asked for advice. He was respected. Here, at home, he was a nobody. His wife made all the decisions.

Fay, too, was upset. Had she not found the perfect place for Jack? Rev. Ornstien was a clever man, respected by Jew and non-Jew alike. Instead of praise from Pinchas for finding a good solution, she was being criticized. Not only was he away for weeks at a time, when he did come back he found fault. It was all too much to bear, yet what option did she have? He was her husband. They had crossed oceans together. They had left behind all that was familiar.

Still, she could not forgive him, nor could he forgive her. Their behavior toward one another was proper, but strained.

The three youngest children, Isaac, Ethel, and Rose, were the only members of the household unaware of the tension between Pinchas and his wife. The older children couldn't understand why there was little conversation between their parents when their father had been away for so many weeks. "Please pass the salt" was the longest sentence uttered by either of them at the dinner table.

In later years, the younger children remembered that first week of that long summer holiday with unalloyed pleasure.

Jack was back at work. He had arranged for David to work with him during the summer holidays, always a busy time at the grocery shop. But the other children were free and so was their father. He took them to different parts of the Cape he had discovered on his travels.

The first day of their holiday they went once again on the long and exciting train ride to Muizenberg. The sea was warm, not cold and tingly like Three Anchor Bay. The beach was long and soft and sandy, not filled with small pebbles. It stretched out for miles in both directions. The picnic lunch, hurriedly packed, was less than substantial, but who could complain about that when everything else was so glorious?

They rode on the train and visited parks in the new leafy suburbs of Wynberg and Claremont. Each day was a new adventure, a new delight. When the shops and offices and factories reopened, they found themselves back at home.

However, even when Pinchas was busy in the morning, delivering goods to the suburbs, he arranged his schedule so the afternoons were free. Savoring these last few hours with his children before setting off again, Pinchas took the children to the nearby park in the Gardens. There they played among the rose bushes and tall shady trees, and their father told them stories from long ago, when he was a little boy.

Pinchas enjoyed this time but was not sorry to be returning to work. Thinking about the upcoming trip, he didn't notice that Joseph had wandered off while the others were playing. He went toward Queen Victoria Street, staring up at the large solid buildings. He crossed the road to examine the stone lions at the entrance up close.

A man came out holding a letter.

"Here you are at last!" he said. "Take this straight away to the address on the envelope, and then come back with the answer."

Joseph read the address. It was only a few doors down. He ran to a smaller building and handed in the letter, then went into the large building and looked around, wondering where to go. How could he tell the man that the letter had been delivered? He knocked on one door, then another, but didn't see the man. Just as Joseph was about to give up, the man came down the passage and shouted at him, "Well, what took you so long?"

The misunderstanding was soon sorted out. Joseph was soon running back to the park, back to Pinchas. He stood beside his father and gleefully told him, "There are lawyers in that big building, and their messenger boy didn't arrive. They don't know why. They said that if I want to be their messenger boy, just during the holidays, I can do it. They'll pay me. I said I would ask Mother."

Pinchas was about to say that the boy needed a break from school, that it was too hot to run around delivering messages. Besides, was it safe? Did he know his way around? But this last sentence gave him pause.

"Yes, certainly. Tell them yes. I will tell your mother."

Fortunately, it had been a good day at the shop. Fay was absorbed in thoughts of orders and new products. Without giving the matter much thought, she nodded her head in agreement.

From that day on, Joseph would spend every school holiday in impressive, oak-lined offices, listening to lawyers talk among themselves and delivering letters to different offices and sometimes to the impressive courts.

That evening, only Frieda noticed the tension at home during the evening meal.

Their father hardly spoke during the meal. He bentched quickly and quietly, and left the table immediately, going out for a long walk alone. By the time he returned the children were asleep.

Jack and David returned late from the shop, pleased with the money they had made and too tired from their work to notice anything amiss.

Joseph, usually so alert to everything around him, was deep in thought as he ate, thinking about all the offices he had been to and the work he would do there during his school holidays.

The younger children noticed nothing.

When the meal was over, the children went to their rooms to prepare for the new school year. They discussed the different teachers they would have and carefully placed their new exercise books into their satchels.

Pinchas was in the bedroom, packing for his trip. Fay hated to see Pinchas leave, but she was too proud, too angry, to allow her feelings to show.

Did he realize how difficult it was for her during the week, and especially on Shabbos? At the Shabbos table she had to be not only the mother, who provided the food, but also the father. She would read the *parshah* of the week from the *Tzena Urena*. Then, she tried to draw a lesson from it, to teach the children about the importance of not speaking *lashon hara*, about the need for total honesty in all their dealings, about being kind and caring to others. She had learned all these things as a child, around her parents' Shabbos table.

But was that sufficient for the boys? She thought not.

In her home her father had spoken so beautifully each week about what could be learned from the *parshah*. How were her children going to learn these things from her? She tried her best. Every week before Shabbos she instructed the older boys to read that week's *parshah*. But though they read it, they could not comment on it like Pinchas. He was a learned man. He had spent years in the best yeshivas, far from home. Every day in the shtetl Pinchas had set aside time to learn. The boys needed their father home, not hundreds of miles away.

So here they were, far from home, in a fine house, with a fine shul nearby and the shop at last doing well, and yet she was unhappy.

Meanwhile, Pinchas longed for the soft, pliable young woman who had followed his wishes without argument. He hoped that before he left, before he traveled far away, his wife would apologize to him for her harsh words. He hoped they could discuss important issues, so that he wouldn't once again arrive home and find decisions had been made in his absence.

Early in the morning, Jan arrived. The shop bell rang, and Fay rushed out of the kitchen. Pinchas waited for a short while, but then he saw the horses were getting restless and Jan was peering into the house, looking worried.

Pinchas couldn't leave with bad feelings between them. He waited until the customer left the shop and then said, "Faigy, I'll miss you. Every day I'll think of you. Soon I'll be home again."

Fay remembered a long-ago admonition from her mother, never to end the day with bad feelings. She thought of how much worse it would be for Pinchas to leave on a long journey while there was discord.

"Travel well," she said. "We all look forward to your safe return."

They parted with words of forgiveness, but the confusion and bad feelings remained.

Chapter 31

"Our Minister, the Reverend A.F. Ornstien, is a popular man amongst all sorts and conditions. He is a distinct Hazzan, an intelligent lecturer, and is thoroughly broad-minded. In fact, he is the right man in the right place..."

— Israel Abrahams, *The Birth of a Community*, pp. 51–52

Jack left his job and returned to school toward the end of January. He felt somehow diminished. He had been a wage earner. He had been valued. Mr. Grocott had seen how reliable he was and had given him more duties, and a slight rise in pay. Now, once again, he was a schoolboy, sitting in a classroom with other boys and listening to a teacher.

The first day he sat quietly in a corner, looking, listening, hardly responding to the teacher's questions. At break time he was drawn to a boy with a deep tan and red-rimmed eyes. Jack wondered about that. Why had the boy been crying?

His whole life he had taken responsibility for his younger siblings. It was difficult to ignore the unhappy boy. Jack took his sandwiches and sat beside the boy in the playground. After a while the boy looked up.

"My name is Itzik," he said. "How do they call you?"

Jack wondered momentarily at the strange accent. He didn't speak in the close-lipped way of those who lived in the Colony, nor was it the Yiddish accent of new immigrants.

"They call me Jack," he said. "Long ago in the shtetl they called me Yaakov."

"Ach, yes! At home I am Itzik. But at school till now, in our *dorp*, they called me Isaac — that is, when they didn't call me '*die kleine joodjie*.'"

"What?" Jack said. He knew English and Yiddish. He even knew a smattering of Hebrew, after years of learning with his father. Well, "*kleine*" he could understand—it was the Yiddish word for "small"—but what did that second word mean?

"You know, the small Jew. I was the only Jewish boy in the school. My father said it was no good. No other Jewish children. No *cheder*. So he sent me here. But at home, we spoke Yiddish. At the school, we spoke mostly Dutch, the new Dutch, in the playground—Afrikaans, they call it—and the old Dutch in the classroom. Also, we had English lessons for an hour a day. But it's hard for me to speak English."

Jack took all this in with amazement. He had been surrounded by Jews in the shtetl. Even in London, most of their neighbors were Jews, and he went to a Jewish school. In the new school his brothers and sisters attended there were mostly non- Jews, but in each class there were a few Jewish children. What was it like to be the only Jew in a school?

"So here, you feel more at home?" Jack said. But the reply was not what he had expected.

"Ach, man, it's so strange for me. I miss my family, my *mamme* and *tatte* and sisters. I miss the big garden. We planted fruit trees when we came, and now this year they gave much fruit. I miss learning each night with my *tatte*. The other boys in this school, well, they're strangers to me."

Jack was silent. His life had been one of change—from the shtetl to London, to those weeks on the sea, to Cape Town—but he had always been surrounded by his family.

"Soon the other boys will be your friends," he said. "Soon you'll find it easier to speak English. There is a saying in Hebrew—*kol has'chalos kashos.*"

"Yes, new beginnings are difficult, but so very difficult," Itzik said.

Jack was impressed by the quick translation. "Look, your Hebrew is good, and you speak Yiddish and new Dutch and also the old Dutch and English. So you're clever, really clever. In no time at all you'll feel as if you have lived here all your life. Your English will be as good as your Yiddish. The other boys will be like brothers to you. Any time you need someone to talk to, I'm here every day. Come to me at break time, or after school, just before I leave."

"Ach, man, but you are good to me."

The bell rang, and they both walked toward the classrooms. Jack felt happier. The boy needed him. Jack felt strange in this new school, but surely not as strange as that lonely boy.

By the end of the day, Jack had slipped back into learning. He found that he remembered much of what had been taught in London. There were only a few boys in his class, and the teacher gave each pupil a lot of attention. There was no time for dreaming as he had sometimes done in his large class in London. His attention had to be focused every moment. He returned home later than his siblings, since the school covered both secular and religious studies, and found them playing in the backyard.

"Look what we found!" they cried.

They parted some overgrown bushes and showed him a door.

"Look, it opens, and behind it there's a big room! What do you think of that?"

"We didn't realize it was there," Frieda said. "The bushes around it were so thick. Then the ball rolled underneath, and we had to struggle to get it. It was so difficult! We had to get a thick knife and cut away branches. We just went on and on, breaking off branches, cutting away bits of leaf and wood."

"It was such hard work," Bertha chimed in. "Then, just as we were about to give up, there it was! The ball was there, and behind it a door! Come inside!"

Jack walked into a large room with a cement floor. A small open window faced the mountain. He shivered. The room was cool, cold almost. Yet outside the sun was blazing.

The kitchen is so hot in the summer, Jack thought. *The coal fire of the stove, and the heat of the sun, make the room feel almost like an oven. Perhaps this room could be used to eat our meals in the summer.*

He walked warily around the room. At school that day some boys had spoken of snakes hiding in long grass and in disused storage rooms. But the room was empty and dark, covered by a layer of dust.

Without thinking if his parents would approve, Jack said, "Come, let's clean this out. Girls, go and get buckets of water. Boys, let's see if we can clear away these bushes, or perhaps just make them shorter, so they don't cover up the door."

"It will be hard work," Frieda said. "Maybe we should change from our school clothes first."

Frieda was well aware of how precious their new school dresses were. The children went inside to put on their old clothes, and then the work began.

As the sun began to set, they heard their mother calling them.

"Children, what have you been up to?" she asked as they went up the back steps. "Just look at the state of your clothes!"

Fay was tired. It had been a long day standing in the shop, and now all the clean clothes, so carefully washed and ironed by Lettie, were covered in grime.

"Come, look what we found," Jack said. "Look what we have done. Now we have a cool room to eat in. When Tatte returns he can make a table and benches."

Fay had been unhappy about eating in the hot kitchen but saw no alternative. She followed him and soon forgot about the dirty clothes.

"Oh yes, now I remember. Mrs. Goldberg down the road asked what we were doing about the servant's room. I didn't know what she meant. Now I see. Lissa, who works for them every day, and who comes to us on Shabbos to light our stove, has a room like this next to the house. Now, into the house and get clean so I can serve your meal."

Jack felt good. He was no longer earning money, but he still had a useful role to play, at school and at home. He wanted to talk to his father, to tell him about his day, but he was far away. His father seemed to be away far more than he was home. Did that make his father unhappy? It certainly seemed to make his mother unhappy. He saw the look on her face when his father left on a journey and the relief when he returned.

His father had said there was nothing to worry about. Jan had been traveling this route for years and knew how to keep safe. Was that true? Some of the boys at the new school came from faraway places. Were these the same places his father traveled to? He must speak to them and find out.

***

Pinchas returned home to find his wife busy in the shop. The younger children were in the backyard. He was happy to be home, pleased that he had parted on good terms with his dear wife. He wanted to talk to her about David's bar mitzvah, and about his plans for the younger boys.

Now, while the house was quiet, he wanted to learn. The trip had been hectic. There had hardly been a free moment to learn. He sat contentedly, immersed in the words before him.

Meanwhile, not far away, at the bottom of Table Mountain, events were unfolding that would unsettle his plans.

***

David was now twelve years old and in the top class at Mr. Thorner's school. Joseph was in the class below. David had been told by his mother that the following year he would follow his brother to Rev. Ornstien's school. David was always at the top of his class. His brother Joseph was also doing well.

Joseph had once been a dreamer and had not always done well at school, but ever since he had begun to deliver documents for the lawyers, he had imagined himself sitting in an impressive office and sending errand boys around town with important documents.

Joseph remembered the advice given to him at the law office. If he wanted to become a lawyer, he must do well in his studies. The result was that his teacher noticed how bright he was and spoke to the headmaster about him.

One day, both David and Joseph were called to Mr. Thorner's office. They went with trepidation. A visit to the office inevitably meant some misdemeanor had been committed.

"Do you think it's about school fees?" Joseph asked.

Now that Jack was no longer working, perhaps his mother had been unable to pay the school fees and they would all have to leave. David didn't know how to answer.

"Let's just go in and see," was all he could say.

Upon entering the office, they were surprised to find a beaming headmaster.

"Come in, boys. Take a seat. There's something I want to talk to you about. Your teachers tell me you're both doing well. Every year there's a scholarship for SACS, the top school here. We feel you should both begin to prepare for it.

"Perhaps we have not left sufficient time for David, but it's worth a try. For you, Joseph, there is still time. You're doing so much better at your studies now. Would you both like to stay on a few times a week for extra coaching?"

David didn't even think to say, "I'll speak to my parents."

"Oh yes," he said immediately. "But what if I fail?"

"It's no disgrace if you don't succeed. Lots of boys take the exam and only one is given a scholarship. If you don't succeed you can still go to the school, but your parents will have to pay the fees."

Joseph remained silent, but he was determined to take advantage of the lessons. He knew from the lawyers that SACS was the top school. They sent their own sons there. He would go there, too. He would get that scholarship. He must.

David and Joseph arrived home that day bursting with their news. Their father was waiting for them.

"Come, sit with me," he said. "Let us learn for a while. Then we must talk about David's bar mitzvah. I will begin teaching you your bar mitzvah *parshah*, and next year you will go to the same school as Jack. Joseph too should sit with us and learn."

"No, I want to go to SACS," David wanted to shout, but he remained silent. What chance did he have of getting the scholarship? It was better not to talk about it now.

Joseph also said nothing. All he could think about was going to SACS. After that he would learn to be a lawyer. He would sit at a big desk in an oak-paneled office and help people in trouble. Although he sat next to David and his father, his thoughts were far away.

Jack returned from school much later in the day. The girls and the younger boys were in the garden, and he found David and Joseph in their bedroom. They looked up when he came in, bursting with their news.

"There's a chance of winning a scholarship for SACS, only a small chance," David said. "But still, you never know."

"How do you get such a scholarship?" Jack asked.

"We must take an exam," Joseph said. "A lot of boys take it, but only one will get the scholarship."

"Well, it's only a very small chance," David said. "But Tatte says we will both go to your school."

"There's nothing wrong with my school!" Jack was offended.

"Your school is fine, but SACS — well, it's famous. I want to take that exam and . . . I know I won't be allowed to."

Just then the girls ran in.

"We found some apples on a tree, behind where the bushes used to be, and also some flowers!" they cried. "Maybe we can plant more flowers."

"Right," Jack said. "Go back to the garden. We'll be there in a moment."

Jack sat, deep in thought. By now the school had realized that each Levine child was two years younger than the rest of the class. Their mother had been called to the headmaster's office to discuss whether the children should be moved to their respective age groups.

She had asked only one question. "Do they manage to do well in their classes?"

The headmaster had simply nodded and said, "Yes, they do well." Then he paused for a while and said, "It would be foolish to make changes now. Do you agree?"

Jack thought about the boys who would compete for the scholarship. They would be from all over town, the cleverest boys—and two years older than David.

"Listen, David, I hope you get that scholarship. But don't raise your hopes too high. Just do your best. There's no need to tell anyone about it. If you win, well, that's the time to talk about it."

Jack hoped he was giving good advice. The chance of success was small, but what harm was there in trying?

Chapter 32

"South African College (SACS) High School and Preparatory School for Boys in Cape. The oldest institution of its kind in Southern Africa... became the South African College High School and continued to occupy the old buildings in the Cape Town Suburb of the Gardens."

— Eric Rosenthal, *Encyclopedia of Southern Africa*, p. 510

Fay had not arranged for anyone to teach David his bar mitzvah *parshah*. She was sure that Pinchas would do that. She was surprised when he brought up the subject later that evening.

"You know, I told you about the *shtiebel* in District Six," he said. "It's just a little room, really, where a little more than a *minyan* davens each day. I met there a very learned man—his name is Reb Mendel Landau. He has no work, and he speaks no English. I can pay him to teach David. He needs the money, and David needs to learn on a regular basis."

To his relief, Fay agreed immediately. He had feared she would want to hire someone from the Gardens shul, or from Jack's school.

Fay was only too happy. The man was learned. That was good. Besides, it would be one less thing for her to do.

The following week all three boys learned with Reb Mendel. He came to their house three times a week. It had been decided that after David spent some time learning to *lein*, Jack and Joseph would join and all three boys would learn Gemara.

Jack found Reb Mendel's approach quite different from the way he learned at Rev. Ornstien's school. He enjoyed the lessons and so did his brothers, sometimes carrying on the discussion even after the teacher had gone home.

With Fay less tired because of Lettie's help, and Pinchas pleased to be able to help his friend financially without embarrassing him, the household fell into a pleasant routine.

When the time came for Pinchas to leave on his next trip, Fay, though she was distraught as usual, kept her feelings under control. This was mainly due to Lettie. She had been with them for some weeks now, and her presence kept Fay calm when worry about Pinchas began to overtake her. Lettie talked about her father and how capable he was, and about the many years he had traveled these routes.

"It's natural to worry when people are far apart," Lettie told her. "My father is very capable, but my mother is much happier when he's home. That is the way of women, to be home and to worry, to wait for the return of loved ones."

Such a sensible young girl, Lettie was. How different and more pleasant life was since she had first come through the shop door.

Slowly, Lettie became an important part of the household. She brought to the house not only a sense of order, but also a wry sense of humor, an ability to laugh at mishaps and diffuse arguments.

Though she had taken on more work and was now in the house every day, from Monday to Friday, Fay never let her help with the cooking. That was one part of her household duties she was not prepared to surrender.

So the year quietly meandered on. All the children were doing well at school. Although Jack had made friends in his class, he still spent some time each day with Itzik, who had slowly settled in to his new environment. David took the scholarship exam without saying a word about it. The boys continued to study diligently with Reb Mendel. The girls were happy and properly dressed, and the shop was doing well.

When Fay wrote her weekly letter to her parents and said that life was good and that they should not worry about her, she really meant it. Before, she'd had so many worries, but never shared them. Now, at last, she wrote the truth. She began to relax for the first time in years.

Fay expected obedience from her children. She needed to concentrate on the shop without disturbance. Once or twice she had heard raised voices, which disturbed her, but her swift rebuke to the children had ended that.

The children spent their time making the room beside the garden comfortable. Pinchas, on his days off, had used the *sukkah* wood to make a table and two benches. He was confident that he would be able to obtain more wood when Sukkos came around again.

The girls had sewing classes in school. Using the skills they had learned, they made an embroidered tablecloth out of plain fabric.

The older boys had made small bookcases during their woodworking class. These now held a few books, won as prizes at school. The children played in this room while Fay was in the shop, so their noise no longer disturbed her.

Not only was Fay more content than ever, the children were also happy.

But everything was about to change.

It all began when David found out that he'd actually won the scholarship. He burst into the house that day.

"Mother, such news I have for you!" he said. "In the whole of Cape Town only one boy gets a scholarship to go to SACS, the very best school in Cape Town, and that boy is me!"

"No, you will go to Rev Ornstien's school, where Jack goes," Fay said. "It's a Jewish school. That's where you belong."

"But Mother, you must pay for that. With the scholarship everything is free."

"What does that matter? It's not a Jewish school. You learn no *limudei kodesh* there. You will not go to that school."

Fay was discomfited. What kind of land was this where children told their parents what they would do? Parents knew what was good for their children, and children were expected to obey.

David was dismayed. For years he'd been in Jack's shadow. He loved his brother, admired him even, but in London, the teachers had always said, "Well, young man, your brother Jack learned with me last year. I hope you will be up to his standards."

Now he had a chance to do something without anyone mentioning Jack's name. Besides, what would Mr. Thorner say if he turned down the offer? Would it prevent him giving other Jewish boys the same chance? No, he couldn't do it.

Joseph, standing by his side, tugged him away. He pulled his brother along until they were alone in their bedroom.

"Soon Tatte will come back," Joseph whispered. "We'll talk to him."

"Why should he say anything different?"

Joseph had been spending any spare time he had at the lawyers' office, acting as a messenger. He received little pay, but he enjoyed the ambience, the people coming in with worried faces and leaving looking cheerful, the lawyers discussing difficult points with one another. Sitting quietly, almost unnoticed, he had learned certain things.

He noticed how, in order to get a client to agree to something they were opposed to, the lawyers sometimes made some small compromises, suggesting something to sweeten the bitter pill.

He remembered one conversation in particular.

"Look here," the lawyer had said. "I know it's difficult to agree to sell that plot next to your house, but I'll get them to agree to plant fruit trees on the border, on your side, so that their house is screened from your view, and you'll also have fruit all summer."

The principle seemed to be: Give a little, and then the big problem will dissolve.

What could they give their father, in return for letting David go to SACS?

"You'll tell him that you'll learn every afternoon with your bar mitzvah teacher, and I will join you. You know he values Reb Mendel's teaching. He doesn't think much of the *limudei kodesh* Jack gets at his school. The money saved on school fees can go to pay Reb Mendel, so he can stay longer."

"You think Tatte will agree? You think he will persuade Mother?"

Another thing Joseph had learned from the lawyers was not to give false hope.

"Who knows?" he said. "But surely it's worth a try. You must try and persuade Tatte that learning with Reb Mendel is much better than learning *limudei kodesh* at Jack's school. It's what he already believes. Also, he's worried that Reb Mendel cannot earn money because he doesn't know English. Tatte will be pleased to help him."

David listened while his brother spoke. Clearly, his mother would not change her mind. Maybe Joseph was correct. Maybe he could persuade his father to let him go to SACS. It was worth a try.

—

Then the trouble with Rose began. She had been begging her mother to allow her to wear her hair in loose ponytails rather than braids.

"All the other girls go like this," she insisted. "No one has hair like mine. I want to cut it a bit shorter, and then wear it in ponytails with ribbons like the other girls."

Her mother was adamant. "No. That's not *tznius*."

So what did Rose do?

She got hold of the sewing scissors and hacked off her braids. But because she didn't cut her hair in front of a mirror, she cut off more than she had planned, and now her hair couldn't even be tied back. Panicking, she ran into the bathroom, wet her hair thoroughly and tugged at it, thinking futilely that this would make it longer.

The result, when dry, was a halo of curls around her face. Fay was horrified, but soon realized that nothing could be done but allow the hair to grow long enough for braids.

As if that wasn't enough, the following day Ethel came home from school very excited.

"A girl in my class, the one who moved here a little while ago — you know, into that big house — is having a birthday party and we're all invited, the whole class."

She had never been invited to a party before, and she was bursting with anticipation.

Lettie, who by now was aware of the laws of *kashrus*, said, "Is this girl a Jew like you?"

"No, but what does that matter? She's in my class. She invited me!"

Lettie usually left when the shop closed, but that day she didn't leave right away.

"Impossible," Fay said. "How can you even think of going? Don't you know we eat differently?"

Ethel ran out of the room, sobbing.

Lettie spoke quietly to Fay. "Maybe she can go, but much later, when the food has already been served and the children are playing games. That's how these things are done. It will look bad for her if she's the only one who doesn't go."

After a few moments, Fay said, "You know where the house is? Will you take her?"

"Yes, and I will wait for her to bring her home."

"Very well!" Fay said, relieved. "Frieda, go and calm her."

Fay was too tired to deal with this tantrum. Her mind was on David and his refusal to go to the same school as Jack. Besides, every time she looked at the children seated around the table, all she could see were the curls bouncing on Rose's shorn head. It was getting too much to handle alone. Pinchas should be home. The house needed him.

"The children all bring presents," Lettie said suddenly.

"Oh no, what will that cost?" Fay said. "Where do I have time to go and buy something? Do I have anything suitable in the shop?"

Lettie thought awhile, then said, "The flower sellers at the bottom of Adderley Street are going home now. The leftover flowers are much cheaper. Give me what you can spare and tomorrow I'll bring the flowers. That could be a good present and won't cost much."

So it was that the following afternoon, Ethel walked up the hill to the large house. She was dressed in her Shabbos best and accompanied by Lettie, carrying a large bunch of flowers.

The present was a great success.

"Oh, what a marvelous idea!" said Susan, the delighted birthday girl. "Flowers for me, just as if I was a grownup lady."

Ethel was happy until Susan's mother said, "We were so sorry you weren't here earlier, but just in case you arrived, I made a little plate of food for you."

Ethel saw a slice of fruit cake and a fancy cream cake, and beside it, a sandwich with a piece of meat wedged neatly into it. She longed for the cream cake, but the meat was practically touching it.

Awkwardly, she refused. The woman looked perturbed. She had saved the food especially for this ungrateful child.

Ethel played a few games, strange games she had never played before. Then, remembering Lettie waiting outside and feeling uncomfortable in any event, she thanked Susan and her mother, and left.

"Well, did you have a good time?" Lettie asked.

"It was good of you to take me and to get the flowers," Ethel said. "Susan just loved them."

After everything Lettie had done for her, how could she say that she just couldn't wait to get home and forget everything that had happened that day?

When Ethel returned home, her mother was busy in the shop. Later, when she closed the shop, she was too tired to ask Ethel about the party. But her sisters asked her what it was like. They had never been invited to a birthday party.

"It was good," Ethel said. "Yes . . . good." She didn't feel brave enough to tell them that it had been an ordeal.

When Fay sat at the kitchen table for the evening meal, she looked around at the children.

Such sullen faces! Why? How could she know that her girls were upset that they had never been invited to a birthday party? Ethel, who had just gone to one, also looked unhappy. Why?

Jack was talking earnestly to David and Joseph, a worried frown on his face. He foresaw a clash of wills. David was determined to go to SACS, and his mother was firmly against it. David wanted him to step in, to persuade their mother, but he didn't see how anything he could say would make her change her mind.

Even the two youngest boys looked glum. Fay couldn't know it was only because they were being ignored by their older brothers. Usually, after school, the older boys gave the younger ones attention. They heard about their day, helped with their homework, and told them stories, but today they had simply ignored them.

Only Rose seemed to be content. She was fascinated by her curls. She hadn't known she had curly hair, since she'd always worn two long braids.

Fay looked at Rose and her curls, and the child smiled at her. What would Pinchas say when he saw her?

She felt despair. These children, they had everything. Pinchas was away for weeks at a time, traveling to dangerous places to earn a salary. She got up early to buy fish and spent the early dawn hours frying it. After that came the long hours in the shop, and what for? So the children would have everything they needed.

Now David didn't want to go to a Jewish school. Rose had cut off her hair. The children were gloomy.

Fay wished Pinchas was home. She wanted someone to talk to, to share her thoughts. She felt like shouting at the children, but how would that help? Instead she said, "If you've finished eating, then *bentch*. I need to finish up some work in the shop."

The children looked at her, puzzled. Usually she asked each one about their day. Jack and Frieda looked at one another, shrugged their shoulders, and began to take on their mother's usual task of getting the younger children ready for bed.

Far away, Pinchas was davening Maariv on his last night away from home in a small shul that had barely a *minyan*. He did his best to keep his thoughts on davening, but they kept straying to the fact that the next time he davened Maariv, it would be with Jack and David by his side.

He couldn't wait for the peace of Shabbos in his own home, for the smiling welcome he always received as he walked in the door. Little did he know that he was about to walk into an unpleasant, and seemingly irreconcilable, clash of wills.

Chapter 33

"In the non-Jewish schools such as the South African College School, The Normal College School, and the Good Hope Seminary for Girls, the Jewish pupils responded well to the … sympathetic attitude of the Scottish school masters and mistresses, and retained a firm loyalty to the schools."

— Saron and Hotz, *The Jews in South Africa*, p. 52

Fay was hardly able to get herself up in the grey predawn. She knew that the fried fish brought customers, yet she hadn't slept well. Had she not vowed that here, she would give more attention to her children? But she was so very tired by the end of the day that so many things had gone unnoticed.

Had David told her about the possibility of winning a scholarship to that non-Jewish school? Had she responded? What had she said, or not said, that encouraged him to attempt to win it? Now that he had been successful, how would she be able to force him to attend the Jewish school?

Then there was the matter of the birthday party that Ethel had so happily attended. Had she spent sufficient time with the children, so that they were aware of the laws of *kashrus*? Had Ethel eaten any forbidden foods?

An image of Rose, with her head of bouncing curls, floated in her mind. Perhaps it would have been sensible to allow her to wear her hair in ponytails. Anything was better than those bouncing curls. Surely this wasn't how Jewish girls walked around.

She no longer had to spend Sunday doing laundry and ironing clothing. It was the shop that was taking up all her time. At last the shop was busy.

Her debts were paid, and now she was making a good profit. But a busy shop meant that she was exhausted at the end of each day. Somehow, she had to find sufficient energy to keep better control over her children. Before she knew it, it would be like living in London all over again, with the children doing all sorts of things she was unaware of.

Fay davened and then walked to the docks. When she returned, she fried the fish and woke up the children. She put out their breakfast and gave a sigh of relief as Lettie entered with a cheerful greeting.

The shop was busy almost from the moment the door opened. Pinchas arrived home in the late afternoon. Fay wanted to talk to him about David and his schooling, about Ethel's birthday party and the possibility that she had eaten non-kosher food, about Rose and her foolish haircut, but the shop was full of customers.

Pinchas walked into the kitchen, where the children were sitting around the table as Lettie gave them their after-school snack.

David and Joseph immediately ran up to him and started jabbering about scholarships and schools.

Ethel looked at her father and burst out crying. What would he say when he heard that she had insisted on going to a birthday party where they served *treif* food?

Then he took in a strange child sitting at the table, a little girl with short curly hair. With shock, he realized that little Rose was looking at him.

Pinchas was tired. The journey had taken longer than usual because a wheel had split and needed to be repaired by Jan before they could continue.

"Children," he said, "let me rest from my journey and prepare for Shabbos. Later we can talk. Lettie, your father is waiting for you outside."

The house slid into its pre-Shabbos mode. There was the sound of water running, of boys shouting, "Where's my Shabbos shirt?" and of little girls shrieking, "You hurt me when you brush so hard!"

Then, at last, the shop was closed, and Fay was able to throw on the white tablecloth and place the food on the slowly cooling stove.

"Frieda, girls, set the table," she called. With a sigh of relief, she began to get herself ready for Shabbos.

Pinchas called to the older boys to get ready to leave for shul. He had set up the candles, and they were ready for Fay to light them. A few times during the week he had been forced to *daven* without a *minyan*, and he was looking forward to shul. It was true that the davening was subdued, but there was a full shul, more than a *minyan*. It would be good to feel the peace of Shabbos come in, with his boys by his side.

David and Joseph had other ideas, though. As they set out to shul, David burst out, "Tatte, you know that next year I go to high school? Well, the thing is, I..."

Pinchas realized that David was dissatisfied with something. He didn't know what the problem was, but right now he wanted only the peace of Shabbos.

"After Havdalah, we'll talk about school," he said. "Now, what do you know about the *parshah*?"

With that, both David and Joseph had to be satisfied.

Back at home, Frieda had given up on trying to pull the curls on Rose's head into a ribbon. Ethel was trying to hide a chocolate stain on her Shabbos dress, made by a careless child. The children gathered around their mother as she lit the candles. Peace and harmony descended on the home.

When Havdalah was over, and the world had returned from *kodesh* to *chol*, Pinchas called David over.

"You wanted to talk to me about something?" he said.

"Yes, Tatte, I do want to talk about something important. Can I go for a walk with you, and can Joseph come? It's easier to talk when we're alone."

As they walked, the boys talked and Pinchas listened.

Joseph spoke first. "David took an exam at school and did really well, and now he can go to SACS for free. It's a wonderful chance."

Then David carefully presented a list of advantages the school offered. He made sure to add that he would learn every afternoon with Reb Mendel.

Pinchas was immediately struck by the thought of how much he would like his boys to benefit from Reb Mendel's learning. His approach was quite different to that of the English-trained rabbi.

He had been worrying about what Reb Mendel would do once he was finished teaching the boys. He couldn't afford to pay him much, but added to the little the man earned from his other odd jobs, it was a substantial sum.

Pinchas had heard of the SACS school. A few of his countryside clients sent their sons there, and they were satisfied.

"Have you spoken to your mother? What does she say?" Pinchas was well aware that he could not make such a decision without consulting his wife.

There was silence, and then Joseph said, "Well...well...We thought... maybe..."

Clearly, Fay had not been happy about the idea. They continued walking in silence.

"Let's make our way home," Pinchas said finally. "I'll speak to your mother. Together we'll decide what to do."

Thinking that all was lost, Joseph turned to his father. "It will be a disgrace if David turns this down. Mr. Thorner will never allow another Jewish boy to take the exam."

Hadn't both his parents always spoken of how important it was not to disgrace the Jewish people with bad behavior, because other Jews would likely suffer?

Pinchas took a deep breath. The boy was right, but he must talk to Faigy. If he couldn't persuade her to agree, he was unsure whether he would insist on something she didn't want.

In spite of his travels, Faigy was now her old cheerful self. When he was home, there was hardly a cross word spoken. He needed her to be happy, especially as he was away sometimes for many weeks at a time.

—

On Sunday morning, the Levine household woke up late.

Before Lettie had become part of their household, Sunday had meant early rising so the laundry could be done.

The previous night Fay had boiled water and added to a mixture of sugar and juice from lemons. She left that in the pantry beside a tin with leftover cake from Shabbos.

Pinchas had returned from his trip with bunches of grapes colored a deep red with a milky white sheen. The farms near Cape Town, with their great white gabled farmhouses, grew grapes that would be used to make wine. Since Pinchas could not accept a bottle of wine from these customers, they gave him grapes instead. Even when Pinchas was not home, there was always fruit in the house, bought from carts that came around selling their wares.

Now, as the children sat around the kitchen table, Pinchas had a chance to talk quietly to Fay.

"David spoke to me about his achievement, getting a scholarship to SACS," he said.

"The boy should not have done that," Fay retorted. "He should have spoken to me. I would have told him not to waste his time and their time. He will go to Rev. Ornstien's school like Jack."

"Faigy, it's true he should have spoken to you first, but now what? What will Mr. Thorner say if he is humiliated, if he has to tell the school that the boy will not attend? How will it affect our children who are still at his school? It troubles me."

"So you want the boy to grow up ignorant of all things Jewish?"

"No, of course not, but he can continue to learn with Reb Mendel. Reb Mendel can teach him whatever he himself learned in yeshiva."

"You think that a few hours of learning after school is as good as being in a Jewish school?"

"Most of Jack's day is spent learning *limudei chol.* David will receive just as good a Jewish education with Reb Mendel. Joseph also enjoys learning with him. Jack too would benefit from learning with him."

"You think he will agree to come every day? What if he finds proper work and can no longer teach?" Fay sat there, thinking. Would it really harm the other children if she refused to let David attend this SACS school? "Well, I don't know," she said finally. "Go talk to Reb Mendel. See what arrangements can be made. Then we'll talk again."

Pinchas knew when to leave well enough alone, so the rest of the day passed in a pleasant but desultory way. In the morning the children played in the garden, and after a late lunch of cold chicken and potato salad, left over from Shabbos, the family crossed the road and spent the afternoon in the Gardens.

It was then that Pinchas asked what had happened to Rose's hair. Fay expected him to be angry, but instead he burst out laughing.

"Oh my," he said, "with these children one must have eyes at the back of one's head. She does look pretty, though, doesn't she?"

Fay looked at the little girl running about, her curls bouncing.

"Yes, but I think she must grow her hair long again. Don't you?"

"I will talk to her," Pinchas said.

With this last little worry taken from Fay, it was a pleasant, restful day. For most of the children, it was delightful. For David and Joseph, who were waiting for an answer from their father, it seemed to last forever.

On Monday morning, as the children were leaving for school, Pinchas handed David a letter.

"Take this to your headmaster," he said. "Last night I asked Jack to help me write it. It thanks him for his kindness, and says you look forward to attending the SACS school."

When little Rose walked out, Pinchas said, "You look so pretty with your hair in curls. Curls look pretty on little girls. Just remember to start growing it long, before you become a big girl who must wear her hair properly tied back."

Rose thought about those words all the way to school. She didn't want to be a little girl. She wanted to be a big girl. She must grow her hair long and wear it in braids again. How long would it take?

As Ethel left the house, she was relieved that her father hadn't said one word to her about attending the birthday party.

So on that day, approaching the end of 1892, the Levine family felt happy and settled in their new country. How could they know that far to the north, gold lay deep beneath the soil, and the greed of men, far beyond the ocean, was to bring strife and suffering not only to the vast, beautiful country and its inhabitants, but also to faraway mothers, who would lose their sons on foreign fields?

How could they know it would also bring discord to their family?

Chapter 34

"The appointment of a young zealous and liberally educated Minister
from one of the older Universities in England, continued to maintain
the position of the congregation as the representative body of Cape
Town Jewry and to continue in the Western tradition of Jewish
Orthodoxy... The new minister, the Rev. Alfred Phillip Bender, born
in Ireland, the son of a minister... was a graduate of Cambridge
University, an exceptionally eloquent preacher and speaker, and an
able scholar."

— Dr. Louis Herrman, *A Centenary History*, pp. 69–70

Looking back, it seemed to Fay that 1895 was the year when
everything began to change.

Rev. Ornstien was no longer alive. Jack had done well at his school and,
guided by him, had applied and been accepted to a new dental school in
London. Now he was working for Mr. Davidoff, earning money for his
education in far-off London.

Pinchas returned from the Gardens shul one morning in a less than
happy mood.

"Rev. Bender davened at the shul today. Nearly everyone in the shul was
so happy. 'Our new reverend has arrived,' they say. 'Son of a *rav*,' they say.

"I asked, 'So his father is knowledgeable, but where did he obtain
semichah?'

"'At which yeshiva did he learn?' asked my friend Yankel.

"You know what they answered? 'Such a clever man, a graduate of
Cambridge University, no less!' That was the answer."

Fay tried to find something good to say about the new reverend.

"If he grew up in a home where his father was head of the Jewish community, he must be a good Jew who knows all the laws. What is the harm that he went to an English place of learning?"

"If you had heard him talk today, you would know! Who does he quote? The Gemara? Rambam or Rashi? No, some Englishman, that's whom he quotes!"

Fay was dismayed. She was hoping that the new rabbi would appeal to Pinchas in a way that Rev. Ornstien had not.

Fay was more than satisfied with the Gardens shul. She liked the way the women were seated in the upstairs gallery and could look down into the shul. She liked listening to the sermon in elegant English. She liked everything about the shul, from the beautiful architecture and lighting, to the stately decorum of the service.

"Give the man a chance. He has only just arrived. Did no one enjoy his first talk?"

"Oh yes, the *Englishers* did, the committee men. 'Such a fine talk!' they said."

"Well then, there you are! He knew he had to please them. Give him time. Wait for his talk on Shabbos. See then who he quotes!"

Pinchas was not convinced. "What I need now is some real learning. First I must go to the factory, to discuss our next trip. After that I will go to learn with Reb Schrire. What a good thing it is that our small *minyan* was able to persuade him to remain here. After he left Johannesburg, he only wanted to return home. He is an able shochet and a fine *chazzan*. We were worried he would not remain, but he is here to stay now that his family arrived. What a business! They came on a Shabbos and had to walk all the way from the docks to District Six!"

"Yes, I remember. You told me. When will you be home?"

"I think I'll stay there for Minchah. Maybe after that I will learn a bit more. I'll be home by suppertime."

Fay thought back to this conversation during lulls in the shop.

Her Pinchas, who had so wanted to leave the shtetl, now longed for the old days. Whenever the opportunity presented itself, he would spend time with Reb Schrire and the men who followed him loyally. Was there nothing in this new land that they could agree on?

More disagreement followed when, due to Rev. Bender's influence, a Jewish school was opened for both boys and girls, and not just for those who could afford the fees.

Fay wanted the children who were still at Mr. Thorner's school to be among the first pupils at the new school, which would begin with the junior grades. Since David and Joseph were both at the SACS school, and Frieda and Bertha attended the Good Hope Girls High School, this meant Samuel, Ethel, Rose, and Isaac.

The children were upset. They were happy in their school. Change was frightening. The girls cried and the boys sulked.

Pinchas and Fay discussed the issue.

"Is it worth making the children so sad?" Pinchas said. "Most of the day the learning will be the same. They will only learn a little Chumash. Reb Mendel is teaching all the boys. He is a learned man, a fine teacher. The girls learn from you. Who could teach them better?"

Fay was flattered, but wanted to continue the argument.

"Look, who knows if the school will be successful?" Pinchas said. "They once tried to open such a school before, and it didn't succeed. Let's wait and see."

Fay was disappointed with Pinchas and his decision. How could the school succeed if it wasn't supported by Jewish parents? However, with the children so upset, and without support from Pinchas, she let the matter slide.

Soon she was dealing with more serious concerns and the matter was forgotten.

Fay, standing in her shop, was the first to hear the news. Far to the north, trouble had broken out. Some British soldiers had invaded the Transvaal.

Every customer was talking about it and everyone had a different opinion.

Pinchas came home from the *shtiebel* to find the house in an uproar. He kept hearing the words "Jameson raid." What was going on?

It was David who sat down with him and told him the latest news.

"Dr. Jameson, a friend of Prime Minister Rhodes, tried to attack the Transvaal in the hope that the *Uitlanders* would rise up and support him and take over the Rand. President Kruger's men watched them all the way and have now arrested them and sentenced the ringleaders to death for invading his land. Some say that Rhodes was behind it. People say he will have to resign as prime minister."

By now, Pinchas had learned to speak the same language as his upcountry Boer customers. It was similar to Yiddish and easy to learn. Because he spoke their language, they trusted him and shared their thoughts with him. He heard their viewpoint when he went on his travels.

"The English, they stole Kimberley when diamonds were found there. Now they want to also steal the Transvaal because of the gold," his customers claimed. "Those English — never satisfied, always wanting more. All they ever want is to fight, to get more."

At home, it was a different story.

"They say President Kruger is unfair to the people who make money for the Republic," his sons said. "He calls them *Uitlanders,* and even though they have lived there for years he won't let them vote."

In the angry comments from the farmers, in his sons' comments, in the slow but steady increase of British troops to Cape Town, Pinchas saw the beginning of a conflict. He hoped he was wrong. Conflict was always bad news for the Jews.

On this occasion the crisis was averted. Prime Minister Cecil Rhodes rode all the way to the Transvaal to plead for his friend, Dr. Jameson, who had been sentenced to death.

The sentence was commuted. Rhodes resigned as prime minister. There would be no war. Pinchas was relieved.

Fay, however, was not. She noticed how more and more of her customers were young soldiers, newly arrived from England. In their small pockets of free time, they would go to the Gardens, perhaps a reminder of the green fields they had left behind in England. They would come to her shop for small items, for matches and cigarettes, and her famous fried fish.

There was more and more talk of how the people who had left many different countries and created a new town in Johannesburg, were making themselves and the Transvaal rich because of the gold deposits far beneath the earth.

They were called *Uitlanders* not only by the president, but by the old-time residents of the Transvaal. They were taxed, and yet had no vote. Many were British citizens. On this issue, it seemed, Britain was prepared to go to war.

On his travels, Pinchas heard angry mutterings from the Afrikaner farmers.

"They care about votes? Nonsense! They want the gold. In Kimberley they found diamonds, so they sent their soldiers and took Kimberley. Now they want the gold!"

"I will go north," muttered a young Afrikaner boy, a son of Pinchas's customer. "The British took our beautiful land from us here in the Cape. So many families left everything to go up north, to live in freedom. Now the British want their soldiers to take that away. We will go to the Transvaal and fight to keep them free."

"Quiet," his father said. "Foolish talk! You will remain here. How can the farm manage without you?"

Turning to Pinchas, he said, "Don't listen to my son. Do you know what harm he can cause just by talking like that? The British say we're British citizens, and if we go against them it is treason. Does my boy want to get shot for treason? Just talking like that is foolishness."

Again and again, similar scenarios played out. What was Pinchas to say?

"You know I never repeat anything I hear," he usually replied. "If it is true that just words can bring harm, perhaps it is better not to talk of such things. Of course, with young men, it's difficult to keep feelings under control. Who knows, maybe everything will calm down. After all, everyone wants to live in peace side by side."

But in this, he was not correct. The reality of war was coming nearer.

The Jews whom Pinchas met during his travels mostly agreed with their Boer neighbors. What would happen if war broke out?

Many Jewish families had traveled north, to the republic of the Orange Free State, or even further to Transvaal. They pursued a variety of occupations. They were shopkeepers, often owning the only shop in the village, farmers, and tradesmen of every description.

In Johannesburg, the new city built on the Rand, sitting atop rich gold seams, the Jews worked in every occupation possible. Some barely made a living while others were amassing great fortunes.

Pinchas was filled with dread. What would happen if there was war? Would Jews join in the fight? Which side would they choose? Would Jews end up facing each other with guns in their hands?

Despite his worries, he didn't discuss the issue with anyone.

Whenever Pinchas returned home, he heard quite a different story. Here the British viewpoint was predominant. There was talk of the unfairness of the Transvaal government to people who brought in money from the gold extracted from the earth and who paid vast taxes, and yet had no say in the government.

The year of 1895 came to an end. Pinchas hoped that the English New Year of 1896 would bring peace. Yet the discontent on both sides seemed to be gathering momentum.

Yet another year went by. Pinchas was home when, in 1897, Queen Victoria's diamond Jubilee was celebrated in the Gardens shul. Pinchas was grateful to this Queen, who treated both Jews and non-Jews alike.

He was more reluctant, however, to attend the Chanukah service for Military Service volunteers later that year. Tension had been growing between the governments of the Transvaal and Britain. Pinchas felt this was not something Jews should be involved in.

The children were dismayed when he said he would not go. Eventually, to please them, he went. After the service, as they were walking home, Jack said, "I think I too will volunteer. Here in this British colony we are not discriminated against as we were at home in Lithuania, or as the *Uitlanders* are in Kruger's Transvaal. We are given full rights. I think that as a citizen of the Cape I owe it to Britain to fight."

Pinchas was horrified. Did the boy not realize that this fight, this attempt by an imperial power to crush a freedom-loving small group of people for the sake of gold, was unethical? Oh, he knew the arguments about defending the human rights of the *Uitlanders*, who were heavily taxed and denied privileges.

But there was another side to consider, that of the Boers. They had left the Cape Colony when the British had taken over. They had traveled far, and under dangerous conditions, to found their own independent states. Did they not have rights to grant or refuse citizenship to others?

Did his foolish son not realize that he was risking his life? Loyalty to England was one thing, but was England correct now to fight the Boers? On his travels, Pinchas had heard the sentiment that this was a war meant to keep rich men in England rich, or to make them still wealthier.

Pinchas remembered how some Jews had talked of fighting on the side of the Boers. Did Jack realize that he could find himself facing a Jewish opponent in battle, a Jew who had thrown in his lot with the Boers? His son was looking at rich English Jews like Colonel Harris and wanting to copy him. Foolishness!

Pinchas thought about what he knew about the man. He had arrived in the country many years earlier and started out as a digger on the Kimberley diamond fields. Later he had joined the British army and distinguished himself, so that by now he had the title of Lieutenant Colonel. Not only that, he was a member of parliament. True, he was an influential man, but that didn't mean Pinchas's own dear son should join the British army.

Pinchas felt that war would come, maybe this year or next year. If Britain wanted the gold, she would not rest until she got it. This was not something a Jewish boy should get involved in at risk of his life. How could he explain all this to his son? What could he say to dissuade him from such rash behavior?

"Think a little before you make such decisions," Pinchas said. "War is about killing people. Do you really want to kill another man, maybe many men?"

"Didn't you listen in shul?" Jack said. "It isn't about killing, it's about honor."

"The war will wait," Fay said. "No one is rushing to fight. It's just foolish men talking big, that's all. First you're going to London, to become a dentist. Book your passage tomorrow. After all this business—application forms, deposits, whatnot—you want to stay here and wait for a war that may never be? Foolishness! While you're there, arrange for David to follow you next year. You will both become dentists—a good profession."

Jack's reaction was to walk away from his family, without a word of farewell, and go down the avenue, down Adderley Street, toward the docks. He needed to be alone. He needed to think how to achieve his aim. How did one enlist?

In truth, he was tired of working to make money to go to faraway London to study. He remembered London as a place of rain and smog and cold. Why should he leave this wonderful place to go there? He wasn't even sure that he wanted to be a dentist. Enlisting meant a chance for adventure instead of his dull life.

Jack arrived at the docks. He saw British soldiers disembarking. He was about to go up to one of them, to ask how he could enlist, when he heard, "Look, there are Jews here too. He's a Jew, I'm sure of it. Hey, Jew boy! What are you doing here?"

Instead of fighting with words or fists, as was his wont, Jack turned around, listening to the hoots of laughter.

"Yes, my mate," he heard someone say. "He's a Jew, alright. Look how he doesn't fight us. Look how he walks away."

This experience was enough to convince Jack that the British army was not the place for him. He walked home and announced, "I will arrange for my passage to England. It's time I studied for a profession."

Oh, but wait until I get a British soldier in the dentist's chair, he thought.

Pinchas was amazed by how easily Jack had acquiesced. He tried to get Jack to agree to small things — to walk with him to the little room that served as a *shtiebel* and learn a bit, to not let the barber cut his *peyos* quite so short — yet the boy would agree to nothing. And here he was, meekly agreeing to his mother's words, letting all the fire die out of him.

Becoming a dentist wasn't a new idea. The day the older boys had received their school certificates, Fay had said, "Now that Jack is finished with school he must go away, to England, to learn to become a dentist. Dentists have nearly as much *yichus* here as doctors, but they work better hours.

"Jack and David must both work to earn money for their training in England. I have been saving money for this for many years. They're still too young to go, but they can earn some extra money."

Pinchas had been amazed then at the way his Faigy simply decided such important matters on her own. What an ambition! Did she really think it would work out like that? Now, just a few years later, he listened as she spoke.

Would a grown boy simply agree to what his mother wanted? Jack, of all the children, was so fiercely independent. But now, listening to the conversation between his wife and son, he saw that what Faigy wanted, she got.

Sweet Faigy, who had bade farewell to her family and traveled with him and the children to London, was gone forever. Somewhere between London and Cape Town, she had been replaced by this stern woman who always got her way.

Pinchas was pleased that she had this influence over his son, that she was preventing him from this foolish deed. But the knowledge that she had this power while he had none cut into him and hurt him, destroying his self-esteem completely.

Tension continued to grow in the land, and it continued to grow in the Levine household.

Chapter 35

"In October 1899, the Transvaal sent an ultimatum to Britain, demanding that troops on the Transvaal border be withdrawn. The ultimatum was rejected and war was declared. The Free State honouring its treaty joined with the Transvaal, and the Boer war began."
— Leo Marquard, *The Story of South Africa*, p. 206

The day that war was declared, Pinchas was away traveling. Although the Cape Colony was not a part of the conflict, Fay was filled with worry. Where was Pinchas? He traveled among Boer farmers. Would they vent their anger on her husband, for what the British were doing to their compatriots in the north?

Worry ate into her. She went through the daily routine, but always, there was the worry. Only late at night, with her worn book of *Tehillim* before her, did she find a little peace of mind.

There were other worries, too. Patriotism to the British cause was in the air. Would David talk about joining the British army just as Jack had?

David had just finished his schooling. She had to send him off to London, to join Jack, before he got any ideas about joining the British in their war.

She needn't have worried on that score. When the younger children were in bed, David came to speak to her.

"Mother, I have decided what I want to do," he said. "I want to be a chemist. You know that big chemist shop on Adderley Street? I spoke to the owner today. He will take me as an apprentice. I just need the money for the apprenticeship, and you need to sign the forms."

"Impossible. Does the shop not work all day on Shabbos? Do you mean to tell the man that you won't work on Shabbos? You think he will agree to that? Foolishness! No, you will go to London. You will become a dentist, like your brother."

David was prepared for this. "Mother, *halachah* allows a Jewish doctor to attend to a sick person even on Shabbos. I'm also helping sick people, by giving them the medicine the doctor wants them to have."

Fay found his words to be a weak excuse.

"No. It is not the same. *Halachah* allows specifically for a doctor to attend the sick on Shabbos. This I know from my father. No one else, except a midwife, is allowed to do *melachah* on Shabbos. A dentist also helps cure people, but he can choose when to work. We decided that you would follow Jack to London and become a dentist."

"No, you decided that, not me. I don't want to travel to London. I don't want to look down someone's mouth all day. I want to be a chemist. I thought about becoming a doctor, but for that I would have to travel far away for many years. A chemist is also good. He makes medicines and helps the sick."

Fay thought for a moment of refusing to give him the money needed for the apprenticeship.

"Well, if that isn't possible, I could always join the army," David said. "I spoke to Colonel Harris about it last Shabbos after shul. Lots of Jewish boys are joining up, including my friends. If you won't sign the apprenticeship papers and pay for me, I will join the army."

This was too much for Fay. She signed the papers and gave him the money. She waited in trepidation for Pinchas to return. What would he say?

Yet what choice did she have? Already, only a few weeks into the war, stories of dreadful losses and casualties had become the talk of the town.

❧

When Pinchas arrived home, the deed was done. His son was absent from the Shabbos table. Until then not a word had been said, but now he asked where David was. Fay hesitated, not quite knowing how to break the news.

"He's becoming a chemist and making sick people better," the children said.

"What, on Shabbos?" Pinchas said. "Faigy, tell me this isn't so."

But one look at his wife was all the answer he needed. White-faced, he left the Shabbos table.

He returned some time later to *bentch,* and then left the house. He returned hours later.

"How could you?" was all he said to Faigy.

The following day he went to shul as usual, but the Shabbos *seudah* was gloomy, with no *zemiros* or *divrei Torah*. The children ate quietly and said little.

Only Frieda had noticed her mother's sadness as she broke the news, and she realized now that her father didn't agree with what her mother had done. Yet he didn't say a word about David.

After Havdalah, when they were alone, Pinchas said to Fay, "We must talk."

Fay was not looking forward to the conversation, but she knew it was unavoidable.

"Where did you get the idea that working on Shabbos is acceptable?"

"I never said it was . . . David said he would join the army if I didn't let him work there. I . . . I was afraid."

Pinchas was dismayed.

"Perhaps it would be better if he were a soldier. He's working in a shop on Shabbos — a shop that sells all kinds of things besides for medicines — creams and lotions, hair tonics and shaving lotion."

Fay groped for some way to defend herself. "David makes medicines. He does not stand in the front and sell these items."

"The place where he works sells these items. It is definitely not permitted for my son to work there on Shabbos. We cannot allow it."

Fay knew this, and she was worried. What could she say?

"I signed papers. I don't think the contract can be broken."

"*What?* How could you?"

"Look, don't stand there and blame me for everything. Did I want my sons to go to a non-Jewish school? Didn't I say they had to go to Rev. Ornstien's school? But then they spoke to you. What did they say to convince you to disobey me, to go to that school? Don't you think they might have been better off learning under Rev. Ornstien and Jewish teachers?"

"Yes, I remember. I also remember that I discussed this first with you. We arrived at that decision together. This is different. You did this without me. Could you not at least have waited for me to arrive home, to discuss with my son how serious a step he was taking?"

"I wanted to wait, but he said if the apprenticeship papers weren't signed immediately, he would join the British army. Lots of Jewish boys from shul are doing that."

"When Jack suggested such foolishness, you were firm. Next thing I knew, he was on his way to England, to become a dentist."

"Oh, but I tried. Do you think I gave in easily? What could I do?"

Pinchas groaned. "What will become of him? Breaking Shabbos! How can that be?"

Fay had been thinking these same thoughts, but now, seeing her husband so distraught, she said, "Our David is a good person and a good Jew. What can he do? This is how things are in this country.

"Jack tells me that on Friday night the shul is almost full. Yet when I go with the girls on Shabbos morning, the women's gallery is almost full and the men's section below is almost empty. Here the Jewish men work on Shabbos morning, yet they still attend shul. They give to charity. They are good Jews. Our David is doing what others do. We cannot blame him. He will remain a good Jew."

Pinchas was not comforted. "It's all my fault! All my fault! We should never have left!"

"Ach, what is the use of looking back?" Fay said. How many times had she felt the same way? No matter how good things were here, she missed her family. She missed the intimacy and warmth of the shtetl.

Now, seeing her husband's despair, she did not voice these thoughts. Instead, she said, "Maybe in time David will realize that it's not good to miss Shabbos. Forcing him to leave now will achieve nothing."

Pinchas, too, saw the futility of trying to force David out of his contract. Fay hoped they were doing the right thing, but like Pinchas, she grieved.

Unspoken between them now was worry over Joseph. Would he too follow in his brother's footsteps? He had insisted on going to SACS school, and within a year he would leave it. What would he decide to do next? Would he too cause them grief?

At present, Joseph was learning each evening with Reb Mendel. Together with David, they had patiently taught their teacher English. The man now had a job, helping to sell merchandise in the marketplace. Yet twice weekly he came to their home when his work was done and studied Gemara with Joseph.

He refused to take money, saying that he now had sufficient income and that learning with a keen young mind was a pleasure to him. He did accept a meal and ate together with the family when the learning session was over.

David had learned with him for several years, and yet he was prepared to break Shabbos. What would Joseph decide?

It was with a sense of relief that Fay and Pinchas learned a year later that Joseph wanted to become a lawyer. The lawyers for whom he had worked as a messenger during the holidays were prepared to give him an apprenticeship. This meant that a contract had to be signed and money paid, but on Shabbos the offices were closed. Not only that, but they had agreed in advance that Joseph could take off for the Jewish holidays.

Fay was thankful. They were fine, upright men, but there was a reason for their generosity that she was unaware of. Of late, they had allowed

Joseph to be part of their discussions on difficult cases. They wanted to make sure he was capable of learning the profession and that he could argue a case.

Joseph, without realizing it, had occasionally applied the logic from his Gemara learning to the difficulties of the case under discussion. On occasion, this had shed a new insight on the matter and worked surprisingly well in court.

The boy had a sharp mind and an amazing aptitude for finding solutions where none seemed to exist. They would have been surprised if he had told them that while studying old Jewish books with a man whose English was less than perfect, he had come across similar arguments and solutions.

Not only that, but the Jewish immigrants were beginning to do well and forming a potential pool of clients. It would be good for their young apprenticed clerk to mingle with them in the large synagogue in the Gardens.

As the new century loomed, Jack in faraway London had almost completed his degree. David continued on his path, unrepentant. Joseph was beginning his apprenticeship. Frieda had just completed her schooling at the Good Hope Seminary for girls while Bertha, Ethel, and Rose continued there with their studies. Samuel and Isaac had followed their brothers' tradition and attended the SACS high school.

Pinchas and Fay were now faced with new problems. Frieda had reached marriageable age. How did one go about such things here, with no *shadchan*?

The war was still raging. What would happen if Jack returned now? Would he again begin to talk of joining the British army?

Fay was more nervous than ever of Pinchas embarking on his travels. British soldiers were marching northwards. Was he safe on his long journeys?

Pinchas had different worries. Trade was slow. Very few people wanted to buy new furniture during the uncertain times of war. He wasn't sure how long he would remain employed.

Only time would tell how the saga of the Levine family would unfold.

Chapter 36

"During the first months of the war, the Boers had advantages over the British but failed to make the best use of them. Britain had only 25,000 troops in the country, and the commando system enabled the Boers to mobilize superior forces and rapidly invade Natal and the Cape Colony, annexing whole districts. Instead of exploiting the initial success which their mobility gave them, by pressing on to the Natal coast and the central Cape districts, they laid siege to Ladysmith, Kimberley and Mafeking, and so gave Britain time to rush more troops from England and India ... Mafeking, where Baden Powell was hanging on with great courage and cheerfulness, was relieved in May."

— Leo Marquard, *The Story of South Africa*, pp. 207–208

Fay was busier than ever. Her shop in Kloof Street was halfway between the rooms where the British officers were quartered and the recently built luxury Mount Nelson hotel, where they were lavishly entertained by the English gentry of Cape Town. The war had taken Fay by surprise. She had been so sure that a compromise would be reached.

At first, life continued as usual. But inevitably, change did come. Instead of Jewish families arriving from abroad, refugee Jewish families began arriving from the Transvaal and the Orange Free State, fleeing the fighting, often with just their clothing. They left their homes and businesses behind. The Jews of Cape Town rose to the challenge of helping their brethren.

The talk had been of British victory within weeks, but instead, the first news was of defeats, and then of British forces besieged in Ladysmith, Kimberley and Mafeking. Now, seven months later, in spite of the troops pouring in, the towns were still besieged. This war, it seemed, would go on forever.

There had been some doubt whether Pinchas would continue to travel during this time. Who could think of such things? Yet after a few weeks, it seemed that Cape Town and the surrounding areas would not be affected by the fighting, and once again Pinchas and Jan set off.

Fay had been dismayed but was unable to prevent it. The days when Pinchas was away stretched out endlessly.

One night, Fay had a terrible dream. She saw soldiers holding guns to Pinchas's head. She woke up, trembling, then said to herself, "Foolishness! Why would soldiers bother Pinchas?"

Now, while there was a short lull between customers and the shop was empty, she would say a few chapters of *Tehillim*.

At that moment, Pinchas and Jan were outspanned near the town of Swellendam. They were drinking coffee and giving the horses a rest before completing their rounds and returning to Cape Town.

Just then, Jan stood up. "Listen! Horsemen!"

Pinchas heard nothing, but moments later a lone man on a horse appeared. He was riding a fine black horse with a white patch on its forehead and white patches on its hooves that looked like socks.

"The British soldiers," he panted. "They're after me ... Mulder's farm, my family ... must get there." Then he slumped forward, unmoving, on his horse.

Both Jan and Pinchas knew immediately what had happened. It was a hanging offense for men from the Cape to go and fight with their compatriots in the Boer republics. Yet young men still did so. This man appeared to be returning from the front. It would be dangerous to help him. On the other hand, could they just leave him? The man was clearly not well, and soon the soldiers would catch up with him.

The young man recovered momentarily. He looked at Pinchas, his eyes glazed.

Jan looked questioningly at Pinchas, who nodded. Jan sprang into action.

"Let the young Baas lie in your bed. Cover him well. Place on his head that small black cap you wear under your hat."

"Come," Pinchas said. He helped the man dismount. He grimaced, and Pinchas realized he was wounded. As he took him by the hand to help him up to the wagon, he realized the man was burning with fever.

"Mafeking," the man said. "Mafeking . . . it is over."

Pinchas noticed Jan go to the back of the wagon and take his writing desk.

"Those white marks on the horse must go," Jan said. "I hope there is enough of that black ink you use."

By the time the soldiers arrived, a pure black horse grazed beside their brown one. Jan was busily adding wood to the fire, the coffee pot was bubbling, and Pinchas was sitting with his account book before him, pen in hand.

The soldiers were resplendent in red jackets, but covered with a fine layer of dust.

"Did a horseman pass by here, a Boer with a gun, on a black horse with white markings?" The man had a high-pitched voice and spoke with a slight lisp and upper-class accent, unlike the cockneys in the East End. The question was rattled out as an order rather than a question.

Pinchas was trembling, but he made his voice firm and cheerful. "Oh, I think so. I think I saw a horseman in the distance go that way." He pointed in the opposite direction to the farm the young man had mentioned.

"Who else is here? We saw him come toward you. Not hiding him, are you? You know the penalty for that, don't you?"

"Now why would we do such a thing?" Pinchas said, trying hard to keep his voice confident. "No, just us here, me and my assistant, and my colored man. My assistant is in the wagon, a bit fevered. Hope we find a doctor in Swellendam. Don't want him dying on me. Knew we shouldn't have stayed overnight on that farm, fresh graves and all."

Pinchas hoped that these soldiers, brave though they were, wouldn't look too closely at a sick man. Soldiers seemed not to fear the idea of dying on the battlefield, but they feared these strange fevers that could overtake one in Africa.

"Go, look into that wagon!" the command rang out. Hesitantly, the soldier went to the wagon, pulled open the cover, and said, "Real sick he is, shivering so much that the blankets are almost slipping off him."

Pinchas struggled to retain his composure. If the blankets fell away, the man's clothing would be revealed. They would all be shot and left out there on the veld, never to be heard of again.

"Right then, won't trouble you. Come away—fever, we don't need."

The soldiers wheeled off and galloped away in the direction that Pinchas had pointed to.

The man in the wagon spoke slowly, with effort. "Soldiers! Gone? Mulders farm. Ma! Help me!" Then he collapsed into silence.

Pinchas and Jan knew of the farm and made their way there. When the farm workers came out to meet them, they asked for the farmer's wife, and then drew right up to the farmhouse door. Pinchas beckoned her to the cart, and she came wordlessly, fear in her eyes. Now the man stirred.

"Ma . . . am I dreaming?"

Looking around the yard to make sure that none of the workers were nearby, Pinchas and Jan helped the young man up the steps.

"We must leave now," Pinchas said. "Your horse—where should we put it?"

"No, take it, get rid of it. Sell it. Give it away. The soldiers will come here."

They left the farm, making their way rapidly back home. On the outskirts of Cape Town, Jan stopped suddenly when he saw a cluster of huts. He went off with the black horse and returned some time later.

"My cousins . . . They accepted the gift with gratitude. Soon they will sell it. No one will know where it came from."

Pinchas and Jan arrived home to find flags waving and people cheering.

As Pinchas walked into his home, the children shouted at him, "Mafeking has been relieved. What a great day!"

Fay came out from the shop. "Mafeking," she began.

"Yes, I know," Pinchas said. He hoped that the solders would never find the wounded young man, would never find the horse, would never find him or Jan. "Don't talk to me of war. I need rest."

Fay and the children stared at Pinchas. The whole town had been in a frenzy of excitement all day. They had expected him only the following day and couldn't wait to tell him the news. Now here he was, not seeming at all pleased to see them, not one bit excited at the news.

"Your father is tired," Fay said. "See how hard he works for you. Quiet now. Let him rest. Frieda, put on the kettle. I'll make a nice cup of tea for him."

Fay was afraid that the children would let slip that their father was a Boer sympathizer, that he didn't rejoice at the news of the ending of the siege. That wouldn't do. Not at all!

"Your father is very tired," she repeated, and then, hearing the bell in the shop and the voices of officers, she turned to leave.

Before she left the room, Fay looked behind her at the rest of the family, home early because of the excitement.

Isaac, now fifteen years old and completing his education at SACS school, was amazed that his father had displayed no excitement.

"Father is tired, Isaac," Fay said. "We must all be very quiet so that he can rest. I must go to the shop."

Something wasn't right, Fay thought. Something didn't feel right, but she didn't know what it was.

For the rest of that week, Pinchas suffered through uneasy days and nightmarish nights. He went to learn in the *shtiebel* in District Six. He went to the factory and discussed the few orders he had made. In times of war, people are reluctant to think about new furniture.

A few days before Pinchas was about to leave again, the shop bell tinkled.

Fay was in the kitchen, frying the last batch of fish to sell.

"Please go to the shop for me," she called to Pinchas. "See what they want. I won't be a moment."

Pinchas was about to comply when he heard voices coming from the shop.

"So the man escaped. We nearly had him. That cursed Boer colonist fighting up north, coming home, and we very nearly had him. Those Boer farmers, with their big white houses and vineyards, live in the Colony. They should be loyal to us. Instead, they go upcountry and fight us. I nearly caught him, that Boer traitor.

"That cursed Jew peddler and his colored man. They gave us the wrong information, I'm sure of it. Oh, if only I could lay my hands on them."

That voice, that high-pitched voice, that upper-class accent, that lisp. It was all too familiar to him. Pinchas froze. There was no way he could go into the shop.

Confirming his fears, he heard another voice.

"Relax, old boy. They had an assistant with a bad fever. You know how the fever travels from one to another. Fresh graves on the farm, the man said. Well, you needn't think about them any longer. Let's enjoy the few days' break we have here."

It was definitely the same soldiers he'd met. Pinchas remained where he was.

"Well, go on then, I won't be long," Fay's voice rang out.

Pinchas walked into the kitchen. He couldn't say anything to Fay about the soldier. It was better that she knew nothing of what had occurred.

"You go," he said curtly. "It's your shop."

Fay pulled off her apron, took the pan off the fire, and rushed past him, glaring at him.

When some time later she returned to the kitchen, the oil was cold and had soaked into the pieces of fish.

"Ruined," Fay said to herself. "Ruined just because he wouldn't go into the shop for a few minutes."

The atmosphere in the house that evening was one of frigid politeness between husband and wife.

Pinchas wanted to explain, but he felt that he would be endangering Faigy by telling her of the encounter. So he remained silent, and the bad feeling between them festered.

Together with Jan, he had saved the life of the young Boer. If he would be recognized now, all their lives would be in danger.

Fay continued to be angry, and Pinchas remained silent. One day, maybe, he could tell her what had happened. One day she would understand. But now was not the time.

After some thought he made a decision that surprised Fay. He took a pair of scissors and trimmed his long beard. He cut it shorter and shorter, until he looked in the mirror and was satisfied.

Fay came in just as he was finished. All she could say was, "Why?"

"Well, you've been remarking on how different I look from the other men in shul for some time, haven't you?" Pinchas said.

"But you were so angry when I suggested it."

The sudden change of attitude troubled Fay. Her husband was acting so strangely. First he had refused to help when she asked him. Then this sudden business with her sewing scissors . . .

What was going on?

For a few moments she was silent.

"It looks good, more like everyone else," she said finally. "But I think that maybe, you should let the barber trim it just a little."

Slowly, the anger began to seep out of her. True, he had refused to help in the shop. Maybe he had good reason not to — though what it could be, she couldn't work out. Yet here he was, trying to please her and cutting that long, wild beard of his.

Pinchas faced yet another problem. He was afraid of bumping into these soldiers if he went out. After all, they had come into the shop. They were in the area. He was wearing the same suit he had worn when he met them. Even if his beard was shorter, he didn't look all that different. But he couldn't remain hidden in his home forever.

"Well, maybe you're right," he said. "But I think I'll change into my Shabbos clothes first."

Now Fay was really worried. He was wearing his Shabbos outfit, on a weekday, to go to the barber!

Just then the shop bell rang as a customer entered. Pinchas exhaled in relief. He had been thinking of a way to explain why he needed to change his clothing. Quickly, he found his white starched shirt, dark suit and black hat. He looked in the mirror. He did look slightly different from the way he had looked that day on the veld. Was he unrecognizable? He hoped so.

He made his way to the barber.

"Tried to save money and do the job yourself?" the barber joked. "Fine mess you made! Don't worry, I'll soon put it right."

Now he needed a new suit, something quite different from the one he had worn during the confrontation with the soldiers. Pinchas walked up the hill to the Malay Quarter and went to the tailor.

"I need something strong for travel over the veld," Pinchas said.

The tailor brought out some material similar to his previous suit.

"No, no, something different," Pinchas insisted. "I need a change. How about brown, and maybe a different cut? I think I need to fit in more with the people I meet on my travels."

The tailor was surprised, as previously Pinchas had been rigid in his desire to keep to the same style he had always worn. Only after some time had a compromise been reached. The suit they had agreed on was black, the style slightly modified from the long black jacket Pinchas had been wearing, but not truly fashionable.

Now, Pinchas rejected plain brown. Eventually, he chose a brown material with a white stripe and was shown a sketch of the latest style. The jacket length was considerably shorter than the previous suit and the lapels were broad. The tailor was surprised when Pinchas agreed right away.

"I need it by Friday morning," Pinchas said.

The tailor was about to refuse, but then remembered that this man worked for the Isaacs factory. These people were all good customers. He nodded and named the price. Pinchas gulped when he heard it, but this was a necessity, not a luxury, so he agreed.

His next stop was the hat shop, where he bought a bowler hat. He felt absurd in it, after the wide-brimmed hats he was used to, but he did look different.

When Jan arrived a week later in the early morning for the trip upcountry, Pinchas was surprised.

"We have a new cart?" he asked.

"No, it's the same cart, I just made it look a bit different," Jan said. "A bit of paint, some wood added here and there. After all..."

"Yes, yes," Pinchas said, aware of Fay approaching them with a packet of food for the journey.

Pinchas and Jan looked at one another, taking in their changed appearances. Whereas before Jan had been clean shaven, he now had a small beard. He wore a large navy flat cap, instead of his wide-brimmed leather hat. His baggy brown trousers and dark blue shirt had been replaced by a pair of narrow dark blue trousers and a sparkling white shirt.

Before Pinchas could say a word, Jan said, "My Sunday clothes. The others, I burned. I'll have to buy new Sunday clothes."

Pinchas nodded.

"You think they'll recognize us?" Jan asked.

Pinchas shook his head worriedly. What more could they do?

Thereafter, there were some things they would never talk of again. It was safer that way.

Fay noticed that her husband, his driver, and the cart had been spruced up. She wanted to ask why, but seeing that it was a change for the better, she decided not to say anything.

Fay suddenly felt upset about the bad feelings between her and Pinchas these last few days. Pinchas seemed to be less than cheerful about leaving. She couldn't know that it had nothing to do with his worries about David, nor about her angry reaction when he had refused to help in the shop.

Since Pinchas had arrived home, she awoke each night as he screamed in his sleep. It was so unlike him. How could she know that the recent run-in with the British soldiers worried him during the day and gave him nightmares at night?

Fay ran back into the house, pulled out the cake she had baked for the children, and ran to him and thrust it into his hands just as he was getting in the cart.

"But you already packed a cake for us!" Pinchas exclaimed.

"Yes, I know, but a little extra can't do any harm."

Pinchas realized immediately that this was Fay's way of saying they should not part in anger.

He replied in a way she knew she would understand. "The sweetness of the cake will be good on our travels. Look after yourself. This isn't a long trip. We'll be back soon."

So, in spite of their worries about David and Pinchas's refusal to help in the shop, they parted amicably.

Chapter 37

"On September the 3rd 1899 the Dorshei Zion Association held its inaugural meeting. It immediately became a rendezvous for the lonely newly arrived immigrants from Lithuania ... and later also for the Yiddish speaking refugees from the Transvaal ... The Reverend Mr. Bender was given the honour as spiritual head of the community, to perform the official opening of the Zionist Hall in September 17th 1901 ... He did not make mention of the new meeting place as a Zionist Hall, but referred to it merely as a library."
— Israel Abrahams, *The Birth of a Community*, p. 104–106

On many Shabbos mornings, Fay listened to Rev. Bender's sermons. She was well aware that he was not a believer in Zionism. When Pinchas returned from his trips, he always went to the *shtiebel*. When he came home from davening one day, he said to her, "The New Zionist Hall is going to have a big ceremony to open it. Rev. Bender of Gardens shul will officiate."

Fay was more than surprised. The man was known for his views against this new ideal of Zionism.

Before she could say anything, Pinchas went on. "You will come to the opening? It will be a great occasion."

Fay was usually too tired after working all day to do anything but rest, but now she was curious. If Rev. Bender was talking, maybe she should go and listen. Had he changed his mind about Zionism? Why?

Frieda, who had nothing much to do during the day except help her mother in the shop, found the idea of an evening out diverting, so she joined her parents.

The hall was packed, but they managed to find three seats together. Pinchas began talking to a young man sitting beside him, who introduced himself as Moshe Lerner. Reverend Bender began to talk, referring to the "library" that was being opened, and deliberately omitting the words "Zionist hall."

This caused some wry comments from the Zionists in the hall.

When the ceremony was over, the family departed from the hall and walked home. The next day, Moshe went to the *shtiebel* where he knew Pinchas davened. He had made inquiries before they parted.

"Your daughter finds favor in my eyes," Moshe said. "Is she spoken for? I don't know how to proceed. There seems to be no *shadchan* here. I come to you to direct me."

Pinchas looked at him. "Tell me about yourself."

"I have a leather shop in Long Street. Back home, my father was a shoemaker, and he also supplied leather to the shoemakers of the surrounding shtetls. When I came, I had little money, but I brought with me some good leather. Now those pieces are gone, but I know where to get good leather, and I supply many different places. I have saved enough to buy a home and care for a wife."

"Let us learn together," Pinchas said.

The two men sat down, and while they talked in learning Pinchas was able to discern more about Moshe's character.

When the time came to part, Pinchas said, "I will talk to my wife and daughter. Let us *daven* again here tomorrow, and after that we can talk."

Pinchas spoke first to Fay, late at night, when they were alone.

"A man we know nothing of!" was her reaction.

"I feel he is a good man," Pinchas said. "When you were Frieda's age, you were already a mother. What are we to do here, in this place, with no *shadchanim?*"

"That is why the Rev. Bender arranges all sorts of activities at the shul for the young people, so they should meet. Frieda goes there. There she will meet someone. Rev. Bender knows the young people who attend. We can rely on his judgment."

Pinchas was horrified. "What?! Our daughter has been going to mixed gatherings? How could you allow this?"

"The rabbi thinks the young people will meet and marry this way."

Pinchas sighed. How strange were the ways of the people in this land.

Frieda, meanwhile, was unable to fall asleep. Once the discussion became heated, she could hear what they said.

She thought back to the young man they had met at the ceremony. Listening to him talk to her father, she had felt some strange affinity. Was it because he had the slightest accent, reminiscent of the shtetl? Was it because he felt so fiercely about his beliefs? She didn't know, but she did want to meet him.

She was about to get up and say, "I want to meet with him," then thought better of it. The next morning she rose early and met her father before he left for davening.

"I heard you talking last night," she said. "I want to meet with him. Perhaps he is my *bashert*, perhaps not, but if we don't meet then how will I know?"

"Your mother is not in agreement," Pinchas said.

"Yes, but you and I together will persuade her," she replied.

Pinchas left the house, bemused. This daughter of his was so determined. Well, was she not Faigy's daughter? Did Faigy give in easily? Had not his Faigy done the impossible by bringing them here to this good land?

In time, Moshe came to visit the Levines. The little garden made a pleasant place to sit and talk. After a few visits, he came for the Friday night meal, where he gave an interesting *d'var Torah*.

Moshe had learned for some years in the famous Mir yeshiva and Fay slowly began to warm to him, even though she had at first felt that she had been forced to agree to the visits because of the pressure from her husband and daughter.

The wedding took place in the Gardens shul. The guests were a mixture of old settlers and new immigrants. The young couple settled in a house not far from the bride's family.

Only Jack was missing from the celebrations. Frieda wrote to him, and so did Fay. Jack only received the letters many weeks later.

As Jack read the letters, he felt a fierce longing for his family. Life in England was difficult for him. He was staying with strangers. The cold weather and persistent grey sky made him long for the sunshine of the Cape.

Not only that, he had missed this momentous event in his sister's life.

He felt an urge to simply give everything up and return, but his mother wrote how proud the family was that he was going to return as a man with a fine profession. Jack sighed and knew that he had no option but to carry on.

BOOK THREE

Jack's Story

Chapter 38

"In a novel entitled Isaac Eiler's Money (1889), Mrs. Sidgwick presents another intimate sketch of community life of Frankfurt Jews in London. The squalid group of money grabbers, and their less repulsive womenfolk, contemptuous and ignorant of anything better than the material interests of life, are put on exhibition before the English reading public, and criticized from the point of view of a cultured Englishwoman."

— Montagu Frank Modder,
The Jew in the Literature of England, p. 323

As his years as a student were drawing to an end, Jack longed to leave London and return to the sunshine and clear air of the Cape. He longed to once again be with his own family. He was tired of living with strangers. True, he had his own room, an unfamiliar luxury after having shared one his whole life, but it was under the roof of strangers.

When he had first arrived in London, he quickly realized that he didn't have enough money to complete the course. He had gone to the only person he knew in London, his old headmaster, Mr. Angel, and as a result he was now living with a middle-class Jewish family. He was a tutor to their son who attended a private school and had missed much learning due to illness.

Though Jack was a good student, dental school was not pleasant for him. He was the only Jew in the class and the top student. He experienced a snide form of anti-Semitism that was new and unpleasant to him. He had to contend with remarks, not directly addressed to him, but just loud enough for him to hear. It wore him down to hear expressions such as "Don't Jew me."

Then there was the war. So many brothers or cousins of other students had gone to South Africa to fight. Each time someone left for the Colony, or a list of fatalities appeared in the papers, or the British soldiers scored a victory, unpleasantness was sure to follow.

"So we send our brave men to fight for the rich Jews on the Rand, while their cowardly sons flee here," some students commented.

It was made clear to him that he should be back home fighting, not in London away from the conflict. His only recourse was silence. Words would have achieved nothing.

Jack longed to use his fists when he heard remarks against Jews, but that would mean expulsion. What pleasure that would give his tormentors!

He longed to explain the complex situation, the rights of the northern Boer republics, their desire for independence, and the feeling that the British were fighting for the control of the gold on the Rand.

However, in the heated atmosphere of war and loss, this would not go down well. Silence, so difficult to maintain, was the only answer.

Instead, Jack concentrated fiercely on his studies, kept his interactions with the other students to a minimum, and went straight from class to tutor his pupil and eat his evening meal with him. Then he went to his room to study.

Shabbos brought some relief. At shul he met people who invited him to their homes. He made a few friends, young Jewish men who were studying for a career at London University, apprenticed to lawyers, or busy working in their father's business. It was good to be with other Jews, but being with other families only made him miss his own family more.

A few times a *shidduch* was suggested, but that would mean remaining far away from everything he missed, or taking a young girl far away from her family, so he demurred. He was counting the days until he could once again board a ship and sail south.

Jack was not worried about his exams. He was sure he would pass. What did worry him was the thought of returning home almost penniless.

A dentist needed equipment—expensive equipment—to work properly. Such equipment wasn't available in the faraway colonies. Everything he would need to set up a practice must be bought in London and transported to the Cape.

It was a conundrum. Without equipment he could not work. Without work he would have no money to buy equipment.

This was solved for him one day after class, when his professor asked him to present himself at his office during the lunch break.

"One of our top dentists needs an assistant," the professor said. "I was asked for my best pupil. I had no hesitation in putting forward your name. You will learn much from this man. He has all the latest equipment and knows the most modern techniques. The salary he offers is more than fair. He would like you to begin the moment you qualify. What do you say?"

What could Jack do but accept the generous offer? Difficult though it was, he must remain in England.

It was some months later that the news of victory in South Africa against the Boer republics was received in London with much jubilation. By now, Jack had enough money to pay for the equipment he needed as well as second-class boat fare on a Castle line to Cape Town. He even had some money to spare to buy gifts for his family.

However, he wasn't celebrating the victory as others were. Instead, he was sitting in a darkened room, listening to a young man, Rob, talk in a low voice. Rob's brother, whom Jack had met in shul, had asked him to come see his brother.

"Thank you for coming," Rob said. "I need to talk to someone who understands. Danny told me you were from the Cape Colony, but instead of fighting you came here, to study. He told me how angry he was with you, that his own brother was fighting your fight. But still, I insisted he bring you here."

Jack wondered why he had been invited and how to respond.

"Of course I came," he said hesitantly. "How could I not? You fought and were wounded. You were so brave . . . I knew I must come."

"Huh, bravery. Poppycock! Do you know what I did there? Do you know what my unit did there? We crossed the Orange River and then went from farm to farm. The men were all away, fighting. The women and children were left to fend for themselves. What did we do? We forced the women and children out of their homes. We set the houses on fire. We killed the livestock. Then we went to the next farm and the next, and when we had enough women and children to make the long journey, we took them to great tented camps surrounded by barbed wire and left them there."

Jack fumbled for a reply. "But you were wounded. You are only now recovering." He had read these stories in the letters the Englishwoman Emily Hobhouse had written to newspapers, after she had gone to South Africa to care for these women and children.

"Hah, wounded! That's right, spit and polish — that's what the officers wanted. Spit and polish. The man next to me was cleaning his rifle. Cleaning a rifle while it was still loaded. Have you ever heard of such a thing? I think, maybe, he was just too tired to think. We had been on a long march through the veld, after burning those farmhouses.

"We were expecting a Boer ambush any minute, and then the officers shouted out that we must prepare for an inspection. Such stupidity! All we wanted, all we needed, was a rest and food and sleep. What can I say, he was careless! The gun went off. The bullet came through my leg.

"Now my family and friends want to talk of bravery. Huh! I find myself unable to utter a word to them. How can I tell them of these terrible deeds I did? How can I speak of brave deeds? I am dumbstruck. At night, I see those women. I see those children. I can smell the burning grass of the veld. I feel blood pouring onto the ground from the cattle and sheep that we slaughtered. Why did we do it? What have we gained?"

Jack thought to himself that Britain now had the wealth of the gold mines, but he said nothing. His father had said long ago that the fight was all about gold. The man lying on the bed wanted comfort. What comfort could he give?

"You were under orders," he said at last. "What option did you have?"

"Yes, kill or be killed. I chose to kill. Well, we didn't kill those women and children, but the stories I heard—about the camps, about the deaths there from disease. We killed all their animals. We destroyed their farms. Perhaps I made the wrong choice."

Jack, aware that he too could have been forced to perform such acts, was thankful now for the anti-Semitic soldiers at the Cape Town docks and their remarks on that long-ago day. He was thankful that his mother had acted so decisively. He had not enjoyed the years in London, but he now had a degree, and he had made sufficient money to return. He was fit and well, and not plagued by the terrible regrets of the man before him.

He thought of his father and what he would say. He thought of his mother, and how she had managed to put those difficult years in London behind her, and start all over again and be successful.

For some time, there was heavy silence in the room. What could he say to bring comfort to this young man? How would he feel if he had done these terrible deeds?

"We cannot change what has been done," Jack said finally. "But we can make up our mind to do better in the future. There was suffering in the war, but now it is over. The women will return to their farms. Their husbands will return, now that the fighting is over. The land will become peaceful again.

"Here too there is suffering, not from war but from poverty. Have you ever been to the East End? No? Well, go one day when you have recovered. There is much good that can be done there by someone who has financial resources and who can show caring. I am sure you can do much good there.

"Go to the Jews' Free School. Ask how you can help. Perhaps you can donate money, or maybe you can teach some skills the boys need to succeed, to pull themselves and their families from poverty."

Rob gave a small smile. "Maybe I can do some good in this world to make up for what I have been forced to do. Maybe! Thank you for coming. I know from my brother that the other students didn't give you an easy time about leaving your country and avoiding the fighting, but you made the correct decision."

Jack left, wondering if in fact he had made any decision, or if the decision had been made for him by his mother. He was determined now to return to Cape Town with all haste.

The war was over; it was time to return. He could buy equipment and travel back in comfort. He would set up his own practice. He had written some weeks before to the shtetl where his grandparents still lived. He had thought, perhaps, to visit before returning to the Cape.

Though he had carefully written his address, there had been no reply. Had the letter reached its destination? Weeks had passed and he had heard nothing. Had he sent it to the correct address? Maybe the family had moved. In any event, now he was in a hurry to get home.

He must go to the Union Castle offices and pay for a ticket home. That was the best way to travel.

Just then he seemed to hear his mother say, "Man decides, but Hashem arranges."

No, he told himself. His plans were made. They would come to fruition.

Chapter 39

"And don't think what they found waiting for them at the ports were ocean liners as we know them today. They were cargo ships designed to take as much cargo as they could possibly hold. Passengers? Passengers were a secondary consideration. Look, the captain didn't send for these people, did he? They came of their own free will."

— Channah Hirsch, *My Llanelli*, p. xii

The following day, Jack gave notice at the dentist. A new crop of dentists was about to graduate and so his notice was accepted. Within a month, another young man came to take his place. Jack was free to return home. He was about to set out one morning when the maid called to him.

"Master Jack, a visitor for you," she said. "He is waiting for you in the breakfast room."

Jack heard the maid stifle a laugh, and went down hurriedly to see what was causing her mirth. He saw, standing awkwardly in the room, a thin middle-aged man, with a long unkempt beard threaded with grey. He was wearing the type of apparel that Jack remembered from his early days in the shtetl. His large black yarmulke peeped out from under his black hat.

For some moments, the two men simply stared at one another.

"Yaakov, grandson of Malka, son of Faigy and Pinchas?" the man said.

Jack nodded. Who was this man? What did he want of him?

"You look like an Englishman," the man said. "I wasn't sure where to go, but this is the address I was given. I have come for help."

The man spoke Yiddish, and Jack had retained his knowledge of the language. Whenever his parents didn't want the children to understand their conversation, they spoke in Yiddish. Jack always pretended not to understand, and so he followed every word. But he had not spoken that tongue for many years. Haltingly, he told the man to sit down, to make himself comfortable and tell him more. He too sat down and listened.

The man told his story in hesitant words.

"My wife, your aunt, your mother's younger sister — well, she saw that others were going to the *goldene medina*. For us, things were not going so well. Things seem to be good for those who went. So we collected some money for me to go ahead and earn more money there, and send for her and the children. Well, I thought I bought a ticket all the way to America. But when I arrived in Liverpool, here in England, the captain came below and said, 'Everyone off.' We came on to the deck. One man looked down. He said, 'This is not America. I have been here before. This is England.'

"What did the captain reply? 'Right, you are in Liverpool, England. Your tickets are for this place. Off you go now, all of you. We take on more passengers here.'

"Well, there was much shouting and arguing, but then all the sailors came, and together with the captain they forced us to leave. In Liverpool I found other Jews and a place to stay. My money ran out. I cannot find work. Now I am in despair. I will never see my family again. I wrote to my wife and she wrote back that her nephew, her sister's son, is in London and that I must go to him for help. So here I am."

Jack was flabbergasted. He couldn't think straight. He couldn't remember an aunt in the shtetl. He could remember uncles, brothers of his mother, but no aunt. He began asking questions, about his grandmother and grandfather, and the house where they had had once lived. The answers were satisfactory.

"How is it that I do not know you or my aunt, yet I remember my family and most of the people who lived there?" he asked.

"We lived in the next shtetl. The distance was not so great, but travel was not easy. We rarely visited."

Convinced now that the man was genuine, and clearly poverty stricken, Jack said, "Come, we will go together and buy tickets for your family to travel to America. But why go there? Why not the Cape Colony? My mother would love to have her own family nearby. The life there is good for someone who is prepared to work."

The man hesitated for only a moment. "No, we must go to America."

Jack escorted his uncle to the shipping office and handed over money for tickets to America, for two adults and five children. In addition, money was needed for the mother and children to travel to London. Jack was thanked again and again for his generosity, and then this man, the husband of his mother's sister, took his leave.

The clerk was delighted with the number of tickets he sold that day. Jack was less delighted. After paying for the tickets, he realized that he didn't have enough money to travel on the Castle line. Yet now, standing in the shipping office, he had a strong urge to return home. He had bought the equipment and tools he needed for his new career. He had presents for each member of his family. What was he waiting for?

"Are there any other boats that travel to South Africa soon?" he asked. "Are they any cheaper than the Castle line?"

"Well, sir, there is *The Windrush*, traveling from Jaffe with oranges and some passengers. It's off-loading here and taking on a few more people. It's smaller than the Castle liners, so takes a bit longer, but cheaper. Not a bad little ship."

Jack sighed with relief. He had enough money for such a ticket, but he barely had any money left for the short time he would have to spend in London.

He began to think of his return to Cape Town, of the warm sunshine instead of the almost constant drizzle, of being once again with his family, instead of always being surrounded by strangers. So he would travel on a less comfortable ship. What did it matter?

But small ships are not only less comfortable; sometimes they are less equipped to deal with inclement weather.

Chapter 40

"That year had been a particularly bad time for shipping. Just off Port Elizabeth, ship after ship had been wrecked that year, twenty at least. Usually it was the sailing ships that were wrecked. The new steamships could use their power to escape dangerous rocks and sandbars. But even those ships had been affected during the past year. Fog had caused the Tantallion Castle to run aground at Robben Island, and a fire had caused the Norham Castle to drift dangerously close to rocks, being saved at the last minute by being towed away."

— *Naval Office, archive section, Cape Town*

Lately, Fay had been dreaming of shipwrecks.

A letter had arrived only the previous day to say that Jack, now twenty-two years old and a qualified dentist, would be returning home on a ship called *The Windrush*. Why should she dream of shipwrecks?

Of course, she was worried about Jack. Foolishness, why should there be a problem? The war was over and he would be home in a few days. He had a degree and good experience. Soon he would set up a practice in Cape Town.

The ship was approaching Port Elizabeth, only a short distance from Cape Town. Jack sat in his cabin, his excitement mounting. Soon he would be home, his degree in hand. In the hold of the ship was everything he needed to establish a practice.

It seemed to him that the waves off the coast were particularly fierce. He peered out of the porthole. Was he imagining it, or was the ship slowly but surely getting closer and closer to the coastline?

As Jack felt the ship roll in the waves, he regretted not traveling on the new steamships of the Union Castle line. Sailing boats were at the total mercy of the elements of the sea. Steamboats could power themselves away from rough seas, yet he had chosen this vessel, powered only by sails. Had he traveled on the Castle line he would have already been home. The journey took half the time. He recalled that when he had traveled to London, the journey had been much smoother. He should have stayed in London a bit longer, made some more money, and traveled home in comfort on a Castle liner.

Still, he was on his way home at last. True, he was practically penniless now after giving his money to his uncle in London. But what choice did he have?

Besides, was he any less able now than when he had first arrived in the Cape so many years ago? Then, as a young boy, he had earned money. Now, as a dentist, he would soon make up the money he had given away. He would rent a room to see patients. All would be well.

It was exactly one month before Rosh Hashanah. Soon he would be davening in the Gardens shul, a place of decorum and beauty, surrounded by his family. He had missed that shul so much.

The ship gave a lurch. Whistles sounded and crewmen banged on doors.

"Onto deck, quickly, onto deck, everyone!" came the call.

Jack grabbed his certificate, pushed it into his jacket, and made his way up the stairs and onto the deck, together with other panic-stricken passengers.

Now, as he stood on deck, surrounded by crying children, wailing women, and pounding waves, it occurred to him that the sacrifice and hard work of the past years had all been for naught. What foolishness it had been to grab hold of the certificate. What good could it do for him now? The ship would go down.

In the distance, he could make out the shore. It was so close yet so far away, taunting and unreachable. Directly ahead of him giant waves pounded the ship, and white spray flew up the rock against which the ship now lay.

Jack found himself next to a woman who was holding a baby in her arms, swaddled in blankets. Standing by her side, clutching her skirt, was a small boy.

"Oy, first the Arabs kill my husband," she moaned in Yiddish. "They killed my dear husband as he walked to the fields near Petach Tikvah. My family sent money for us to join them, so we wouldn't starve, and now this, now this. Soon we will all be with my poor dead husband."

Just then a line came snaking onto the ship, shot apparently from the shore. The crewmen ran to it, tugging at it, until a much thicker rope, attached to the first thin one, came on board. A crewman tested the rope and clung onto it, making his way to shore. The passengers were instructed to follow.

Jack looked at the woman, heard her moans.

"I can't do it," she wailed. "How can I with two children?"

Though he too felt fear, he forced himself to speak soothingly.

"I will tie the baby onto you, very tightly, with your shawl," he said. "See, like this. You can do this. Hashem will help you, and soon you'll be safe on land. I will follow with the boy and care for him as if he were my own."

The Yiddish words seemed to calm the woman. She looked at him.

"I will do as you say. I lost my husband. I will keep our children safe. For his sake I will do it."

Jack watched as she held onto the rope, as she moved one hand forward and then the next, as the spray hit her. He marveled at her strength and courage.

Now Jack bound the boy to him and clutched the rope. The cold sea hit them and the rope swayed. The weight of the boy dragged him down, pressing the rope into his hands, cutting into them. He was no longer aware of anything but the need to place one hand in front of the other, to cling to the rope with his feet, to keep going. He felt his strength leave him. The boy was heavy.

Had he not promised the mother to take the boy to safety? He could not give in.

Slowly, carefully, he moved one hand in front of the other.

Just as Jack felt his whole body would collapse, he heard shouts, telling him they were nearing the shore, but his hands were raw and his strength was going.

He gave one last desperate attempt and found himself grasped by strong hands, then dumped down. As he staggered forward, more hands took hold of him, leading him away from the blinding water, wind and sand.

It took some time for the news of the wreck to reach Cape Town. When it did, there was gloom in the Levine household. Only Fay kept a cheerful countenance.

"What, my Jack, not coming home? Nonsense. My Jack can look out for himself."

—✐—

Table Bay harbor was calm as a lake, glinting in the grey of the early dawn. The ship bringing the survivors of the shipwreck from Port Elizabeth slowly made its way to the docks.

The newspaper had written the day before of their arrival and included a list of passengers. Those waiting on the dockside were subdued as they hoped and prayed.

Jack stood at the rail, looking out toward the mountain, the outline a clear, deep grey against a pale grey sky. He thought back to his arrival here.

Then, he had been surrounded by family. Now, standing at his side, was a young widow with a baby in her arms and a young boy beside her.

"Look!" the boy said. "See that strange mountain, with its flat top!"

Those had been the same words Jack said when he first arrived, dressed in his Shabbos suit and confident that all would be well. Now he was wearing a slightly shrunken, sea-stained suit. In his pocket was a crumpled, blurred certificate.

He had no instruments with which to practice his profession. He had no gifts for his family. All his work was lost. He was no longer an optimistic young boy. He was worried about how he could practice his profession with no instruments and no money.

As Jack gazed at the mountain, he saw the sun, slowly rising, shining on the landscape. It illuminated the bright colors of the red-roofed houses, the green of the mountain slopes, the clear, bright blue sky. Jack's optimism returned.

Beside him, the woman had her own worries.

"Do you think our families know we are arriving today?" she asked.

"Well, there seems to be a fair number of people there," Jack said. "Apparently, they published a list of our names in the Cape Argus, so that people would know we were arriving today. But don't worry. If they're not there, you'll come with me to our home. We'll find them."

Soon the gangplank was down and the passengers began to disembark, unburdened by luggage. People surged forward, and there were cries of joy as families and friends were reunited.

Jack saw his mother, standing stoically, watching. He ran to her, pulling the boy with him as the mother and baby followed. He had almost reached her when a tall, well-dressed man came striding toward them.

"Channale, is it really you?"

The woman turned to Jack. "My family! I am safe now."

She took the boy by his hand and went with the man.

Jack walked to his mother. She saw him coming but stood still, waiting for him.

"You are home," Fay said, and Jack gave a deep sigh of contentment. Yes, he was home, away from the smog of London, away from the snide remarks of his fellow students, away from living with strangers. His books, clothes, and instruments lay at the bottom of the sea, but he was home.

It was difficult to find a cart to get home, so Fay and Jack walked up Long Street. Jack looked this way and that, taking in the old familiar sights. Standing on that wind-lashed deck, surrounded by screaming women and children, he had thought he would never see these familiar places again.

Fay walked beside him. There was so much she wanted to say, but the relief at finding her son on the quayside, safe and well, filled her now and silenced her.

"They all wanted to come and meet you, but I insisted on coming alone," she said finally. "After all, I sent you away. Maybe I shouldn't have done so. Did I think then that I was putting your life in danger? I thought I was sending you away from danger."

"Well, you wanted me to be a dentist, and so I am." Though what good would that do him, with no instruments and no money?

They entered the house through the shop entrance. They found the family sitting around the kitchen table, the fire in the stove burning, teacups on the table but no food.

Fay entered first and worried faces turned toward her. Jack followed and suddenly the room was filled with a clamor of voices.

"Jack, it's really Jack! Oh, Jack!"

"Well, didn't Mother say her Jack would come back safe and sound?"

"Tell us what happened! What a worry you gave us!"

"Why did you change your plans? Why didn't you go on the Castle line, like you first wrote?"

"Children, calm down," Pinchas said. "Let my son be seated. Give him some time to answer all your questions." His face shone with happiness.

"Now, don't we both at least deserve a cup of tea, after our long walk from the docks?" Fay's voice rang out, clear and practical as usual.

No one had dared say a word to Fay during the last troubling days. The reports in the newspapers had been dramatic. They had been afraid that Jack had not survived the shipwreck, but they listened despondently, unbelievingly, to Fay as she immediately declared, "There are survivors. My Jack is a survivor. He will be home soon."

Fay gazed triumphantly at her family. "See, my Jack is home. What did I tell you? Now, let's have tea and something to eat. Then Jack will tell all."

Jack was pleased that his mother had taken control. He felt overwhelmed. He looked around the table and noticed how the years had brought change. The family was secure financially, that much was clear to him. Their clothing was of good quality. The food on the table was abundant.

Suddenly, he felt like a stranger. He had left a house of children. Some of them were now adults, and the others were already in high school.

"Welcome home, my son," Pinchas said. "Tomorrow we will go to shul together and you can say *Birchas Hagomel.*"

Jack was home. No one could have guessed how Pinchas had worried about his boy, back in London, in the place that had made him so ill. But Jack looked well. The black smog of London hadn't affected him. Pinchas was silent, letting everyone else talk, ask questions, answer Jack's queries, and enjoy being together once again.

Jack looked at Frieda. She was a married woman now, her little girl on her lap and her husband beside her.

Opposite her was Bertha, more beautiful than ever at nineteen.

Beside her sat Ethel, a child no more. He hardly recognized her, with her upswept hair and elegant dress.

Rose, sixteen now, was getting food and placing it on the table.

Jack drank the hot tea and looked around the table. "Before I tell you about what happened, let me first hear about you. What have you all been up to? You wrote letters, but letters don't tell everything."

So Bertha told of how she had long ago completed her schooling and now helped her mother in the shop.

"Oh, and I paint a little," she added. Jack thought he detected sadness in the way she spoke. Did she long to paint more and work less?

Ethel spoke next. "I've been out of school for a year already, since we all finished school at sixteen instead of eighteen!"

"What about you, Rose?" Jack asked.

"Oh, nothing to tell! I'm still in school."

"And what about when you finish school?"

"Oh, I don't know. I haven't really thought about it. I'm not as good as Bertha at art. Every year she was given the art prize at school, but I do like to draw and paint. My friends will be eighteen when we finish school, and all they can talk about is who they will marry!"

"I must leave soon, for college," Samuel said suddenly. "Can't be late! You know I thought of becoming a doctor. Then your letters came, and I remembered how cold and dark it was in London. Not for me. So now I'm studying science at the South African College. At one time there was talk of establishing a medical school, but so far, that's all it was—talk! Pity!"

"I must also run," Isaac said. "At SACS they don't let you give excuses for being late. You know, in just one month it's my bar mitzvah. I know the *parshah* backwards now. How marvelous that you're home! I was so upset to think you would be away."

Jack noticed that everyone was there except David. Joseph, sitting beside him, said quietly, "David is working. He will see you later in the week." Jack wondered why his brother was working so early in the morning. He wanted to ask more, but one look at Joseph quieted him.

Jack thought back to their arrival, all those years ago, and the way they had nearly lost all their possessions. Even after the long sea voyage, away from the smog of London, his father had not recovered completely.

Everything was so much better now. What if he had not collected stamps? What if they had not been able to travel that long distance?

Later, when they were alone at the table, as everyone left to carry on with their daily routine, Joseph said, "I must also go off to work, but first I want to tell you about David, so you don't ask anyone about him."

"Why? What happened to him? None of the letters I received gave me news of him!"

"No, it isn't what happened to him, it's what he did. David insisted on being apprenticed to a chemist in Adderley Street. Of course, that meant working on Shabbos, even though David said it's permitted because he's healing people. But Mother knew the store sells all kinds of other things, too, and she was against it.

"What do you think David replied? 'If you don't agree, I'll join the army and go upcountry to fight the Boers.' Well, that was the very worst thing he could use as a threat, and it worked. Mother gave in. When Tatte returned, he was not pleased. I heard them talk late at night. 'How can you let such a thing occur?' Tatte said. 'How can a son of mine break Shabbos and then come home? What influence can this have on the other children? What would your father say to such a thing?'

"The reply was a surprise to me. 'He would say: Your child is forever your child. Overlook his faults. Treat him with kindness. In time, he will return to the mitzvos.'"

Jack listened, astonished.

"So Tatte let it be?" Jack said. "He let his son violate Shabbos and he did nothing?"

"What could he do? Think about it. Now David is through with his apprenticeship. He works now for the same man, but for money now, a good salary. We hardly see him because of the long hours he works. Now that he's qualified, he sleeps in an apartment above the shop, so that if there's an emergency he can attend to it. But I'm sure David will want to see you."

Jack found this incredible. How could his brother have embarked on a career that meant working on Shabbos? How could his mother have allowed it? He had faced many difficulties during his time in London, when there had been requirements to work on Shabbos, sometimes for a special lecture, sometimes for work in a clinic for the poor, but always he had managed to explain why it was not possible for him and his explanation had been accepted.

"Well, what about you?" he said. "Mother always wrote about how well you were doing. Is that truth or motherly pride?"

"Well, you know how determined I was to study law and work in those offices where I was a messenger boy. What can I tell you? I worked really hard there for five years, and soon I will be able to work as a lawyer. I turn twenty-one this year. Below that age they won't allow anyone to practice law."

"So, where will you work once you are qualified?" Jack asked.

It seemed as if his brother, too, needed to go out and launch himself into the world.

"They have already asked me to remain with them, maybe to become a partner in the future."

"They offer every clerk a job?" Jack asked.

"Oh no, but it seems they are pleased with me. You remember Reb Mendel? We still learn together once a week. He says I have a real *gemarakup*. Now he has a job selling in a shop, so it's good of him to continue to learn with me.

"Every now and again something occurs to me at work, a solution to a legal problem that is puzzling everyone. When I suggest a solution they're amazed. 'What a fine idea! How did you think of that?' I don't tell them that I learned this in the Gemara. They asked me to remain with them. So maybe Mother is not bragging for nothing!"

Later, when Jack was alone and the house was quiet, he walked into the garden and looked up at Table Mountain. It was a clear day, and the sharp outline of the flat mountain stood out against the clear blue sky.

Jack thought back to when his family had arrived as strangers, dressed differently and speaking differently. Now his family was fashionably dressed in light fabrics and spoke with the soft Colonial accent, which sounded strange to Jack after his years in London.

They had become part of their new surroundings, content with their lives.

It felt as if he had never left. It had been so difficult being away. There had been moments on that storm-tossed sea when he had felt that he would never again see his family. He hoped to never again leave the beautiful Cape.

More than that, he remembered the tension in the family, the girls wanting to dress like the others in their class, the boys wanting to attend SACS. He recalled the friction between his parents over his father's traveling upcountry, how he davened in the little *shtiebel* when he was home, rather than the Gardens shul.

His father no longer sported a long, unkempt beard. With his trimmed beard and smart suit and bowler hat, he looked like any other member of the Gardens shul, and he apparently davened there regularly.

The family seemed so united, at peace.

But where did he fit in? He had one tattered, stained suit and a blurred certificate. He had not a penny to his name. He had no instruments with which to start a dental practice. Where did he fit into this successful family, so at ease in these beautiful surroundings?

Chapter 41

"Although by the turn of the century East European Jews constituted the majority of Jews in South Africa, there emerged a synthesis of the two traditions, characterized as "the pouring of Litvak spirit into Anglo Jewish bottles ... One consequence was that most Jews left their traditional Lithuanian way of pronouncing Hebrew for the Anglicised pronunciation."
— David Sher, "Nusach Anglia," *Jewish Affairs,* 2014, p. 53

Jack was sleeping with his brothers. The room seemed so crowded. He was ashamed of himself for wishing for his own room again. He felt ill at ease. He was with his family again. Did that not count for something?

"Hurry, boys," his father said. "We don't want to be late for davening."

Jack suddenly felt worried. How could he go to shul in his battered suit?

He sat up. "Maybe just today I will *daven* at home," he said.

His father looked at him in surprise, then took in the crumpled suit folded at the bottom of the bed.

"Yes, that is the sensible thing to do. I'm not working this week. Later today we will go to my tailor and do some shopping. You'll need shirts. You lost everything ... You'll need new *tefillin* as well."

"The money ..." Jack said. "When I begin to work, I can repay you."

"Ach, such talk! What better way is there to celebrate your safe return? Money is no longer a problem for us, here in this good land."

Lettie arrived just as he finished davening. Jack went into the kitchen. She gasped when she saw him and said, "So the sea didn't get you! I knew it. Your mother, she also knew it. The others, how they worried." She looked Jack up and down and laughed out loud. "Well, the sea didn't improve that suit of yours."

Jack thought of the quiet, submissive little maid in London. How different Lettie was, with her exuberant remarks, quick wit, and jokes. What a pleasure it was to be here again.

"So you don't like my suit," he said, laughing. "But don't you worry. We're going to the tailor so I can look respectable again. I wouldn't want you to feel ashamed!"

Later, after breakfast, Jack and his father set off for the Malay Quarter. Jack noticed how his father walked up the hill without having to stop even once. How different from the first time they had walked up the same slope to be measured for their first new suits.

Three suits were ordered, two for weekday and one for Shabbos. The tailor looked at Jack as he finished measuring him.

"One suit will be ready tomorrow evening," he said. "You need it badly, yes?"

"That is good of you," Jack said. "But how will you manage in such a short time?"

"Oh, do not worry. My boys are at school in the morning, but afternoons, they help me. We will leave aside everything else. Call tomorrow evening."

By the time Shabbos arrived, Jack was newly outfitted and had everything he needed. The men of the family walked to shul as the sun began to set. Jack remembered his first time in the Gardens, his encounter with those well-dressed Jewish men.

Now his father and brothers were well dressed and talking to one another in English. But more than that had changed. When the service began there was no longer the near silence of men murmuring their prayers. Now there was a hum, not as loud as it had been back in the shtetl, but a distinct melody of men's voices, rising and falling. Apparently, influence was not a one-way street. The men from afar had learned to modify their tone, but it seemed they had influenced others to *daven* with more fervor.

The shul was crowded. Many more Jewish immigrants were now living in the town. Clearly, they had brought into the shul the old intensity of their prayers, slightly toned down to conform with the *"Englisher Rav."* Not only that, besides for men dressed like his father, with smart suits and bowler hats, there were men who had recently arrived, wearing long black shtetl clothing.

Everything, it seemed to Jack, had changed: his family, the shul, everything. Where would he fit in?

As they walked down the avenue, his father sighed.

"I was hoping ... I was hoping that David would be there," he said. "Surely he could leave early just this once."

Later, when they returned home, the talk around the table was about Rev. Bender,

who was now firmly in control at the Gardens shul.

"Rev. Bender gave an interesting talk today, don't you think?" Joseph said.

"He's a clever man," Fay said. "I so look forward to hearing him when I go to shul."

Pinchas, it seemed, thought differently.

"You should know, Jack, that there is a learned man named Rav Schrire, who lives in District Six with his family. He gives really fine *shiurim*. I go whenever I can. We also have a fine library in Roeland Street, because of those people who came here during the war. We have a committee that collects money to send to the poor Jews of Palestine. What do you think of that?"

Pinchas looked around the table. "Of course, Rev. Bender has other ideas. He says this is not the time to talk of returning to Eretz Yisrael. He says we are loyal British citizens and that talk of our homeland is harmful to us."

Jack noticed his mother tense up. His brothers exchanged glances and began to sing *zemiros*.

But Pinchas could not forget his dismay. "Him and his strange ideas! Did you hear in shul an announcement for a bas mitzvah for some girls this week? What foolishness. He wants to make girls like boys. If the boys have a bar mitzvah, then the girls must have a bas mitzvah. They will stand up in shul and talk. Surely it is not *tznius* for a *Yiddishe maidel* to stand like that in front of a mixed gathering. Were we not created for different roles? What next? Will he want the girls to wear *tallis* and *tefillin*? Foolishness!"

Fay suddenly spoke up. "Now what is wrong? A little ceremony to mark the transition of a girl to her age of responsibility for the mitzvos, when she turns twelve! Is that not a charming idea? Who said anything about *tallis* and *tefillin*?"

Jack expected his father to argue, to say something. Instead, there was an uneasy silence.

Jack wanted to change the subject but could think of nothing to say. Then Bertha said how good the food was and began to talk of Frieda's little girl and how she was just beginning to walk.

Joseph told of a thief, caught red-handed, who in shock had said to the man confronting him, "Oh, Mr. Brown, it's not me you see."

Slowly, the atmosphere around the table lightened again.

Joseph began to hum a Shabbos song. Jack joined in, and then his father and brothers joined too. The Shabbos joy was restored to the table.

The following day, the family walked together to shul—except David, whom Jack had still not seen.

The weather was balmy, warm without being too hot. The sun shone down through the leaves of the trees in the avenue, making a shifting pattern on the ground. The girls, dressed in their Shabbos best, discussed who would be in shul. Jack saw his mother look at the girls with pride.

Jack wondered why his father davened at this shul, rather than the *shtiebel*, like old times. As if his father was reading his thoughts, he said, "It makes your mother happy that we all go to shul together on Shabbos. Sometimes on weekdays, I go to the *shtiebel*, but I usually go here, so that the boys and I can *daven* together before they go to their studies."

They returned home to a fine *seudah*. Jack was surprised to find that what he had thought were potato latkes were spicy, meat-filled triangles that burned his tongue. His mother noticed his reaction.

"Oh, I should have warned you. Lettie taught me how to make them. They're called samosas. Aren't they tasty? Maybe they take getting used to."

For dessert, there was compote, and also an array of fruits that Jack had never seen in London.

"Try the pawpaw and the pineapple," Samuel said. "I convinced Mother that they are good, quite good. We buy them now, and also guavas, lychees, and mangoes when they're in season. Just wait until it's really hot, real summertime. You'll see how delicious they are."

Jack thought back to his first days in Grocott's grocery, and how he had learned about all sorts of new fruits and vegetables. Now these foods were part of his family's diet. How things had changed since those early difficult days.

Toward the end of the meal, feeling relaxed and happy, Jack thought of the man to whom he had given his money in London.

"Why did you come home on that small ship?" his father asked, almost as if reading his thoughts. "We thought you would return as you went, on the Castle line. They have a good record."

"I had money saved," Jack said. "I bought presents for you all. I bought dental equipment to bring back with me. Then a man came to see me. He said my grandmother gave him my address. He talked about our family in the shtetl. When I asked him to describe the house we used to live in, and my grandparents, he knew everything. He told me he was married to Mother's sister.

"He told me how he had bought a ticket to America, and instead had traveled to England. Now he wanted to send money to his family, so they could travel together from London to America, but he didn't have enough money.

"I was suspicious. Married to a younger sister? Mother had never mentioned a sister, only brothers. So I questioned him closely, and in the end, I was convinced he was telling the truth."

Jack didn't notice that his mother had turned pale.

"Well, how could I not help my own family?" he continued. "We went together to the shipping office and bought tickets for his family. After that I only had enough money to travel on a sailing ship, instead of a Castle steamer."

"You nearly lost your life on that boat," his mother said, her voice tight. "Once again, my sister causes me harm."

She got up and left the room. After a few moments, Pinchas followed her. The family sat, stunned.

"What did I say?" Jack asked.

The children looked at one another and shrugged their shoulders.

After a while Bertha spoke. "I never knew Mother had a sister. Brothers, yes, and they're married with children. But she never mentioned a sister. Are you sure he said he was married to a sister? Are you sure he didn't say he was a brother?"

Jack thought back to the conversation. The man had clearly said he was married to Jack's mother's sister.

There was an uneasy silence. Bertha and Ethel removed the plates from the table. Rose brought cake to the table. Bertha brought hot tea and Ethel brought teacups and saucers.

"There must be some explanation," Joseph said. "We will soon know. Don't worry, Jack. Perhaps you were cheated of your money, but even if you helped a stranger, you helped a poor Jewish man. Giving *tzedakah* is always a blessing."

Their father reappeared just in time to hear his words.

"Correct," Pinchas said. "You gave *tzedakah*. It's not important who you gave it to. Now we will all forget about this matter."

Later, Jack spoke alone with his father.

"There is more to this," he said. "There is something I can't understand. Surely Mother wouldn't have reacted in such a way if I was merely cheated out of some money. She was white when she left the room. She looked like one of my patients after many teeth had been extracted. She was in terrible distress."

"My son, I don't ask you for much. You're a good son. I ask you now to forget this matter, never to talk of it again."

"But there must be an explanation. Why can't you give it to me?"

"It's not mine to give. I ask you now to leave it be. Forget these events as if they had never happened."

Jack thought of the terrible voyage, when he nearly lost his life. He thought of his hard-earned money, gone. He thought of the troubles he would now have as a result. But he looked at his father, saw his pain-filled eyes, and reluctantly agreed.

Chapter 42

"I have no prejudice against Jews as Jews, and I cannot think who has given rise to such an idea ... I have known Jews as excellent colonists at the Cape, industrious, law-abiding, and thoroughly loyal." (Lord Milner, The High Commissioner, July 1902)
— Saron and Hotz, *The Jews in South Africa*, p. 91

On Sunday morning, when the men and boys returned from shul, they were surprised to find the girls sitting alone at the table, looking worried.

"Mother says she is tired," Bertha said. "She is staying late in bed. She said we should see to the food."

"Mother, tired, still in bed!" Isaac exclaimed.

In all his young years, his mother had been busy and brimming with energy. The older boys and girls looked at each other, but though they said nothing they were in agreement.

"Sit, eat," Pinchas commanded them, and then went to see Fay.

Jack was sitting nearest to the bedroom and could hear snatches of the conversation.

"... So maybe he was not your *bashert* ... maybe ... forgive her after all these long years ... Is life here not good? ... How do you know she started the gossip? Was she not too harmed by it?" Then, in a slightly louder voice, "Jack is safe and sound ... that is all that matters ..."

That night, Jack woke up to hear his mother shouting, "You ruined my life. Such embarrassment! How could you do this to me?"

Then his father's soothing words. "Shh, shh ... You're having a bad dream. We're safe here. We're here with all our dear family. Sleep now. No more dreams."

On Monday morning, there was no smell of fish frying in the kitchen.

His mother was still in bed and the girls were preparing breakfast. Lettie arrived.

"Where is the madam?" she asked.

"Mother is in bed," Bertha replied. "She doesn't feel well."

Lettie said nothing, but a worried expression crossed her face. "No fish frying! Still in bed! She must feel really bad. I must see her."

The children looked at each other, not knowing how to respond. Lettie marched past them and into the room. They thought she would walk out moments later. Fay had been curt with the girls when they had gone into the room to inquire if she wanted anything.

There was a low murmur of voices. Then, surprisingly, laughter, and Lettie emerged. She wasn't smiling, but she looked less somber.

"Your mother, she just needs some rest," she said. "You two big girls will look after the shop this morning. After lunch, I think, your mother will be much better."

She took the cleaning supplies from the cupboard and began her usual routine.

Jack was slightly mollified by Lettie's words, but worry remained. Something he said had caused his mother unhappiness. Why had she been so affected when she heard he gave his money to a stranger, who said he was married to his mother's sister?

Did his mother have a sister? She had never mentioned one. Had the man, desperate for money, made up a family connection? But then how had he known where Jack was staying? How had he known so much about the shtetl and Jack's family?

What had caused his mother to leave the table, go to her room, and stay there?

Apparently, she blamed this man for the fact that Jack had traveled on a different ship, and the shipwreck that followed. But didn't the fact that he was home and safe count for anything?

His father clearly understood why his mother was so disconcerted but would not share his knowledge. Jack felt his old confidence leave him. When they had first arrived at the Cape, he had saved their luggage from theft. Now, his luggage was gone, and he had arrived home with nothing except a stained, shrunken suit and a wrinkled, smudged certificate.

When they had first arrived he had made money, enough to keep them going, until the shop began to make money. Now, his father had paid for every stitch of clothing that he owned.

When they had first arrived his mother had sometimes shared her worries with him about his father's health, about finances, about his siblings' schooling. Now he was out of the picture, unknowing, while his father knew of things that he, Jack, knew nothing of.

There seemed to be little he could do by remaining in the house. Jack went to his room, placed his certificate in his jacket pocket and his new hat on his head, and said, "I think I will go to Adderley Street, to the dentist who advised me before I left."

Jack crossed the road to the Gardens and then turned right and walked down the long avenue of oaks, with little red squirrels darting up and down, and out into the broad, dusty shop-lined Adderley Street. He wondered if Dr. Martin even remembered him.

He wondered if, like his fellow students in London, Dr. Martin looked down on him for not remaining in South Africa to fight. He wondered if the man would remember the advice he had given him long-ago.

A patient was leaving as Jack entered. The man was clutching his jaw, looking miserable. The dentist stood at the doorway, watching the man leave.

"Good morning," Jack said. "I—"

"Jack, my boy, you're back, I see. How did it go?"

Jack passed his water-stained certificate to the dentist.

"This was all I could save, when the ship was stuck on a rock," he said. "I just grabbed it and ran for the deck."

"You were on that wreck? What an experience! You managed to keep hold of your certificate! Well saved! Of course you can write and get a new copy, but this is good. It means you can take over here for a while. I badly need a rest.

"The troops are leaving. There aren't so many left now, but it seems to me that every other soldier needs a dentist, and they're unwilling to use their own medics. Mind you, seeing the results of one or two of their extractions I'm not surprised."

"Me?" Jack said. "Take over? You need a rest? You'll stay here and watch while I do the work?"

"What kind of rest is that? You have your certificate. You were at the best place in the world to learn the art of dentistry. Of course I won't be here."

Jack hadn't expected such a quick response. Suddenly, he felt nervous. He had always worked under supervision. He was worried about being on his own, but it was too good an opportunity to turn down.

"Where will you be?" he asked. "In case . . ."

"Me? I'll be away, in St. James. Lovely little place, soft white sands, calm little bay — ideal place to get some rest. We have a small holiday cottage there. Come now, there's a spare coat in the cupboard. Take it to cover your clothes and let's see what you can do."

By the end of the day, Jack had done most of the work while being carefully watched.

"Right then! Tomorrow you go solo! Best way to gain confidence. I'll tell the wife we can be off tomorrow. She can send the maids ahead to see that everything is ready."

Jack was about to ask the man how many days he would be working on his own. Before he could even open his mouth, Dr. Martin said, "About a week should do it. No cure like the sea air."

Jack was about to accept, when he remembered that a whole week would include Shabbos. David had broken Shabbos to work for the chemist. Jack knew that he could not do this.

"There is a problem," he said. "I'm happy to work for you all week, but Saturday...that day is our Sabbath. I cannot work then."

"Oh, not to worry! This week I didn't accept Saturday bookings. I was planning to leave on Friday afternoon, so no problem there. First thing Monday morning I'll be back. I watched your work. You'll be fine."

On Jack's first day alone, a young British officer stumbled in, looking miserable. His face was swollen and there was a blue bruise on his jawline. His stiff red officer's coat seemed to be the only thing that was holding him up. Jack led him to the leather dentist chair and the officer slumped down on it.

"Bad tooth," the officer mumbled. "Army surgeon tried to remove it, but no success...Heard about the old chap here...good man, they say. Where is he?"

"He's away. Now open up and let me see."

"What you? A youngster like you? Younger even than me, it seems!"

"Yes, maybe, but look up there. See that certificate with my name? Now open up."

The man gave a helpless shrug but obeyed.

Jack saw where the army dentist had dug in to try and extract the tooth. All he had done was badly damage the surrounding gums. Now they were ragged and bleeding. The tooth itself showed some signs of decay. Drilling and filling would solve the problem. The gums would take some time to heal, but properly cleaned, and with soothing cream, the prognosis was good.

Not too long ago, barbers had extracted teeth. Then, a new profession called dentistry had sprouted, and aspiring dentists had trained by being apprenticed to other dentists. Only very recently had professional courses, such as the one he had taken, been introduced. Clearly, the army dentist belonged to the old school—no apprenticeship or proper training.

Jack worked slowly and carefully. The soldier lay there, tense and worried. When Jack said, "Right, all done, five shillings, please," the response was, "But the tooth is still there."

"The tooth had decay. I filled in the hole. Keep your mouth clean by using a salt solution three times a day. Apply this cream. In a week or so you should be just fine."

"I came to have a bad tooth taken away. It's still there. I'm still in pain. Now you want five shillings!"

"I did what was needed. No extraction is necessary. The pain is from the drilling. In a few hours it will be gone. The gums will take a little longer to heal properly, but you must do as I said—gargle with salt water and apply the cream."

"Five shillings! Absurd!"

"Look there, the fees are written up very clearly."

The officer hobbled off the chair and made for the door, but Jack was there before him. "Perhaps your senior officer would like to pay instead."

This had the desired effect. Jack had noticed the deference with which Englishmen treated their seniors. He thought it had something to do with the school system, the way the upper classes sent their boys away to school at a very young age. Now he hoped his ploy would work, since he had no way of finding the right officer.

To his great relief, the man paid and stalked out. One by one patients arrived, and slowly Jack gained confidence as he followed what he had been taught. By the time the week was over, he was sorry to relinquish the job.

On the following Monday morning, he was at work, waiting for Dr. Martin. He had kept a list of patients, their treatment and the fees received. He had agreed on a salary for the week and saw that he had made far in excess of that during the time there, but he felt no resentment since it had been an ideal learning opportunity for him. But where would he go now?

At nine thirty the dentist walked in. He was slightly tanned, and his eyes no longer looked dull and tired.

"Well, my boy, how did you get on?"

Jack handed the accounts book over and waited for his response. Just then, a soldier walked in, stiff and upright in his bright red coat. At his side was a frightened-looking youngster—a private, by the way he was dressed.

"Grand job you did for me," the officer said. "Brought young Tomkins to you. Too scared to go to the doc. Can't say I blame him. Grand job you did for me, grand job."

Jack was about to say that he was no longer the dentist, that the old, experienced dentist was back, when he heard, "Well then, Dr. Levine, take off that jacket and get kitted out. Let's work together today."

By the end of the day, Jack was happy to tell his family seated around the table, "I am now a partner in a dental practice."

His mother was still in the shop, but the rest of the family beamed at him. The congratulations came thick and fast.

Only Joseph, now in his final year of training to become a lawyer, had a worried look on his face. After the meal he spoke quietly to Jack.

"A partner! But how are you buying into the practice? I thought you told me you returned here without capital."

"Stroke of luck. It's a busy practice and the dentist is overworked. There's no one suitable here to take on. I will get the fees of the people I treat, less twenty percent, which will go toward buying into the practice."

"How many years will that take?" Joseph asked.

"Three years, more or less," Jack said, beaming. "It's all worked out, signed and sealed."

"You should have let me look at the contract first," Joseph said.

Jack realized that in the years he had been away, people had changed. His younger brother was now proficient in legal matters. Although he wasn't worried about his signature on the piece of paper, he realized that it would have been both sensible and polite to let his brother look at it before signing.

"Yes, maybe . . . I won't sign anything again before letting you look at it. But I'm happy now that it's signed. I have work and I can make plans for the future."

Jack wanted to tell his mother the news, but he was worried that she was still unhappy or annoyed with him. Just then his mother came bustling in.

"Well, where have you been all day?"

Jack was pleased that his mother was her old self again. He was happy to share his news. He was earning again. His mother was feeling better. All would be well.

Chapter 43

"The Cardarga temporary Synagogue was the place of worship for 'corporation Sunday' in September 1904 when the newly elected Mayor, Hyman Liberman, and the Corporation attended the Divine Service in their robes of office."

— Dr. Louis Herrman, *A Centenary History*, p. 79

The year 1904 was an important one for the members of the Gardens shul. They had collected enough money to build a large new shul. This had necessitated breaking down the right side of the old shul, to make room for the new one. In the meantime, they had rented a large hall in the Cardarga Hotel to use for worship.

On a bright spring day in September, the shul members came together with the dignitaries of Cape Town for Corporation Sunday, in honor of the newly elected mayor, Hyman Liberman. Rev. Bender gave an impressive sermon and a collection was made for the hospitals. Everyone who was anyone was there. Naturally, Fay had made sure that all the Levines, dressed in Shabbos clothing, were there too.

Even Pinchas was there, for was not Hyman Liberman of like mind? Had he not come over from Suvalki, a small town in Lithuania, and to this day spoke with an accent that was considered "foreign"? Was he not a fine Hebrew scholar? Did he not treat all his fellow Jews with respect? Did he not help many new immigrants to find their way in the new land?

Oh, the stories about this man Liberman! Not only had he made a lot of money in his business enterprise, he was well known for his contribution to the town council, to the shul, and a myriad of different activities.

Now he was mayor. What a marvel! Could such a thing have happened anywhere else in the world, that a Jew, an immigrant, could be mayor?

Of course, he, Pinchas, would attend the service and honor the man.

The new Gardens shul wasn't yet built. They were now passing the old Gardens shul, and Pinchas remembered how awestruck he had been the first time he had seen it. Now they were building an even bigger, finer shul. But it would be nothing compared to the new shul building that had gone up that year in Roeland Street. What a building! Yet there they davened as if they were back home, back in the shtetl. There they felt themselves at home, among *landsleit*, rather than stiff English and German Jews.

There, in the new Roeland Street shul, all the mitzvos would be strictly observed. In the *talmud Torah* behind the shul, their children would be taught in the old way.

The bedraggled immigrants had arrived from the depths of the steerage accommodation in the ships. Their language, Yiddish, had for a short while been challenged. It was not a "European language" and had nearly prevented their entry to this land. Yet these people had triumphed. They made a living. They created their own shul. When he was among them, Pinchas felt at home.

Nevertheless, he only went there occasionally. His Faigy preferred that he go with the boys to the Gardens shul, and so, to please her, he usually went there. Pinchas was slightly less comfortable in the Gardens shul, but it was nearer to home, and his boys were happy when he went with them.

Pinchas was pleased to attend this ceremony for Hyman Liberman, this new immigrant, this upright Jew, wherever it would take place. Now he walked proudly down the avenue, his wife by his side. Their children walked slightly ahead of them, laughing and talking as they went. He watched them, filled with fatherly pride.

By now, Jack had a good reputation as a dentist and was on his way to becoming a full partner.

He felt a twinge when he thought of David, now a qualified chemist, saving to open up his own shop. Many Jewish men, who had once observed all the mitzvos meticulously, didn't keep Shabbos in this new land, yet the thought of his son joining their ranks pained him each time he thought of it.

Joseph had qualified as an attorney and was working for a prestigious firm. Samuel was completing a degree at the university.

Bertha, Ethel, and Rose, with their schooldays behind them, were fine young ladies, resplendent in brand-new outfits made especially for the occasion.

Only Isaac looked unhappy. He was fifteen years old, just finishing school and thinking about his future. He longed to be with his friends now by the seashore in Sea Point, instead of heading to an afternoon of speeches.

The family arrived at the hall and split up, the men going in one door and the women in another. The speeches were many, the prayers long, and the choir wonderful.

As they came out, Jack saw a young woman walk toward him. She was smiling brightly and waving at him. Only when she was nearly in front of him did he recognize her as the woman he had helped during the shipwreck.

How different she looked, so smartly dressed, with a tall, distinguished man by her side.

"Morris, come Morris," she said. "Here is the young man who saved us, that day of the shipwreck."

Jack was soon introduced to her new husband. As the rest of his family caught up with him, he introduced them.

"Oh, how brave he was that day," the woman said. "If not for him, if not for him . . ."

By now, the rest of her family had joined them, and they too were introduced. They had sent tickets to Palestine to take the woman and her children away from the scene of her sadness, the tragic death of her husband.

Both families now stood in a small group, talking.

Fay looked carefully at these people and realized that they were none other than the Bernsteins, the most successful jewelers in Cape Town, one of the founding families of the congregation.

The matriarch of the family looked at the Levines. She knew precisely who they were. She had daughters, marriageable daughters, and these Levine boys . . . well, they were professionals. A dentist, a chemist, a lawyer, and another at the university . . . They were presentable young men, well spoken, well dressed, not bad looking at all. Well, not quite the social equals of the people she had mixed with as a girl, but then, here, far from Europe, one couldn't be all that fussy.

As the two families mingled and talked, Fay was elated — so elated, that she was less aware than ever of Pinchas, standing beside her, distinctly unhappy.

Pinchas had retained his shtetl mentality. He didn't approve of this easy mingling. These young people, talking and laughing together, opposed all his feelings of what was correct and seemly.

The *d'var Torah* he had just heard, with its many references to English literature, felt like some alien entity. But of course, it reflected the educational background of the reverend of the shul. Not that the sermons in the new Roeland Street shul were any better, in his opinion, with the young lawyer, Morris Alexander, and his academic gown and Latin quotations. He sometimes spoke since they had no *rav*.

In the Gardens shul, there were men who wore top hats, who sat in the front seats. These men were wealthy. They had arrived many years before and mixed with the elite society. Their level of Jewish observance was not exactly something Pinchas admired.

Then there were those who had come from the shtetl or from England, poorer Jews, who came to improve their lot in life. They worked hard, taking every opportunity that came their way, even if that meant forsaking Shabbos. They now lived good, comfortable lives, but not affluent ones.

These men wore bowler hats and came to shul on Friday night, but not on Shabbos morning. These families associated with others like them, Jewish families making their way in the new world. The men might violate the laws of Shabbos, but their wives kept kosher homes, herded the children to shul on Shabbos morning, and did their best to follow what they had learned long ago from their mothers.

Wearing long beards and shtetl clothing, the third group generally took seats at the back of the shul. These men were recent arrivals, coming alone and saving money to bring their families away from poverty, to hope of a good life in this vast land.

Though Pinchas was working and had integrated even into the Gardens shul, he felt most at ease with the third group. These men wore flat caps and old-fashioned suits, and felt uncomfortable in the Gardens shul. Like Pinchas, during the week they found refuge in a *shtiebel* with others like them, where they could *daven* loudly and fervently, and lose themselves in learning when davening was over.

As these thought went through Pinchas, he stood silently, watching, listening. He wondered why these men with their top hats and these women with their rich dresses were talking so animatedly to his family.

Frieda stood with her husband, and beside them stood Bertha, Ethel, and Rose.

Joseph was gazing at everyone but saying nothing. Why had this quiet son of theirs decided to become a lawyer? Surely, talking to people who came in asking for advice was an important part of his work.

Samuel was standing a little to the side, seemingly not taking part in the discussion.

Isaac was scuffing his newly polished shoes, clearly anxious to get away.

Pinchas noticed Jack talking to a young woman. He also noticed the girl's mother looking at them.

Pinchas was surprised when, moments later, the woman issued an invitation to the Levine family to join them for tea, and together they walked the short distance to a large home on the slopes of the mountain.

Pinchas was concerned. What did he and his family have in common with these people? Was their food kosher?

Fay noticed Jack the dentist, as she always thought of him, laughing at a joke made by one of the jeweler's daughters. Was this discussion the makings of a *shidduch?* she wondered. Was that why they were being invited to visit?

Once they were seated in a large room, Jack became engaged in an animated discussion about London with the younger son, who was about to travel there for his family's business.

The daughter was talking animatedly to Frieda about the latest fashions.

The oldest son, James, was seated beside Bertha. He had been taken by her quiet demeanor and shy smile, and was determined to know more about her.

Bertha had always been stuck between her older and younger siblings and had rarely been asked her opinion. Her early years had been dominated by her ability to charm people with her sweet smile.

"Listen, stand next to me," was a familiar refrain. "Smile. Don't say anything."

Nevertheless, Bertha was intelligent. She listened to everything that went on around her. James found that she had decided views on Zionism. She was in favor of the Jews returning to their land, but while she admired those who traveled there, she worried about the dangers they would face. This seemed to him an eminently well thought-out and balanced approach, especially considering how his aunt had suffered in that faraway land.

They discussed recent events: the return of the Jewish refugees to the Transvaal, the aftereffects of the war, and the speeches they had heard that day.

By the time the Levine family left for home, both James and Bertha wanted to meet again. He arranged for his sister to invite the Levine girls for afternoon tea. Dinner invitations followed. Not long after that first meeting, the engagement between James and Bertha was announced.

Pinchas was worried about Bertha marrying such a suave young man, a man who, in all probability, couldn't speak Yiddish. A man who, he surmised, would be more familiar with the English classics than Shas. And what about Shabbos? Surely his father's shop was open on Shabbos.

They needn't have worried. Bertha spoke to her parents soon after the announcement.

"James's family has a special arrangement for Shabbos," she said. "They have a non-Jewish partner who goes on Shabbos to the shop and takes the profits from that day. A rabbi approved this arrangement."

After her marriage, Bertha moved to a large house in Sea Point. There, she closely supervised the workers in her kitchen, was a generous hostess, and quietly helped many Jewish families as they began their new life in the Cape.

Fay began to worry about Ethel, who was twenty already. There was no *shidduch* in sight.

Bertha made sure to invite her sister to her house often. It was in Bertha's home that Ethel met a new immigrant from England, a young man who had been sent to join his cousin in Cape Town. Their business of selling fruit and vegetables from the outlying farms to retail grocers was expanding. His cousins were older than him, and were tiring of traveling to the outlying districts. Since this work was done only during the week, once again, both Pinchas and Fay gave a sigh of relief.

The year 1904 ended with only Jack, Rose, Isaac, and Samuel still at home.

David was now living above the chemist shop. He had completed his apprenticeship and was registered as a pharmacist. If an emergency arose during the night, he dealt with it. Confident that David would handle any request competently, the chemist bought a house in the Gardens area, a large house surrounded by a fine garden, and moved there.

Chapter 44

Jack worked hard, but was only slowly accumulating enough money from fees to pay for the practice. He was beginning to find the work repetitive. He felt despair as he watched men who had arrived only a few years before learn the language of the new country and embark on ambitious entrepreneurial enterprises that made quick fortunes.

In addition, he was troubled by a confidence that David had shared with him. The chemist's daughter had visited the shop many times and become friendly with David. One day, when the shop closed, her father had asked David to accompany his daughter home. Since then, he had visited her several times at her home.

Now the chemist had spoken to David.

"If you're serious about my Annabel as she is about you, then the two of you should marry," he said. "I will give you half a share in the shop and buy you a house, and we will employ another chemist to live above the shop."

David had been taken aback. The girl was pleasant. He enjoyed her company. But marriage! What would his parents say? If he didn't accept this generous offer, he would have to leave his job. What would he do?

He had no finances to set up shop. He doubted that he would find work elsewhere in the Cape. Should he leave and try his luck upcountry? But what could he do there without financial backing?

David was thinking about the offer when Annabel came into the shop.

"Can we meet later, when you finish work?" she said.

"But it is so dark then. It's not safe for you to be out."

"Hasn't Papa spoken to you? Today you can leave at four. It's all arranged."

David left the shop that afternoon, as arranged. "Annabel, we must talk."

"Oh, but that is exactly why Papa gave you the time off."

"Let's go to the Gardens. We can sit on a bench and talk there."

Soon they were seated. "Your father made me a generous offer, but all this is too soon. We hardly know one another."

"But we do. You have worked in the shop for more than five years. I have seen you often during that time."

"But I was on one side of the counter and you on the other. There were always customers in the shop."

"Well, these last few weeks we have seen more of one another, and not just over the counter." Annabel smiled sweetly.

David began to feel flustered. "Yes, we spent such pleasant times together, but surely, not sufficient to consider marriage."

"You don't want to marry me? I thought...I was sure...I..."

"Annabel, we shouldn't rush into such an arrangement. Come, let's sit down on that bench."

As they sat in the Gardens, David began to think that perhaps marriage to Annabel wasn't such a bad idea. But how could he do such a thing to his parents? They had been devastated when he worked on Shabbos. They would be even more upset if they knew that he didn't always eat kosher. But this—how could he justify this to his parents?

As they stood up and walked away from the Gardens down Adderley

Street, they passed passed the flower sellers. David decided to buy flowers to soften the fact that he had disappointed the girl.

"I'm so flattered that your father approves of me, but we need a bit more time to come to an understanding," he said. "Let's choose some flowers for you to take home."

Annabel smiled, and David felt confusion. Such a pretty, amiable young woman! Did it really matter that she wasn't Jewish?

They stood up and walked toward the Adderley Street flower sellers. Annabel pointed to a small bunch of bright yellow flowers. The woman wrapped them in newspaper and said, "Sixpence, please."

Annabel pouted. "What? For such a small bunch? Don't Jew me."

David recoiled. "Jew me? I'm a Jew."

"Oh, David, don't be so sensitive. It's only an expression. Everyone uses it."

———

Later that day, David asked Jack to take a walk with him and told him what had happened.

"How can you do this?" Jack said. "Think about our parents... Think about your future children."

"Listen, I always take off for Yom Kippur. Besides, I didn't mean for this to happen. I thought the family was just being hospitable by inviting me for meals. I thought the girl was just being kind and friendly to an employee in her father's shop."

Jack wondered at his brother's naivety, but withheld comment. Instead he said, "So, just tell her you aren't ready for marriage. Tell her it's no more than friendship you feel for her. She'll quickly stop seeing you and find someone else."

"No, you don't understand. It's awkward for me now at work. My employer expects me to marry his daughter. I cannot continue like this. I must decide soon, one way or another."

"Listen, I have some money saved up. You have some leave. Go away for a week. I'll pay for board and lodging. How about Muizenberg? I hear there's a kosher boarding house there."

"How will being away for a week help me? I'll come back to the same problem."

"It will give you time to relax, to think. Better that than to rush into a decision because you feel awkward."

A week had passed, and Jack had heard no word from David. Where was he? What had he decided?

Jack returned home from work in a glum mood. He should have shared what David had said to him with his parents, although David had asked him not to. They were wiser than him. They would have known what to do. Maybe David was already back at work, making plans with the chemist's daughter.

He was determined now to share his worries with his parents. He entered the house to find the kitchen crowded with strangers.

Joseph got up and went over to Jack.

"Reb Mendel sent home for a bride," he said. "She arrived this morning at the docks. Mother was there as usual. The boat arrived a day early, so this poor girl had no one to meet her.

"Mother was just about to leave, when she saw a girl crying. Now how could she leave a Jewish girl there, newly arrived and distressed? She came home with Mother, and when she said Reb Mendel was supposed to meet her—well, you can just imagine!

"Lettie came to my office with a message for me. I couldn't leave work immediately since I was with a client, but I did leave early and went to find Reb Mendel—and now we're celebrating their *tenaim!*"

Jack didn't know whether to feel relieved or disappointed that he couldn't talk to his parents about David that night.

The following week, after days of worry and indecision, Jack found he had an hour free during the morning. Normally he never left work, not even for lunch. Now he told Dr. Martin that he had urgent business to deal with and would be back within the hour.

David should have returned from Muizenberg. What decision had he made?

Jack walked down Adderley Street toward the chemist shop. He entered with some trepidation and walked up to the counter.

"Could I see my brother David for just a moment?" he asked.

A young man frowned at him, said a curt "Wait here," and disappeared into the dispensary.

Moments later the chemist appeared. "Your brother no longer works for me. He asked for a week off, and I agreed. On the day he was supposed to return I got a letter from him, saying he needs another week off. I straight away wrote to him and told him not to return. Such an ungrateful young man! After all I have done for him, after all that I offered him!"

Jack left hurriedly. He would just have time to go home and then be back for the next patient.

Fortunately, his father was home, having just returned from a trip upcountry. He caught him just as he was leaving to the *shtiebel*.

Pinchas listened carefully and then said, "I must go to David in Muizenberg. I know the boarding house. He'll be upset about losing his job. I don't like that he works on Shabbos, but still, to be suddenly told not to return? He must be feeling despondent. He needs me.

"I will leave immediately. Tell you mother that I had some free time and decided to go out for the day. No need to worry her with all this."

Jack returned to work. He forced himself to concentrate, to put all thoughts of his brother aside.

At the end of the day he walked home with some trepidation. Would his father be back from Muizenberg? How was David? Why had he not returned? The money that Jack had given him could not have lasted for longer than a week.

Jack found his mother busy in the shop, no look of concern on her face. He found Isaac at the kitchen table doing homework.

"Tatte left a note. He might be back late," was all he said, and then went on writing.

Though Jack still went to Shacharis each morning, he no longer went regularly to Minchah or Maariv. His parents had nagged him at first, but then realizing it was futile, had let him be. Now he craved the comfort of prayer.

"Just going to the Gardens for Minchah," he said to his brother.

"Oh, really," Isaac said. "I'll join you."

Jack realized then how bad an influence he was on his younger brother. Once his parents had lost the battle with him, they soon gave up trying to force his younger brother to attend shul after school. They had to remain satisfied that at least he went regularly to the Talmud Torah in Roeland Street each afternoon.

The shop closed at eight. When it was finally quiet, the family sat around the kitchen table.

Joseph had sent a messenger boy with a note saying that he had to see a client who was not available during the day, and he would be late coming home.

Pinchas had left early that morning and told Fay there was a possibility he wouldn't be home in time for the evening meal, maybe even returning only the next day. Fay had assumed this was a short business trip, and so was unworried. The long trips, far into the interior, still bothered her, but these short trips meant that he was in a small village nearby, maybe Wynberg or Simonstown, or some other safe place.

Everyone except Jack spoke cheerfully of their day. He forced himself to eat, to make conversation, to smile and carry on as normal.

When would his father return? What news would he bring?

Chapter 45

> "Muizenberg...a holiday resort built by the British Empire and a set of Eastern European immigrants who were arriving in a new country and who adopted this holiday resort even as the colonials abandoned it and remoulded it to their image..."
>
> — Dr. Mervyn Rosenberg, *Jewishgen.org*, 2010

It was a day later, when the family was again seated around the table, eating the evening meal, when David and his father arrived. Neither man looked too happy.

When the meal was over, Pinchas asked for everyone to leave except for Jack and David. He said he needed to talk with them and their mother privately.

David spoke first, telling of his involvement with the chemist's daughter and the offer of a partnership. He also related how Annabel had said, "Don't Jew me."

"I followed Jack's advice," he said. "I went to the Jewish boarding house. Immediately, when I met their daughter, I realized that she was my *bashert*. I knew I would have to tell the chemist and his daughter. I was cowardly. I couldn't face it. I asked for another week of leave."

No one interrupted. They simply sat and listened. After a few moments, David continued.

"Well, the chemist sent a reply that I need not return to work. He would hire someone else. I think he must have realized that if I was staying another week, an extra week's holiday that I was not entitled to, I would not marry his daughter. I don't know why she took it so for granted."

"How often did you meet with her?" Fay asked.

"A few times a week. She would come to the shop at lunchtime and we would walk in the Gardens. I would sit and eat my sandwiches. She would eat something she had brought from home, cake or fruit. I was invited to eat with them a few times. Yes, I know it wasn't kosher, but ... well ... that's how it was."

"For how long has this been going on?"

"A couple of months, I would say. I didn't expect her to think that meant I would marry her. I didn't expect the chemist to take it as a done deal and offer me a partnership. So I spoke to Jack and took his advice to go away for a week."

"You have upset this poor girl," Pinchas said. "Of course, after all those meetings she thought you were serious about her. She must have asked her father to offer you a partnership."

David had always thought that his father, with his old-fashioned way of thinking, was stuck back in time in the shtetl. Yet here he showed he understood current mores only too well.

"Well, now I am in a fine mess," David said. "No work. The family in Muizenberg doesn't approve of me because I work on Shabbos. Their daughter won't oppose her family and have anything to do with someone who doesn't keep Shabbos."

"You must write to the chemist and his daughter, and ask them to forgive you," Pinchas said. "Only after that can you consider your future and make plans."

"You forget why I didn't want to see her again. You forget that she said, 'Don't Jew me.'"

"And if she hadn't said that you would have gone ahead?" Fay said. "For this you broke Shabbos in the chemist shop?"

David looked shamefaced. The truth hit home and hurt him.

"The girl was prepared to marry you," Fay said. "The father was prepared to make you his partner. Is that not more telling than using a phrase that is common to such people, almost meaningless to them, though hurtful to us?"

"I will write the letters and show them to you right now," David answered.

Some time later, he handed over two letters. Fay took one and skimmed it.

Dear Annabel,

I am sorry if I hurt you. I am sorry if you thought I meant marriage. I enjoyed our time together but didn't mean anything serious by it and thought you felt the same way.

Your friend, David

Fay read it and said, "Your letter to the father is similar?"

David nodded, pleased that the unpleasant task was over.

Fay responded by tearing up both letters. Pinchas nodded his agreement.

Jack watched as David turned white. "Why did you do that?"

Fay spoke angrily. "You want to harm the girl forever, don't you? You want her to feel rejected? How could you write such a thing? Write this down: 'Thank you for the time you spent with me. It was kind of you to take pity on a lonely worker even though our backgrounds are so different. I had to leave your father's employ. I will miss working for him. I thank you for those few moments you spent with me. I ask you to forgive me for taking up so much of your time. But I will always treasure those moments.'"

Jack and David were both amazed at how their mother, who had arrived in the Colony speaking only very little English, was now so fluent.

"Now, write that down nicely. Write something similar to the father. Leave them both their pride. Once pride is ruined, character changes, and not always for the better! I know."

Pinchas looked at Fay and began to speak.

Fay interrupted. "Not now! Later! Not now!"

Jack was mystified. He thought back to the time he had spoken about giving money to the stranger. Once again, his mother and father looked discomfited. What was it that was upsetting them?

"Give me the letters," Fay said. "I will deliver them myself."

"No, Mother. You cannot do that. Why should you do that? The postal service is totally reliable."

"Because when she sees your writing, she'll tear the letter up. I don't want that to happen. I will deliver it and she will read it. She'll feel good again."

"Why should she do that? Why should she tear the letter up?"

"Don't ask stupid questions. Just do as I say."

For once David didn't argue and did as he was told.

Jack watched as the letters were carefully written. He watched as his mother read them, and then, with a determined look, she took them and left the house.

⌐

Later, Fay returned. She said nothing to anyone. No one dared to ask what had happened, not even Pinchas.

David's clothing was in the apartment above the shop and he knew he must collect them, yet he lacked the courage. He borrowed clothing from Jack and went to shul each morning and evening.

Three days later, a boy arrived, carrying three large boxes. "Sign here. Clothes for Mr. David Levine. Left behind, they were. Oh yes, I almost forgot! A letter for him! Here. Sign for me!"

David was relieved to have his clothes, but nervous about reading the letter.

To his surprise it said:

Your mother was kind enough to come to our house. After she spoke to our daughter for some time, and my daughter read your letter, she was all smiles

again. I am pleased that this little misunderstanding has been cleared up. I hear
that Somerset Hospital needs a chemist. Maybe you should apply.

David gave a sigh of relief. Then he went into the shop and waited until his mother was free.

"You gave me good advice," he said.

"I'm at fault," she said. "I should not have allowed you to work on Shabbos. No good can come of it. Please promise me you won't do such a thing again."

Now David was in a quandary. He wanted to work as a chemist, or all those long years of training would be wasted. What was he to do?

Could he apply for a job and mention that he couldn't work on Shabbos or the Jewish holidays? It didn't seem feasible. But he was tired of doing nothing, so he took his hat and straightened his tie, and walked to Somerset Hospital.

An hour later he found himself in the dispensary talking to the chief dispenser.

"I heard you need another pharmacist," he said.

"Oh, so they told you, did they! I was speaking to the people in the chemist shop in Adderley Street yesterday, in case they knew of someone. Your name came up."

David gave a start. What had the man said about him?

"It seems he was pleased with your work! Well, here our hours are slightly shorter than a retail shop, but there must be someone on duty every day, including Sundays and holidays. No one likes to work on Sunday or on a day like New Year, but there it is. Would that suit you?"

David took a deep breath. Here was a chance, a slight chance, but worth taking.

"If I worked every Sunday, and all those holidays, could I take off Saturday instead?"

"Well, it would suit us, but what an idea! Are you sure you want that?

Oh! I see ... Levine? Oh yes, you must be one of those Jewish fellows who keep all those strange laws. Well!"

David bit his lip. His one chance of getting work was gone, but what could he do? He had promised his parents he wouldn't violate Shabbos. He braced himself to hear that he would not be given the post, when he heard, "Splendid. No more forcing people to work on Sundays. Right, then! When can you start work?"

Later, much later, Jack listened as David said, "Well, as Shakespeare said long ago, 'All's well that ends well.' I have work. I don't have to violate Shabbos. I can offer my future wife a home where *halachah* is observed. Do you think the young lady I met will accept me?"

"Let us hope so," was all Jack said.

Chapter 46

"The valley of the Eerste River, as its name (first) indicates was the first of the inland valleys to be settled by farmers from the Cape. . . . Scenically it is superb. Stellenbosch, which lies at its upper end, is without doubt the prettiest of all the small towns in Southern Africa, while the wines, wild flowers and fruits of the valley are the finest in the world."

— T.V. Bulpin, *Discovering Southern Africa*, p. 89

Jack looked back on a year that seemed to be a whirl of activity for his family.

David had begun to work in the hospital pharmacy. He moved home and slowly picked up the different strands of observance that he had ignored over the years.

He wanted to visit Muizenberg again, but since he worked every Sunday and couldn't travel on Shabbos, this was difficult. Besides, Fay strongly discouraged him.

"Give it time," she said.

When she finally relented, David was overjoyed and wrote immediately to Muizenberg. The letter was not well received. A letter from the father of the young woman came back a few weeks later.

So now you keep Shabbos because your work allows it, he wrote. *What if in the future you change to different work and once again transgress halachah so blatantly?*

Through perseverance, David succeeded in calming the man's fears, and some weeks later a wedding was held in Muizenberg.

Soon after the wedding, Joseph was sent to Stellenbosch to meet with a Jewish client who had a boundary dispute with his neighbor over an adjoining vineyard.

This was one of the first cases Joseph had been trusted to handle on his own. He traveled by train, taking with him law books on land ownership.

The scenery through the train window was magnificent — lush forests, rivers, and in the far distance, soaring blue-hued mountains. Joseph was so engrossed in his books that he hardly noticed.

He was met at the station in Stellenbosch by the farmer's driver and taken by cart to the farm.

They drove many miles until they entered a large gate, surrounded by tall white walls on either side. They drove through long lines of vines to reach an imposing, white-gabled Cape Dutch house.

Joseph felt himself tense up. He had always worked in Cape Town. There were always older, more experienced men, to ask for advice. Now he was quite alone. What if he failed?

A woman came out to greet them.

"Welcome, Mr. Levine. Come inside. You will need some refreshment after your long journey." She turned to the driver. "Pieter, thank you for bringing the lawyer here. You can see to the horses. I will send someone to call the master."

Joseph walked into a home, similar to those of other wine-growing clients near Cape Town. The only difference was the *mezuzah* on the front door and on the door of the large sun-filled salon.

But thereafter, he noticed not the antique table, nor the tapestried chairs, but only the young woman who came to greet him.

"Sit, rest," she said. "While Mother gets someone to call Father, I'll ask our maid to bring tea and cake. I'm Esther Gold. You are?"

Joseph momentarily forgot about the laws of borders and properties. "Joseph, Joseph Levine. How do you do?"

He sat down, entranced by the girl's calm demeanor and merry laugh.

She went out and came back a few moments later carrying a tray. "They're so busy in the kitchen. I thought it quicker and easier if I just brought this myself."

Joseph had been entertained in many homes where the young ladies sat while maids staggered in with heavy trays. It was thoughtful of her to take on the task herself.

"Mother says she will be here in a moment."

They sat alone in the salon, drank tea from fine china cups, and talked. Esther told of the days when she had boarded with other Jewish girls and attended The Good Hope Seminary for girls.

"At first, I longed for my family, for the farm. But when it was time to return, I longed to be back in Cape Town, with my friends."

Joseph marveled at how she had been unafraid to leave her family. By the time her father arrived, he had to pull himself together to concentrate on the case.

"You see, it's like this . . ." Mr. Gold began.

Joseph listened, occasionally taking notes, while a long tale evolved of fences broken and fences mended, and sudden rain creating a furrow between the fence and the vines.

"See, here we make sweet red wine. My neighbor has green grapes, which are less sweet. He makes a dry white wine. There's a big empty piece of land between our vines, and he put up a long fence in the middle. Now, that isn't right. That's my land, not his. How can he just take half of it like that?

"I was planning to use that land to grow strawberries. They're an early summer crop, and the vines are only ready to be picked in the late summer. Strawberries in Cape Town would make a fine profit."

"Do you have the deeds to the farm?" Joseph asked.

"Yes, of course, but I don't need them. When I bought this farm years ago, the seller walked me all around the boundary. He told me quite clearly that the land on either side of the vines was mine."

"To convince your neighbor, the deeds must be brought out and shown to him. Certainly, when going to court we will need the deeds. Can we look at them now?"

Time passed. It was already noon. The dinner gong rang out, and all work on the farm came to a stop. Workers returned to their cottages, and mother and daughter came into the room.

"Come, hurry," Mrs. Gold said. "You know that the cook doesn't like to be kept waiting."

Later, after a leisurely lunch accompanied by fine wine, Joseph was shown the deeds. The demarcation line was less than clear.

"I'll need to see your neighbor's deeds," he said. "Who is his lawyer?"

"Look, I don't know. Lately there have been bad words between us."

Esther came into the room with cups of lemon tea. "Why don't I go to the farm with Mr. Levine? Surely he can see the deeds there."

"No, that won't do. He's angry with me, though it should be the other way around. He won't agree. He'll just send you away."

"Why would they turn me away?" Esther said. "Sannie and I practically grew up together, meeting each day at the farm school. We're still friends."

"Well, I suppose it's worth a try. The sooner that fence comes down and I can start planting, the better."

"Right," Esther said, smiling. "I'll arrange for Pieter to be ready for us early tomorrow."

Joseph set off the following day, Esther by his side. He was filled with a sense of trepidation. He surely represented the enemy to this farmer. Was what he was doing now wise? Surely it would have been more sensible to follow the correct procedure and make contact only with the farmer's lawyer.

He had simply agreed to a naïve young girl's arguments. Foolishness!

They arrived at a house, very similar to the one they had left behind. The farmer's wife came out. She looked at Esther in surprise, but invited them in and sent for her husband.

It took a little persuasion for the farmer to agree to Joseph's request to show him his deeds.

"Man, a lawyer, for that man who wants to take my land. Why should I show you?"

It was Esther who persuaded him. Joseph didn't understand everything she said, but he understood the words "friends" and "honest" since they were similar to Yiddish.

Esther left the room to find her friend.

The deeds were brought out. It became clear to Joseph that the man was within his rights. In fact, he had been generous. All the land beside the vines belonged to him, yet the fence had been situated not at the edge, but in the middle.

He would have to explain this to his client. He would be angry. Joseph would leave and never see the girl again.

"Thank you for being so helpful," he said. "I feel all this can be easily solved."

"What, that man, whose children played with mine, wants the courts involved now! I also have lawyers, good lawyers. Tell him that!"

Esther was called and the cart was brought to the front door. She talked merrily all the way back to the farm about how her friend had been so pleased to see her. She hardly seemed to notice that the young man beside her was deep in thought and hardly responding to her chatter.

They returned to find Mr. Gold pacing in front of the house.

"Come, let me hear what occurred," he said.

Joseph followed him into the house and took a deep breath.

"His deeds are quite clear," he said. "All the land between the vines does belong to him. In fact, by putting the fence in the middle, and not at the edge of his property, he has been more than generous. He told me he heard about your plans for growing strawberries there. The workers from both farms talk often to one another. He didn't want arguments in the future, when you had already taken that land, so he thought it better to fence his land off from yours.

"He wanted to leave some space for you and the new plants. He thinks it's a foolish idea to grow strawberries, but since you have been friends and neighbors for so many years, he thought he would give you the land to try it out."

To Joseph's surprise, once all the details were explained to his client, he was far from angry.

"So he was right and I was wrong. I must go to him and ask him to forgive me."

There was one sour note. The lawyers in Cape Town were less than pleased with the outcome of the case.

"The correct procedure, for future, is to meet in court and decide the case there," they said. "Your unusual action turned out well on this occasion, but it could have played out a whole lot differently. The protocols have been developed over many years. There is good reason for them. Never mind, it's early days. You will yet learn."

Joseph was unhappy. He had acted incorrectly. This was his first case, his chance to prove himself, and he had satisfied the client but not the seniors of the practice. They would hesitate before letting him attend a case without supervision for some time to come.

Not only that, it was clear to him that his acquaintance with the farmer's daughter would not go any further. The case was settled. Stellenbosch was far away. There was no chance that he would once again spend time on the farm.

To his surprise, an invitation came in the post only a few days later inviting him to spend the following Shabbos at the farm.

We would like to spend some time with you, to thank you for preventing a bad mistake, Mr. Gold wrote. *Good neighborly relations are important. I was too hasty, and you set me on the correct path.*

Well, it was soon apparent that there was more to the invitation than met the eye. Not long after, Joseph married Esther and started a legal practice in Stellenbosch. The Jewish community in that little town was not large, and Joseph found himself very much involved in shul affairs.

In the once overflowing house, only Jack, Samuel, and Isaac remained in one room, while Rose, now eighteen years old, had a room to herself.

Samuel had completed his science degree at the South African University College, but finding work in his field was proving impossible. He was considering taking a teaching degree and becoming a science teacher, but maintaining discipline over a classroom of rowdy boys was not something he really wanted. He had hoped that talk of a medical school would by now have turned to reality, but that was not the case.

Rose helped her mother in the shop on some days and visited her sisters on other days. Frieda always welcomed her help with her growing family. Bertha had a cook, nanny, and gardener, but her baby was sometimes fractious and Rose seemed to have a calming, soothing effect on the little one.

Isaac had hoped to study medicine. He considered science, like his brother, but realized there would never be a medical school in the Cape and that there was little opportunity for work with a science degree. He decided that the only option was to travel to England and study at a medical school there.

Jack had left and come back with qualifications. He would do the same. Unfortunately, it was more difficult than he had anticipated for a Jew to be accepted into medical school in England, but quite suddenly, in midyear, he was accepted to study medicine in Edinburgh, in faraway Scotland. Since the term there began in September, he found work in a department store and began to save for his studies.

So everyone was busy and happily occupied except for Samuel. His science degree looked good on paper, but it seemed that scientists were not wanted or needed. Since he could not sit idly at home, he went from one unsatisfactory job to another. He served behind a counter for a few weeks, and then left. He worked for a Jewish wholesale merchant for some time, but then left that too. He considered opening a business and looked around for various possibilities, but eventually decided the only option was to go to college and get a teacher's certificate.

Early one morning, as he was sitting at the kitchen table filling in forms for admission, Fay arrived home with a tearful young girl.

"Meet Ruth from Australia," she said to Samuel. "I went to the docking area as usual, to buy the fish, and what do I see but a young girl crying? I thought it was the usual trouble — suitcase taken after the promise of transport. But no, this time they left the suitcase and slashed the ribbons of her reticule.

"Now all her money and a train ticket to Johannesburg is lost, but more important, she doesn't know her family's address. So run along now, Sammy, my boy, and ask Rev. Bender to find out where family Schneider lives in Johannesburg."

"What are their first names?" Samuel asked.

"Well, that's just the trouble," Ruth said in a low voice. "In the shtetl, they were my Tante Bracha and my Fetter Yechezkel. But since they came to this country, they changed their names. It was all written down, and now I can't remember."

Samuel went off to the Rav's house. He returned some time later to find Ruth installed in the girls' bedroom and chatting happily with Rose.

By the time Jack returned home from work, it seemed to him as if this young girl had always been there.

This was not the first time his mother had brought home friendless Jews. Since Fay went very early each morning to the docks, she was often there when passengers were disembarking. Remembering their own experience as new immigrants, Fay would glance around to make sure that no Jewish woman was standing there, alone and anxious.

The family had long ago become accustomed to arriving home and finding strangers sitting around the kitchen table, talking volubly in

Yiddish. Sometimes there would be a lone woman; other times there would be a mother surrounded by her children. Usually the stay was short.

This girl was different. She spoke English, although it had a slightly different accent than the English spoken in London and the Cape Colony. She was clearly upset, but forced herself to smile and talk, as though she was just on a pleasant afternoon visit.

When Samuel came home each day, unhappy at work and gloomy at the thought of studying to become a teacher, he found the girl pleasant to talk to. He listened to descriptions of all the strange creatures she had seen and as she spoke wistfully of her family. He spoke to her of his hopes of finding work in his profession instead of becoming a teacher.

Fay was well aware of this. Though she was in the shop for long hours, she kept a careful watch on the girl.

Each day, Ruth inquired if news had come of her family in Johannesburg.

"My dear," Fay said. "I am sure we will receive a reply soon, but I'm not sure how long it will take. It will do you no good to sit here worrying. Mrs. Borenstein, who lives just a few doors away, has young children and no family here. If you would move in with her and help a little with the children, she would be so grateful. Would you like that?"

Ruth was happy to agree with whatever Fay suggested. Samuel helped carry her luggage to the new place of residence. He returned home looking none too happy.

"Why could she not remain here?" he said. "We have plenty of room!"

Fay was not to be provoked, though she understood the reason for his anger.

"I must do what is best for the girl. There she will be busy, not pre-occupied with worrying about finding her family."

Fay was kind to everyone she brought into her house, usually asking no questions. This time, however, she wrote a careful letter to the shul in Australia, asking what was known of the girl and her family. She sent the letter to Rev. Bender, since she had no address, and Lettie delivered it on her way home.

Jack returned home and heard that Ruth had left. He was surprised but didn't react angrily like Samuel.

The weeks went by. Fay invited Ruth for a Shabbos *seudah*. The girl spoke happily of the days she spent with the Borenstein family.

"The children are so sweet," she said. "I never had brothers or sisters, and it's such fun to be with them. They like the stories I tell them and let me dress them in the morning. Since losing my parents, it's the first time I have begun to feel some happiness."

When Samuel heard this, he smiled at his mother for the first time in days. He knew nothing of the letter she had written, now making its way across the ocean to Australia.

Chapter 47

"Australia's first voluntary Jewish settler was ... Barnet Levey ... who arrived in 1821 ... By 1881, the Jewish population had reached nine thousand ... At no time did they encounter serious prejudice ..."

— Howard M. Sachar, *Diaspora*, p. 169

The first letter that arrived from Johannesburg brought disappointing news. Rev. Bender had contacted a number of Schneider families, but none admitted to having family in Australia. However, he did not give up. He had some leads and was following them.

Fay was concerned. Samuel had been accepted as a student in the teacher's college the following year. Meanwhile, he had found work as a clerk in a Jewish wholesale business. During the day he was busy, and at night he went to visit Ruth.

He returned late each night. True, Ruth appeared to be a fine girl. However, there was so much she didn't know. Nowadays there were few women and many men in the new Colonies. Intermarriage was not uncommon. Who were the girl's parents? Was she truly single? Why couldn't they find her family in Johannesburg? Had she told the truth about losing her tickets and money?

At long last, a letter arrived from Sydney, Australia. The rabbi there wrote of how a young couple with a little girl had arrived from his shtetl. He had known their families for years and he kept in touch with them when they went to live in a small settlement to open a shop.

After several years, tragedy struck. First the husband and then the wife succumbed to fever. Ruth had been brought to his house, and he had contacted her aunt and uncle in Johannesburg. Their name in the shtetl had been Schneider, since the husband was a tailor. In Johannesburg they had opened a general dealer shop and changed their name to Taylor. He still had their address.

Fay sent the letter to Rev. Bender. Soon another letter arrived from Johannesburg, this one addressed to Ruth. Fay took the letter to the girl that evening. She waited while Ruth read the letter.

Ruth thanked Fay, but seemed subdued. "They were very worried when they didn't hear from me," she said. "They sent tickets and money for the journey, and asked that I come as soon as possible. Thank you for all your help."

"Would you like me to book your ticket?" Fay said.

"Yes, that is kind of you."

"Today is already Thursday," Fay said. "You don't want to risk travel over Shabbos. So would Monday be suitable?"

The words were barely audible. "Yes, thank you, that would be good."

Fay noticed tears escaping slowly but said nothing. She wondered how Samuel would take the news. She wasn't surprised when he turned red, and without a word, put on his jacket, picked up his hat and stalked off.

He returned a short while later, Ruth beside him. Without preamble, he said, "Ruth and I wish to be married."

Ruth blushed furiously, looking worried. Fay said not one word.

"We will make a *vort*," Samuel said. "Then Ruth will go to Johannesburg, and when she returns we will marry."

"What, make a *vort* and then see her off?" Fay said. "What foolishness is this? Either marry here and you two will go together, or there will be no *vort*."

"But my family . . . they're expecting me!" Ruth said.

"Do you want to marry my son?" Fay asked. "If you don't, it's better to say so now. If you make a *vort* and then later change your mind, it will be very complicated. Speak now. Tell how you feel."

"Of course I want to marry Samuel. It's just that I don't want my family to be angry. They sent money for the tickets and offered me a home. They've spent months worrying about me. I have a duty to them."

"No marriage, no *vort*," Fay insisted.

Jack was watching and listening. He wondered at his mother's strange insistence.

There was a long silence. Then Fay spoke again. "I have seen tragedies caused by such arrangements. I will not allow it."

Jack wondered anew at his mother and the things he didn't know about her. What tragedies was she referring to? He had no knowledge of such happenings. He wished his father was home, not far away on one of his trips upcountry. Perhaps his father would enlighten him. His mother was in no mood to be questioned.

"I have only the simple clothing I wore in the outback in Australia," Ruth said. "If I go to my family, and then later Samuel comes to Johannesburg, I am sure my family will take care of everything for me. That way would be better."

"Oh, you are sure! Maybe they're struggling financially and it was a great sacrifice to send you a ticket. There's a shortage of Jewish women on the goldfields. Maybe they already have someone in mind for you. What will you say to them then?

"No! Either you marry now straight after the *vort*, or you go to them free from obligation. We can make the arrangements here and give you a wedding gown, but you must be very sure that this is what you desire. You must not allow my son to pressure you into a step you do not wish to take."

Samuel looked at his mother. "Now why would I do such a thing?"

"Ach, who can understand the ways of men? Give the girl time to think."

Ruth spoke in a calm, firm voice. "There is no pressure. I want to marry Samuel. If he agrees, we will do as you say."

The wedding took place two weeks later. One week after the wedding, the young couple were on their way to Johannesburg. They planned to spend some time there before returning to the Cape to set up home.

"But what will they live on?" Pinchas asked Fay. "What work will Samuel do?"

A month later Samuel wrote that he had found work in Johannesburg assaying gold. People with his qualifications were in short supply and much needed. His science degree was useful after all.

—

The next year, Isaac left for Scotland. The house seemed empty. Jack had the boys' room all to himself. Rose was just turning twenty-one. With no school to attend and no sisters for company, time was heavy on her hands.

Whenever Pinchas had time, he went to the *shtiebel* in Constitution Street. One day, he came home flushed with excitement.

"Yesterday the first rabbi with proper *semichah* arrived! His name is Rabbi Mirvish, and he will be the *rav* in District Six. Now what do you think of that? After all these years, we'll have a proper *rav*, with genuine *semichah*! That makes us a shul, not a *shtiebel*, don't you think?"

Fay was less than impressed. "Why the excitement? There's nothing wrong with Rev. Bender or the Gardens shul!"

Jack wanted to meet the new *rav*. He still had memories of his grandfather.

"Maybe tomorrow morning we can both *daven* there?" he said to his father.

Pinchas nodded.

"He came with his family?" Rose asked.

"Yes, they all came together. The community found them a house in District Six."

"I will walk with you tomorrow," Rose said. "We'll pass the flower sellers on the way. I will take a bunch to welcome the Rebbetzin."

For Rose, any departure from the boring routine of her days was welcome.

The decision was to prove a fateful one. On that same day, a young man was en route from England to the British colony of Natal. He made a brief stopover in Cape Town and stayed at the Jewish boarding house in District Six. He had heard about the new *rav*, so he too went to that *minyan*.

Pinchas bade farewell to Jack, who left to work. Noticing a new face, he introduced himself.

"You are new here? My name is Pinchas, and what is yours?"

"Solomon. Good to meet you. I know no one here. I arrived yesterday, but I'm only here for a short while. Soon I will be on my way to Natal, to Durban."

"Why Durban? Why not here?"

"My brother is already there with his wife. He writes that with the money from the small house they sold in London, he has bought a fine large house and a large plot of land. He wants to open a fine shop and will take me as a partner."

"Are there many Jews there?" Pinchas asked.

"Oh yes, would we go there otherwise? They have a shul and a *rav* who came from Russia, a fine and learned man."

"When do you leave?" Pinchas asked.

"The goods for the shop were delayed. Once they arrive, I will travel with them to Durban. Meanwhile, I think I'll look around Cape Town. Who knows when I'll return?"

Since Pinchas was off that day, resting from a long trip, he offered to show the young man around. Suddenly, he remembered Rose.

"I must collect my daughter from the Rebbetzin's house and then we can leave. Would you mind?"

Solomon shook his head.

"I will show you the Gardens," Pinchas said. "We live nearby so I can see my daughter home. We can have a bite to eat there, and then I'll take you over the peninsula. We have a fine tram service and a train service."

As they walked home, Rose said little but kept glancing at the young man. Solomon spoke about his family and how he was looking forward to seeing the Colony of Natal, after all he had heard of it.

Pinchas walked between the two and said little. His breakfast was usually a simple affair, since Fay was already in the shop. He hoped the young man would be satisfied.

As it turned out, Solomon was more than satisfied. Rose saw to it that the food was ample. She prepared eggs on the stove and brought cake and fruit from the pantry.

When the meal was over, she said to her father, "I have no plans for today. Maybe I can also go around with you?"

"First check with your mother that you are not needed in the shop," was his reply.

Would Fay have agreed had she known that the result would be a marriage, with her youngest daughter leaving to faraway Natal? Who could have known that quiet Rose, the baby of the family, could be so impulsive and stubborn?

The wedding took place not long after that first meeting in Bertha's home.

Solomon was surrounded by Rose's family but was bereft of his own. He waited impatiently for the goods to arrive, and soon he boarded the ship with his new wife smiling happily beside him.

Fay and Pinchas returned from the docks. Fay went to the empty bedroom, once filled with her daughters' shouts and laughter. She lay on Rose's bed and sobbed.

"Faigy, why? He's a fine young man. Why do you behave so?"

Just then the loud shop bell was heard.

"Go, go to the shop," Fay said. "Tell them we're closed."

Pinchas went to the shop and stood behind the counter. He found a box of matches and the flour that the woman requested. The prices were written on a board beside the money drawer.

One customer followed another. Pinchas continued to work, wondering all the while if he should close the shop and go to his wife. When there was a lull in customers, he went back to her.

"You, in the shop!" Fay said. "Before today you never helped, not even that day when I was frying the fish and I needed another pair of hands!"

"Faigy, how do you feel now? Why the tears?"

"Simple. Now I know how my mother felt the day I left. I was so hurt when she smiled as we waved goodbye. Now I see that she was smiling just as I smiled, to give my daughter courage, while inside, my heart was breaking."

"This is different. Then we left forever. Now our girl is only a few days away by steamship."

"Ach, men! What can they understand? But why did you not close the shop? You have never worked in the shop."

Pinchas sat down and told her of that day in the veld, of how he had helped the enemy and the danger of being accused of treason. For Fay, it was as if a pebble that had been rubbing against her foot was taken away. Pinchas's behavior on that long-ago day had not caused irreparable damage, but there had always been some resentment. Even when Pinchas was home and the shop was impossibly busy, she had never again asked for his help.

On that day, when her daughter traveled far away, to a new life, Fay regained her trust and admiration for her husband.

<hr>

Only Jack and his parents remained in the empty house.

Since his return from London, Jack felt as if he had been surrounded by a storm of events. He had played no part in them. He had simply gone to work each day and returned home to find something new was in the air.

Now bereft of his siblings, with his father mostly away from home and his mother busy from early in the morning till late at night, he suddenly felt alone. Alone! In Cape Town! How he had longed to return. It was foolishness, to feel so alone.

In grey, smog-filled London, surrounded by people and fellow students, he had felt alone. He had longed for the fresh clean air of the Cape, for the bright sunshine, for the waves breaking on the yellow sand — and most of all, for his family.

Yet now, he once again felt terribly alone.

Strangely enough, he felt most alone when he was invited to eat with a family that had a young girl of marriageable age. Why could he find nothing in common with these pretty young women?

Each day he went to shul and to work. When his father was home, they learned together. He went for long walks in the cool evenings when his father was away.

His days were busy since he was now no longer a partner, but sole owner of the practice. Dr. Martin had retired happily to live by the sea in St. James.

Jack recalled a saying from his school days. "All work and no play makes Jack a dull boy."

That was exactly how he felt — dull. The future stretched before, bleak and lonely.

Chapter 48

"As late as 1904, the proportion of males to females among Jews in South Africa was 25,864 males, to 12,237 females, or 2 to 1. Single men would go back to find a bride, and sometimes a bride would be sent out to a South African immigrant whom she had not met before."
— Saron and Hotz, *The Jews in South Africa*, p. 75

In 1908, many Jewish immigrants came from Eastern Europe, bringing with them news of great poverty and hardship, as more and more restrictions were placed upon the Jews. Both Pinchas and Fay wrote home, enclosing money and encouraging their families to join them.

With only Jack at home, and with him earning a nice living, they were able to send money to their family. They waited anxiously for news, hoping they could make preparations for their family's arrival. If all went well, they would need to rent another two houses.

Yet there was no reply.

They were not the only ones anxiously waiting to hear from their loved ones. It seemed that unrest in Eastern Europe was affecting postal services.

There was another worry. As spring slowly edged into summer, Pinchas said, "Jack is nearly thirty. When will he marry? Why have all the others married and not Jack?"

"You forget Isaac," Fay said. "He's not married."

"Ach, now, don't change the subject. Our Isaac is much younger and far away. Jack is working and doing well. He has a good name. People stop me and say, 'What a fine son you have. What a good dentist he is! You must be so proud of him!' That's what they say."

"Is something wrong? You're not proud of him?"

"Of course I'm proud of him. Yet not a word from him about marriage! He's turning thirty soon, and he's not married!"

Fay was all too aware of this. Her Jack was good looking, with a good profession. He was smartly dressed. He was invited to eat with many fine families, and all of them, she suspected, had eligible young daughters.

If here, there were many more Jewish men than women, surely it was not affecting her son. Not a week passed by without a dinner invitation.

Pinchas continued. "Look, when I was his age . . ."

Fay, angry that all her plans to marry off her son had come to naught, spoke without thinking. "Yes, I remember it well. We were in London. You were ill. We were living in terrible conditions. When Jack marries, he will buy a fine home. There will be no problems with money. So he's marrying a bit later than you did. So what!"

Immediately, Fay was sorry that she had said these bitter words, but her worry over Jack had caused her to lash out. She wished she could take the words back.

"What can we do?" she said more gently. "This is not the shtetl. There's no *shadchan*, no one to talk to." Abruptly switching topics, she said, "My sister's husband took money from Jack to go to America. That's why he was on the shipwreck."

"What exactly does that have to do with Jack finding his *bashert*?"

"Ach, men!" Fay muttered. "What do they understand?"

Would Fay's bitterness toward her sister never end? Was marriage to him so disappointing that she was so unforgiving?

"Faigy, listen, Jack is a good man. He did a good deed. Was it not because of the woman he saved on the shipwreck that Bertha met her *bashert* that day as we walked from shul? And where did Ethel meet her husband, but in Bertha's house? Can you not see a pattern to the rewards for our son's good deed? What does it matter that it came about because Jack was helping your sister's family?"

Fay was unimpressed. "Still, why are all the younger children married and not our Jack?"

Pinchas sighed. "One thing has nothing to do with the other." He was about to say more, but bit back his words. He was angry with Fay, angry that she had pulled up again those years in London, angry that he had failed his family so miserably and that only Fay's courage had brought them here to a safe, good life.

Why had she married him so many years before? He had always felt it was because she truly cared for him, just as he cared for her. Now he began to wonder if she had married because of hurt pride.

Too angry to voice his thoughts, he said, "I must go now." He put on his hat and left the house.

Jack occupied his thoughts. How did one go about these things here, with no *shadchan*, where young men and women mixed so freely?

Mixing with so many people had not brought Jack a wife. There were fewer women than men in the Colony, and many men sent home for a wife. Yet he knew that Jack would not do this.

Pinchas soon found himself walking down toward Adderley Street, where Jack worked hard from early in the morning until late in the afternoon. Pinchas had reached a decision. Since there was no *shadchan*, *he* would be the *shadchan*. So then, how did a *shidduch* begin? Usually the parents were asked, "What do you seek?"

Here, things were different, so he would be the one to ask his son that question.

Pinchas arrived at the dental clinic to find an empty waiting room. He could hear the sound of drilling. He sat on a chair and planned what he would say.

Some time later, Jack emerged together with a young man holding his hand to his cheek.

"Well, we saved your tooth," Jack said. "Now, be careful! Don't eat any food for the next few hours, and then only something soft. By tomorrow you should feel just fine!"

Jack noticed his father. "Tatte, why are you here? No problems with your teeth, I hope."

For a moment, Pinchas felt shy. These rooms were impressive and his son was a professional man. Who was he to interfere? He gathered up his courage and said, "No, no problems, but I wanted to talk to you. With the girls married now, and all the boys married except for Isaac, I was wondering what it is you seek in a wife and cannot find."

Jack felt angry. For much of his life his father had been absent, and Jack had taken charge of the family. Now suddenly, his father was asking these questions.

What should he tell him?

He spoke at last. "You know how often I am invited out for the evening meal. I suppose you realize that there is usually an unmarried daughter or niece at the table. Somehow, I don't feel comfortable with them. Why? I don't know.

"Maybe it's not the girls I don't feel comfortable with. Maybe it's just that at home we eat in the kitchen. Mother and the girls bring the food to the table. My sisters also have a lot to say for themselves. They are so aware of everything going on in Cape Town, perhaps because they help in the shop when it gets busy.

"At these meals I'm invited to, we sit in a grand room, and every now and again a small bell is rung, and a servant takes out the dishes and brings in the next course. It feels so strained. The girls talk of such superficial things — the latest play they saw, how charming the weather is. I don't want to meet with them again."

Pinchas was quiet for a few moments.

"Many young men here send back home for a girl to come over," he said. "Our families back home would see that a suitable young woman could be persuaded to come here and be your wife."

What was Jack to say? "Yes, send for a new immigrant who cannot speak English, who would be baffled and lost in the new world of the Colony." Instead he said, "I cannot do that, to take on a stranger like that. Some do it, but I cannot."

Pinchas had expected that, but still thought it was worth a try.

Jack looked at his watch. The next patient was due momentarily.

"Tatte, don't you see? I need someone like my sisters, as familiar with the Cape as they are, not a new immigrant, and not someone who has always lived here in a big house on the slopes of the mountain."

Just then a young woman walked in with a tall boy by her side, his cheek swollen and his forehead furrowed in pain.

Pinchas knew it was time to leave. He stood up quickly. Surely the type of girl his son described did live in Cape Town. Many new immigrants had arrived in the past years, people like them, people whose daughters Jack would feel at ease with. Surely the right woman was somewhere in Cape Town!

He was determined to find such a young woman for his son.

As Pinchas walked toward District Six, toward the *shtiebel*, he was deep in thought. Perhaps one of the men who davened at the *shtiebel* had a daughter of marriageable age who would fit these guidelines.

It was so simple! He must look for a girl who had grown up in this town, but was familiar and comfortable with the old ways. Maybe if he went to the *shtiebel* to learn for a while he would find a man with such a daughter.

But his hopes were not met. The men he met that day were all alone, without their families, working to make money to bring them over.

So Pinchas resorted to the only thing now in his power. He davened fervently that he would be successful in his mission to find a wife for his oldest son.

On his way home Pinchas met Jacob Gordon, one of his clients from the country, walking down the avenue with his family.

"What brings you here?" Pinchas asked.

Jacob walked with Pinchas ahead of his family, soon outpacing them by a small distance, before replying.

"My son is old enough to look after the shop for a few days, so we came, my wife and my daughter, for a little break. We can visit our younger sons who are at school here. We miss them so. We're staying with my sister in Kloof Street."

Jacob sighed. "There in the veld, there are no suitable Jewish men. My daughter has met with the single men who live in our district, but . . . well, she went to school in Cape Town. Three times a year, together with her brother, she traveled here. How her mother cried each time the holidays ended.

"Now she's home. She helps her mother. She helps in the shop. The young Jewish men she met don't find favor in her eyes. Who knows why?

"We wanted to send for a young man. After all, we're comfortable now. He could join us in the shop, or we could set him up somewhere, but no, she won't consider it. She says, 'I cannot do that, to take on a stranger like that. Some do it, but I cannot.'"

The words resonated with Pinchas. Had Jack not said the same words just a little earlier?

Pinchas remembered how he had stayed with the Gordon family on his travels inland. There had been no hotel in that small town, and the family had reserved a room for Jewish travelers.

The picture flashed through his mind of a large kitchen and a black coal stove. He remembered Jacob's wife, bringing in delicious, piping hot food. There were three little boys seated around the table, but no young girl. Now he knew why. She had been away then, at school in Cape Town.

The girl sounded suitable. How could he arrange for Jack to meet her? This wasn't something he had done before. How should he begin? Could he invite the family for a meal?

What would Fay say? "After a hard day in the shop you expect this from me?"

No, that wouldn't do!

Pinchas knew where the family was staying. Several times Jacob had sent fruit with Pinchas to his sister in Kloof Street, and she had sent back gifts, goods that were unattainable in the countryside.

"If I send something to you this evening, a letter maybe, can you make sure that it is your daughter who receives it? I will send it with my son."

There was a moment of incomprehension — "A letter? Now, why?" — followed by realization. "Oh yes, definitely. Yes, that can be arranged."

Later, after supper, Pinchas set his plan in action. The English liked to say, "Nothing ventured, nothing gained." Would the girl accept the letter, or someone else? Would they talk at all, the two young people? It was so much easier in the old days, with the young couple knowing exactly what was expected of them, as they sat talking while the girl's parents watched.

Jack agreed to deliver the letter. It was strange that his father was too tired to walk the short distance, but still, how could he refuse him?

Some time later, Jack began to understand. The girl, Hannah, accepted the letter and offered him a cup of tea. They sat in the front room, where her mother was sewing. Hannah had been educated at Good Hope Seminary, like his sisters, while boarding with her aunt.

She was well spoken and fashionably dressed. She told how she helped in the shop her parents ran, and she spoke of Cape Town and her friends. She listened as Jack spoke about his time in London. Time flew by. Suddenly, Jack pulled out his watch.

"Oh, look at the time. So sorry, I didn't realize . . ."

Hannah looked at him and said, "Neither did I."

When Jack returned, his father said nothing. Pinchas wanted to ask about the girl and what had taken so long, but what was he to say?

Jack looked at his father and laughed. "Tatte, don't ask why, but maybe tomorrow night you will have another letter to send over?"

Pinchas understood at once what Jack was telling him.

Chapter 49

"In the vast majority of South African synagogues, English influences
meant that wedding ceremonies were held before the Ark ... and as
opposed to having the solemnization outside as was the custom in
many Eastern European congregations."
— David Sher, "What We Learn from 'Nusach Anglia,'"
South Africa and Its Threatened Anglo-Jewish Heritage Jewish Affairs

When something is meant to happen difficulties fall away.

Jack and Hannah met again and again, and found much in common.
The decision to marry came easily, but where to hold the wedding was
a problem.

Hannah's father had attended a family wedding in the Gardens
shul, quite unlike any wedding he had ever attended. Back home the
weddings had been outdoors. The groom wore a white *kittel* and walked
up to the *chuppah*, escorted by the two fathers. Then came the bride,
heavily veiled, the mothers carefully guiding her on each side. She
walked around the groom seven times, and then stood beside him as
the age-old ceremony began.

In the Gardens shul, things were done quite differently. The *chuppah*
was indoors, in the shul itself. The bride was accompanied by her father
to the *chuppah*. She walked around the groom only three times.

Somehow, this hadn't seemed like a real wedding to him. Halachically,
there seemed to be nothing wrong with it, but what about the customs
that had been passed down through the generations? He didn't want his
dear daughter to marry in such a way. There also there was the problem
of who would attend the wedding. His close friends and family, the

brothers he had brought out, one by one, all lived in small villages close to him. How could he ask them to leave their shops and travel all the way to Cape Town? Yet how could they not be present?

It was the custom for the wedding to be held where the bride lived. But these people in Cape Town would not travel to a small, faraway village. The groom also wanted his family and friends to be present. While the *vort* was celebrated in his sister's home with great joyousness, Hannah's father was worried.

The problem was solved quite unexpectedly when Jack's brother, Joseph, came over to him with his father.

"My son has invited us to make the wedding on the farm that belongs to his wife's parents," Pinchas said. "You see, there is a new baby, and it would be difficult for his wife to travel. She would be so upset to miss the wedding."

"Stellenbosch isn't so far from where we live," Jacob said. "But where would all the family stay? They would have to sleep there overnight."

"We already thought of that," Joseph said. "The house is large with many rooms. There are also five small houses, built for people who come to the farm temporarily — the *shochet*, the man who repairs the vats for the wine, and others."

"What do you think?" Pinchas said. "Would your family agree? I think mine would be agreeable. We wanted to see what you think of this idea before we asked anyone else."

Both families were in agreement. Fay wanted Jack to marry this fine girl. It didn't matter to her whether the wedding was in Stellenbosch or Cape Town.

The wedding was held a few months later in the open air. Jack approached his bride, to pull the veil over her head. The look that passed between them was long remembered by those near enough to see it.

Under twinkling stars, Jack, a white *kittel* over his suit, walked to the *chuppah*, flanked by his father and father-in-law. As Jack stood, his eyes closed, davening fervently, his bride came, escorted by their mothers, and made the seven circuits.

The night was quiet as the age-old ceremony took place.

Later, much later, when they were at last alone, Pinchas said to Fay, "That was so like our wedding ... Such memories. How happy I was that the wonderful girl I had seen in the *rav*'s house had agreed to be my wife. When the *shadchan* spoke to me and I told her that only one woman was for me, I never thought such a miracle would come to be."

"But, I thought, I thought ..."

"What did you think?"

Fay thought back to that time, how she had wondered why Pinchas had been so insistent on meeting her. Then she remembered how she, too, had noticed Pinchas that day. She had wondered who would be fortunate enough to become his wife. Though she had been hurt by her sister, her heart had given a leap of joy when the carpenter's son sat at the table opposite her.

In that moment, the long-ago hurt, the anger at her sister, melted away. How could she have been so foolish not to realize that everything happened for the best? Of course, she and Pinchas had always been meant to be together.

"I must write to Dina," she said. "Her letters ask always for forgiveness, but I must tell her that there is nothing to forgive. Each of us married the one who was destined for us."

When Pinchas heard these words, his heart filled with joy. All these years he had worried that he had been accepted, not for love, but only to prevent humiliation.

It was time to remedy the bitterness he saw in his wife's heart each year as a letter arrived before Rosh Hashanah and was left unread.

Unfortunately, not everything works out as planned. They traveled home by train the following day and took a cart home. Arriving there, they found a young man slumped on the steps next to the closed shop door.

He jumped up when he saw them.

"Oh, at last. You are Pinchas? Good! The ship came in very early this morning. I am Yechezkel, son of your brother. My father sold his carpenter's tools for profit and soon the rest of the family will join me."

When they were seated around the kitchen table, Pinchas asked, "Why did only you come, and not the others? Why the delay?"

The young man looked down, fumbled a bit with the edge of his shirt, and then said, "Well, it's like this ... There was a bit of trouble in the yeshiva. New ideas, you know — Zionism, Socialism! It came to the knowledge of the Rosh Yeshiva, what I was reading, what I was saying! I had to leave and go home.

"I should have learned from what happened in the yeshiva. I shouldn't have talked again of such things. But talk I did! Next thing I knew, there was news that I was in trouble with the authorities. So I left right away."

Fay brought the teapot to the table. "What news is there of my family? They were also sent money for tickets. When will they come?"

The young man looked more discomfited than ever. He looked down at the table. At last he spoke.

"When I left your brothers were sitting *shivah* for your parents. It was such a long, hard winter. There was such poverty. What can I say?

"Your brothers' sons are doing well in Mir. Your brothers will use the money to make their lives there more comfortable. There was talk of buying a cow, so they would have milk, maybe even make cheese and sell it. They were going to give me a letter, telling you of their plans, thanking you and explaining why they don't wish to leave."

"Why didn't they give you the letter?"

"Well, like I told you, I had to leave suddenly, in the middle of the night."

Fay was devastated. Her parents — gone, without any warning! It was a double blow, delivered so quickly and unexpectedly.

Her family had decided not to come. So many Jews were arriving. They all told of poverty, of harsh edicts, of wanting to leave. They spoke of the difficulty of saving money for fares. Yet the fares had been sent to her family, and now the money was being used not to travel, but to remain. The rejection was painful to her.

Later, much later, after an exchange of letters with her brother, she realized that only her parents had known her sister's address in America. There was no way to tell her sister that she had forgiven her.

BOOK FOUR

Alison's Story

Chapter 50

Alison, Jack's granddaughter; Cape Town, 1954

Well, in the end, though my great-grandmother Fay would not talk of old times, I found on subsequent visits that she could talk of many other events—local events, international events, and more. She was a keen observer and interesting to listen to, and I began to visit her regularly on Sunday mornings.

Her children were more than happy to recall those first years in Cape Town. Lots of work it was, and I took careful notes, until I felt I had a full story.

But a thesis is more than a story. I spent a lot of time in the library in the Gardens and in the Zionist Office library in town.

Once I had a good background in the history of those times, I delved into sociology books, theories of immigration, theories of all sorts of things. My, but such fancy words, such impressive sayings, and somehow I had to pull all these threads together. It was no easy task, I tell you. I was reaching the end. I needed just a little more time in the university library, and then I could get everything typed and bound into three books, and handed in to the department, and then, hopefully be rewarded with an M.A. degree.

I knew that what my parents and grandparents really wanted for me was a different kind of M.A. They wanted me married. My friends were mostly married, and some already had children. They wanted me to be "Ma," not "M.A."

Of course, I also wanted to be married, to be a mother, but it seemed that a husband was not coming my way.

Those were my thoughts on that fateful Saturday morning.

Usually I went to the Gardens shul on Shabbos—by car, of course. This morning, however, was different. Debbie, my friend in Vredehoek, had invited me to her brother's bar mitzvah. She had warned me not to park near their shul, which consisted mainly of people who observed everything, just like in the old days.

I knew, because of my studies, that they were descendants of the congregants of Rabbi Mirvish, who was the first rabbi with *semichah* to arrive at Cape Town from Eastern Europe. He and his congregants had lived for years in District Six.

When they could afford it, they moved as a group up the slopes of the mountain to Vredehoek. I understood why Debbie had requested me not to park near the shul and accepted it.

That morning I went to the car and realized I had forgotten my gloves. I walked back into the house, found my white lace gloves, and then absentmindedly closed the door. As I heard the lock click, I realized that my purse and keys lay on my bed, with no way of retrieving them.

My parents were out. The maid, Annie, was off that day. I couldn't get into the house.

There was no bus linking Oranjezicht and Vredehoek, two adjacent suburbs lying on the slopes of Table Mountain. I had promised Debbie I would be there. It was getting late. I would have to walk. So in my best Shabbos dress and white gloves, I began the walk along the lower slope of Table Mountain that led to the shul in Vredehoek.

The Rebbetzin noticed me as I walked into shul and smiled at me. Later, much later, I realized that she apparently noticed that I had no handbag, and since there was no *eruv*, she falsely surmised that I was mitzvah observant. After the service she asked who I was, and where I came from, and made sure that I had walked to shul by asking, "How long did it take you to walk here, my dear?"

Well, having established that I was "suitable," I later realized, she introduced me to Bernard's mother. Then, as the *kiddush* was ending and Bernard walked over to his mother, both women watched as Bernard and I were introduced to each other. The hall emptied, and I went off to join Debbie and her family at the bar mitzvah lunch at their home.

Later that evening, Bernard called and invited me out for Sunday morning.

We played half a round of mini golf, and as neither of us was much good we gave up and went to the car. Then we drove to the nearby fishing beach, which was almost empty that morning. Bernard had cookies and tea in a flask. I thought it was such fun, so different from my usual dates, and then I said the wrong thing!

"This all makes a pleasant change from parking at the Doll's House drive-in."

Well, that took Bernard by surprise.

"You eat *treif*? You eat at the Doll's House?"

"Sure, why not? Just the milkshakes, or the chips, not the meat or hot dogs..."

"I thought, well, if the Rebbetzin introduced us, and my mother agreed, well... aren't you *shomer mitzvos*?"

"Aren't I what?"

"You know, don't you keep all the laws? Shabbos, *kashrus*..."

"Our home is kosher. I usually go to shul on Shabbos."

"But you eat at the Doll's House? Why did you walk to our shul last week? Don't you usually walk to shul?"

So then the whole story came out — about the car, and the keys locked into the house.

I learned then that in that shul, it wasn't only the rabbi and *chazzan* and maybe the Hebrew teachers of the shul who kept all the laws. All of the families who prayed there kept them, Bernard's family among them. Well, that came as a surprise to me.

I remembered the intense discussion that followed. We agreed not to see each other again, that our lifestyles were too different, but somehow, I was intrigued by this man. I wondered what it would be like to always eat kosher food, to never travel in a car on Shabbos.

If I couldn't use the car on Shabbos, how would I go to the Gardens shul? It had been our family shul for three generations. The walk downhill, in the early morning, would be no problem. It would probably take no longer than a quarter of an hour. In the cool morning, that would be fine. But what about walking back home in the summer, in the midday heat, up the steep incline of the mountain slopes? That was another matter altogether.

What would I eat on weekdays at the university? Usually I ate with a group of Jewish students in the university cafeteria. Not kosher food, of course, but most of us avoided meat products. What would my friends think if I suddenly brought my own sandwiches?

Then there was the beach. Saturday afternoon was "beach time," or what some people called "Jewish social time." Muizenberg, with its long stretch of white sand and warm water, was still popular with Jewish families from all over South Africa, but for us, who lived in Cape Town, the icy Atlantic water and towering cliffs of Clifton beach was our favored spot.

By car, from Oranjezicht, it was a short drive up past Tamboers Kloof, with its steep streets and quaint old houses, then over Neck, the mountain pass where Lion's Head and Table Mountain meet, and then down a curving road to the beach.

Rocks divided the long white sands of Clifton into four different coves. First Beach, the one nearest to Sea Point, had become the meeting place for Jewish youth. Second Beach was mainly occupied by non-Jewish families, Third Beach, by non-Jewish singles, and Fourth Beach, with its large changing rooms and less steep path, was the place for Jewish families with young children. How did this come about? Now, that's an interesting question to which I have no answer.

I sometimes met suitable young men at First Beach. We would be introduced by a mutual friend, and later in the week I would get a call with an invitation to go to the cinema on Saturday night. That's how young Jews of Cape Town met, and quite often this led to marriage.

So, if there was no travel on Saturday, where did one meet? After all, unlike Tevye's shtetl, in the stories of Shalom Aleichem, there was no matchmaker in Cape Town to bring a suitable couple together.

The beach on Sunday was a less suitable time for meeting new people. So how did someone like Bernard meet a suitable girl? How would a Jewish girl who didn't travel on Shabbos meet a suitable young man?

It was all very puzzling. On Monday I went to university as usual, and at the cafeteria that day I noticed, for the first time, a corner table where some Jewish students were sitting together, eating food brought from home. How strange that I had never noticed them before. Did they not like the canteen food, or were they too, like Bernard, who kept the mitzvos?

During the week, Mervyn, whom I had been out with once before, called.

"Long time no see!" he said. I tried to remember why, and failed. Had I refused him? Had he stopped calling? Anyway, when he asked me out for Saturday night I accepted.

My parents were pleased. Mervyn was from a good family. He was an accountant, a good profession. Maybe something would come of this renewed friendship.

Why, then, did I find the whole evening so tedious? Why did I feel, as I stepped into his luxurious car, when the sun was still in the sky, when it was still Shabbos, that I was doing something wrong?

Why did I accept a midweek invitation, and why did I feel bad as I dug into chocolate cake, my favorite, as we sat in an Italian coffee house?

At the end of the evening Mervyn invited me out for the following Saturday night, and I couldn't believe it when I heard my voice say, "That would be nice, but only if it is after sunset. I don't really want to travel on Shabbos."

"But that would mean we get to the film well after it starts," he said. "Who wants to see half a film? What is this, all of a sudden?"

Well, the upshot of it was that I stayed home that Saturday night.

My family watched with amusement as I slowly changed the way I lived.

I stopped driving to shul on Shabbos and walked instead. I spent my afternoon reading a book instead of going to the beach. Then I stopped switching lights on and off over Shabbos.

I wasn't ignorant of the laws of Shabbos. Had I not gone to Hebrew school? Did my grandparents not observe these laws? It was just that my parents didn't and neither did I. Well, that wasn't strictly true. Of course we kept kosher. Of course we went to shul for all the festivals. While I did travel on Shabbos, I never sewed or cut with scissors. Why?

It was quite puzzling to me, once I began to think about it.

Then there was *kashrus*. Our home was strictly kosher, yet we all ate out. We didn't eat crayfish, as some of my friends did. We carefully refused the cheese topping on the meaty sauce in the Italian bistro. Why?

So I began to take sandwiches to university, though I still sat at the same table.

I heard my mother say to my father, "What's our little '*rebbetzin*' going to do next?"

"Ach, man, it's just a phase," my father said. "It will pass. Leave her be."

Two months later, I woke up one Shabbos morning with the thought of yet another day of walking to shul alone, trailing back up the hill alone, reading a book. I hadn't been on a date for weeks. I hadn't been to the beach to meet friends on Saturday afternoon. By the time Shabbos was out, the cinemas had already begun, so I refused invitations. In any event, how would I explain that I didn't want to go to the Italian coffee bar afterwards?

All this wasn't getting me anywhere. Bernard wouldn't go out with me again. That was clear. He hadn't called, not even once. It was time to get back into my familiar routine—driving to shul, then the afternoon at Clifton Beach, meeting someone there, going out that evening.

I didn't want to prove my father correct, that these past few weeks had just been some sort of "phase," but there was no point in carrying on like this. So I dressed for shul and took my car keys, and then something strange happened. I couldn't get myself to walk out through the front door.

"Nonsense," I said to myself.

But I stood there, not taking a step forward or back, until at last, I went back to my room, put down the keys, and walked down the road to shul.

Standing in shul that day, I decided that if I was going to change the way I lived, I would do it properly—not for Bernard, since he was clearly no longer interested in me, but for myself.

Chapter 51

The Rebbetzin at the Gardens shul had noticed that I walked alone up the hill, and that day she invited me for lunch the following Shabbos.

"Your parents will worry if you don't arrive home on time," she said. "Since we can't call them, come next week for lunch."

That was something I hadn't thought of. Not using the phone on Shabbos?

The following Shabbos, after the service, I walked with the Rebbetzin and her family to her home, not far from the shul. Such a marvelous experience it was!

At first I felt strange. I should be with my family, not with strangers. My grandmother expected us for lunch on Shabbos, yet she hadn't objected.

The meal itself was a slow, relaxed affair, with much discussion about the *parshah*. The men sang such wonderful tunes. I was relieved that the women sat quietly, since what would I have done had they joined in? Shabbos songs weren't a part of my grandmother's Shabbos meal.

After lunch, the Rebbetzin asked me if I wanted to learn with her. I agreed and we discussed some of the laws of Shabbos, not just what was forbidden, like my mother had taught me. We learned the very basics, and it all sounded so clear, so logical.

I stayed until the sun had set and the Rabbi made Havdalah. Well, that was an experience. I had never before seen the braided candle, with the many wicks. The flames, the sweet smell of cinnamon, the beautiful words — it resonated within me. The extinguishing of the flames in the wine, to signify the end of the day of holiness and the transition to the ordinary, was so beautiful.

Why was I ignorant of this custom? Probably because I was never around when my grandparents performed this ritual.

How did my grandparents feel about the way they observed the day, and the way we did? It was so different. Yet they had never said anything critical, as far as I could remember.

I was familiar with lighting candles on Friday night, of course. Didn't every Jewish woman do that? But ending Shabbos with Havdalah was new to me.

Did my grandparents still do this? Had my grandfather ever worked on Shabbos?

I was reluctant to speak of these things to my parents and grandparents. Slowly, I came to the conclusion that the parts of Shabbos that I kept—not sewing, not cutting, watching as my mother lit the Shabbos candles—belonged to the domain of women.

Havdalah, the domain of men, had vanished and that was understandable. The men in our community had often come alone to South Africa. Many were just barely out of their teens. In a land of many Jewish men and few Jewish women, and little if no communal structure, they were adrift.

They had been faced with the difficult choice of working on Shabbos, these lonely young boys, these men without families. What could they have done? Could they have found other work? Now, after all this time, who can know? Alone, far from their family, their community, desperate to make a living, they found themselves violating Shabbos.

Perhaps they did so reluctantly at first, with a feeling of guilt. Then later, seeing others do the same, perhaps it was with less trepidation.

In those far-off days, with so few Jews of substance and so many new immigrants, life was hard, and if the situation was work or starve, who can judge them?

For the women it was different. They usually came later. Sometimes they came with young families, having been left behind while the men worked to establish themselves and save money for fares. Sometimes they came as a result of a *shidduch* made across the sea. There was little they could do to change their menfolk, but in the home, they ruled, and there they kept the laws, passing on to their children every bit of Yiddishkeit that they could.

Sons would follow their fathers, and if their father worked on Shabbos, it was likely that they also would. Perhaps more influence could be exerted on the girls, so they too kept what they could — lighting candles, the festive evening meal, the prohibitions such as cutting and sewing.

Yet I had handled money on Shabbos. I had thought nothing of traveling by car, and in our home, lights were switched on and off and food was cooked.

Why? How did mothers who had arrived straight from the shtetl handle such matters? How did successive generations of Jewish women differentiate between one "forbidden" and another?

Was it due to the women, past and present, that the community retained its strong Jewish identity, even though it broke many laws of Shabbos?

It seemed that in Bernard's family there was no such dichotomy. The men obeyed all the laws. Why was his family different? How had those who came before him managed to keep all their customs intact? What work did they do that allowed them to take off all of Shabbos? How had they managed to establish generations of mitzvah-observant families, descendants who proudly adhered to their precious tradition?

The families who lived in Vredehoek, who had moved there from District Six with Rabbi Mirvish — how much of their determination was bolstered by Rabbi Mirvish? How did they resist social pressures to change and integrate, right up to the present?

These thoughts puzzled me all week as I sat with the words of Great-Granny Fay's children before me, and the pile of notes I had written in different libraries about the early days of Jewish immigration.

The Rebbetzin of the shul called me once again on Thursday night with an invitation for Shabbos lunch. So began a regular routine: shul and lunch and then learning. Slowly, week by week, I learned more. There were so many small details to keeping Shabbos and kosher. Immersing dishes — well, that was a new concept for me!

Some things that I knew surprised the Rebbetzin. Take the laws of *lashon hara*, for example. As we went through them, I found that I knew them all. My mother encapsulated them by saying, "If you have nothing good to say about a person, say nothing." But our whole family, the Levine family, was very particular about how we spoke of others, and particularly when in the presence of Great-Granny Fay.

I took on each new mitzvah slowly, considering each aspect. This meant not only taking my own sandwiches to the university, but also discarding some of my dresses and taking others to the dressmaker to be altered.

I was now spending lots of time alone, since my friends went to the beach over the weekend. I no longer ate at non-kosher establishments where they socialized. My parents began to worry. If I didn't socialize, how I would I meet someone to marry?

Shabbos was marvelous for me. Sunday was lonely. Like my parents, I wondered how I would meet someone, since my social life was totally barren by this time. I too began to worry about my future.

How did Bernard hear that I was now living a different lifestyle? I never did find out. All I remember is that one day he called me, and we went again to the mini golf course, but we never played golf that day. Instead, we walked by the sea and talked.

So we began to go out, and my mother was proved wrong — my new way of life was not something temporary, but a new and more satisfying way of being Jewish. I felt fulfilled. This was a worthwhile life, without the previous contradictions. There were no double standards, no knowing what was required but behaving differently, because, well, because that was the way Jews behaved here, now, in this time and in this place.

By the time we announced our engagement, I was comfortable with the new way of life. Our marriage cemented this feeling of contentment. Bernard never asked anything of me that I was not more than happy to comply with. Our home was strictly kosher. Annie, my parents' maid, had come to work for me. I taught her the extra laws of *kashrus* that had been ignored in my home. She knew not to turn on the oven, but to let me do it. I learned from Bernard's mother how to make cholent, and then taught Annie.

The Rebbetzin had taught me well, but still, there was so much to know when running a home. Bernard was patient with me. That first year, whatever Bernard asked of me I did.

We bought a house in Claremont. Why Claremont? Well, it was the fashion then to move farther out to the suburbs. My friends had bought homes there. Bernard went to the shul in Claremont one day during the week and felt comfortable there, so he agreed.

We found a beautiful old house built in the Cape Dutch style, with a large, curved gable and a front porch running the length of the house. To the right of the house was a long garden sheltered by a high hedge and a mature old oak tree.

In the corner, surrounded by another hedge, was a swimming pool. The house itself was not large, just two bedrooms, and a lounge and dining room. The kitchen was old and would need modernizing. In fact, the entire house needed work, but it had potential, and we could afford it precisely because it needed work. And so we bought our home.

By now, I had received my M.A. degree, but the "Ma" part eluded me. Even those friends who had married after me seemed to have no trouble in this regard.

Chapter 52

Our home was beautiful, but after a few weeks I realized that it had been a mistake to move so far away from our families. Very few Jewish families in the surroundings kept the laws of Shabbos as we did. We were lonely. We began inviting guests who shared our lifestyle. Sometimes Bernard's two younger sisters came. Very occasionally, his married brother and his family stayed with us.

That meant we had company. The problem was it meant a lot of work for me. Annie was off on Shabbos. On Sunday morning she would come in, tidy the house, wash the dishes left in the sink from Shabbos, and then go off again.

Bernard said he would help, yet this proved difficult. How can both host and hostess get up from the table to take away the dishes, and leave the visitors sitting alone?

I tell you all this so you can understand how I paid less than my full attention to the conversation in our home on Shabbos.

The trouble began with a young man called Yitz, from Jerusalem. He became a fairly regular Shabbos visitor. Like Bernard, he was an actuary. He had been sent to Cape Town by his firm to sort out a complex problem that was quite beyond my understanding.

When Yitz spoke of Jerusalem, his face seemed to glow. He spoke of the peace that descended upon the entire city as Shabbos came in. He spoke of his years in yeshiva, and how most evenings after work he went there once again to engage in serious learning.

I mostly nodded in agreement to his words, or said something bland but pleasing to him. After all, he was our guest. I wanted him to feel good.

When he said one evening, "Wouldn't you like to live in Jerusalem?" I unthinkingly replied, "Well, it does sound a good place to be."

I was just being polite, but apparently, my words were taken quite seriously by both men. When I later brought in the coffee, I heard the tail end of a conversation.

"Maybe my firm could use your expertise," Yitz was saying.

Bernard smiled and nodded. I didn't take much notice. People often said things to be polite.

Some weeks after Yitz returned to Jerusalem, as we were waiting for Annie to bring out the first course of supper, Bernard said, "I need to learn more."

"Why, that's a good idea," I said. "When do you plan to do that?"

I thought maybe he would spend more time with his father, or perhaps he would learn with the Rabbi of the shul on *motzaei Shabbos*.

What followed took me by surprise — or perhaps shock would be a more appropriate word.

"Actually, Yitz found work at his firm for me, an afternoon job that will pay enough for us to live on. They need an actuary with my experience. He also found out that there's a new yeshiva in Jerusalem that has a special class for people like me, and . . ."

"Jerusalem!" I said. What was he talking about, this husband of mine? He continued even after Annie came in and placed bowls of soup in front of us. "This yeshiva takes people like me, who have some knowledge of learning, but not sufficient for the mainstream yeshivas. After a year or so I should be able to join a regular group at Mir.

"Isn't that great? I didn't want to tell you until all the details were worked out, in case you would be disappointed."

"Jerusalem! You're talking about Jerusalem? I thought, well, I thought . . ."

"Yes, what an opportunity! Just think — next year we could be saying, 'This year in Jerusalem.' What do you think of that? Isn't it marvelous?"

"What gave you the idea that I would agree to this?" I burst out.

"But you did agree. We discussed it with Yitz, and you agreed. Don't you remember?"

It hit me then. Both men had taken my polite words as an agreement! Now let me explain why this came as a shock to me.

Don't get me wrong—Jerusalem was precious to me. Every year we contributed money for an orphanage there, and for a forest on the hills outside the city. But to go and live there? Well, it took my breath away.

I'm as interested as the next person in Jewish things. Didn't I choose to pursue a degree specializing in Cape Town Jewish History? Did we not live a lifestyle that encompassed the fulfillment of the mitzvos? But to move to Jerusalem?

I had not yet begun to work. Truth be told, I was a bit worried about finding a job. Fascinating though the subject was, how could it help with employment? The small department of Jewish Studies at the university had a full staff. My friends, who had taken the more usual courses of medicine, law, and social work, had all found jobs soon after graduating. Now they generally worked part time, or not at all, since marriage had been followed by children. We had been married for three years, and as of yet, there were no children...

All I said was, "I don't want to go. How could you arrange all this without first discussing it with me?"

"I didn't want to say anything in case it couldn't be arranged. I didn't want to disappoint you if everything fell through. It's not easy arranging a job from so far away. I wouldn't consider going if I didn't have a job that provided a living. I was so sure you would be thrilled."

Finding no argument from me, Bernard started talking about where we would live and how much we could expect from the sale of the house, detail after detail. I let it all flow over me.

Eventually, I recovered enough to voice my feelings. Bernard was horrified.

"Why didn't you say at the time that this wasn't what you wanted?

How can I tell Yitz now that I've changed my mind? Besides, I want to go. I want to live there. I want to work there and learn there, in Jerusalem."

Even though she was old, my great-grandmother was an early riser, probably because of all those years she had gone to the docks, to meet the fishing boats as they came in.

By the time breakfast was served in the dining room, she had already davened, said *Tehillim*, and gone for a short walk by the seafront.

As soon as Bernard left for work, I called my great-grandmother and asked if I could visit that morning. She told me that would be nice, but not before eleven.

I had a quick swim and then dressed, looking in the mirror carefully. Sloppy dressing was another no-no for Great-Granny Fay.

As I arrived, a tall, distinguished, dark-haired man was just leaving. He nodded politely at me and continued walking. I entered the room and saw biscuits laid out on a small table and a teapot standing nearby.

"Two visitors, one after the other! Well, sit down, sit down!"

"Who was your visitor? I've never met him before."

"Lettie's grandson. You know about my friend Lettie?"

"Yes, Lettie came to your house to do the laundry and clean."

"Right, she came to help me for several years until she got married. We remained friends over the years. We kept contact, her children and grandchildren too, even after . . . well, they always kept contact.

"Her grandson came to say goodbye. He's the principal at the top colored school and his wife is a nurse at Somerset Hospital. They're leaving this week for Canada."

"But why, if they have such good jobs?"

"My dear, how would you like it if you had to use a special entrance to the post office, if you couldn't sit on certain seats in the park, if . . . well, you know, all these new laws . . . Canada wants good people, well-qualified people. His wife's nursing qualifications means they have been accepted.

They're such a close-knit family, all his cousins and their children. He's sad to leave them, but as the laws tighten still further, he feels they will follow him."

That took the wind out of my sails. Not only Bernard wanted to leave this beautiful place.

"Well, maybe for them it's sensible to leave," I said. "Now that I think about it, there *are* all these new laws. But they don't affect us and now Bernard wants to go to Israel, not just for a holiday, but to live there."

"All of a sudden! You never spoke of this before. What does he plan to do there?"

"He says he will learn in the morning and work in the afternoon. He has it all arranged."

"So you'll have an income and you'll find somewhere to live. What a morning! Everyone's leaving, it seems!"

"But I don't want to go. I don't want to leave my family. I don't want to leave my house. I don't want to go to a strange place where I don't even speak the same language."

Fay thought back to that long-ago time, when she spoke to her mother about going to London with Pinchas.

"Why are men never satisfied?" she had said. "Why does this husband of mine want to leave? What can be wrong here? We're surrounded by family. We have enough to live on. We live in pleasant surroundings. How can I go so far away?"

The words echoed in her head as she listened to Alison. What was she to say to this girl?

She felt so close to her, closer to her than any other grandchild or great-grandchild. Why? Perhaps it was because Alison had always made time each week to visit her, or maybe because only Alison had returned fully to the old ways.

Fay had never criticized her grandchildren when they began to violate

Shabbos. It wouldn't have done any good. She remembered her father saying, "If someone is going to transgress *halachah* because he is ignorant, but he will continue in his ways even if he is informed, it's better not to tell him. Telling him changes the sin from one committed without knowing to a much worse sin of knowingly doing something wrong."

Of course, in those days, everyone in the shtetl had been knowledgeable, so it was just a theoretical discussion. Who could have known that so many a years later it would apply to her own life?

Bernard was a determined young man, she knew. How would this disagreement end? She must somehow convince Alison to see her husband's point of view. It was difficult for Alison to go so far away, and it would be even more difficult for her mother. But it would be even worse for Alison and Bernard to lose one another.

"My dear, at your wedding you stood under the *chuppah* with your husband. That means that your husband is now your closest family—not your parents, or your grandparents, or me."

"He *is* my family. I never said anything different. But why can we not stay here? Why go so far away?"

Fay thought back to the early years, when the new Jewish immigrants spoke of the return to the Holy Land. Then, it had seemed an impossible dream, yet now, it was a reality.

She remembered how Rev. Bender had at first been against it, saying the time was not right for such ideas. In his later years, he had done an about-face and spoken from the pulpit about return to the Holy Land.

In time, nearly all the Jews of South Africa had embraced the idea, yet they remained where they were. Only a few individuals made the long journey to live in Jerusalem.

As cries of "Next year in Jerusalem" echoed each year after the Seder, she sometimes wondered why they didn't make the journey there. What was preventing them from going? But of course, she knew the answer.

Life was good for the Jews in this beautiful land. They had come with the early pioneers and had been involved in the formation of commerce and factories, and the creation of universities. They were an integral part of society.

If, over the years, there had been some outbreaks of anti-Semitism, this had quickly been forced under the surface. Life was good here. Why leave?

"Grandma, did you hear what I said? You seem to be far away."

"Yes, I heard . . . I was thinking. Why does Bernard want to go?"

"He says . . . he says . . . there our children will live a full Jewish life . . . but . . . but . . ."

"Children will come. When the time is right, they will come."

"But so far away, far from everyone and everything I know?"

There was a small, battered *Tehillim* on the table. Fay picked it up.

"What happens in life is for a reason, a good reason," she said. "All will be well, for you, for all of us. Even the great King David had difficulties. Listen to these verses he wrote.

"'A psalm of ascents' — Bernard wants to ascend to Jerusalem, not only to live there, but to learn. Is that not ascent? A few sentences later, it says, 'Your wife shall be like the fruitful vine' and then 'May you gaze upon Jerusalem all the days of your life.' Maybe Bernard is doing what is correct for you both.

"Besides, today, when you leave a place, you can always return. It's not like the old days, when leaving was forever. You can even talk from one country to another. Don't think of this as leaving — think of it as a long holiday. Do you think Bernard would insist on staying if you are unhappy? Who knows, maybe you will be happy there."

At last I found my voice.

"Maybe Bernard will be unhappy there," I said. "Perhaps he will miss everyone here. After all, his brothers and sisters and their children all live here, and he's very close to them. Yes, maybe we will go for a short time only."

"Of course, my dear! The same plane that takes you there can bring you back again. What have you got to lose?"

"Well, what you say is correct. Besides, what choice do I have? Bernard is so determined."

My great-grandmother stood up and went to her wardrobe. She took out money and wrote on a piece of paper, "For forgiveness, from me to you, and you to me. From Faiga bas Malka to Dina bas Malka." She put the money and paper in a large white envelope and wrote on it "For charity in Jerusalem."

"When you get there, give this to charity for me. These words should be written on the receipt."

I took the envelope.

"I want another favor from you. There's a place in Jerusalem called Yad Vashem. It has a list of all the people killed in the war. I want the names of my family written there. Every year I light *yahrtzeit* candles for them. I always mean to get their names on that list, but somehow, I never get around to it. Will you do this for me?"

I nodded. It seemed to me that our departure had already become an established fact. My great-grandmother picked up her *Tehillim*.

"My mother gave me this to me before I left," she said. "It has been my comfort. Use it in good health."

She handed it to me along with the list of her relatives' names.

"It is yours," I said. "It's precious to you."

"Don't worry. I have others. This one helped me over the years, and it will also help you."

Just then the gong sounded, announcing lunchtime.

"Will you stay for lunch?"

But now I was in a totally confused state of mind and wanted only to go home. I had been so convinced that here, in this room, I would get sympathy and advice on how to speak to my husband and persuade him not to go so far away.

Instead, I had been given no encouragement to remain. More than that, I had been given tasks to fulfill once I was far from home.

"Thank you, but no," I said. "Annie must have made something. I didn't tell her I would be away."

＝

Annie had cleaned the house while I was out and was now sweeping stray leaves from the front porch.

"You're home for lunch?" she said. "I made nice curried fish."

My first thought was, *How will I manage without Annie if I go far away?* My next thought was, *How will Annie manage if we leave?*

Annie came from the Transkei. Her whole family lived there. Her mother looked after Annie's children and the money Annie sent to them each month was their only income.

Because of government regulations, Annie was only allowed to remain in Cape Town if she was working. Even if we found another place for her, she would have to go to government offices and get her papers changed. If she was refused she would have to leave, and then there would be no money to support her family.

Annie had worked for my parents since I was very little. Now my mother had someone else working for her. What would become of Annie?

"Come now, Miss Alison," Annie said. "Stop eating your heart out. Whatever is troubling you will pass. I will bring you the fish and a nice salad, and then you will feel good again."

Annie was her usual perceptive self. Throughout my childhood, she had been the one who saw when I was troubled and soothed me, giving me the courage to deal with whatever problem I was facing.

Now I was about to abandon her. I felt terrible. I washed my hands, looked in the mirror, and saw dark rings under my eyes, the result of a restless sleep.

Annie came and stood before me. "You are worried. The master wants to take you far away. Yes?"

How did she know? I nodded.

"He spoke to me. When I began to work for you, he gave me a little book. Before you go away, he will place a lot of money in the bank. Each month I will take the little book and the bank will give me money. As long as I take out the same amount each month as my salary here, the money will not go down. I can choose to go home to my children or remain here."

Listening to these words, I realized that Bernard had been thorough in his preparations. What would he do if I refused to go? Would he leave me? Unthinkable! No, I must go. After all, my great-grandmother was correct. We could always decide to return. Only a few generations ago, leaving meant forever. This was no longer true.

"So what will you do, when we leave?" I asked. I noticed I had said "when," not "if."

"So you have decided! That is good! The master, he was worried, I think. But of course you wish to go, just like I wish to return to my homeland."

"My homeland?"

"Oh, I am not ignorant. I go to church and the women's class. I know the Bible. Yes, you must be so happy to go back to your homeland just like I will go back to my land, to my children. They will be so happy. All these long years, and only once a year do I see them! You will have children who grow up in their own land. You have much luck to be married to the master. He's a good man. He thinks of me and my needs."

I wanted to say, "But I must leave my family. How can I do that?" Then I realized the foolishness of such a statement. Annie had left everything behind — her family, her husband, her children, everyone. How could I complain when I would be going with my husband?

She looked at me for a moment. "We will part, but it is for good reasons."

She bustled out, and I watched her leave, stunned. How little I had appreciated this woman, who had done so much for me over the years. How fortunate I was to have in my life two such feisty, clever women — my great-grandmother and my long-time helper, Annie.

So, that was how the decision was made.

Bernard was relieved when I told him that we would go — although the next few months were not easy.

We listened to our mothers' tearful words. We endured the wondering, almost cynical voices of our friends.

We argued. Oh, how we argued. I wanted to rent out our home. Bernard wanted to sell it.

"Renters are risky," he said. "They can stop paying. They can do damage. We need the money to buy a home in Jerusalem."

"Maybe we won't be happy there. Maybe we will come back. What then?"

"Simple. We sell, and buy again here. Why should we not like it? Why even think so negatively?"

In the end I gave in. We sold the house. We called in the shippers and our furniture was packed in enormous containers. We took a last slow, long drive around the beautiful Cape peninsula. We left on a day when the sun shone and Table Mountain was clear and beautiful. Though I smiled, I felt as if my heart was breaking.

Chapter 53

We arrived on a burning hot summer day.

Yitz had rented for us a small apartment, near the central bus station. Can you imagine leaving a spacious house, with a massive garden and swimming pool, and living instead in a three-room apartment? The rooms were tiny. The noise from the traffic was unceasing. Fortunately, Bernard was as unhappy as I was.

Instead of attending the yeshiva, he devoted his spare time to finding somewhere more suitable to live. He refused to say how unhappy he was in that tiny apartment. Instead he said, "It's no good leaving money lying in the bank. We need to find a place to buy."

Who was I to argue?

We found a small house with a patch of garden in Bayit Vegan, the so-called "garden suburb" of Mandate times. In those long-ago days, apartment buildings had not yet replaced all the little houses.

We somehow managed to fit in most of the furniture. Bernard became Baruch, and I became Aliza. I think Bernard felt "blessed," as his name suggested, but I didn't feel all that "happy," as my new name meant.

Bernard started going to the yeshiva in the morning and to his new office in the afternoon. I was left alone. We had no phone, and there was a long waiting list to get one. Letters seemed to take forever, but they were my only link, and so I wrote to everyone — to my parents and to Bernard's and to my grandparents, and also to my great-grandmother.

The letters were cheerful. What was the point in writing differently? But without language skills, and struggling with cooking and cleaning, I felt alone and inadequate.

Truth to tell, I was still hoping the stay would be temporary. All I would have to do was cope with my new surroundings and not complain, and in time Bernard would want to return.

We received letters from friends asking about our life in Jerusalem. We had left a short while before the terrible Sharpeville incident, in 1969. Opposition to the harsh laws restricting the movement of colored people had grown. Even Annie, sweet, soft-spoken Annie, had spoken bitterly about these laws.

The African leaders organized peaceful demonstrations against these laws. During one of these demonstrations in Sharpeville, the police panicked and shot wildly into the crowd, killing sixty-nine people. The African population could be passive no longer. The government took strong countermeasures. The calm of the country was shattered and many people saw a future of chaos and began to leave.

Surely everything would calm down, I told myself. The government would make concessions. What choice did they have? Everything would return to normal. Struggling with cleaning, cooking, and laundry, all new to me, I felt like telling everyone not to be foolish, to count their blessings and remain where they were.

We had no need of an extra income, but being alone all day was not pleasant. It was time to find work, something to do in those long hours when Bernard was away.

Everyone said I should go to an ulpan to learn Hebrew, but I resisted. That would mean admitting that we would remain here. I was determined to find work where I needed to use only English. Not easy, I tell you!

Looking through the papers I would need, I came across the envelope Great-Granny Fay had given me. How could I have forgotten her request? Who should I give the money to?

The calendar on the wall of our apartment was from the Diskin orphanage, so I went to the house next door and asked my neighbor for directions. An hour later I stood in an office and took out the money and paper.

I handed over the paper. "Please write this on the receipt."

"No problem" was the response.

But *I* had a problem. Faiga bas Malka was surely the name of my great-grandmother. If so, who was Dina? No mention had ever been made of a sister.

My great-grandmother's brothers and their families had all been killed in the Holocaust, and I had heard these names from time to time. But a sister? I decided to write to my grandfather and ask him.

It was only mid-morning when I completed my task, and I was reluctant to go home. Perhaps this was a good time to begin job hunting. Where to start? My Hebrew was far from perfect and my degree not particularly relevant.

What could one do with a Master's degree in history that focused on the Jewish immigration to South Africa? Very little, I thought. Still, I had to begin somewhere. I had taken with me a small map of Jerusalem, in case I couldn't follow the instructions my neighbor had given me. Looking at it, I saw that there was a museum a short distance away.

Maybe there was a job there for a historian. In any event, it would be good to look around, to spend some time away from home and housework.

I managed to find the correct bus and walked into the building, preparing what I was going to say.

With some difficulty, I found the correct office. As I walked in, a woman looked up from her desk and said, "Did you fill in the forms? Mr. David knows you have an appointment, but he was called away to deal with an urgent matter. Wait. He'll be here soon."

What was she talking about?

Just then the phone rang. "What, you're late? The bus got stuck in traffic? Is this some sort of a joke? Hello? Hello?" The woman stared at me. "You're Dina Finkelstein, are you not? You majored in history in America and now want to work here. Right?"

"Well, I do have a degree in history and I do want to work here. But my name is Aliza Berger."

Just then a woman came rushing in.

"Sorry I'm late," she said. "Is he still here? I filled in the forms."

She saw the woman looking not at her but at me, and she turned to me. We both stared at each other, mouths open.

"Well, you can see why I made that mistake," the woman said. "Why didn't you tell me you were Dina's twin?"

A man came rushing through the door.

"Miss Finkelstein. Please come to my office."

"Whatever you do, don't leave," Dina said to me as she followed the man into the office.

I sat and waited. I asked for no forms and responded vaguely to the questions the woman asked.

After what seemed like forever, Dina came out, beaming. "After six long months, a job at last." She turned to me. "Come, we must talk. The cafeteria is just down those steps."

Once we were seated, a cup of coffee and a slice of cake before us, she said, "You must be from Faigy's family, Faigy who married Pinchas."

I nodded in confusion. How could she have known?

"My great-grandmother was Dina. She was married to Aharon."

"Who are these people?"

"You don't know? They never told you? Faigy's son Jack saved their lives. When Aharon was stuck in London, penniless, Jack gave money to send for Aharon's family, and they all went together to America. That's how they survived."

"Jack is my grandfather, but why did he give so much money away?"

"Oh, you really know nothing. I'll tell you the story. I never knew my great-grandmother. She died a few years before I was born. My mother said the terrible conditions in America when the family first arrived ruined her health. But my mother told me the story of Dina and Aharon. It was family legend. It happened like this . . ."

I sat forward as Dina told me the story I had never heard before: of Dina and Aharon traveling on the same wagon, of the carpenter's son marrying the older sister.

"I never heard of such a thing!" I said. "But I did give charity for Faiga bas Malka to forgive Dina bas Malka. Dina and Faigy—well, I never! That would make us family! But can this really be correct? Maybe there was another Dina and another Faigy?"

"Why are you so doubtful? Didn't that woman in the office think we were twins? Besides, Malka was the name of both Faigy and Dina's mother, you know."

For some time I simply sat and thought. When we first arrived, my neighbor had said, "What family do you have here?"

My reply? "None, absolutely no one."

She looked amused. "No, that's not possible. Every Jew has someone here, someone who is family."

It seems that she wasn't wrong.

I sipped at my coffee, not knowing what to say.

That's how I made my first friend in Jerusalem. Dina was alone and single, and, like me, had no other family around. She was our first Shabbos guest. It was so good to have a guest for Shabbos.

Shabbos had been such a difficult day for me, with Bernard so satisfied with how his week had gone, and me so disgruntled, so lonely and unhappy.

Dina knew far more than me about the family that had remained behind. She told me about Malka, the daughter of a *rav* who had married a *rav*. She told me about their sons. This reminded me that I had fulfilled only one of my great-grandmother's requests.

When Havdalah was over, I turned to Dina. "I need to go to Yad Vashem. Will you come with me?"

Bernard overheard. "Why?" he asked.

Once I explained, we decided that we would all go together.

―

Bernard missed a session of learning. Dina had one day off a week. Me? I had all the free time in the world! We arranged a time to meet in town and from there we traveled to Yad Vashem together.

Once we had gone through it, I was so relieved that I had not come alone. The inhumanity laid before us was too dreadful to confront without support.

We then went to the office, where I made my request. We were given forms. Bernard, whose Hebrew is so much better than mine, filled in all the names.

A woman took the forms and told us to wait a few moments. She came back sooner than expected.

"All these names . . . we already have them. Look!"

There they were! Beside them was a name: Mordechai Guttman. Below it was an address in Jerusalem.

"I remember him, a middle-aged man," the woman said. "Is he family?"

"Everyone was killed!" Dina said. "How can it be?"

Well, of course, the only thing to do was to find a taxi and go to that address.

―

Mordechai Guttman wasn't home, but his wife was. She sent her son to the yeshiva to tell his father that there were important visitors from abroad and that he should return home.

He turned out to be the grandson of my grandmother's oldest brother! He told us his story.

"I wasn't home on that terrible day. I was learning in the Mir Yeshiva. I escaped with the yeshiva to Japan . . ."

He told of the long train journey across continents, of the miracle of finding a shul with the correct number of seats for the yeshiva refugees. He told of the difficulties of getting to Jerusalem, once the war was over.

"I was determined," he said. "I knew there was only one place I wanted to go to, and here I am!"

"Did your family ever talk of family in South Africa, of family in America?" I asked.

"Yes, they did, but what were their names after marriage? Where did they live? That I didn't know. This meeting is such a miracle!"

As I looked around at my family, the family I hadn't known I had, I could only nod in agreement.

Chapter 54

That year, Great-Granny Fay celebrated her hundredth birthday. The family made a grand party.

"No presents," she had said. "Give to charity if you insist on giving."

I went back to the orphanage and made another donation. I sent the receipt to my great-grandmother, together with the receipt of her charity donation. I also sent a photo of Dina, myself and Bernard, and Mordechai and his family.

As I carefully wrote the names of all the children, it seemed to me that there was a soft, sad echo of those same names I had seen in Yad Vashem.

We have been away from Cape Town for only a short time, I wrote in the birthday card. *I have left behind one family, only to find another. It is all due to you.*

Surely that was correct! Had not the charity money given me courage to go to the museum? Had not the list of names forced me to go to Yad Vashem?

Having family made all the difference.

Dina helped me to find work. When another department in Yad Vashem needed a historian, she was quick to let me know. I went with a copy of my thesis and letters from my former lecturers, and the next thing I knew, there I was, working.

Some time later, I had to give it up. At last I had fulfilled the wishes of my family back home. I was no longer just M.A., but Ma.

On Pesach, we went to the Guttman family. All the occasions we had previously shared with family in Cape Town, we now enjoyed with our cousins. Dina joined us many times on Shabbos, and we were overjoyed when, a short time later, she married and moved near us.

Some years later, my parents came to visit. They brought with them my great- grandmother's candlesticks and a silver Kiddush cup.

"She left it for you," my father said. "She said that you turned her sadness to joy. Whatever did she mean by that?"

I was reluctant to tell them. I knew her secret, her joys, her hopes, and also her regrets, and so did Dina. It was ours to keep.

Epilogue

Jerusalem, 2000

Who can believe that a new century is here? The years have gone by so rapidly.

How different the land is from when we first arrived. Then, we could only view the Kosel from atop a tall building, peering through binoculars. Now we can visit it anytime, day or night.

We came alone, Bernard and I, and now we're surrounded by family, our children and grandchildren, and close relatives who followed our example many years later.

We very rarely returned to the beautiful Cape over the years, and I do miss it. But I am not unhappy here. Far from it! The years here have been good to us.

Eventually, I learned Hebrew. Bernard followed the routine of work and learning for many years, and now sits and learns in the local *beis midrash* all day.

Yesterday, my twelve-year-old granddaughter came to visit me. It is a tradition here that upon becoming bas mitzvah, a girl investigates her family background.

I talked and talked. By the time she managed to leave, her eyes were glazed! Perhaps I talked too much. All the family history came pouring out.

Soon her cousins would also come. I would have to find a different approach.

After much thought, I took the notes I had written so many years before about the arrival of the Levine family in Cape Town and made copies for each of my children.

Now, when anyone wants to know some family history, they can simply go through the pages. Besides, it's painful for me to recall a foolish young woman who was so afraid that she wanted to remain with all that was familiar, instead of settling here, in this marvelous land.

My children think of us as brave pioneers, coming here and leaving everyone behind. The truth is, Bernard was brave, but I was terrified. I gave in only when I had no other option and hoped that our stay here would be a short one.

How wrong I was. How grateful I am to my dear husband. Our children and grand-children lead full secure Jewish lives. And "Next year in Jerusalem" is not just a phrase at the end of the Seder, but our reality.

Glossary

Agunah — woman who cannot remarry because her husband has not divorced her

Aliyah — the honor of being called up to make a blessing over the public Torah reading

Arba kanfos — lit., "four corners," referring to the strings attached to the corners of a Jewish male's four-cornered garment, as per the Torah commandment

Aron kodesh — the holy ark in the synagogue that contains the Torah scrolls

Bachur — unmarried man

Baruch Hashem — thank the Almighty

Bar mitzvah — celebration of a Jewish boy coming of age at thirteen

Bashert — destined mate

Bas mitzvah — celebration of a Jewish girl coming of age at twelve

Bein hazmanim — yeshiva intersession

Beis midrash — Torah study hall

Bentch — recite Grace After Meals

Bereishis — the Book of Genesis

Bimah — platform in the synagogue from where the Torah is read

Birchas Hagomel — blessing recited publicly after surviving a dangerous situation

Brachah — blessing

Bubbe — grandmother

Chagim — the Jewish holidays

Chavrusa — Torah study partner

Cheder, chadarim — Torah primary school(s)

Chol Hamoed — the intermediate days of the holidays of Sukkos and Pesach

D'var Torah, divrei Torah — Torah insight(s)

Daven — pray

Davening — prayer

Der heim — lit., "the home," referring to Eastern Europe or Russia

Dorp — a small rural town or village

Drashah — speech

Eibishter — the Almighty

Eishes chayil — woman of valor; chapter from the Book of Proverbs recited on Friday night

Frum — religiously observant

Gehinnom — place of suffering

Gemara — the Talmud; volume of the Talmud

Gemarakup — clever person

Gonif — thief

Halachah — Torah law

Hamotzi — blessing over bread

Kavanah — intent

Kichel — type of pastry

Kittel — white robe worn by men on Yom Kippur, at the Pesach Seder, and by a groom at his wedding

Kodesh — holy

Kol has'chalos kashos — all beginnings are difficult

Kosel — the Western Wall in Jerusalem

Landsleit — fellow countryman

Lashon hara — gossip

Lashon kodesh — the Holy Tongue, Hebrew

Lein — to read from the Torah using the tune of the cantillation

Limudei kodesh — Torah studies

Luchos — the Two Tablets given to Moshe by Hashem at Mount Sinai

Maariv — evening prayers

Maaser — to give a tenth of one's earnings to charity

Maidel — young girl

Mamme — mother

Mechitzah — partition between men and women in the synagogue

Melachah — activity that is forbidden on the Sabbath

Minchah — afternoon prayers

Minyan — quorum of ten adult men needed for public prayer

Mitzvah, mitzvos — Torah commandment(s)

Motzaei Shabbos — Saturday night, after the Sabbath ends

Neitz — at sunrise

Parnassah — livelihood

Parshah — weekly Torah portion

Peyos — sidelocks

Rabbanim — rabbis

Rav — rabbi

Rebbetzin — rabbi's wife

Rebbi, rebbeim — Torah teacher(s)

Sefer, sefarim — Torah book(s)

Semichah — rabbinic ordination

Seudah — meal

Shabbos — the Sabbath

Shacharis — morning prayers

Shadchanim — matchmakers

Shalom aleichem — welcome

Shalom bayis — marital harmony

Shalosh seudos — the third Sabbath meal

Shidduch — marital match

Shidduchim — the stage of life when one seeks a marital partner

Shiur — Torah lecture

Shomer Shabbos — Sabbath-observant

Shtetl — village

Shtiebel — small, homey synagogue

Shul — synagogue

Siddur — prayer book

Smous — a peddler

Sukkah — holiday that commemorates how the Almighty protected the Jewish people in the Wilderness for forty years following the Exodus

Sukkos—huts in which Jews
eat their meals and sleep on
the holiday of Sukkos
Talmud Torah—
elementary Torah school
Tatte—father
Tefillin—boxes with small Torah
scrolls worn on the head and
arm by adult Jewish males
during morning prayers
Tehillim—Psalms
Teivah—the ark that Noah built
so that his family and a rem-
nant of all living creatures
would survive the Flood
Tenaim—engagement contract
Tosafos—commenta-
tors on the Talmud
Treif—not kosher
Tuppence—slang for two pence, a
small money denomination

Tzena Urena—Torah work
favored by Jewish women
Tzitzis—strings attached to
the corners of a Jewish male's
four-cornered garment, per
the Torah commandment
Tznius—modest, modesty
Vort—engagement party
Yahrtzeit—annual commemoration
of the date of a relative's passing
Yamim Noraim—
the High Holy Days
Yamim tovim—Jewish holidays
Yeshiva, yeshivos—
Torah school(s)
Yidden—Jews
Yiddishe—Jewish
Zeide—grandfather
Zemiros—songs sung at
the Sabbath meals